7/9/09

Ken,

Have a good time in your retirement.

You always been a great friend and call me if you need anything

Ray

Wave Upon Wave

Isaac Green

authorHOUSE®

AuthorHouse™
1663 Liberty Drive, Suite 200
Bloomington, IN 47403
www.authorhouse.com
Phone: 1-800-839-8640

First published by AuthorHouse 5/18/2009

ISBN: 978-1-4389-6392-1 (sc)

Library of Congress Control Number: 2009902236

Printed in the United States of America
Bloomington, Indiana

This book is printed on acid-free paper.

For my father and mother

Dr. Morris N. Green and Blanche J. Green

PART ONE

CHAPTER 1

It was late afternoon as the sun began to set behind the dam, turning the water in the lake a pale yellow. There was no wind, which created stillness in the surroundings. The day became cooler and a haze started to build across the lake. A boy's head emerged from the water, creating concentric waves. The boy kept his head at the water level; his eyes stared at the wake of a water glider as it skated on its four legs across the placid surface. As he tracked the insect's graceful movement, another head suddenly appeared from underneath the water.

"I wish I could glide across the lake all day," Nick said as his friend Tommy came out of the water beside him.

"I want to be other things than a bug," Tommy said in a dismissive tone as Nick started to swim across the lake, trying to imitate the glider. Nick spoke about animals and insects as if they were his friends, but Tommy thought he should be getting out of the habit. After all, Nick was turning seven and should be familiar with more adult things such as baseball or football. At eleven, Tommy was more mature and aware of the world around him.

Tommy saw Nick swim more than fifty yards ahead and was amazed how a smaller kid could be more of an athlete than he. Tommy was five-five with a lanky body. He hoped in a few years, with his long arms and legs, he could be a state champion swimmer or basketball player. Nick had a more compact, muscular frame with a crawl stroke that enabled him to move the water efficiently around his body. Tommy swam after Nick and was exhausted when he finally reached him in the middle of the lake.

"We should go. I don't want any trouble with my folks," Tommy said.

"You're such a wuss," Nick said defiantly. "We've just got here and I haven't even started exploring." With that, he began swimming towards the base of the dam. Nick was a risk taker and adventurer, whereas Tommy was more of a thinker. These complementary qualities formed much of the basis of their friendship.

Swimming in the lake had been prohibited ever since a high school senior drowned on a prom night while skinny-dipping with his date. Ever since, signs had been posted warning of fines for bathing and other activities taking place near the water. The signs had served less of a warning than an enticement. On occasion, some teenager would be seen in a police car being taken back to town after a swim. The fine had been a small punishment compared to the ridicule heaped on the offender for being caught in the first place.

After a few crawl strokes Nick was able to reach the boulders that framed the base of the dam. He pulled himself out of the water, climbing the rock riprap lining the interior slope of the embankment. Nick loved to climb and he negotiated the sharp-edged rocks in bare feet to the top of the embankment without losing his balance. Looking down over the railing, he saw the grey shotcrete surface that formed the downstream face of the embankment, vertical at the top, and curving as it went down towards the river. Nick leaned over as far as he could and then spat, watching in satisfaction the white gob of spit travel down until it bounced off the curved concrete.

Nick raced along the embankment to where water flowed out of the dam over a flat granite shelf twenty feet below the top. The surface of the water seemed smooth and dreamlike. Nick simply stood there entranced by the sound of the waterfall and was distracted when he heard Tommy's heavy breathing as he struggled up the slope.

"This is so cool. I can see the entire town," Nick called out to Tommy, who was still on the embankment rocks. On the right was the steeple of the Pope's Mills Baptist Church and to the left was the factory with its two smokestacks. In the center was the clock on the cupola of the High School and the "L" shaped Clark Memorial Hospital. Even though the town was two miles away, Nick stuck his arms out pretending to touch the buildings, moving them around in his head as if they were part of some large plastic model set one would see in the stores at Christmas.

The afternoon was quickly becoming evening. Tommy rested on the open, rocky slope shivering and feeling vulnerable. Out in the distance he could hear the blaring, cough-like honking of Canadian Geese feeding in the cornfields. Soon they would descend on the lake to take refuge for the evening. Tommy looked overhead and saw only a single goose above him. He had been at the lake when the sky was dark with the geese; the sound they made was overwhelming. His father had been with him, the two of them standing in awe of this force of nature, while he covered his ears to muffle the noise.

Tommy eventually reached Nick at the top of the slope and was immediately drawn to a concrete marker with a weathered bronze plaque bearing the inscription:

"DAM #304 ON THE KENDALL RIVER

DESIGNED AND CONSTRUCTED BY
THE U.S. ARMY CORPS OF ENGINEERS
1955

CAPACITY 900,000,000 GALS, 2760 ACRE-FEET
HEIGHT TO TOP OF SPILLWAY 55 FEET"

Nick peered curiously over Tommy's shoulders for a few seconds and, bored by the plaque, started to run across the crest of the dam

Tommy called after him, "I was supposed to be home by six. If I'm not, my father will have a shit-fit and get the Sheriff to look for me. Then we'll both be in trouble."

Nick stopped in his tracks and replied with a playful taunt, "Why don't you come and get me?" It had been Nick's idea to go to the lake and Tommy realized it would take more than a threat to get him to leave. It was Saturday night and after a day's work at the plant, Nick's father would be drunk and getting into a fight with his mother. Nick never talked about his parents, but his father's bouts of drunkenness were well known throughout the community. Tommy felt sorry for Nick. Being at the lake was the only escape from his dismal home life.

Tommy started to run after Nick to get him when he saw a red pickup truck coming up the road. The truck abruptly turned off onto the access road for the dam. Tommy pointed at the truck in the distance and said, "Let's get back down to the lake." Nick realized the danger of being discovered and they instinctively climbed back down the riprap and swam hurriedly toward the shoreline for cover.

The truck continued up the road and parked adjacent to the top of the dam. Two men got out of the truck, took off the white tarp that covered the bed and began unloading crates. One man seemed to be directing the other and pointing to things on the dam.

Tommy and Nick crouched under the shrubs that covered the shoreline. Tommy had gone duck hunting before and learned about using vegetative cover to blend into the surroundings. The shrubs formed the perfect natural camouflage for watching the activity at the dam. As part of being a hunter, Tommy had a talent for staying motionless for hours. He couldn't vouch for Nick who was more restless.

Nick stared at the men and said, "I wonder what the hell they're doin?"

Tommy put his hand over Nick's mouth and whispered in his ear, "Shut up, stupid." The boys crouched in the water and watched as the men finished moving the wooden crates from the pickup truck. Nick looked fascinated while Tommy stared ahead, wide-eyed, his heart pounding with fear.

***

Sheriff Sam Johnson Jr. pensively sipped coffee from a cracked mug as he sat on the circular, red padded stool at the counter of the Collins Hotel, four seats from the end. It was all part of his daily afternoon ritual of working in his office until four thirty in the Municipal Building and then walking across the square to the Collins. It was the same routine his father, Sam Sr., had followed for the fifteen years he was Sheriff of Pope's Mills.

The Collins Hotel was the oldest building in town and was not really a hotel, rather it was a restaurant and community meeting place. It was the only place in town serving reasonable food other than Christine's, a bar located next to the railroad tracks. Constructed in the 1850's as a country store, the Collins was the best example of Greek Revival architecture in town with its brick exterior and large arching windows that seemed to dominate the first floor of the restaurant, providing an unobstructed view of the grassed square.

Sam daydreamed for a moment as he looked out the windows and then felt a stabbing pain in his head. It was all the stress from spending three hours at the computer, reviewing rows of figures. He was a cop, not an accountant. He withdrew a small plastic bottle out of his gold uniform shirt and shook out two aspirins that looked like microscopic dots in his baseball mitt-like, coffee-colored hands. He winced as he swallowed the pills, alternating them with sips of coffee. Trying to take his mind off work, he spread out the Pope's Mill Gazette in front of him as he uncomfortably hunched his two hundred and fifty pound muscular frame over the counter in a stool too high for a man of his stature.

The pain in his head still would not subside.

A few seats away, Thelma Parson stood behind the counter gossiping in a hushed tone to Sally Holiday, a retired high school counselor. Sally was there for her daily free cup of coffee provided in exchange for information about anyone in town. The acknowledged rumor queen of Pope's Mills, Sally would know anything that occurred within the town so that many people did not depend on the newspaper; they simply contacted her for any news. Sally enjoyed the attention this provided, since she was a spinster in her sixties who had never been married and needed the contact with people. Most of the information she would obtain first hand, and on most days she could be seen sitting in her rocking chair on her front porch that overlooked the town with her six dogs looking at people passing by.

Thelma, a short gray haired lady wearing a dirty white apron, stuck her head away from the conversation with Sally and finally ambled over to Sam. "The usual hot dog and coffee today, Sam?" she asked.

"No, just a Coke, I don't feel like I want nothing much." He said with a twinge of anxiety in his voice.

"You look down. Is there anything I can help you with?" Thelma asked sympathetically.

"Maybe, if you could find a million dollars buried somewhere." Sam hesitated, "Actually fifty thousand will do." Sam thought about how he spent the afternoon in his office balancing the department's budget. His father, Sam Sr., seemed to understand the procurement process much better and did it without the help of any computers or spreadsheets. Sam Sr. was the first black Sheriff of Pope's Mills. Son of a sharecropper, he had only a rudimentary high school education, but was the Einstein of common sense and could solve complex problems through intuition.

"You can look at this place and see what I'd be spending money on." Thelma said.

She was right, the restaurant had seen better days, Sam thought. Sam looked around and saw the broken, discolored plaster on the ceiling where a water pipe had burst the previous spring.

There were only three people in the dining area. It was still early, but on a normal Saturday night the restaurant would be half to three-quarters full. Sam realized the lack of business was due to a conflict with the First Baptist Church picnic that night. It was a semi-annual event that drew three to five hundred people. Sam remembered going with his parents when only thirty people would show.

Thelma quickly passed Sam a glass of Coke and said as she leaned over the counter, "A lot of people are going to the picnic. How about you?"

"I've got my evening rounds," Sam said.

"Nothing ever happens here. Why don't you go? It will be good for you to see some people."

"That's all I do all day is see people," he retorted.

"You know what I mean," Thelma said. "You need to socialize. It's been one year since your divorce."

"I don't have the time to meet women," he said, trying to seem more interested in the paper. Sam understood Thelma's maternal feelings towards him, and was one of the few people in town he tolerated discussing his social life. Thelma, who had known Sam for all his life, would tell stories of when his father, Sam Sr., used to carry him into the restaurant when he was a baby.

"Ellie will be there. She always comes in here asking about you," Thelma said.

"Oh no," Sam thought, "she's trying to fix me up again." Ellie Booth went to high school with Sam; he knew her to be overweight and always chewing gum. Sam found it distracting that she couldn't utter a sentence without taking part of the gum out of her mouth and twirling it around. Sam remembered Ellie sitting in the stands at football practices. She married Rodney, a wide receiver. Rodney had died two years ago from a rare form of liver cancer and she was on the hunt to find a successor.

"So Sam, are you going to start dating Ellie?" Sally asked from three stools away. She had an obnoxious talent for listening in on three conversations at one time.

Sam was noncommittal. "She seems to be a nice person. I really do want to start a family of my own."

"You're not going to do that sitting in your police car, now will you?" Thelma quipped.

Sam realized he was not going to win the debate. "Thanks for the advice. You should start a romance column for the Gazette."

Quickly placing some coins on the Formica counter, Sam got up to leave. He ambled over to Sally. "I would appreciate if you would not start any talk around town. I would like to keep my social life…private," he said with emphasis on the last word as he trotted out to start his rounds.

As Sam exited the Collins, he crossed Poplar Street, the main thoroughfare that divided the town in half. Adjacent to Poplar Street was a grassed square that marked the center of town. In the middle of the square, surrounded by park benches, was the bronze statue of Thaddeus Pope, the original owner of the parcel of land in which the town was situated. Dressed as a Confederate infantryman, he held a rifle in one hand and had the other outstretched in the air pointing towards the horizon. In 1860, after the Civil War, Pope, a moderately successful businessman, constructed the original grain mill on the Kendall River for which the town was named.

The half dozen stores on the square were closing for the day. Before the economic recession in the late 1990's, all the storefronts had been occupied with businesses, but now the area was mostly vacant. Sam made a cursory inspection of the empty storefronts to check for any break-ins. At times, vagrants would occupy the empty stores and start fires in the winter to keep warm. One of the fronts served as a charity mission and had a large, ornate cross painted on the glass. The store had not been occupied in ten years, and the cross looked chipped and warped. Sam took out a white handkerchief, wiped away the accumulated grime, and saw the remnants of the benches and a piano.

Sam got into his six-year-old blue and white Mercury police cruiser parked on the square. He hastily drove over the railroad track, down the nearly dark residential street lined with modest wooden A-frame structures topped with mordant-brown asphalt shingles built forty years ago from kits purchased from Sears. Sam knew the houses; each had two rooms on the first floor and another two on the second that passed as bedrooms. Lined up in one monotonous row after another, they were painted various colors: red, pink, blue, and even purple, but in Sam's mind, nothing could disguise their sterile appearance.

Still early in the evening, Sam made a left onto Spruce St, headed west toward the river and noted on the right a narrow, bituminous road shaded with Sycamore trees. He could briefly see in the direction of the river a mansion house that had four white columns supporting an overhanging porch. The stately "Clark" house served as a library and meeting hall for Pope's Mills. For over twenty-five years, the mansion was home to Matthew Clark, the former owner of the Pope's Mills Paper Company. Sam remembered the place from when he was young, going to elaborate Christmas parties there and meeting Clark, a tall man with a large head of slicked back white hair and a long grey beard. At the time of his death in 1994, Clark had accumulated a fortune estimated at twenty million dollars. Since he had died suddenly of a heart attack, and left no will, the mansion was turned over to one of Clark's nephews. Two years later, the nephew decided he did not want to live in Pope's Mills and had promptly sold the house to the town for half its value.

The road made a sudden decline down to a one-lane, hundred-foot long concrete bridge spanning the Kendall River. Slowing the car to a near crawl as he crossed the bridge, he briefly looked upstream towards the dam and tried to decide if it was worthwhile to make a stop to enforce the ban on bathing. He made a left onto River Road, which paralleled the Kendall. Adjacent to the road were cabins that appeared to be randomly placed. They were austere, with rough-hewn oak logs and tar roofs, heated only from a wood stove and no running water. All of them were previously used as hunting lodges by businessmen. Discarded for more luxurious accommodations, they became dwellings for plant workers on a budget.

Sam sped past a dozen houses, all dark and showing no signs of life except for the largest one, which had its lights on. Sam glanced at the house curiously and then cruised up the road for another two thousand feet. Seeing the vague outline of the dam through the trees, he unexpectedly veered the car onto the shoulder and turned off the ignition with a dismissive flick of his hand. Sam had always thought River Road to be the most scenic section of town, especially in the spring when the Yellowwood trees were ready to break into full blossom. He rolled down the window and the car filled with the sweet scent of the white fragrant flowers hanging from their branches in clusters resembling bells. He leaned back in his seat and closed his eyes, smelling the scent of the flowers and hearing the sound of birds. It reminded him of when he was a boy, clipping the branches with his parents for Easter ornaments. It was a much less complicated time when he did not have to deal with the public, the Mayor, or the Town Council. Why waste the effort, he thought, the kids won't be swimming here today; they will be at the picnic. Despite the warm weather, it was still early in the year for swimming. After a few moments, Sam started the engine, turned the police car around, and headed back towards town.

* * *

The water in the Kendall River tumbled over the boulders creating circular eddies and currents. Charlie Stewart sat on his front porch drinking a beer. He stared at the water as an occasional trout came up to feed on a fly at the surface. He thought it would be a perfect time to go fishing. Charlie held back the impulse and stayed on the porch swing. His daughter, Tonya, had gotten sick during the day and his wife, Eve, would need him close by to help out with any housework.

Charlie got up to get another beer and proudly eyed his home, a somewhat eclectic mix of building materials. The front of the building was made of logs cemented together, which contrasted with the smooth white planks of the rear addition. Over the years, he had added a kitchen, bathroom, and two bedrooms, doubling the living space. All the work he did himself on evenings and weekends. Charlie was a maintenance man. The project allowed him to make use of all the knowledge of carpentry, plumbing, and masonry he had learned while working at the paper plant. With his job, all he could afford was a company owned home, not more than fiberboard with a thin layer of plaster. They were drafty in the winter and hot in the summer. Now, he was in possession of a comfortable home that was previously owned by a wealthy white man from Louisville.

There were drawbacks to life on the river. About five years ago, nearly a foot of rainfall fell in a six-hour period. The water in the lake had come within six inches of the top of the dam. Sam Sr. evacuated him before the maintenance people released the floodgates. It required some pushing and pulling to get Charlie and Eve to leave the house. Waiting out the storm, Charlie did not know if he would have a home to come back to. He prayed to the lord asking not to have put so much time and labor in vain. The entire first floor was flooded and the living room set ruined, but when he saw that the house had survived intact, he went to his knees and kissed the ground. As a commemoration, Charlie painted a black line on the white doorsill six feet off the ground, the highest level reached by the river. He also put a crucifix onto the door with St. Jude.

A figure of a delicately shaped woman with long graceful legs and smooth brown skin wearing a tan cotton jumper appeared in the doorway. "I think the worst of it is over. Her fever was one hundred and two this afternoon, and now it's down to one hundred. Maybe with a little bit of rest she will be back to normal tomorrow," Eve said with a note of worry.

"That's a relief," Charlie said. He did not want to think about spending the evening in the emergency room, or having to spend his small paycheck on the doctor's bill. "Do you know what brought it on?"

"I don't know. I took her over to the playground earlier this afternoon and she was playing well with the other kids and then she came over to me complaining of chills. I checked her temperature and she seemed to be burning up. I spoke to Doc Rolland and he said it was probably a twenty-four hour virus and to give her a nice bath, cool drink, and some cold compresses to reduce the fever. If it persists, I will have to take her over tomorrow."

"Looks like we're going to spend a quiet night a home rather than going to the picnic," Charles said, looking disappointed. "I was looking forward to trying Martha Jones' sweet potato pie."

"No problem, you can go to the picnic, and I can stay here with Tonya," offered Eve.

"I don't think it would be the same without you. Everyone there would be asking about you and Tonya, and I would wind up talking about Tonya's illness all night. Probably the Reverend Nixon would take me aside and tell me about my fatherly responsibilities. I don't need a lecture from him today."

"Well then, it looks like you're stuck here with me tonight," Eve said with a sly smile.

Charlie stroked his chin in the middle of a thought. "Maybe, I can start figuring out my next project. I think I'm going to build the addition to the back of the house. It would make a great play area for Tonya."

Eve got a sour look on her face. "Not another addition…you promised you would not spend any more money on the house and start saving for Tonya's education. I want her to go to Gottlieb Heights Christian Academy next year." Eve had previously discussed the possibility of sending Tonya to a private church school in the next town.

"I think the public schools around here are good enough. I made it to the university."

"You got there on a Track and Field scholarship. I don't want her to depend on sports to get into college. If anything, I want her to succeed because of her education. All I'm thinking about is her ability to leave Pope's Mills when she turns eighteen, and not work for Pope Paper." Complaints about the company were becoming a common theme in their discussions, and it was apparent Eve was having second thoughts about living in a company town.

Charlie finally said, "Do you have any regrets about living here in Pope's Mills? I'm powerless to change anything that has happened. You know the only thing I think about during the day is the both of you."

"I know you love me, but I am trying to think about Tonya's future." Eve said walking away.

Charlie got up from his chair and grabbed his wife's arm, turning her around, his muscular six-foot frame towering over his wife. He confronted her almost becoming defensive, "I asked you a question and you did not answer it. *Do you regret coming here?*"

Eve made an angry face and pretended to ignore the question and said, "I'm going into the house to start dinner. I think there is some leftover ham I can make into a casserole."

Charlie went back to the porch swing and took another gulp of beer. Tonya slowly emerged from the front door carrying a worn brown teddy bear with a near grin on its face. The more Charlie looked at her, the more she resembled her mother with her delicately curved eyes, oval face, and light complexion. Teddy bear in her arms, Tonya climbed aboard the porch swing and put her head in his lap. "Can we can go fishin' tomorrow?" she asked.

Charlie smiled, and thought Tonya could not be as sick as Eve had described if she was asking about fishing. He reclined in the wooden swing and stroked her head as he looked out toward the river. "We'll see, baby. We'll see," he said as he rocked her rhythmically back and forth.

After a few moments, Tonya burrowed deep in his lap to sleep as Charlie took long sips of beer. He was about to fall asleep himself when he heard the sound of a car pulling into the driveway. Opening his eyes, he saw Sam stride out of the car and with a note of recognition he sat up, mildly surprised. "Good evening Sam. To what do I owe this visit?"

Sam had a worried expression on his face as he walked over to the porch. "I saw your lights on. I thought you guys were going to the picnic."

"Tonya's sick and we thought we should spend a quiet night at home," Charlie said as he kissed Tonya on the forehead.

"I hope it isn't anything serious. Is there anything I can help you out with?" Sam offered.

"I think she spent too much time out in the sun today. She'll probably be back to normal tomorrow, but thank you for your concern."

"Maybe I could pick up something for her in town. I don't mind."

"I don't think that's necessary. Take a break. I've got plenty of cold beer here," Charlie said pointing at the red Styrofoam cooler under the swing.

Sam heard a noise in the house and Eve appeared smiling in the doorway. "I thought I heard someone out here. How you doing Sheriff? It's been a while since you visited. Why don't you sit down and have some dinner with us?"

"Eve, I've always enjoyed your cooking but tonight I think I'll take a rain check. I see Tonya is holding my teddy bear. I hope she likes it."

"You know she does. It's her constant companion," Eve said.

Sam reached out as Charlie handed him the sleepy Tonya. "How's my little princess today?" he said as he coddled her and gently kissed her on the forehead. "Little Princess" was Sam's nickname for Tonya since she was three years old, and liked to act out parts of the fairy tales Sam would read to her. She would put on a pink ballerina outfit with a wand in hand and pretend to change butterflies to frogs. For her fourth birthday, Sam bought her a small silver bracelet monogrammed with "My Little Princess." Tonya smiled, faintly putting her arms around Sam's waist as the chain clinked around her wrist.

"How about next Sunday I take you over to Gottlieb Heights?" he said softly. "I hear they opened a new ice cream parlor there and we can have banana splits together if it's okay with your mom and dad."

"No problem, Sam. It will give us a chance to catch up on our housework," Eve said with the understanding that Sam loved to spoil Tonya. He was Tonya's godfather, and Eve realized how protective Sam was of her, as if she were his own child.

Sam looked down at Tonya and said, "How about it sweetie?"

"I would like that fine, Uncle Sammy," Tonya said in a tired voice.

Sam set Tonya down and said, "I better get going. I will leave you folks alone to eat dinner."

Sam heartily shook hands with Charlie, hugged and kissed Eve, and said, "See you all next week then."

When Sam drove away he saw all three of them smiling and waving at him through his rear view mirror. He regretted leaving them to spend the next few hours making small talk and playing politics.

***

"It's the most damned strange thing I've ever seen." Tommy whispered to Nick as they crouched together in the water.

They had been watching the two men at the top of the dam for nearly three- quarters of an hour. The tall man had a harness around his shoulders and a pouch fastened to his chest. A thick rope was tied around the metal safety railing while the other end was attached to the harness. Tommy watched curiously as the tall man disappeared from sight down the face of the dam. Occasionally, the tall man would climb back up and the second man on top of the dam would hurriedly put dark circular objects in the pouch. The boys watched intently as the tall rappelling man and the shorter man swiftly moved along the dam face.

"I don't recognize either of them." Tommy said in a concerned voice. The sun was low in the horizon and Tommy could not see their faces, just their builds. Tommy had met all the people who had done building and road maintenance for the town. Tommy's father, Ted Armstrong, was the Director of Public Works. Being director was a significant job, and during the economic boom Armstrong supervised ten people. Now in a recession, Armstrong's staff dwindled to four. None of them had any motivation to do their job in an expeditious manner. Tommy's father would come home and would consume the dinner conversation with complaints about the speed his staff worked. Tommy was certain his father did not employ the two men he was seeing.

"They're probably fixin' the dam," Nick said innocently.

"If they were, they'd have my father with them."

"Your father doesn't know everything that goes on."

"He knows enough. He's involved in all the construction projects here." Tommy would sometimes go along with his father when they fixed a section of water pipe or repaired the curb section of a street. If there had been a project at the dam, his father would have been an active part of it.

Tommy strained to see the pickup truck. The truck did not match any of the semi's the town owned and did not have any government insignia, or any lettering indicating ownership. The more Tommy thought about it, the more he became concerned; nothing seemed to be right. He put his arms across his chest shivering from the cold. He needed to leave and get the Sheriff. "I'm making a break for it. I'll tell you when," Tommy whispered to Nick. He would have to leave the water to get on his bike hidden next to him under the shrub. He would be visible momentarily from the dam, and would need about five seconds to get beyond the rise adjacent to the lake to pedal down the slope to River Road.

Nick looked back at Tommy and said, "I'll stay back here and find out what they're doing."

"I don't have time to argue with you. There's something wrong and we need to get the hell out of here."

"I'm staying. When I get to school on Monday, I'm going to tell everyone how scared you were. You won't be able to live this down for a week."

Tommy did not pay any attention to Nick. He was finished playing games with his friend. Nick would just have to take care of himself. Tommy needed a diversion to get clear of the lake without being noticed, and did not have any immediate ideas. A flock of Canadian Geese were gathering on the water, feeding on insects. Tommy looked at the birds and finally thought of the course of action.

"Last chance. I'm going now," Tommy whispered.

"See you later, you wuss."

Tommy searched for a stone and picked up an eight-inch round, smooth piece of granite along the shore. He stood up and moved slowly from behind the shrubs going down to a crouch as he got to his shirt, pants, and shoes. He quickly put them on and glanced up; the two men on the top of the embankment were looking over the face of the dam. As Tommy lifted his bike hidden in the shrub, the tall man with the pouch on his stomach turned around staring down toward the reservoir surface where Tommy and Nick were hiding. Dropping the bicycle, Tommy immediately went down to his stomach, diving under a shrub, covering himself with leaves. The tall man hesitated for a moment, muttered something to the other person as he started to climb down the stone riprap. He got to the mid-point approaching the location where Tommy was hiding. Nick was another ten feet further from the base of the embankment hidden securely under a thick mass of cattails. Tommy tensed and started to scout the area for a potential weapon. The tall man took another two steps and Tommy got a glimpse of his face. The man was wearing a hooded sweatshirt but he could see the cropped, sandy blonde hair underneath. The face was rather angular with a wide brimmed nose and almost hollow cheeks. Tommy decided it was an unpleasant face. Tommy felt his heart beat heavily in his chest as the man got within a few steps from him. He heard a muffled noise sounding like, "Come back up here, we don't have time for this bullshit" and the tall man made a quick retreat up the slope.

Tommy waited five minutes and the shorter man was back to looking down at the face of the dam. With all his strength, Tommy threw the granite into the lake. The birds scattered making a loud flapping sound as they moved into the air. Leaping onto his bike, Tommy pedaled as fast as could as he catapulted himself up the slope. The short man, initially startled as the birds began to fly around the dam, began to concentrate back on the business at hand, not noticing the bike. Tommy shot out onto River Road, standing upright on the bike, getting as much power as he could out of each turn of the pedal, not looking behind at the dam as he raced back towards town.

***

Sam felt the emptiness in his stomach as he looked at the vast array of food on the foldout tables. There were three types of chicken: roasted, barbecued, and fried, along with ham, pigs feet, ten types of salads, corn on the cob, and a dessert table of decorated cakes, pies and cookies. Thelma was right. He needed to get out and see people having a good time rather than dealing with their problems eighteen hours a day. It was going towards six thirty and all the teens in attendance had finished dinner and were playing touch football in the meadow adjacent to the Baptist Church, a whitewashed structure with a slanted roof that reached a point with a steeple and bell tower on top.

Sam saw a picnic table under a Juniper tree, grabbed a plate of food and started to watch the boys throwing the ball. A discarded, retractable plastic pen bearing a sketch of the Mayor sat on the table. Sam felt a twinge in his stomach thinking about the Mayor being at the picnic giving out cheap plastic pens. Over time, Sam grew to hate the Mayor. Actually "hate" was a polite term for their relationship. Despised, abhorred, and detested would be more accurate. To Sam, Larry Williams represented the wealthy population that constantly patronized the blacks in the community. Williams was completely incapable of telling the truth, always took credit for Sam's work, and was the first to blame him for anything that went wrong. Williams had the only furniture store in town, and the visit was part publicity for the store, and part politicking for the next election. In some ways, it was humorous. Everyone would be dressed in blue jeans and a casual shirt, while the Mayor would show up in a black suit with white socks and shirt looking like a sweating penguin.

Sam was about to take a bite of his fried chicken when a football hit him in the chest. Annoyed he couldn't even finish his dinner without something happening, he gave an irritated glance at the boys playing football and they seemed to snap to attention in fear. Sam was about to throw the ball back into the crowd when he thought what it was like when he was their age. He stood up, unceremoniously taking off his uniform jacket saying, "Let me show you how the game is played."

A tall teenager whom Sam recognized as deputy's son, said disgustedly, "Oh no, we're going to get a lecture."

Sam entered the huddle, signaling to the boy who appeared to be a receiver to run a "J" pattern. Even though he never played quarterback in high school, he knew enough to call the play. When the ball was snapped, he threw a crisp pass two-thirds down the field.

The tall boy clapped and said, "Pretty good for an old man."

Sam started to return to the table and noticed the minister watching him. Reverend Nixon put his arms around his shoulder, "I knew you couldn't resist playing football."

"I just like to see kids play the game," Sam said tersely, sensing the Reverend was about to ask for a favor.

"We're starting a community league on Sundays and we need you to work with them. They seem to respect you, and it's quite apparent you could teach them more things than football."

It was difficult to say "no" to the Reverend. "I'll have to see how my schedule works out." Sam said.

"Looks like a project both you and Charlie could do together."

Sam thought back to his high school football days with Charlie, and decided not to try to relive them. "I can't speak for Charlie; he's back at home tonight..."

"I hope I can count on you both to come through for the church," Reverend Nixon said, not listening to Sam stumble over his words.

"You know... I'll do anything I can," Sam said in a low voice.

The picnic was beginning to wind down with people in small groups talking loudly, engaging in gossip about meaningless current events. Sam recognized the Mayor's high-pitched voice from across the lawn, and felt secure he was listening to him from a safe distance. The Mayor would sometimes show up at these events with his wife and children, but this time he was solo. Sam continued making small talk with the Reverend and the Mayor's voice become silent. Feeling a hand slap his shoulder, Sam turned around and found himself face to face with Williams.

"Howdy there, Sam. I'm glad you could make it," the Mayor said, making a concerted effort to convey a sickeningly sweet, folksy image.

"What a surprise, I didn't realize you were here," Sam lied.

"I just wanted to come over and tell the Reverend what an excellent job you've been doing for the town."

"Thank you, Mayor. It wouldn't be possible without the support of yourself and the Council," Sam said, trying to hide his sarcasm.

"Did the Reverend mention the project to you?" The Mayor continued to grin as if he were selling a piece of second hand furniture from his store.

Sam shook his head, and the Reverend said, turning to the Mayor, "I was about to bring it up, but maybe it would be more appropriate that you talk about it since it was your idea."

The Mayor put his hand on the lapels of his suit and gloated, "The Reverend and I were talking and it came up that the town government and the church should join forces with regard to policing the community, especially after the increase in juvenile crime we've seen here. I mentioned I would support any work you would do with the church. After all, the church men's committee pitches in every year to beautify the area around the municipal building. Don't you think it's time we return the favor?"

Sam hated when the Mayor used the pronoun "we," since it meant he would do the work. "Yes, the idea was discussed at a couple of Council meetings," Sam said. "But I thought the project was put on hold until next year's budget passes." Sam mistakenly thought he could, at least, be partially compensated for his time.

"I don't expect it to cost a whole lot of money. It's just a few hours a week and I think both you and the kids will get a lot of it. We can discuss it further at the next meeting." The Mayor looked at his watch. "Looks like I have to run, I've got a dinner date with State Senator Blake over in Gottlieb Heights regarding a grant. Anything you need please contact me."

The Mayor quickly shook the reverend's hand and walked off to his car. Sam was amazed that an hour at the picnic potentially obligated him to another forty hours of community service. Sam smiled, trying not to look upset, "That is the best food I've had in a long time. I think I still have some paperwork to do back at the office. Thanks again for everything." It was too late to undo the damage done and Sam decided it was probably a mistake to have come. As the sun was starting to set behind him, Sam walked back to his car, feeling tired and looking forward to the end of the day.

***

Nick tracked the progress of the men as they moved two-thirds across the length of the dam. As the sun sank in the horizon, the water turned from a golden yellow to a shade of orange crimson matching the hues of the sunset. Nick stuck his head down towards the surface of the water moving out of the protection of the cattails to get an unobstructed view of the men. He got to a spot where he finally satisfied he could see and hear everything that was happening.

The short man on the dam was giving abrupt instructions to the tall man on the rope. "You're too close; move another five feet towards the west."

The man on the rope gave an inaudible response, and the man in charge said, "You've got two more to place. Move your butt; we're running out of light"

After couple of minutes, the man on the rope came up to the top of dam, winded.

The short man looked down at the embankment, pausing to admire what was done. He said, "Okay, let's move out of here, I want to be five miles from Pope's Mills at seven."

Both men started to pile the rope and crates back into the pickup truck. After a minute of collecting the debris from the crates, the men hurriedly got into the truck and sped back down the access road.

Nick swam again over to the embankment and climbed up to the top. The town had a surreal, peaceful look. Nick bent over the railing and saw about thirty silvery objects one to one and half feet in diameter in diagonals along the face of the downstream embankment. The embankment was fairly steep and high, but Nick was certain he could risk it and try to pull a silvery object off of the concrete as a trophy to show everybody how brave he was for not leaving. He strained to put his hand near the object. As he got closer to the grey disks he could see there was a clock on each of their faces. He could barely make out the numbers. They seemed to be counting down from 3:39, and by the time he was able to grab an object off the dam the clock had counted down to 2:30.

***

Not speaking during dinner, Charles and Eve sat at the table and both shot glances at Tonya who had eaten a hot dog earlier and was asleep on the couch with the teddy bear in her hand. Moving towards the couch, Eve picked up Tonya and carried her upstairs.

Charles went outside to have another beer. Feeling tired himself, he closed his eyes and watched the trees rock with the spring breeze. He heard footsteps from behind him, felt Eve's arms move under his shoulders and her head on his back. "I'm sorry. I didn't mean to be bitchy with you this afternoon. I was worried about Tonya," she said.

Charles turned around and kissed her on the mouth, "You don't need to explain anything to me, baby. I understand."

Eve stared into Charles' eyes, "Yes, I want to be here in Pope's Mills with you. There is no other place I'd want to be."

"I'm flexible about Tonya. We'll figure things out."

"I know we will. I think I'll go upstairs to do some knitting," Eve said.

"Have a nice time. I'll be down here drinking beer."

"I haven't figured out what I'm knitting, and I can be 'interrupted' if you know what I mean," Eve said with a grin on her face.

"Okay, I'll be up in a minute after I finish the beer."

"Don't take all night," Eve playfully admonished.

Charles went out to the porch swing to finish his beer. Boom…Boom….Boom…Boom. A series of loud explosions from the dam shook the house. Charles felt the wood plank floor vibrate as if a large semi-truck was barreling down the road. The entire house began to shake and Charles fell to the ground as if there were no more solid foundation. Plaster came down from the ceiling and shattered near the spot where he lay on the ground. Grabbing onto the sofa, he stood up and stumbled over to the entry. The scene was beyond his comprehension. A wall of water nearly as high as the trees traveled down the river, picking up velocity and debris as it careened through the riverbanks. Trees were upended. Roots became battering rams. He stood frozen at the entranceway, his mouth wide open. He heard Eve and Tonya scream from the upstairs. As he turned his head to look in their direction, the leading edge of the wave lifted him off his feet, throwing him into the wall of his home. Within a fraction of a second the house was lifted off its foundation and disintegrated.

***

Sam parked his car in front of the municipal building and was looking forward to taking a shower and relaxing on the couch in his office when he heard the explosions. He craned his neck and tried to determine their origin. Sam guessed some of the kids at the picnic were setting off M-80's. The blasts had a muffled tone and sounded more like munitions as if a physical object was being blown apart. There was a series of four more loud explosions and Sam realized they were not coming from the south where the picnic was, but from the north toward the dam. Sam got back in the patrol car and drove off towards the river.

Sam came within fifty feet of the bridge crossing and saw an empty gap over a rumbling void. Sam grabbed an electric lantern out of the back seat, slowly got out of the cruiser, and stood on the pavement, motionless, trying to understand the scene in front of him. He smelled the fetid stench in the air. Everything was quiet. There was no sound of birds or animals, as if some terrible force had displaced them. A calm, warm spring evening had become a nightmare. Within the space of minutes, a five-ton concrete bridge deck had disintegrated leaving only the abutments. His first thought was that someone had blown up the bridge. He walked towards the abutments and looked upstream. He could not see the road. Everything within a hundred feet of the stream was flattened. Trees and telephone poles had been thrown over, flat on the ground.

Sam figured out the object being blown apart was not the bridge, but the dam.

People from the picnic began to gather behind him and some of the children started to walk towards the stream to look at the floating debris. Knowing the potential panic if he were to announce to the crowd that the dam had been blown up, Sam's thoughts turned to protecting the public. Sam saw Deputy Butler Cox in the crowd and hurriedly said, "Get these people away from here. Call Colonel Gredling of the State Police, and tell him we have an emergency; the dam has probably collapsed. Tell him to get a helicopter with searchlights and call the fire department. We need all the volunteer deputies to cordon off the area and keep people away until we figure out what has happened."

Sam stood nearly helpless for twenty minutes waiting for the water to recede and looked upstream to try to make a quick assessment of the damage. By that time, the area was completely dark. State police troopers arrived from the barracks outside Gottlieb to set up massive floodlights to illuminate the zone of damage as helicopters circled overhead with search lights on the ground. As the water receded, he recognized blue siding from one of the houses along River Road. Sam realized the houses adjacent to the road must have been destroyed. Intermixed with the uplifted trees were cars, sofas, the remains of desks and bureaus, stoves, and washing machines; all the telltale remnants of people's lives. Maybe the Stewarts had seen the dam failing and had time to get to higher ground. He reached for his cell phone and dialed their number; he heard a recorded message that the call could not be connected. Sam became very anxious and started to look through the debris, searching for any items from their house. The helicopter circled above him shining a spotlight where he walked. He saw the blue flowered couch from their living room off towards the edge of the debris field. A small object toward the left of the sofa attracted his attention. He turned on his lantern and started walking towards it. Sam felt a wave of nausea as he approached the object and finally saw what it was.

The teddy bear.

The nausea intensified as Sam tried to grab the bear. He fell to his knees, tears streaming down his face. Sam forced himself to look down to see what was holding the bear in place and saw it was a tiny hand with a bracelet engraved with the words "My Little Princess."

CHAPTER 2

Water began filling behind the dam accompanied by "Let It Be" playing in the background, making the splashing sound seem more dramatic. A man's voice sang along in a weak baritone, repeating the words, seconds out of phase with the music. As if on cue, the water stopped at the crest. There was a pause of a few seconds and then a mechanical unlatching sound. The plastic door that held back the water instantaneously exploded outward. The water whooshed out of the structure and a translucent curved wave traversed the sand channel downstream. As it did, a computer monitor on a nearby rusted metal stand plotted the wave location versus time. A gap in the plot gave the illusion of a crack in the screen.

"Oh shit, the laser is out of alignment again," a voice called out over the singing.

Joseph Hamiz, a short, wiry, modest looking man with curly hair looked up at the rectangular tank that held the water. He inspected closely the electronic release mechanism that controlled the door. He stopped singing and muttered to Kevin Crowley, the graduate student standing next to him, "Didn't I ask you to lubricate the door lock after the last trial? It did not release cleanly."

Kevin responded impatiently, "I told you, we didn't get the data. The laser is out of alignment."

Joseph's face turned red. "What did you do? It is the most sensitive piece of gear we have, and it doesn't take much to mess it up…we will have to set up the trial again."

Kevin threw up his hands, pleading innocence, "I did nothing, man; I was just standing here."

Joseph nodded his head and thought the entire problem was just that, Kevin was just standing there. No one in the department seemed to want Kevin for an assistant. Joseph, a recent doctorate from Colorado State University, was the "lowest part of the food chain", and never really thought he would have top notch graduate students working for him. He considered himself fortunate to find a post doctorate position at the Kentucky Institute of Engineering and Technology, and, overloaded with work, would take what ever was handed to him.

With a plaintive glance towards Joseph, Kevin said, "I want to hit a few bars. I still want to go back to my apartment to take a shower and wash all the dirt off of me. I don't feel like spending all Saturday night in this dungeon."

"It's only nine o'clock and you still have plenty of time for your debauchery at the local taverns," he said to Kevin, who was sulking in the corner. Joseph learned to tolerate Kevin's constant complaining about the hours and the conditions in the lab. Kevin's description of the lab as a "dungeon" was fairly accurate. The hydraulics lab, located in the basement of the Civil Engineering Building, dated back to the early 1900's. The room was oblong, measuring sixty by twenty feet with gray granite block, load-bearing walls. During times of heavy rainfall, the walls felt moist. Joseph would find himself wearing a heavy sweatshirt during the summer to fend off the cold and dampness. The ventilation was virtually nonexistent with the only fresh airflow coming from two small three-foot windows at the top of the wall. The dampness and the humidity also aggravated Joseph's allergies, and for weeks he would have sinus problems so severe, he lost the ability to smell or taste. The environmental conditions were a small drawback compared with the room not having been cleaned in years and inhabited by small armies of roaches and mice. The advantage to working in a foreboding place was that it kept visitors to minimum. Bob Sorenson, the head of the department, never came down to the lab to supervise the experiments. Joseph enjoyed the solitude of the work, without the interference of others.

As a child, Joseph dreamed of becoming a teacher like his father, and he envisioned being a professor at a prestigious university working in a paneled office with a Persian rug and a fireplace. Instead, he was stuck working at a tedious job at a second tier academic institution, performing manual labor in filthy conditions, and taking grief from a graduate student.

The wave had created dunes in the sand channel. Joseph took a swig of coffee from his thermos, trying to gather the energy to reshape the channel back to its original trapezoidal shape. "Okay, you fix the laser while I set up the trial," Joseph said as he attached the leather harness to his shoulders to pull the plywood form over the wet sand, like a horse plowing a field.

As Kevin began work unscrewing the head of the laser, he saw a dark object in the sand. He grimaced and then suddenly jumped back. "Oh fuck, there's a turd in here."

Walking over, Joseph took a small plastic shovel and dug out the object and deposited it in the metal garbage can in the corner of the room.

"I hope the cat doesn't show its face around me because I swear I'm going to break its fuckin' neck," Kevin said.

"Why should you kill the cat when it actually does some work around here?" Joseph replied. Joseph's relationship with Abercrombie was the most satisfying he had in his current life. He had complained about the rats and the janitors put out traps that were completely ineffective in controlling the problem. A couple of months earlier, in the middle of winter, Joseph noticed a stray cat in front of the building and fed it. The gray haired calico cat kept on returning. On a freezing, rainy night Joseph brought it into the lab. Abercrombie turned out to be a good mouser, controlling the rodent population. It had also provided him companionship on long nights.

Kevin tinkered with the realignment of the laser and then stood back watching Joseph grade the channel and said, "Don't you feel guilty sometimes about doing this type of work?"

The question seemed to come from nowhere and Joseph set down the form. "I don't know what you mean."

"Come on, you know what I mean, Joseph. You're aware what the Army will do with the information we develop about dam failures."

"They are going to use it to create better methods for predicting the height of the waves after catastrophic failures. Actually, there were a half a dozen or so failures in the United States last year, so the research is quite topical."

"Do you really believe that? The army will probably use the information to destroy dams in China or Russia, to inflict the maximum damage on the civilian population."

Joseph shrugged his shoulders and said, "All I know is the research will be applied to flood prediction and the creation of better alarm systems for failures.

Kevin was still adamant. "I don't understand the peacetime applications. Let's say you can predict within a half-hour that a dam will fail. Do you really think all this disaster preparedness stuff really makes any difference? What can the authorities do in a half an hour or even an hour? The Feds knew the Grand Teton dam was going to fail and still there were eleven people killed."

"That was back in the 1970's and we have made many advances in emergency preparedness since that time. Even a bad plan is better than no plan. I don't believe we should do nothing...and watch people die."

"Let's suppose you knew a dam was going to fail. What would you do? Would you have access to some crazy dam safety plan and be able to do anything within an hour?"

"That is a stupid question since I don't know about a particular dam failing. There are a lot of variables involved. I cannot make a general statement."

Kevin sat on the desk sipping a soda. "I meant it as a rhetorical question. To be honest, I don't think we are going to come up with any answers for these issues doing experiments."

"You really do not like your work down here, do you?" Joseph asked in an unemotional, non-judgmental voice.

"It's like any other job. It pays the bills and it gets me my master's degree. You can't say you are completely happy working in this dungeon"

"Part of the reason I did a doctorate was to do research and this type of work does give me valuable experience." The answer seemed canned and phony, but Joseph did not want to give Kevin the satisfaction of complaining about the project. After all, the published scientific papers would have Sorenson's name on them so Sorenson would receive all the credit for the research. Joseph would be the second name on the papers and would not qualify for any literature citations even though he did all the work.

"I try to have a life outside this place. I plan to get out tonight, to get drunk and laid— not necessarily in that order. You can come along if you want," Kevin said with a smirk on his face.

"Thanks, but I am tired. I have been up since six this morning."

"There are a lot of beautiful women on the campus. I bet shacking up with one will stop you from worrying about the project. I even know the pickup line for you. All you need is a key chain from a BMW. You can put it on the bar and I can introduce you as a nephew to a Saudi prince."

"There is no truth to the statement since I am Lebanese. My uncle was a tailor in Beirut and I own a 1980 Dodge K car. "

"It doesn't matter. She would not be able to figure out the difference in your nationality and you'd be walking her back to your apartment rather than driving."

"I have enough of a life outside the lab. I do Lebanese cooking on Tuesday night at the Student Center." He added hastily, "I also do Karate on Thursdays at the Physical Education Center."

Kevin laughed. "If you call that a life. Somehow, I can't imagine you studying Karate. I can't even see you in a street fight." Kevin got up from his chair, making Karate chops and spastically leaping in the air while kicking and making yelping sounds doing a comic Bruce Lee imitation.

Kevin did the routine for a minute and finally Joseph smiled and said, "Okay you can stop now. I don't do Karate to get into "street fights." I like the workout it gives me. It improves my balance and coordination, and it clears my mind."

"It sounds like too much exertion to forget what I am doing. Anyhow, if I really want to clear my mind I will watch the girls sunbathe on the quad."

Joseph saw Kevin was not going to accomplish anything else that night. "Why don't you do your bar thing? I can finish up here."

Kevin feigned politeness, "Are you sure? I can hang around for a few minutes to help out with another trial."

"I think you have helped out enough today," Joseph said, trying to get Kevin to leave so he could get some real work accomplished.

"See you on Monday then." Kevin picked up his coat and strode out the metal door to the corridor, which closed with a clang.

With the distraction out of the way, Joseph thought he could do the rest of the trials he had scheduled for the night. Rock music from the 1970's filled the room and, humming along with the songs, he reached over to the wall turning the valve to release the water into the tank. He heard a meowing from the floor below him and felt Abercrombie gently rubbing against his legs. Joseph picked up the cat and the meowing changed to a purring. He took a bowl out of the lab desk, poured some milk from a carton on the desktop, and set the cat in front of it. Joseph started to sip the milk out of the carton. Staring at the cat contentedly lapping at the bowl of milk, he said, "Looks like we have a long night ahead of us, my friend."

CHAPTER 3

The press corps invaded Pope's Mills at dawn. There were ten trucks from the local news stations with their ubiquitous satellite dishes and as a dozen vehicles from the national news services such as CNN. The scene in front of the municipal building was pandemonium with all the news people competing for a spot. Sam had the state police clear them out and move them to the other side of the square. The traffic was becoming gridlocked with one continuous line of cars coming into the center of the town. It was the first time Sam could ever recall that the square required any form of traffic control and he telephoned Colonel Gredling of the state police for help.

By nine a.m., Sam had retreated to his office in the municipal building to take a brief respite from managing the crisis. He spent all night coordinating emergency activities with the state police and at two o'clock in the morning got a call from the parents of Nick Palmary regarding the disappearance of their son. The mother started yelling and crying inconsolably. At three a.m. he called Doc Rolland to administer a sedative. Out of sheer exhaustion, between four and four-thirty, he took an hour-long nap on the red leather couch in his office and afterward took a shower.

Sitting behind his desk, Sam was astonished that it only had taken five minutes for his small, nine by ten office to fill with people. Looking over his desk at the crowd he tried to participate in two conversations at once. It was a useless exercise since every person had his own agenda.

A Red Cross official was talking to the high school principal about arranging a shelter for the people made homeless by the dam break. "The school gymnasium should be good for at least a week until we can make permanent arrangements."

The high school principal was unhappy. "That may be difficult for us since we have classes and having the families stay at the school will disrupt everything. Maybe the motel on the edge of town would work better for you."

"We tried there, but that is where the police have set up their operation."

"Have you tried the Lakemount Motel?" the principal countered.

The Red Cross official shook his head. "It's fifteen miles outside of town. It would present a severe hardship to the families."

The two men were continuing their dickering while the equipment operator from the public works department, who was removing the debris from River Road, argued with Deputy Cox. The equipment operator, a large man wearing overalls, had been working all morning and was at an impasse. "We've been dumping the debris at the vacant lot on the south side of town but people are complaining about the foul smell."

"Why don't you use the landfill?" the deputy suggested simply.

"There isn't enough space in the landfill. We've been running out of space for the past two years."

The deputy scratched his chin, trying to brainstorm an acceptable location. "Maybe we can find another spot for you to dump, outside of town…"

The operator was at the limit of his patience. "I don't have a a permit to haul it outside of town. I think the town should set aside…"

After spending the night searching for the bodies of his friends, and being yelled at by a hysterical woman, Sam couldn't listen to any more loud arguments. He abruptly got up from his desk, put his arm around the Red Cross official and said to the principal, "I think we have enough cots in storage to put up the six families at the school for tonight. It is a Sunday night and they'll be out of the way by Monday morning."

The principal started to make a retort and Sam turned his head to the Red Cross official, "I want to thank you for your offer of help, and certainly we will need it. I'm going to talk to Reverend Nixon at the Baptist Church and see if we can find some families with room to spare for a week. That ought to buy enough time for you to figure out any permanent arrangements." He went over to the equipment operator. "I'm going to call the Gottlieb Heights town engineer and see if he can send up some trucks and backhoes to help us out. When they had a fire a couple of years ago, we took all the rubble in our landfill. I'm certain they can help us out now." Sam made a general announcement in the center of the room. "And now I've solved all of your problems, I trust all of you can take your discussions somewhere else. I need some time alone."

"Is there anything else you need? Anything I can bring you from the Collins?" the deputy inquired.

"Thank you, no. Too much as happened in the past twelve hours and I need some time to think."

Sam went back to his desk, pulled out a large jar of aspirin, took a couple and threw them into his mouth. The noise in the building was still loud from the press conference in the Mayor's office across the hall. Sam tried not to listen, but it was unavoidable.

A newswoman in a blue pants suit asked, "Earlier this morning the Governor took a helicopter tour of the disaster scene. Did he fill you in on what he will do?"

Mayor Williams stood in front of a desk lined with microphones. All the attention was focused on him and he had been waiting for the opportunity to act as the hero providing leadership in a crises. "I've met with the Governor and the state police. The Governor is prepared to use all the emergency personnel at his disposal to aid in the town's recovery. Furthermore, he said there would be a full and complete investigation into the cause of the failure. I have told all the town departments to fully cooperate with the police and the agencies investigating the incident."

Another newsman broke in to ask, "There were widespread reports of explosions prior to the collapse. You think the failure was the work of terrorism?"

"That's for the state police and the law enforcement officials to decide. It wouldn't surprise me if it was a terrorist act. There is no better way to strike at America than to go into a God-fearing community like ours and murder our citizens. In light of recent events, we all have to be on guard for terrorism. As a community, we have a responsibility to protect our citizens. I believe if we all stand together, we can defeat the forces that strike at our country. In addition..."

The Mayor was beginning to ramble, and a newsman, wearing a tan shirt with a red tie, mercifully interrupted, "There are three confirmed deaths with one missing. What has the response been from the town?"

"I knew all three members of the Stewart family who perished. They were very, very dear close friends of mine. I plan on establishing a fitting memorial in their names...I just want to say as a community...we will pull together and recover from this tragedy... I've been busy coordinating the disaster relief plan and I assure you that...."

Sam could not stand it anymore and tiredly got up from his desk, closing the door to the hall, muffling the Mayor. He wanted to go back to his house to privately mourn the deaths of his friends. He was certain there were explosions prior to the collapse and an examination of the site would yield the evidence. He searched his mind trying to understand why anyone would blow up the dam. Charlie Stewart never harmed anyone and the entire act seemed senseless. He knew his place was at the office and somehow, he thought if the Stewarts were alive they would understand. Clearing his mind, Sam took out a notepad from his desk and started to list the things he had to do within the next twenty-four hours in response to the emergency. The first item on the list was finding Nick, the missing boy. He drew up a list of people to interview, writing down the names of teachers at his school, and any people seen with the boy.

The wooden office door swung open and two dark-suited men walked in. One of them was a short, thin, balding white man with a close cropped hair cut, and the second a tall, athletic, black man with wire rim glasses. Sam leaned over in his chair in the middle of writing down his thoughts and hesitated as he gazed up from his notes. Peering over his reading glasses, he gave a dismissive glance at the men. "I'm afraid I'm not taking any questions from the press at this time. If you're interested, there is a press conference in the adjoining office."

The short thin balding man reached out in his pocket and flashed a badge, "I'm George Sattler from the FBI and this is Mike Jefferies from the ATF. We're from the Federal Anti-Terrorism Task Force and will be leading the investigation of the incident."

Embarrassed, Sam quickly got up to shake their hands. "I thought the state police were going to be in charge. I've given Colonel Gredling a full report of what happened last night."

Sattler mechanically responded, "The alleged illegal use of explosives is a federal crime and gives us jurisdiction over this investigation. We've spoken to Colonel Gredling and have reviewed your report. We need some additional information, if you have the time."

Sam said, "I'm sorry, no one told me the FBI was going to lead the investigation. Why don't you both take a seat on the couch? I will be happy to help out any way I can. Can I offer you some coffee? As you folks can understand, I've been up most of the night and if I don't have another cup, I'll fall asleep trying to answer your questions."

The two men sat down in unison on the beaten leather couch as Sam handed the agents two cups of black coffee in weathered mugs. Jefferies reached in his briefcase and took out a piece of paper with typing on both sides. Sattler studied the paper for a moment and said, "The report says you were the first man on the scene."

"Yes, it was around 7:05 pm. I had just had some dinner at the church picnic and I was about to head back to the office to do some paper work before returning home. That's when I heard explosions that sounded like ordnance. It's all in the report."

Sattler looked at Sam concertedly, as if trying to make a detailed assessment. "Well, let's go back in time. You were in Pope's Mills all day? Can you tell us what you did?"

"I don't see how the question has anything to do with whatever happened at the dam."

"Just answer the question," Sattler said tersely.

"Let's see, I woke up." Sam smiled hoping to break the tension. Neither Sattler nor Jefferies got the humor of the statement, and both of them shot back a blank stare. Sam continued, "The first part of the morning I went on an accident prevention inspection of the mill. When I got back, Ms. Andrews called to report a sprained ankle and I took her to the hospital since there was no ambulance available. I had a bag lunch and read the newspaper from twelve to one. From one to five, I did paper work related to the budget. At five, I went to the Collins Hotel for a Coke, and then I took a tour of the town to make certain everything was alright. I went up River Road and visited the Stewarts." Sam was back in his car for a moment, seeing them wave goodbye to him as he drove down the road. His eyes became moist and his voice choked up. Recovering from the momentary lapse, Sam said, "I'm sorry if I get a little emotional. I'm still in shock. They were really close to me."

Sattler said, "I understand. I've lost friends in the line of duty and it's tough to recover."

"Anyhow, I spent ten minutes with them, and then I went on to the picnic."

"How long have you been Sheriff?" Jefferies asked.

"I was elected to office two years ago."

"You've been living in Pope's Mills all your life?"

"Yes. I've lived here my entire life excluding the four years I spent at Kentucky State University."

"So you know everyone in town. It's a relatively small place." Sattler said taking over the line of questioning. Both men seemed to be working in tandem.

"The last time I checked, the population was thirty two hundred, and yes, I've probably met everyone in town; just don't ask me to recite their names," Sam commented in a tired voice.

"So, all the places you were Saturday, including your trip to the mill and down River Road, you didn't see anyone who you haven't seen before, or anyone doing something out of the ordinary?"

"It was a pretty ordinary day except for the dam collapsing."

Sattler put down his coffee, ready to get to the serious questions. "You said you were on River Road. Did you notice anything about the dam?"

"I try to visit there on a daily basis to make sure no one from the town is up there."

"Isn't it state property?" Sattler asked.

"Yes, it is, but it adjoins the town boundary and I have an informal agreement with the Natural Resources Police that I would go there periodically. They've got limited personnel and they've had trouble patrolling the area. A couple of years ago, a kid from the high school drowned there, and he was from our town. The town solicitor said water from the dam goes to the town and that there was a potential for a lawsuit. We convinced the state to post signs prohibiting trespassing or swimming. A handful of times I've caught kids drinking and screwing around. Otherwise, nothing serious goes on up there. Even though it is a couple of miles from here, it is a state park and a relatively remote area."

"You did not visit there on Saturday?" Sattler asked in an accusatory manner.

"I didn't have a chance. I scheduled myself to go to the picnic and I was late." Sam was in the middle of a crisis and he hadn't thought about how he could have helped prevent it. He thought there would be plenty of time to assess blame.

Jefferies saw how uncomfortable Sam had become and decided to switch topics. "You are completely certain you never saw anything out of the ordinary? Maybe a strange vehicle?"

"Sometimes I notice an out of state car here and there. Most of the time they're lost and I have to direct them back to the main road. Judging by your questions, I take it you are proceeding on the assumption that the dam was blown up."

"Yes, we are going by that assumption and we currently have a team at the site taking soil samples. We should have the preliminary results of the spectrographic analysis by tonight. Do you know why someone would want to blow-up the dam?" Sattler asked.

The idea of someone from the town murdering people was beyond him. "No sir, I do not. I can't imagine anyone from Pope's Mills doing this. You have to understand, we don't see much crime here. Most of it is petty theft, vandalism, and public intoxication. A few years ago we had a case of manslaughter when a mill worker got drunk behind the wheel, ran over and killed a fifteen-year-old boy on a bicycle."

Jefferies asked, "You don't know anyone who would have a reason for an act of retribution against Pope's Mills? Maybe it's someone who filed a lawsuit against the town, or someone convicted of a serious crime."

"I don't know anyone who fits the profile. Anyhow, I don't know if I agree with the theory in the first place. So you think anyone who has sued the town would be a suspect?"

"It's a start," Sattler said.

"A few years back, a seventy-year-old woman tripped over a soda bottle on the sidewalk in front of the Town Hall. I took her to the hospital where she was treated for a minor sprain. A week later she showed up with a lawyer suing the town for a million dollars. Of course, she only got a few hundred dollars for her medical bills, but it took a few months of legal wrangling. She now lives in a nursing home outside of Louisville. I suppose she's going to be a suspect."

"We're not eliminating anyone. In short, we need a list of lawsuits against the town and felony arrests for the past ten years."

"The list of lawsuits would be at the office of Wayne Cauldill, our Town Solicitor for the past twenty years. He works for us on an hourly, as-needed basis. He handles a dozen small communities throughout the state. I think this time of year he's vacationing in Florida."

"I'm sure he can be contacted and someone from his office can look through his files," Sattler said.

"The list of felonies would take me back into my father's records. Most of them are archived and in storage. It's going to take me a few days to go through them and I'm busy trying to take care of the emergency," Sam said as Sattler and Jefferies shot back a vacant gaze. He became more defensive, "Look, we're in a complete state of shock here. I'm trying to coordinate the relief efforts and I've got a missing seven-year-old boy to look for. So I hope you understand why I'm not jumping out of my seat to pull the files."

Sattler was undeterred. "I can make matters easy for you. Hand the files over to us and we can go through them."

Sam did not like the idea of some stranger going through the town's arrest files. To him, the issue centered on the privacy of the people in the community even though arrest records were technically considered public information. "I'm the only person who understands my father's filing system. I'm afraid anyone else would be lost."

"I would like to have it within forty-eight hours. I would consider any time longer as impeding my investigation. I would hate to embarrass you with a court order. It would look real funny for you in the press." Sattler was accustomed to using leverage to get what he wanted. In previous investigations, he had dealt with journalists who had provided him with information "quid pro quo" and then would use the opportunity to leak material back to them.

Sam knew he had lost the argument and said in a conciliatory manner, "I will see what I can do.... The only felony arrest I can think of offhand is the episode with a "Reverend" Adamson that happened here about ten years ago. My father handled the arrest personally. It involved a kidnapping and there were some federal charges filed."

Sattler was one for looking at the details and did some quick database research before traveling to Pope's Mills. "Yes we have it in our records. Three other people were arrested with him; the charges against them were eventually dropped."

"Then I don't need to tell you about it. It was a major case around here and the newspapers reported it for a couple of weeks. Of course, the "Reverend" himself is dead and I think two out of the three people who were involved have died as well. The one person who still alive has been institutionalized and would probably be of no help…"

"We may want to interview anybody who knows about the incident. We'll see how things develop in this case. I think the items we discussed ought to keep you busy for the next couple of days." The agents got up to leave and started to open the door. "By the way, I would like all the directives for future clean-up efforts to go through my office. We had to stop the backhoe operator at the river." Sattler said.

Sam exploded, "*Why did you do that?* The equipment is costing the town three hundred dollars per hour."

"You forget it's a potential crime scene and anything there is evidence. We want to be present during any cleanup operations and use our own backhoe operators," Sattler explained as if lecturing a schoolboy. He turned around and said, "One other thing—we need a place to work. I noticed the municipal building is fairly booked up. Is there any place in town we can use?"

"There is a lot of empty storefront space on the main street," Sam replied. "The problem is, many of those buildings haven't been used in years, are half falling down, and have no working plumbing. Maybe I can talk to the commissioners about you folks using the library for an office. It's out of the way, and you can proceed with your investigation without any distractions."

"Thank you for your assistance, Sheriff. We will call if we have any more questions," Sattler said formally.

Sam, upset and still shaken by the interview, stood by the office window and saw the agents driving away in their black SUV. Sam was looking forward to working with the state police in the investigation. Sam had met Colonel Gredling during the courses he had taken at the state police academy; they had coffee together and talked about hunting and fishing. The FBI did not want to deal with him as an equal and simply came to his office making demands, talking down to him. He had no experience working with the FBI and was feeling anxious about any future relationship.

***

"Gentlemen, we've got a lot ground to cover today," Agent Sattler said as he stood in the middle of Poplar Street, using the washed-out bridge over the Kendall as a dramatic backdrop. The agents crowded around him creating a human amphitheater. Sattler liked being in charge during an important investigation that would be reported in newspapers across the state. He tried to play the role accordingly. "I would like all of you to canvas the community and see if anyone was at the dam on Saturday. I need to know if any person saw anything suspicious in town during the past two days. I also need a list of the people who had houses destroyed by the flood, and I need their whereabouts. I would like to interview them personally." Sattler pointed at one of the agents. "Have the technicians finished taking the soil samples and shooting the photos of the dam?"

"Yes sir, the samples were sent out about half an hour ago. We should expect the results to come back by ten tonight," the agent answered eagerly.

"Were you able to catalog any physical evidence at the scene?"

"There were some tire tracks left on the portion of the embankment that was not washed away. We have some people taking molds and will have the tires identified by tonight."

"Good. I know it's a long shot but we need a group of agents to start sorting through the debris for any remnants of explosives. The future of the investigation is riding on all of you doing your best, and what we do during the first forty-eight hours is critical to finding our suspect." Sattler made a dramatic pause trying to make eye contact with everyone in the group. "Okay, we will meet at the library at ten p.m. to discuss any findings."

The agents scattered and Sattler saw a state car at the scene. He walked over and introduced himself to the middle-aged man writing notes on a legal pad. The man gave Sattler a firm handshake, "I'm Bob Dickey from the River Authority. I was up in the helicopter surveying the damage. It's quite a mess out there, isn't it?"

"I've wanted to talk to you. Are you are the person who's been responsible for maintenance of the dam?"

"Yes, I'm *one* of the people involved in the maintenance."

"We would like to have the maintenance records. We want the names of all the people on the maintenance crew."

"The dam was transferred to us from the Corps of Engineers. They have most of the records for the forty-seven years the dam has been here. For the other three years, the records are at our field office. I will to check with the office manager regarding their availability. I don't know the people who have done the maintenance work, but I can give you the phone number of the personnel department," Dickey explained hastily.

"I also need to know the depth of water behind the dam at the time of the incident," Sattler said as Dickey began to walk away.

"We had a telemetry gauge on the dam, but I don't know if it was in good working order before the failure. The information we give to you may be faulty. I don't want to mislead the FBI…"

"Let us decide the accuracy of the information," Sattler said.

"We're legally responsible for the validity of the data. We check the water levels versus the releases of the dams upstream and publish all the water records at the end of the month. I only have two people working for me and it takes time to process any data. Anyhow, I cannot release it early without the written approval of the Commissioner."

"Are you suggesting we wait a month for you to provide us the information? I was hoping you would cooperate," Sattler said trying to control his anger.

"I want to help, but I've got internal procedures to follow as much as you do. I suggest you direct all your inquiries to the Commissioners office. I have to give him a preliminary report about the failure, so I'm pretty busy. I trust we're finished here."

Sattler watched Dickey walk away, astonished at the raw nerve of the man. He was about to confront him when his mobile phone rang. It was Jefferies reporting the residents of the destroyed homes had assembled for a meeting at the high school auditorium. Sattler had more important issues to deal with than Dickey, who he considered at best to be a minor civil servant. He spoke back into the telephone and said, "I will be there in five minutes," and got into the car, leaving the group of agents to sort painstakingly through the debris field.

***

Later that night, the conference room of the Pope's Mills library was filled to capacity as thirty weary investigators from the FBI, ATF and state police gathered around the oblong mahogany table strewn with papers and coffee cups. There was complete silence as George Sattler sat at the head of the table reading the results of the lab tests. He methodically checked through a binder's worth of tabular data, then turned to Colonel Frank Gredling of the state police, a short, gray-haired man with a muscular build sitting next to him. "The tests came back with a positive result for TNT and RDX, a major component of plastic explosives. There's no doubt the dam was blown up. I don't want to be in your position when you call the Governor with the news."

Gredling calmly took a sip of coffee before responding, "Thanks for the sentiment. I think the Governor's expecting bad news. He met today with the Emergency Preparedness Division of my office. The next step is to call a news conference declaring a state of emergency and to call on National Guard to provide twenty four-hour protection for all the dams and reservoirs in the state."

"I think that's the prudent thing to do. The sabotage was most likely carried out by a team of people, and if they have the resources to blow up *this* dam, others may follow." Sattler tried to hide his frustration about the first day's lack of progress. The only physical evidence obtained at the dam site was the tire tracks that were later determined to have come from a pickup truck. The task force interviewed over a hundred and fifty people in eight hours. His own questioning of the families that lived along River Road proved fruitless. None of them knew anything about what had taken place at the State Park, or the dam on Saturday.

Sattler stood up from his chair and announced with a grave tone, "Looks like we have a real conundrum here: we've got no eyewitnesses, no physical evidence other than the type of explosives used, and the possibility that a pickup truck was used to transport the explosives to the dam. More importantly, we have no apparent motive. I'm willing to open the floor for any ideas about the investigation."

A young agent to the right of Sattler spoke first, "I find the choice of the target interesting: Why choose a reservoir, rather than a bridge or a building?"

Another agent answered. "Perhaps the perpetrator thought he was impacting the entire community by removing the water supply."

Sattler, acting as a moderator, answered in an authoritative voice, "I had a talk with the town engineer. According to him, the town no longer obtains its drinking water from the reservoir. The town stopped using the reservoir ten years ago when the wells were drilled. Since then, the reservoir has served as backup water supply and used solely for flood control."

Colonel Gredling said, "Possibly the persons involved are not from this area and did not know this."

A young agent from the far side of the table said, "I found it interesting all the people who had their houses destroyed were black. Do you think there's a racial motive?"

"Hmmm," Sattler said, giving a worried look. "That motive also occurred to me, although it may be just a coincidence. That's why I reviewed the last census data and found that demographically, the town is thirty-one percent black. What I'm saying is that even though blacks are a minority, there's a significant likelihood the victims would have been black anyway. We may want to consider investigating it in the future though. I'm relying on everyone's discretion about discussing this with the media. I certainly do not want it published anywhere that we're considering race as a potential motive. I don't want to be blamed for creating racial tension within the town."

Jefferies stated his theory, "Maybe there's no motive, and this was completely a random target. Maybe the perpetrators chose the dam based on opportunity—it is in fairly remote area."

Sattler responded, "No, I disagree. It took a considerable level of engineering expertise to blow up a dam that size, to create a wall of water flooding down a stream valley. Whoever did this planned the job for a long time. I would also gamble that whoever did this had a college education. At this time, it may be best to create a profile of the person who had the knowledge and experience to pull off the bombing."

Jefferies noted, "The Sheriff said no one from the immediate area could have done this. We are missing the obvious fact that it was possibly someone overseas who did it as an act of terrorism. Why don't we do a database search of INS records to see who meets the profile, someone with an engineering education and experience with explosives?"

"The profile is still too general. There are several engineering specialties—civil, electrical, and mechanical. The Middle East is the center of terrorism activity. Why don't we do a computer search of anyone who has knowledge of water resources engineering, comes from the Middle East, and has experience dealing with explosives?" Sattler replied.

Jefferies added, "Judging by similar cases we've experienced, psychologically, the person is non-confrontational and probably lacks the social skills to deal with problems with other people. He would hold a grudge for a long time, vowing revenge. I would think he is a loner and unmarried."

Sattler put his hands on the table trying to make a summation. "I think our job over the next day is to continue canvassing the community. I don't care if we interview each and every person in Pope's Mills. Agent Jefferies, I would like you to contact INS and do the database search. I would also like someone to coordinate with the state police to see if they've issued any traffic citations to anyone in the immediate area Saturday. I need a group of people to check on anyone who would have access to explosives, and check any type of construction wholesaler that sells blasting caps or demolition products. If we trace the explosives, we will get to the responsible party. I would like to thank all of you for your hard work. I think we have enough on our plate for the next day. I will see all of you tomorrow."

As the agents and state police officers got up from their chairs and started to leave the room, Sattler motioned Jefferies over to talk. "Mike, you're my right-hand man in this investigation. I thought the both of us should brainstorm about a problem that developed today."

"Sure thing, George. How can I help?"

"No one on the team has any knowledge of dams and I think we need someone with this know-how."

"What about Dickey from the River Authority?"

"I talked with him earlier today, and I nearly knocked him on his ass. He was getting bureaucratic with me and I don't feel like taking shit from someone like him. It looks like he's scared that if he cooperates with us he'll lose his job."

"That's unfortunate. Maybe we should look for someone from the Corps of Engineers or the U.S. Geological Survey."

"I don't have the time to do the personnel search and go through the paperwork to get someone on loan. Keep your eyes and ears open."

"Will do. I'm going back to the motel to try to get some sleep. I suggest you do the same."

"Thanks for the motherly advice. I think I'm going to stick around here for a while and do some reading." Sattler sat down, grabbed his leather briefcase, took out a file two inches thick, and started thumbing though the papers. He thought he must have missed something in the interviews with the townspeople. Out of the corner of his eye, Sattler saw a twenty-six-year-old agent making phone calls to the state police to check out traffic citations from Saturday.

Sattler remembered his early days at the FBI as a special agent when he would work sixteen-hour days on a case for weeks at a time. He was much older now and his body could not stand the strain. The days seemed longer years ago when he worked on the Brinkman investigation out of the Atlanta office. Recently married to an attractive secretary, he was a bright, new prospect out of the academy handling embezzlement and telemarketing fraud cases. The mob had been trying to gain a foothold on the waste management contracts for the city. Clarence Brinkman, a tall, soft spoken man from the comptroller's office, had come to the FBI with reports of people in City Hall taking kickbacks from the mob on trash disposal contracts. Sattler knew he had a near perfect opportunity to gain advancement in the FBI, and he had lobbied his supervisors to be the agent in charge. When Sattler made his pitch, he left out one important detail: he knew Brinkman from his undergraduate days at Temple University. During the investigation, Sattler not only befriended Brinkman but also spoke frequently to his wife and family of three kids. They called him, "Uncle George." The investigation ended when Brinkman was found shot three times in the head in a parking lot a few blocks from City Hall. The saddest, most humiliating day as a FBI agent was going to the funeral and having to look at his wife and kids.

The upper-echelon of the FBI blamed the failure of the investigation on Sattler, claiming that he had not provided adequate protection for Brinkman. Reassigned to a tedious job in the administrative branch, Sattler started drinking. His marriage faltered; he was divorced and lost the house. Arriving to work drunk after an all night binge, his superiors warned him he was about to be terminated. Sattler became active in Alcoholics Anonymous and was reassigned to the Lexington Field office where he compiled an impressive record of solving bank robberies in Kentucky.

It was three o'clock in the morning. Sattler rubbed his eyes after re-reading the interviews. The Pope's Mills bombing was his chance to become an inspector and regain his upward mobility in the FBI. This time, he was determined to succeed. Sattler stared across the empty mahogany table. Nothing made any sense. The questions still burned in his mind: Why would anyone destroy an old relic of a dam, and why did they pick a piss-ant town like Pope's Mills?

CHAPTER 4

The marketplace was crowded with men in turbans, skullcaps, and cloaks, walking slowly and deliberately through the wooden stalls as the shafts of sunlight descended from the canopy overhead. Joseph sat alone at a café, eating roast lamb on a plate decorated with ornate red and blue flowers. He shifted his head quickly, nervously looking around him. Each of the passing men gave Joseph a stern gaze as they walked by his table. There was a pool of blood on the plate from the meat and his hands were dripping with crimson. There were no napkins so he had to resort to wiping the blood onto his white linen shirt, now stained with dark red streaks.

The men continued their slow motion walk in front of the market. In the line, there suddenly appeared a boy wearing white baggy pants and shirt. He stopped and beckoned to Joseph with his hand. The boy stood there for the longest time, continuing to motion. With his curly black hair and sharp nose, the boy looked familiar, almost too recognizable. Finally, he started to walk away.

Joseph called out, *"Who are you?"* as he stood up to pursue the boy through the market. Joseph sped up his pace, but the boy managed to stay ahead. Merchants reached out of their stalls trying to grab him saying, "Do you want to buy some shirts, some slacks? Name your price." Joseph ran through the barrage of offers, avoiding the hands reaching out to him.

The boy was now standing at a busy boulevard lined with palm trees. Joseph asked more emphatically, *"Who are you?"* Effortlessly, the boy crossed, avoiding all traffic. Joseph ran across the street, dodging the cars as their horns sounded. Joseph traversed the hot pavement falling to his knees in exhaustion as the boy was about to disappear in a group of bombed out buildings. He held his hands out imploringly, *"My existence depends on it. Who are you?"*

The boy turned around, his brown eyes glaring ahead in the muted sunlight. Silently, he mouthed the answer. Joseph already knew what the boy was going to say since he had heard it many times before. As it turned out, he knew the boy's identity from the beginning, but could not accept it. The boy saw the disbelief on Joseph's face and repeated it out loud: his voice echoing through the urban landscape.

"I am your brother."

A bell rang in the distance as the boy's image faded. Joseph could hear footsteps coming towards him, sounding louder as he opened his eyes. He had fallen asleep in his office chair with his face resting on his hand, his fingers becoming numb. Rubbing his face, he reached for an empty pot of coffee, but instead, tipped over the mountain of papers on the desk in front of him—they hit the ground with a "thwack." The clock on the wall showed eight as the bell rang again announcing the first class of the day. There were more student footsteps in the hall, and the clamor outside of his office became louder.

It was Tuesday. He had one hour and fifty minutes to get a book at the campus library and shower at the Physical Education Building. He had to teach a hydraulics class at ten. He ran his errands and arrived back at the building at a quarter to ten. In the fifteen minutes before class, he decided to get coffee and a sweet roll in the small cafeteria located in the first floor of the engineering building. Fellow professors gave him polite "hellos" and "good mornings," eyeing him suspiciously and keeping their distance.

Joseph got his food and started to head for his office.

Climbing the stairs to the third floor, he was startled to see two men in dark suits standing in front of his office door.

The men retrieved their badges out of their suit jackets. "Are you Joseph Hamiz? We're Agents Sattler and Jefferies from the FBI Lexington office.. Would you be able to answer a few questions for us?"

Joseph looked at them cautiously and responded, "I am sorry, but I have to teach a class now. Maybe after eleven o'clock I can speak to you."

"We've made arrangements with Dr. Sorrenson for someone to take over the class. Why don't you come down to the conference room with us?"

The small conference room was a windowless, poorly ventilated byproduct of a building rehabilitation years ago. Measuring a mere ten by twelve feet, the room was big enough for a small rectangular conference table and chairs. Sattler threw his hand towards one of the metal chairs, inviting Joseph to take a seat. The two agents remained standing. As Joseph nervously glimpsed around the grey steel table, he noted that neither of them were smiling and steadfastly gazed at him.

Agent Sattler was first to speak, "We came here to discuss some things about the Pope's Mills Dam. We thought we could talk here informally and not downtown. You know about the dam? Dr. Sorrenson says you studied it as part of an inventory project for the state."

Joseph relaxed in his chair and smiled anxiously, "That is a releif. I thought you gentlemen were here to talk about my parking tickets. Parking is tight on campus, and I have ten tickets I have always been meaning to pay…"

Sattler interrupted, showing irritation, "We don't care about your outstanding tickets. What do you know about the Pope's Mills Dam?"

Somehow this question did not seem to be a general information inquiry. Why would the FBI travel to the university when the question could be better answered at the River Authority? Joseph hesitated and put his hands to his head trying to concentrate. "I have done many studies since that time. I am sorry if I have trouble remembering. Maybe I can get the inventory to refresh my memory…" He started to get up, but saw both agents staring at him. Joseph slowly went back to his chair and could feel the acid from his morning cup of coffee churning in his stomach. He vaguely remembered doing the report two years ago. He thought the inventory project was a "make work" activity serving no real purpose since all the information could be found in the files of the Corps of Engineers or the River Authority. It would be something to be shelved and forgotten. Now a mundane, two-year-old project had come under close scrutiny of the federal government.

The image of the dam came into his mind and Joseph said, "I believe it's a compacted earth-fill dam with a Shotcrete face constructed by the Corps of Engineers in 1955. It is approximately sixty feet high with a seventy foot long ogee concrete spillway. Is there anything wrong?"

"We're not interested in playing games. Are you saying you don't know what happened there?" Sattler asked tersely.

"I am sorry. I do not listen to the television or radio. I was in the hydraulics lab most of the weekend."

"So you did not hear that someone blew up the dam, and that two counties are under a state of emergency?" Sattler made a dramatic pause, "I find that difficult to believe."

Joseph's face registered shock. "I never heard anything about it." His voice became defensive. "I have a tight deadline on the present study I am doing for the Army, and I have two classes to teach, so I am fairly busy."

Jefferies asked, "Was there anyone who saw you working?"

"I was with a graduate student on Saturday night." Everybody sat motionless, unimpressed with the answer.

Sattler said, "Let's digress here for a moment. Your file at the INS says you were born in Beirut, Lebanon. Is that correct?"

"I actually was born in Jounieh, a suburb of Beirut. At thirteen, I immigrated here to the United States with my parents."

Sattler paged through the file and recited in a mechanical voice. "Just confirming the information we have: You're the only child in your family. Your father was a professor at American University in Beirut, and after emigrating to the U.S., he got a job teaching in Ithaca, New York. He stayed there for two years and then taught history at Oberlin, a small college in Ohio. Your mother died in 1998 of Leukemia, and then you moved around the East Coast another three times. Your father's last residence was in Louisville, where he sold oriental rugs. He died in 2002. You have a bachelors degree in Civil Engineering from Penn State, masters from Ohio State, and then a doctorate from Colorado State. You worked for about six months for the Gladstone Mining Company here in Kentucky, and you have been teaching here at the Kentucky Institute of Technology for the past two years. You have never been married."

Joseph listened, amazed how someone could summarize his life in one paragraph. "Well…I guess that's true."

"Just looking at the description, you must have lived in over ten states during your time here in the U.S."

"Eleven to be exact."

"Okay then. Why all the moving?"

"My father was a university professor and it is difficult to get tenure, especially in subjects many people consider to be arcane, such as Persian History. Not very much demand for this type of course in the first place. He spent most of his career at the American University in Beirut and had a reputation there as a scholar of Arab Literature. It can be difficult to go to another country and re-establish academic credentials."

"The State Department went to great lengths to find the jobs, and your father had trouble keeping them," Sattler said condescendingly.

Joseph did not like strangers to pass judgment on his father, but was in no position to complain. "Academia has a separate set of rules from other types of professions. There is a tremendous amount of politics involved…," Joseph cut short his explanation. He did not want to say his father was a proud individual and could not tolerate the behavior of his superiors who had not treated him well.

"Your father had a good knowledge of politics, didn't he?" Sattler asked in a derisive tone.

Joseph decided to play along. "You must be talking about the time he was a representative in the National Assembly."

"That's a very high office in Lebanon. I would say it is equivalent to that of a congressman's here. He knew a lot of people in Beirut and stayed in touch with them. I see in front of me some of the contacts he had back in Lebanon. Some were in the Baath party. These are some of the people involved with terrorism in the country."

Joseph did not like the inference about his father and tried to be diplomatic. "Probably he did not know they were engaged in those activities."

"Maybe the reason he moved around so often was that he did not like it here and was feeding information about the U.S. back to some operatives back in Lebanon," Sattler offered.

"That's completely ludicrous. I would think if the INS really thought this to be true, they would not have allowed my father to stay here."

"It seems your father was fairly smart and would not overtly show his sympathies. Sometimes it takes years to establish these patterns. That's why we maintain these files over long periods of time. Another troubling thing I noticed looking at the file is that neither you, nor your father, had ever applied for U.S. citizenship. Why is that?"

"My father was always busy working. My mother got sick, and he spent a lot of time taking care of her before she died. It never really occurred to me to get citizenship since I have permanent resident status and I have always been going to school. You can see that looking at my record. I guess I could take some time and apply."

"You still have relatives back in Lebanon, don't you?"

"Yes, I have an uncle, an aunt, and some cousins."

"Your records indicate you still keep in touch with them."

"Yes. I do call them a few times a year. They were not allowed to emigrate over here with my parents. I didn't know my telephone calls were a matter of public record."

"We make periodic checks of telephone records as a matter of national security. Maybe you don't like it here and plan to move back to Lebanon."

"I am deeply involved in my work. There is no reason for me to move back there."

"So what is the nature of your work?" Jefferies asked.

Joseph didn't feel like going into a long-winded explanation. It was only ten minutes into the interview and he was already getting tired. "You must have heard it from Sorrenson."

"Answer the question," Jefferies prompted again.

"We have a contract with the Army Corps of Engineers to study the characteristics of a flood wave that results from a catastrophic dam failure." Joseph put his hand to his forehead and mused, "It would have been fairly interesting to have seen the wave created by the Pope's Mills Dam."

"We're not interested in scientific theory. We're investigating the death of three members of a family."

Joseph's face became flushed, embarrassed that he had not asked about any injuries resulting from the dam collapse. "I am terribly sorry," he said with a sad look on his face. "I did not know there were people who died."

"So you consider yourself an expert in dam failures?" Sattler asked, getting to the crux of the discussion.

Joseph felt instantly more at ease speaking about his area of expertise. "Yes, you could say that. I have studied the case histories of many different types of failures, including breaches, seepage, and catastrophic failures where the entire embankment fails at once. As part of my doctorial thesis at Colorado State, I studied the types of waves created from dam failures. I suppose that is why I was hired to perform research for the Corps of Engineers."

Jefferies thumbed through a grey file folder. "I see here from your transcripts that you've had several structural design courses."

"I was in college and grad school for about eight years or so, and, of course, I took a variety of subjects, including structural engineering among many others. I have been what most people would categorize as a "professional student, pursuing undergraduate work for about six years prior to getting a masters and doctorate. I took nearly every course offered in the Civil Engineering curriculum."

"So you would know how to do a structural analysis for a dam?"

"I guess so. I am fairly familiar with dam design."

"I also find it interesting you worked for the Gladstone Mining Company after your doctorate degree."

"After I went to Colorado State University, I moved back to the Louisville area to get a job. My father was living around here and I wanted to be close by. I was fairly broke after my doctorate. There were few jobs at the local universities, and I saw a newspaper advertisement that the coal companies needed people. As you said, I took several courses in coal mining. I knew what it entailed, and I went to work for a company in the vicinity of Pikeville in eastern Kentucky where they do surface mining for coal."

"By any chance, did they do any mining using explosives?" Jefferies asked, thumbing through his folder.

"Yes, it is an efficient way to get at the coal. Sometimes, I was asked set up the explosives prior to detonation. We purchased the dynamite from a construction supplier, and other times it was cheaper and more convenient to use fertilizer-based explosives we made ourselves."

"Why did you quit the mining company?"

"My main interest was teaching. Anyway, I did not like the hazards of the mining industry. I saw that many people who worked there had only two to three fingers on their hands. Many of the accidents happened as a result of working with explosive charges, and I prefer to go home with the same number of fingers I have when I wake up in the morning."

"We asked the question because whoever was involved with the Pope's Mills dam had some experience with explosives," Sattler said casually, not knowing how Joseph would react.

"I have thought about the problem of using explosives to demolish a dam. I believe if a group of individuals set out to blow up a dam they would most likely use plastic explosives."

"Plastic explosives?"

"When the allies broke up the German dams in World War II, they had the advantage of five thousand pound bombs. Of course, a group of terrorists would find it difficult to place such a large bomb on the dam at the proper location. I would say they would have to have accomplished it with smaller charges. These charges would have to be lightweight and shaped so that the explosive force was directed inward towards the dam embankment. Plastic explosives have additional advantages as well: they are relatively stable, can be stored for longer periods, and they can easily be transported to a site. Generally, an explosive of this type is composed of three parts: detonator, booster, and a bursting charge. Maximum efficiency can be achieved by having a small amount of TNT as a booster charge, initiating a shock wave that would in turn set off a high velocity explosive usually composed of RDX. You probably found traces of TNT and RDX in the soil?"

There was complete silence in the room and no one had an immediate reaction. Joseph continued speaking, "The explosives would have to be placed so that a group of charges would destabilize a portion of the dam until all the weight of the dam becomes concentrated at one location, which then fails. In the case of Pope's Mills, the dam was probably blown up towards the evening hours probably at about seven o'clock or so when there would be a maximum volume of water in the lake."

"Where would the terrorists get the explosives?"

"I am certain someone could obtain C-4 illegally. If one could not buy the explosives, there are a whole lot of 'recipes' for plastic explosives on the Internet using common materials such as potassium chloride, gasoline, and laundry bleach."

"Is that what you used in blowing up the dam?"

Joseph hesitated for a moment, recovering from the shock of the accusation and started to laugh out loud. "You think I did this!"

"Did you?"

"Of course not!"

"You seem to have the knowledge and expertise," Jefferies said.

"So do many people. Anyway, would I have sat here and explained about the placement of explosives if I had been involved?"

"I don't know. I've interviewed many criminals who liked to brag about how they did their crimes. I am curious about how you knew about the plastic explosives and finding traces in the soil? The information was never released to the news and wire services. You pretended not to know what happened, and then you gave the time of the failure almost to the minute. You seemed to know a lot of information about the dam when you say you never have been there."

"That's right, I have never been there. I learned everything from the inventory project. The information I gave you about the plastic explosives and the time was an exercise in logic."

Sattler made a disgusted face and said, "An 'exercise in logic' huh? You would make things easier on yourself if you tell us whom you are working with. "

"I am not working with anyone because I did not do it in the first place."

Jefferies said, "Is there any way for us to verify your whereabouts on Saturday?"

"I told you, I was in the lab all weekend."

"You said a graduate student was with you on Saturday night. Pope's Mills is only three hours west of here. That gives you plenty of time to go there, place the explosives, and then come back. Nobody else saw you on Saturday?"

Joseph sat back and stared ahead for a couple of seconds trying to clear his mind. "There was an incident in the lab on Saturday afternoon. There was an obstruction in the drain line in the lab, and, during one of the tests, water overflowed into the hallway. I saw the head of maintenance, Ralph Barger, who came with a crew, buckets, and pumps."

Joseph had almost forgotten about the incident. He remembered the maintenance man was fairly annoyed, saying, "It takes a hell of a water resources genius to fuck-up a drain system.." Barger threatened to report the incident to Sorrenson and now Joseph was hoping the maintenance man had kept his promise.

"When did this happen?"

"About two in the afternoon."

Jefferies said, "We'll check it out. I guess it will help us clear things up if we could search your car and your apartment. If you do not give us permission we can place you in custody for twenty-four hours while we obtain a warrant."

Joseph said in an exhausted voice, "Looks like I have no other alternative. I have nothing to hide, so go ahead and do your search."

Sattler reclined in his chair with his eyes staring down at Joseph "Now that's the type of 'logic' I like to hear."

Agent Sattler stood in the middle of the sparsely furnished living room in the basement apartment with a small loveseat and a black and white television set. "How about the bedroom? Anything there?"

Jefferies shook his head. "Just a double-bed and a closet of clothes. This place defines spartan," he said, as he motioned two other agents to go through the dirty clothes piled in the corner, neatly folded in a stack.

The apartment was a twenty by forty-foot efficiency. The bare white walls made the room seem larger. In one corner, there was a sofa bed covered with a purple cloth that had a rip in it. In the opposite corner, there was a kitchen with a small stove and a white porcelain sink. Two clean plates and a chipped saucer rested by the kitchen sink. The faucet dripped. Ten pizza boxes were arranged in perfect alignment beside the dinette set. The sole item on the kitchen counter was a silver-plated espresso machine with delicate, hand-painted flowers. A set of enamel espresso cups on a matching oval serving tray rested beside the machine. Jefferies started to open the kitchen cabinets and found two cans of tomato soup and three cans of coffee. "At least I can safely venture a guess as to what he drinks in the morning," he said, smiling.

There was a small, two-drawer, oak dresser next to the sofa bed and a black and white television at the foot of the bed. An unfinished, wooden bookshelf stood against the wall and was filled with dog-eared textbooks. There were notebooks of handwritten papers filled with mathematical equations with vector diagrams of water flow. Sattler thumbed through the sheets, dropping them on the ground where he found them.

Jefferies said, "We've spent the past two hours combing through his junk and everything checks out. There are no electronics here to speak of, or anything resembling the equipment needed to create explosives. It looks like a place where a bachelor, college teacher making thirty-five thousand a year would live."

Sattler commented, "Not a whole lot to live on. I never realized teachers make so little. How about the car?"

"It's one of those 'K' cars from the early eighties. It's filled with newspapers and textbooks. It definitely doesn't match the description of the pickup truck used to carry the explosives to the dam. We called Sorrenson regarding Joseph's story about the accident in the lab. That all checks out too. I'm sorry for the wasted effort. It's uncanny: his profile matched the one created down to the detail that he's a loner with little family or friends in the states. But now it looks like he is in the clear. He did seem though to have a lot of intuition about the dam," Jefferies said, examining the detail on the espresso machine.

"Yes, it was strange that he guessed plastic explosives were used—not to mention the timing of the explosion."

"He also seemed to know a lot about dam design."

"Yes, he did." An uncharacteristic smile came across Sattler's face. "Maybe, it was not such a waste of time after all."

***

Joseph sat on the chair in front of the conference table and could not help playing with the pencil in front of him. It had been six hours since the FBI agents left to conduct the search of his apartment. It had been the longest six hours of his life. Joseph thought about how he had spent almost all his life studying and preparing for a teaching career, and now everything he had worked for was at the mercy of the judgment of strangers who spoke to him only for a few minutes. The door to the conference room opened: Sattler and Jefferies entered with Sorrenson.

Jefferies took a seat next to Joseph and said, "We'd like to thank you for your patience and cooperation. Your story checks out."

Joseph sighed with relief and said politely, "You're welcome. I have no hard feelings. I am only happy to help the FBI. If you need any more information regarding dams, you know where to contact me."

Jefferies leaned over to Joseph, "Funny you should mention that. We could use some help in this investigation."

"I am flattered, but I am sure the federal government has at its disposal a lot of people with my knowledge."

"But not on a local level like you. You not only seem to know information about individual dams, but also where to obtain it."

"Is this part time…or full time assistance?"

"We want you to come down to Pope's Mills, and advise us as to any dam issues regarding the investigation," Sattler said, leaning back in his seat.

"That is impossible. I have a tight deadline on the project I am working on for the Corps."

Sorrenson broke into the discussion, "I was just in touch with the project manager at the Corps. He's willing to extend the deadline to next year."

Joseph had been working twelve hours a day in the lab. Now it all meant nothing to his boss. He started to think about his self-respect and said, "I am also teaching two classes."

Sorrenson responded, "I'm going to have Norris teach the classes for you."

Ben Norris was an adjunct professor who had only six months teaching experience. Joseph worked evenings to prepare for the classes and felt insulted that Sorrenson thought Norris would be a suitable replacement. "Norris is not familiar with the material I am teaching."

"You needn't worry. I'm certain Norris will get through the course well enough," Sorrenson retorted.

Across the table, Sattler was beginning to lose patience and his eyes began to narrow. "You're single and have no family obligations. It seems like you're in a very good position to help us."

"Going over to Pope's Mills is a little extreme," Joseph said plaintively.

"Dr. Hamiz, it's my observation that all you have allowing you to work in this country is a Green Card. According to our records, you're still a citizen of Lebanon."

"So, what do you mean by that?"

"What I'm saying is, you're still a guest in this country, even though you may have been here for over eighteen years. You like it here?"

Joseph responded immediately, "I certainly do!"

"All I need to do is take ten minutes and fill out an INS form. I could fill it out saying you have been uncooperative in our investigation and recommend rescinding your green card: or I can fill one out saying we should give special consideration, allowing some of your family to come over here from Lebanon. The bottom line is, you help us, and we solve your family's emigration problem."

Sitting there waiting for the other shoe to drop, Joseph said, "Or you..."

"...or we send you back to wherever the hell you came from," Sattler said, as if closing a trap.

CHAPTER 5

Sam Johnson gazed over the town square, sipped his coffee from the Collins Hotel and felt encouraged to see only one news truck, rather than the three that were parked there for the past four days. He was hopeful the outside world would lose interest in recent events and that Pope's Mills would return to normal. Sam avoided publicity whenever possible. He wondered how his father would have approached the crises. Sam Sr. was more daring and brazen in his work, and, in the first place, would have told the FBI to go screw themselves. For the past two days, he had two part-time deputies, Travis Cox and Butler Cole, handle all the law enforcement while he combed his father's archives for all felonies of the past ten years. By the end of the two days, Sam had enough material to fill two file boxes…and to keep the FBI happy.

Reverend Nixon pulled up driving his blue and white, 1960 Ford Fairlane in front of the Town Hall. He saw Sam lingering on the square and walked over. "Good morning, I thought I would check to see how you are doing. Every time I called I got your answering machine."

Sam thought the Reverend to be intrusive, but understood the kindness behind his motives. "I'm sorry. I haven't had the chance to talk to anyone in the past few days. I hope you understand I'm not trying to avoid you. I've got fifty different things on my mind."

The Reverend gave Sam a concerned look and said, "I thought I would offer you my services. I figured you needed someone to talk to."

Sam put his arm around the Reverend's shoulder and spoke directly into his ear, "You 're one of the few people in town I can trust, but some other time."

"I understand. I've been organizing the Stewart's funeral arrangements. I needed a public official to speak and you were their closest friend."

"You know me. I'm a terrible public speaker,." Sam said modestly.

"I've had a few people ask about you speaking. People need a sense of closure, and they respect you. I don't think it would be nearly as appropriate if I had Mayor Williams say something."

Sam winced as if someone stuck a needle in his leg. "The Mayor has enough on his mind. I suppose I can give a few thoughts."

"Thank you. I will see you tomorrow." The reverend shook the Sheriff's hand and was about to leave when a K-Car entered the square sputtering, coughing, and trailing a plume of gray smoke. The side of the car was dented and the hood was beginning to rust through.

Sam looked at the car and said, "I wonder who that is?" The car lethargically circled the square and was starting to make a second pass when it slowed down. A man with a foreign accent Sam could not recognize stuck his head out the window and asked, "Is this Pope's Mills. I almost got lost on Route 33 a few miles ago."

"Yes it is. Is there any place I can direct you?"

The man had trouble hearing Sam's response over the engine noise, and Sam had to repeat his answer.

"I have an appointment with the town engineer…a Mr. Armstrong."

"He works out of the Town Hall building right in front of you."

The man found a parking spot across the square and turned off the ignition. The car kept on running and sputtering. Sam and the Reverend gazed at the K-car in amazement as the man exited wearing a worn brown tweed jacket. He stumbled over to the Sheriff. "May I inquire on which floor he is located?"

The Sheriff looked at the small, two-story, brick Town Hall and thought the man must truly be a stranger since it was the first time anyone had asked him which floor anyone was located.

"Second floor," Sam responded. The man was walking away when the Sheriff said, "You know, your car is still running."

"Yes, I know it is. It must be the cheap gas I give it. I am sure it will stop soon. I have timed it and it doesn't run more than two minutes."

Before the Sheriff could say anything else, the man hurriedly went across the street toward the double doors of the Town Hall. The man, preoccupied and seemingly in his own world, did not notice a woman walking her Dalmatian on the sidewalk. He appeared to be surprised when the dog barked at him, and he dropped his brown leather briefcase, spilling it contents onto the concrete. Quickly, he bent over shoveling the papers back into the briefcase as the woman offered to help. He ignored her and rushed into the building.

Both the Sheriff and the minister smiled as they saw the scene and then looked down at their watches as the car kept on shaking in its parking spot. The car gave a last cough, discharged smoke from the tail pipe, and was finally silent.

Sam gave an amused look to the Reverend and said, "One minute and thirty-five seconds. At least we know he's honest."

***

Ted Armstrong scrutinized the foreign looking gentlemen sitting in the chair reserved for visitors. The man seemed uncomfortable in the office surroundings as he crossed and uncrossed his legs. The office was small with an oak desk, drafting table, and file cabinet. On the desk were two pictures: one showed Armstrong with his wife, Betsy, and the other, Armstrong with his son Tommy holding geese shot on a hunting trip.

"Dr. Hamiz, Agent Sattler contacted me about your visit. He said to show you the plans we have on file for the dam. You understand, it's not a complete set. The originals are at the Corps district office. If you need more plans, you will have to call them."

Joseph said, "To be honest, I don't even know what exactly I am looking for, but I need to get acquainted with the design so I can answer any questions from the FBI. By the way, what do people do around here?"

"Economy-wise, this town has an industrial base. Most of the people work at the Pope Paper Company. The company makes paper products including paper towels, napkins, and it even has a division that makes construction products, like the formed wood panels found in homes. It's quite an operation. It runs continuously three hundred and sixty five days a year, twenty four hours a day. Railroad cars full of wood pulp show up in the back of the factory and out comes reams of finished paper distributed to various parts of state.

Joseph remembered seeing the factory when he came into town, a windowless red and white rectangle about one thousand feet in length running parallel with the Kendall River. There were five smokestacks of varying heights that seemed to sprout from the roof. He wasn't really interested in a mundane industry such a paper making, but to make polite conversation he noted, "I would have thought a paper operation would be located in the forested , western part of the state where the wood is harvested."

"That's a good point, but sometimes the forests are in remote areas. It just makes more sense to have a plant in a central location, serviced by highways and railroads. Even though Pope's Mills is in a rural community, it is close to the railroad. We've got a spur going through town and we're near Route 68, a major east-west road about ten miles away." Armstrong kept on looking through the storage bins. He finally put his hands on a set of yellowed drawings and said, "Aha, here they are."

Joseph took the drawings and started to unroll them on the drafting table. The blueline paper was crinkled with age and smelled of mildew. Armstrong looked over his shoulder and commented, "The dam was in excellent shape, and it probably would have lasted another fifty years if someone didn't blow it up. They really did an excellent job building it. I think I have an archive of the pictures taken during construction. Do want to see it?"

"I would like that." Joseph examined the plans in detail as Armstrong searched for the photograph book. Out of curiosity, Joseph looked at the lower right corner of the plan sheet and saw the designer's initials were "MPC." He said whimsically, "I wonder if the initials stand for Matthew Clark?"

There was no response from Armstrong as he busily checked through piles of albums.

Joseph said, "I am sorry—that was a silly thing to say. While I was passing through town I kept seeing his name. I saw Matthew Clark's name on the hospital wing and the gymnasium for the school. I thought perhaps he designed the dam, too."

Armstrong retrieved a photograph book and said, "No, it wasn't a silly thing to say because he *did* design the dam. I'm not used to hearing the question because it is pretty much common knowledge around here."

"Did he design the dam before or after he got the hospital wing named after him?"

Armstrong was becoming impatient with the questions. "Before. He did all the engineering for the dam early in his career while he was working for the Corps. He was responsible for most of the progress made around here. You have to understand that without the dam, there wouldn't be a community called Pope's Mills."

"The dam made that much of a difference?"

"After the grain mills died out in the late 1920's, there was no economy to speak of. The town's land was all fields of corn and alfalfa for animal feed. The paper industry came here after World War II and brought back the economy. The dam made it possible for all of it to happen. Do you realize it used to take about fifty gallons of water to make one pound of paper? So imagine producing thousands of tons a day."

"He must have been a remarkable man to create a basis for an industry like that," Joseph noted, trying to be diplomatic.

"He was a visionary. He saw a viable community with churches and schools when the area was still just dirt roads." Armstrong glanced at the papers on his desk and gave a worried look. "I'm sorry, I'm fairly busy. There are a lot of failed utilities and clean-up related to the emergency. Why don't you take the plans and the photographs with you? Maybe we can talk some other time when things settle down."

Taking the black, leather-bound book, Joseph walked onto the square, realizing the invitation was not genuine. He felt his stomach twinge. He had started out at five o'clock in the morning and needed some hot food to continue. Joseph saw the Collins Hotel in front of him and ambled across the square.

***

Joseph stood in the doorway of the Collins Hotel, weighing the options of sitting in the dinning room or at the counter. It was about eight thirty in the morning, and the restaurant was still full. Joseph could tell from the insignia on their clothing that most of the people were from the FBI. A number of heads turned as he entered. Many people seemed curious about the visitor.

Joseph took a seat next to a man in his early thirties who had long, brown hair kept in a ponytail. He spent about two minutes pouring over the menu as Joseph noticed the man giving him a cursory look. In a low voice, Joseph asked shyly, "What do people eat around here?"

"Generally, most people order the biscuits and gravy, grits, and the scrapple," the man responded.

Joseph had never eaten many of the items listed on the menu, and decided it was rude to order something different than what everyone else was having. There was country music playing loudly on the jukebox. Joseph tried the nearly impossible task of ordering breakfast meticulously by reciting the individual menu items "biscuits, gravy, grits" over the sounds of the jukebox and the people in the restaurant. The man saw Joseph trying to get the waitress' attention, leaned over the counter, and in a loud voice boomed, "HEY THELMA, GET THIS GUY A NUMBER ONE BREAKFAST." He turned to Joseph, "You can't be bashful around here or else you could go days without food. By the way, the name's Anderson, Dutton Anderson."

"Joseph Hamiz," Joseph said, as he shyly extended his hand to Dutton, who shook it.

"You don't look like you're a Fed," Dutton said, eyeing Joseph from head to toe.

"Actually, I am a professor from Kentucky Institute of Technology. I am here to help the FBI with any technical issues with the dam, or, shall I say, what *was* the dam."

Dutton smiled, "I teach high school science. About a year ago, I did some research on the dam. Gave a lecture on it to the local Sierra Club. Before they built it, there was a large bass fishery upstream in the Kendall Creek Watershed. Ask the old timers. They'll tell you how many stripers they caught in the headwaters. I have pictures of the river before and after the dam."

Joseph showed Dutton the leather bound scrapbook of photos given him by the town engineer. Dutton proceeded to leaf through its contents and said, "These are great. We ought to compare notes sometime. I have class at 9:30. Look me up if you need any more info." He got up from the stool and shook his head as he looked at the FBI agents drinking coffee. "This place was a lot better before the fucking FBI showed up." he said in a hushed tone. He quickly put money on the counter and went out the door.

Staring at his plate for about a few seconds, Joseph tried to figure out the origin of the food. He tasted a forkful of grits and made a slight grimace. He looked around the counter and eventually found the item for which he searched: a bottle of Louisiana hot sauce. Inverting the bottle over the plate, Joseph was disappointed the reddish liquid came out only in small drops. Joseph took the bottle and banged on the plastic insert on the top. After tapping the bottle on the counter, he gained the attention of the two middle aged men wearing John Deere hats, both men looking at him as if Joseph was in some form of street theatre. Joseph finally succeeded in twisting the top of the bottle and loosening the insert. He poured a quarter of the bottle over the food and started to eat contentedly, while the two men gawked.

They continued their conversation. The older man, who had a head of white hair and wore a plaid shirt said, "Shit. I've lived here all my life and the dam blowing up must be the single biggest event ever to happen in the history of Pope's Mills."

The younger of the two men responded, "I don't know Earl. I guess you're right if you judge it by sheer magnitude. I still think what happened with the Reverend Adamson ranks up there. I mean it happened over a period of months, and we got to read about it in our newspapers every day—kinda like a soap opera. Hec, you blow up a dam ... bam, its over in one minute, and you read about in the papers for just a week."

Earl thought for a moment, "You know somethin', the day they arrested the Reverend, April 17th, is the same day the dam was blown."

"You're shittin' me. What a weird coincidence."

"Know how I remember it? When he was locked up we had a big party because it was our twentieth wedding anniversary. Last Saturday, when it all happened, was my thirtieth wedding anniversary. Do the math...that makes it about ten years ago the 'Reverend' was put away. The old man spat his tobacco juice into a coke can on the counter. "What a sick piece of crap he turned out to be. He fooled us all."

"I guess it's all history. The good thing is, it's over and done with, and we don't have to deal with him anymore," the younger man said before sipping his coffee again.

* * *

Joseph was terrible with navigating new places and figuring out where he needed to go; but he knew he had right place when he saw a black SUV serving as a checkpoint in front of the macadamized driveway. The driveway was so full of black SUV's, they almost blocked the road. After parking nearly halfway between the main road and the library, Joseph grabbed the heavy leather briefcase with one hand, the set of the construction plans with the other, and laboriously hiked to the building. The library, an old mansion, loomed ahead with its white, wooden columns supporting a curved, overhanging porch. An electric lamp hung gracefully from the second floor lit the double, front entrance doors. The sign on the doors, in old style script letters, read, "Clark House."

Joseph was searched by two sets of agents before he could enter the library. He reluctantly handed his notebook PC over to a female agent in a business outfit who brusquely took it out of his hands for a thorough check. The long, oblong main room that had once served as a living room for the house had an unkempt appearance with its wooden bookshelves moved off to the side toward the wall. Joseph could see the indentations on the floor where the bookshelves once stood. Five four-by-three foot foldout tables were added to provide desk space for about twenty people.

Out of boredom, he walked across the foyer and started to examine the paintings of Clark and his family. The two-by-three foot oil painting of Clark was twice the size of the small one-foot-wide family picture. It was the family portrait that caught his attention. In the portrait, Clark stood over his wife and his daughter both sitting in plush red chairs in a room that resembled the foyer. The mother and daughter were holding hands while Clark stared ahead, as if he had no association with the two women. The daughter bore no resemblance to Clark, but had a lot of the eyes, nose and cheeks of the mother.

Joseph was busy concentrating on the family portrait when a voice from behind said, "You find them interesting?"

Continuing to examine the painting, Joseph said, "The town engineer told me about Matt Clark, and I was curious to see what he looked like. He didn't tell me he had a wife and daughter."

He turned around and found Sattler looking over the portrait with him. Sattler corrected him, "I believe that's his step daughter. Why don't you bring all your information over to us? We're ready for you in the conference room." Joseph followed Sattler into the paneled room where Jefferies was waiting at the table.

Sattler said, "Let's see what you have." Joseph gave Sattler a tour of the plans for the dam. He started out with the plan sheet indicating the location of the principal and emergency spillways. The principal spillway, used to discharge storm flows through the dam, was a ten-foot diameter concrete pipe. The emergency spillway was the long weir constructed five feet above the lake surface and served to convey the runoff from heavy rainfalls without overtopping the dam. As Joseph described the emergency spillway, Sattler looked through his file and pulled out a field photograph of the dam remnants showing the spillway after the explosion. It resembled a concrete tongue elevated thirty feet above the stream.

Joseph looked at the picture and observed, "I guess they built the spillway to be structurally separate from the dam."

Sattler said, "I've got another meeting in ten minutes, so let's get down to business. First, we need to know what exactly happened here. Sorrenson said you could tell how long it took for the reservoir to dewater and for the flood wave to travel down the river."

"Yes sir, that's correct," Joseph answered as if taking orders from a commanding general. "But, I would need to get the flood elevations in the stream. I could get those from the high water marks left on the trees."

Sattler droned on, "Secondly, I would like for you to work on a database of dams that could be potential targets. We would like to know of any dams that would present the greatest hazard if sabotaged like the one here. The National Guard is providing twenty four-hour protection, but our resources are not unlimited. I know there are existing databases, but I need one geared towards our investigation. For example, one of the variables you could work with would be the proximity to Pope's Mills. I'll be busy managing the investigation, so you can discuss the exact details with Agent Jefferies."

Busily taking notes, Joseph said, "I can get data for the public dams. However, most of the dams in Kentucky are privately owned. For these structures, I need some information from the state."

"Agent Jefferies will give you the contacts. We were promised cooperation from the River Authority. If there are any problems, you can work with him." Sattler smiled, and said in a dismissive tone of voice, "I'm happy you found the time to help us out. Jefferies will show you to your office. Thank you, that's all I've got for the time being."

Joseph wanted to stand up and salute, but instead decided to follow Jefferies out of the room. Jefferies took Joseph up the spiral wood staircase to a long hallway that traversed the second floor. Acting as a tour guide he said, "This was where the family lived. We've taken over the first floor, which was used as a library. The basement serves as a records repository for the town newspaper, the *Gazette*. The second floor has five bedrooms and three full baths. The town used three of the bedrooms for storage areas for their accounting records and their miscellaneous archives, and another bedroom as book repository, which leaves the room they use as an office." Jefferies ceremoniously opened the door. The room was a modest size of twelve by eight feet. The pink walls had become dingy and a there was faded flowered border toward the ceiling. It was obvious the previous occupant was the daughter in the painting. The room had not been cleaned in months and layers of dust covered the floor. Joseph felt his allergies kick in and held back a sneeze. Jefferies said, "I'll let you get set up."

As Jefferies left the room, Joseph let out a large sneeze. He proceeded to noisily blow his nose with the handkerchief he took out of his pocket. The room was stuffy and he walked over to the window to get some fresh air. The window would not budge and after straining for a couple of minutes, Joseph got it cracked open about three inches. Joseph inhaled the spring air, wiping his nose and looking over the room layout. The room was bare except for the desk adjacent to the wall and the small, metal filing cabinet in the corner. He went over to the closet to hang up his tweed jacket. The corner of the closet was filled with boxes of old books. He thumbed through them and saw classic titles such as *Little Women* and *Gone with the Wind*. He also found a copy of the *New Testament*. Joseph hung up his coat with the lone wire hanger and was about to close the door when he brushed up against a small piece of yellowed paper pasted to the door with heavy tape. It was the type of thing that could have been easily overlooked if hadn't laid his finger on it. The print on the page was faded but still legible:

> When I want to fight, to rebel, to flee, I know that you are there. No matter how violated and angry I have become, your love will surround me. You will provide your sustaining courage regardless of the future. Please grant me and all my loved ones the courage to face future uncertainties. Help me come to you to lay all my burdens at your feet. In Jesus' name, Amen.

The closet presented an intriguing mystery to Joseph. As he interpreted the passage, it was not a prayer glorifying God, or a blessing for the house; it was a petition for assistance. Joseph stood at the closet for a minute asking himself what would have prompted a teenage girl of affluent parents to post the prayer in a hidden spot. At that point, Jefferies entered the room with his portable computer. "Our expert looked it over and you're clean," he announced. Jefferies saw Joseph stare at the closet and added, "By the way, we're putting you up in a motel, so you don't need to worry about storage of your clothes. Sattler needs the model analysis of the dam by the end of the week. He advises you to get assistance from the town in making any surveys of the stream." Jefferies hurriedly left leaving Joseph to do his work.

As Joseph started up his computer, he forgot about what he saw in the closet. The screen was filled with graphs and figures and he was soon lost in the complexities of the numerical dam. The realm of mathematics he could easily figure out, but was not so comfortable making sense of the motives of people.

***

A deep voice reverberated through the empty hallways of the municipal building, "I have been asked by the Reverend to heal the wound that cannot be healed, provide comfort for the weary of ... uh ...heart, and make sense out of a...a senseless act.... I cannot possibly do this. I...I...am just like everybody else here in the past week who has felt a tremendous loss, as if a limb of our body has been amputated ...um I mean 'cut off.'" Sam shuffled through his note cards, made a notation. It was seven thirty at night and the municipal building was vacant. Everything was too quiet; he could hear his own heart beat. If he felt this nervous in an empty room, he wondered about his speaking abilities during the funeral with nearly the entire town in attendance.

The front door of the municipal building opened and someone came up the staircase. Sam was too involved with the eulogy to hear the footsteps. His voice choked up, "...Tonya became as close to me as if we both saw the world out of the same pair of eyes. She... um ...she... was such a...a...light and every moment I spent with her represented joy. One time, I came over her house and she gave me a poem she wrote for me. I thought I could read it for you all:

A flower grows in the garden
When I think of you
With petals of white and blue
You are so big
Riding in your shinny car
I can see you from near or far
I like the smile you make
Eating the cookies
I help my mother bake
When you take my hand
I want to kiss you on the cheek
Most of all
You are my very favorite friend."

He barely completed reciting the verse when his eyes started to get moist. Shaken, he started again, "Her life to me is like an unfinished poem…" Someone knocked on the door. Startled, Sam said, "Who is it? I am kinda busy right now."

"It is Joseph Hamiz…the consultant to the FBI." The voice on the other end of the door replied.

Sam had heard about Joseph from Armstrong, who simply described him as a "funny, little, absent minded professor." Sam did not want to see anyone, but out of politeness said, "Hold on for a moment. I'll be right with you." He went to the bathroom and washed his face. Feeling back to normal, he opened his office door and saw Joseph standing in the hall, leaning on a wall.

"I have been looking for Mr. Armstrong. I guess he is gone for the day," Joseph said, looking tired.

Sam said, "I just saw him leave. You can come back tomorrow morning. He starts at seven. Is there anything I can help you with?"

Joseph had a perplexed face. "I am doing a survey along the river and need someone to hold the other end of a tape."

Finding Joseph's reaction to the problem amusing, Sam smiled and said, "That doesn't sound too difficult. I'm sure we can find someone to help."

"Thanks, I didn't want to trouble anybody; especially with the cleanup work going on around here."

"We believe in helping each other out. That's what type of community this is. I'm sure you're more used to the large metropolitan areas where everyone is crowded together and pretend to be strangers."

Joseph perked up. "I know exactly what you are talking about. I was raised in a small community on the outskirts of Beirut, Lebanon. Living here in the United States presented a major adjustment for me."

Sam was taken by surprise. "I didn't figure you to be an Arab. You have a European accent, like someone from Brussels."

Sounding indignant, Joseph said, "Sheriff, I don't exactly know how to take that…"

"I like people to call me 'Sam', not 'Sheriff,'" Sam interrupted, as he took a seat behind his desk.

"Fine then. Sam, I have been living in the U.S. for most of my life and whatever accent I had when I was child has most likely changed. Up to a few days ago, I used to consider myself a resident of the U.S. until someone told me I was only a 'guest.'"

Needing a momentary diversion from practicing the eulogy, Sam said, "Lebanon—must be an interesting place to grow up. I never knew anyone from that neck of the woods. Why don't you take a seat and tell me about it." Sam went into the bottom of his desk drawer and pulled out a bottle of ninety- four proof Bourbon. "Care to join me for a drink?"

"I generally thought law enforcement people were prohibited from drinking on the job."

"Who said I was on the job? I generally drink beer and don't go for the hard liquor. I get this stuff directly from a distillery near Lexington. During prohibition, they bottled it for 'medicinal purposes.' I've had a shitty week and have some serious 'medicinal purposes.' I gather you had the same week and need a belt yourself."

Producing two small juice glasses from the bottom of his desk, Sam poured the caramel-colored liquid. Joseph took the glass to his nose and gave it tentative sniff. He then proceeded to drink the liquor in one gulp. His face turned red and he started to cough. Pulling out his handkerchief, he blew his nose. "I see now why you said 'medicinal purposes.' That was strong, but it did a good job clearing out my sinuses. Can I have another?" Joseph asked timidly.

Filling his glass again, Sam said, "You're supposed to sip it. You say you have been here most of your life and you haven't ever tried bourbon?"

"I am really not an alcohol drinker. I really love coffee though. I have my father's silver espresso machine in my apartment. It is my most valued possession," Joseph added with pride.

Sam saw the alcohol's relaxing effect on Joseph and said, "You were going to tell me how it was growing up in Lebanon."

Joseph settled back in the red leather couch and took a sip of the bourbon. "Actually, we lived in the most picturesque house in town of Jounieh, on the side of a hill looking down on the Mediterranean Sea. The house was essentially a square with a courtyard in the center. Compared with the Clark House, it was fairly modest. We had only one floor with a kitchen and a combination living and dinning room. On the sides were the three bedrooms and the one bathroom. But most of the houses in the neighborhood had just one bedroom with no courtyard, so our house was considered to be fairly extravagant. Both my parents were teachers by profession, but my father came from a wealthy banking family. We had enough money to hire a maid to free my mother from doing chores."

"I gather you didn't have any brothers or sisters."

"I had a younger brother who had died in childbirth when I was four years old. My mother was thirty-five at the time and the baby was head up in the womb with the umbilical cord wrapped around its neck. My mother couldn't deliver the baby vaginally and needed a cesarean section, but there were no hospitals or clinics in the area that could take her, so she had to make the drive into Beirut. Her water broke about midway to the hospital on the coastal road and the baby was coming fast. My mother's taxi came up on a Druze checkpoint about five minutes from the hospital. The fifteen-year-old child manning the checkpoint didn't understand that my mother was in labor and in dire need of attention and would not allow them to pass. The cab had to take a three mile detour, and, when they got to the emergency room entrance, the baby was stillborn on the floor of the cab." Joseph took a long sip of bourbon, "I more or less consider him a casualty of war."

"Aside from what happened to your brother, it sounds like you had a nice childhood," Sam noted.

"Yes, I was fairly spoiled. My father took me on many trips to all the neighboring countries—Egypt, Israel, Syria, and Jordan—when he gave seminars at universities. He taught me to love books; I spent many long afternoons reading under the palm trees in the courtyard."

"It sounds like you were ready to follow your parents' career in academia in Lebanon. What happened?"

"My father decided to have a career in politics. He had bad timing, and being a representative in the National Assembly was a dangerous profession after the Civil War in 1984. He wound up angering the wrong people and his life was in jeopardy. He made some friends at the U.S. Embassy in Beirut, and was able to convince them he was more valuable to them alive in the U.S. than dead in Lebanon."

Sam reclined in his chair and said, "At least it seems we have some things in common. I am an only child, too, and my father had to put up with bullshit from the Klan. But I don't know if his life was ever on the line like your father."

Not believing he had finished the bourbon, Joseph looked dreamily at his empty glass. Feeling woozy, he got off of the couch almost falling onto Sam's desk. Sam got out of his chair to help steady him. "Are you alright? Do you need someone to drive you back to the motel?"

"That's okay Sheriff…I mean Sam. My feet fell asleep while I was sitting. I will be back to normal once I am outside and get my legs," Joseph said, massaging his calves.

"Really, it's no problem. I can call a deputy to give you a lift back."

Joseph extended his hand dismissively, "Thanks for the hospitality. Its getting late and I should let you get back to your work." Joseph shut the door and Sam was again alone in his office to finish his eulogy.

Getting into the K-Car, Joseph saw Sam practicing his speech through the window. He turned the key and, after a couple of attempts, the car coughed to life. The main street now was completely dark, except for the light that was on in Sam's office. Joseph drove down Poplar Street until the light faded from view in his rear view mirror.

The cemetery, located on a high bluff overlooking the Kendall River, was filled with men dressed in black wool suits and women in full-length black skirts. Ironically, the Stewarts were going to be buried fifty feet from the river that killed them. Joseph, wearing only a tweed jacket and tie, felt out of place in the crowd, George Sattler and Carl Jefferies stood beside Joseph, trying to create dignified poses. Neither wanted to be there, but they wanted to be seen as sensitive and sympathetic to the people in the town.

As the service drew to a close, Sam separated himself from the throng of people and was up at the caskets trying to get one more chance to say goodbye. He removed a plastic bag from his suit, retrieved a fabric onto which was embroidered a blue cloth football, and laid it on the dark wood of the casket. Sam moved onto the second casket, kissed it, and lay upon it a red rose. He uttered a few words and moved onto the third, child-sized coffin.

The small coffin was closer to the ground alongside piles of earth. Sam knelt to the ground in the freshly dug soil and hugged the wood coffin. He put a teddy bear on top and visualized Tonya growing up, graduating from high school and college, getting married, and having children of her own. Feeling empty, he got up and looked forlornly at the river rampaging within the gorge beneath him. Reverend Nixon walked over, looking concerned. He put his arm around Sam and said, "You did good today. They would've all been proud of you."

"Thank you, Reverend, you don't need to worry about me. I'm going to be okay. I would like to thank you for allowing me to get everything off my chest."

"Is there anything I can do for you?"

"No. Not at this moment," Sam said as he looked at the mourners and saw Sattler and Jefferies going back to their cars. "If you'll excuse me Reverend, there is something else I must do."

Sam waded through the mourners and caught up to Sattler and Jefferies about twenty feet from their cars. Sattler noticed him approaching. Feeling awkward, he said in an official sounding voice, "On behalf of the Bureau, I want to extend to you our sympathies for your loss."

Not wasting any time on pleasantries, Sam said in a semi-demanding tone of voice, "I want to talk about my future involvement with the investigation. I thought I could help out with things and be on the team."

"I don't think we should be talking about this now. You need some time to grieve and help the town recover."

"I think I'm the best judge of my fitness to work. The best thing I can do for everyone is to be productive."

"The last time we spoke, you said you did not have enough time to help us out."

"That was a couple of days ago and a lot has changed since then. The Mayor and the Council are now administering the recovery effort. My primary responsibility is law enforcement and I have three deputies who can take over for me."

"I cannot reimburse you for your time. I don't know if the town would want you to be part of the investigation."

"Let me concern myself with the Mayor and the Council. I can do it on my own, personal-vacation time. I'm familiar with the area, and I know a lot of the folks personally. I've handled their problems for the past two years."

"I'm sure you're familiar with everyone in town, but as you said, the perpetrator is an outsider."

"My familiarity with the region will be a help to you."

"This is the 21st century and we have GPS to help us navigate. We also have a chopper at the airfield to help us with any aerial reconnaissance."

"I'm aware of all of technology you guys have, but you need to understand that you've never been on some of these roads. Many of them are just glorified mule trails."

Sattler was beginning to loose his patience. "I'm certain our vehicles can navigate your trails. We've got people who're experienced with this type of terrain." Sattler started to walk towards his car but Sam followed on his heels.

"The terrain is trickier than what appears on the map."

Continuing to walk to his car at a brisker pace, Sattler said, "Again, we'll manage." Sattler paused and finally gave the real reason. "To be honest, you were a friend of the victims, and I don't think you'll be able to conduct yourself in an objective manner…"

Sam broke in and started to raise his voice, "I'm just as much of a professional as you. Just because I don't walk around in a suit and tie doesn't mean I can't handle myself."

Sattler arrived at the car and started to fumble agitatedly through his suit pocket for the car key. "I really don't care how professional you are. You're not part of the investigation—*period*." After sorting through twenty keys of varying shapes and sizes, Sattler found the car key, opening the door and slamming it behind him. Sam was five feet from the car when it sped away on the gravel parking lot, pebbles spraying over his suit pants.

Sam turned around and saw that a crowd of people had gathered to watch his confrontation with Sattler. Not saying anything, he got into his police car and drove home.

Chapter 6

It was the day after the Stewart funeral and all the school children were enjoying the day without any cares or worries. Sam stood at the chain link fence observing them running in the playground in the noonday sunlight. The children had divided themselves into groups: the girls playing hopscotch in the shade and the boys having an impromptu game of kickball with bases of coats and book bags. For Sam, watching children play was a welcome diversion after spending the day investigating the disappearance of Nick Palmary. Sam had his directive from the FBI to stay out of the investigation, but for the time being, the disappearance was considered a local issue, and the FBI showed no interest in pursuing the matter.

The whereabouts of Nick had been a loose-end from the onset. It was not known whether the boy died as a result of the dam break, or had been a victim of foul play. Only two people remembered seeing Nick on Saturday. His mother saw him leaving the house at three p.m. to ride his bike. A pharmacy clerk recalled Nick buying two chocolate bars. Sam questioned Nick's classmates and teachers about any friends he might have been with on Saturday. The only lead was that he had been seen with Tommy Armstrong, the son of the town engineer, riding a bicycle and practicing baseball in the schoolyard.

Scanning the playground, Sam did not see Tommy participating in any of the games. Out of the corner of his eye, though, he noticed Tommy leaning against a stone wall of the school building, sullen, looking away from the other children. For a brief moment, the Sheriff made eye contact with Tommy and started walking slowly toward him. Tommy saw Sam approach and ran into the school. Trotting down the hall, Tommy ducked into an empty classroom. Sam opened the metal doors to the building and walked steadily down the hall methodically checking the classrooms. His hard-soled leather shoes made an echoing sound that could be heard throughout the building.

Sam poked his head into one of the empty classrooms and saw an array of wooden desks and chairs facing an oaken table. At the rear was a gray steel book closet with splotches of rust. Sam saw the closet door move a fraction of an inch.

Flicking on the light switch, Sam sat at the teacher's chair and put his black leather shoes on the desk. He started talking out loud to the seemingly vacant room, "It is interesting you chose this classroom. I took fifth grade American History here with Miss Halloran. She had these deep wrinkles on her face and large mole on her chin she had tried to cover with pancake makeup—it only made it stand out more. Anyhow, I had never liked American History. I thought it was complete bullshit. My father got a newspaper from Louisville everyday. I used to steal his sports page and bring it to school. I developed a fairly slick technique for reading the sports page; I would fold it into my history book. I used to underestimate Miss Halloran. One time, I picked my head up out of the sports page and saw her standing over me with a look that would turn most mortal men to stone. Miss Halloran called my father. He was creative in giving me punishments. He didn't allow me to play football for two weeks and instead, forced me to study American History. The moral of the story was: I was only eleven at the time and I thought I was smarter than everyone else. I was sure that no one knew what I was doing, when exactly the opposite was true." Sam paused for a moment. "I think I've spent enough time talking to a closet. Maybe I will sit here for the next fifteen minutes and wait for the other kids to come back from recess. I'm sure your classmates will get a big kick seeing you walk out of the book closet."

After a minute of silence, the closet door opened and Tommy nervously stepped out. Sam asked, "Why did you run away from me?"

"I didn't feel like being outside anymore, and I didn't want to talk to anyone," Tommy said, crossing his arms.

"Why don't you sit down and we can chat."

"I said I don't want to talk about anything. Am I being arrested? I know from TV that if I'm being arrested, I don't have to speak to you."

"Did you do anything wrong that would cause me to arrest you?"

"I did nothing wrong, Sheriff," Tommy said, still looking at the ground.

"Look at me when I am talking to you!" the Sheriff said in a booming voice.

Tommy glanced up and yelled back, "I said I did nothing wrong! Can I go now?"

"No, you can't. I want to ask you about Nick Palmary."

"I know Nick. We hung out together," Tommy said in a nonchalant manner.

"I've spoken to your classmates and they say you two are inseparable."

"I've got a lot of friends at school, Sheriff." Tommy started looking down at the floor again.

"Do you know where he is? His parents are worried sick about him."

"I don't know where he is."

"Didn't you see him on Saturday?"

"I don't remember!" Tommy said, almost leaving his seat.

Sam decided to take a risk and said, "Let me refresh your memory. I've been talking to people in town who say they saw you both on bicycles heading towards the river on Saturday before the dam broke." Of course, Sam had no such information; he hoped Tommy would take his bluff.

Tommy was caught off guard and his face became flushed. Sam knew he was getting to the truth. "I know that the both of you were swimming in the river before the dam blew up. Don't you feel it's unfair to keep this a secret? Nick's parents need to know what happened to him."

Tommy's eyes started to tear and he said very softly, "I left him there."

"Where did you leave him?"

Tommy's voice started to quiver. "He didn't want to leave. I had no choice."

"*Where did you leave him?*"

"I was so scared. We were swimming in the lake and we saw everything. Honest to god, I raced back to tell you, but the dam had exploded soon after I got to my house. I'm so sorry."

At that moment Sam realized Nick was dead, and the bombing had claimed the life of yet another child. Tommy, quietly sobbing, put his head on the desk. Sam got up, put his arms around Tommy and tried to comfort him. "It's okay; it's alright; nobody's going to arrest you." Sam said slowly stroking Tommy's shoulders. "There was nothing you could've done. Believe it or not, I know how you feel."

***

Agent George Sattler looked down at Tommy Armstrong sitting at the conference table in the library and said, "Can you tell me again what exactly you saw? Every little detail counts. You want us to find who killed your friend, don't you?"

"All I know is that there were the two of them in a red pickup truck," Tommy said, his eyes glazed over.

Agent Sattler went down on his knees and looked at Tommy directly. "We're not here to arrest you; we just need to find out what happened. You said you like to play baseball. I have a son your age and he also likes to play baseball." Actually, Sattler had not seen his son in a year, ever since his ex-wife took him to Chicago, but it was a convenient story to make up. The story didn't work and Tommy sat nervously at the table, looking as he thought someone was about to put a metal hat on him, strap him to the chair, and put fifty-thousand volts of current through his body.

Agent Jefferies sat at the table operating the tape recorder. There were a group of four agents sitting at the table, leaning on every word Tommy said. Sam and Bill Armstrong stood at the head of the table, looking nearly as frightened as the boy. Sam was concerned an interview with the FBI might be too much for Tommy to handle. Sam found it interesting that after five days and interviews with hundreds of witnesses, the only tangible lead was an eleven-year-old boy. He broke in, "Just try to relax. Forget about all the people here. Close your eyes. Pretend you're back at the lake."

Sattler threw an annoyed look back at Sam.

Tommy closed his eyes. "We left town about three-thirty and arrived about half an hour later. We ditched our bicycles on the shore so nobody would notice us and started swimming. We swam for a while, and then climbed on top of the dam when we heard a truck come up the access road. "

"When did that happen?" Sattler asked.

"We didn't have watches. I don't know what time it was."

"How did you know it took a half an hour?"

"I rode my bike there before and I know how long it takes."

Sattler said, "Maybe you remember the location of the sun on the horizon when you noticed the truck come up the road."

"The sun was low, probably two thirds down."

"It must have been between four thirty to five o'clock," Sattler observed. "Tell us about the truck. Did you notice any license plates?"

"We had climbed back down to the lake. We must have been a hundred feet from the embankment, and I couldn't get a good look at the license plates."

"What about the truck? Was there anything special about it?"

"What do you mean by 'special?'"

"Imagine if you were in a big parking lot and you had to find it. How would you do that? For example, did it have any markings or dents you could notice?"

"No sir; none I could notice." Tommy still had his eyes closed. Pausing for a moment, he visualized the overall shape of the truck body. "I think it was a 1978 Ford 150."

Knowing the make of the truck was one thing, but knowing the year was extraordinary. Everyone in the room dropped their jaws except for Sam and Bill Armstrong. It was a popular truck amongst some of the more infamous people in town. Sattler, taken completely by surprise, said, "How do you know that?"

"That's easy, I have a Matchbox car collection at home and I like to collect model trucks. I have all the Fords from 1950 to 2000. Sometimes my father would allow me to trade them on the Internet."

Armstrong chimed in, "I can attest to that, officers. That's all he spends his allowance on. He loves trucks."

"How did you know it was a 1978, rather than, say, a 1980 model year?" Sattler asked.

Tommy finally at ease said, "Hec, everybody knows in 1980 they changed the body style from a straight-back body to a flared out body over the rear wheels. In 1979 they went to a rectangular headlight. They aren't nearly as cool as the circular 1978 headlights. I can spot a 1978 Ford 150 a mile away."

Sattler said, "I'm sorry, I didn't know I was dealing with a truck expert. Do you remember anything about the men?"

"One of them I saw up close when he walked down the slope. He had a thin, mean looking face and very short blonde hair. I could only see the outline of the second one. The sun was in back of him and the only thing I could really tell was he was a little muscular and had longer hair. I would say it was black. He was the one who stayed on top of the dam all the time I was in the water. The first man was about five inches taller and looked skinnier."

"Can you tell us exactly how tall were they?"

"I don't know," Tommy said, his expression perplexed.

Sattler found Tommy relaxed when he started talking about trucks and immediately got back on the topic. "How tall were they in comparison to the back of the truck?"

"The shorter man was about a foot and a half taller than the top of the tailgate."

Sattler did some mental arithmetic and figured one of the men was around five feet nine and the other, six foot two.

"Were they young or old?"

"Everybody looks old to me." Everyone in the room laughed and Tommy continued, "But, if I had to guess, I'd say they were in their twenties."

The boy yawned and half closed his eyes sleepily. Sam took notice and said to Sattler, "Maybe you can continue this tomorrow, it looks like we're loosing him."

Sattler hesitated, "Okay, we'll break for today." Sattler patted Tommy on the back and said, "You're a big help and all of us here are very proud of you. We'll send a sketch artist over to your house first thing tomorrow morning. He is going to draw the man you saw up close. After he does that, I'm going to take you out for an ice cream soda and we can talk some more. How does that sound?"

Bill Armstrong made an insecure smile, put his arm around his son and said, "Of course, we'll do everything to cooperate." Father and son eagerly left the room.

Waiting for the conference room door to close, Sattler turned to Sam and said testily, "I wish you wouldn't stand there and tell me how to conduct an interview. I've been in law enforcement for ten years and I've questioned hundreds of people. I was doing you a courtesy allowing you to be here while I interviewed him. Now, I've got to put up with your bullshit."

Sam had had his limit of Sattler's bullying and responded in kind, "Personally, the presence of outsiders does not inspire a great deal of trust around here. I tried telling you that at the cemetery, but you were stubborn and walked away. If it weren't for my involvement, you wouldn't have a witness, and you folks would be sitting here with your heads up your butts. So don't stand there and talk to me like I am some second-rate asshole."

Both Sam and Sattler were staring at each other like two angry bulls ready to clash. During the confrontation, Jefferies phoned the Lexington office. He yelled over to Sattler, "Good news, I've checked the automotive data base and the tire size we got from the tracks fits the 1978 Ford 150. Looks like partial confirmation of the boy's story."

"Of course, the boy's right. Don't you know, we all 'truck experts' 'round here." Sam said in a mocking, southern accent.

Sattler turned away from Sam and said to Jefferies, "Contact the MVA and get a list of all red 1978 Ford Trucks within a twenty mile radius. I want agents to canvas the town. Ask people if they saw a red truck and anyone matching the general description given by the boy."

Sam was about to leave when he said, "I'm already aware of one owner of a 1978 Red Ford Truck in Pope's Mills. Cecil Millar—and I can give you his address. He doesn't meet the general physical description, though; he's about fifty five years old now."

"Okay, we'll put him on the contact list." Sattler did not care what Sam said and started to sort papers on the conference table.

"My father dealt with him mostly. Cecil is Grand Wizard of the Klan."

With the word 'Klan,' Sattler's face perked up. "Does he live alone or do I have to worry about people with him who'll interfere with us?"

"He lives alone."

"I'll get a few agents, go out to his house, and interview him."

"Blowing up a dam doesn't sound like anything the Klan would do," Sam noted. He thought that more than anything else, the Klan involved itself with general nuisance and intimidation such as cross burning and defacing black churches. When they wanted to make a serious statement, they would turn to arson. Sam had heard the story that thirty years ago they had tried to burn down the First Baptist Church. The close proximity of the sprinkler system to the front of the building had saved it from major structural damage.

Sattler gathered up his notes. "Maybe they've changed their strategy, or they know of someone who'd be involved."

"I don't think Cecil would volunteer any information about…anyone."

"Let me worry about that."

Sam wanted to be generous with Sattler. He offered, "I'll bring him in for you. I know his tactics. "

"I think we can handle this," Sattler said confidently as Sam shook his head and left the room.

Sam recalled the confrontations Cecil had had with his father over the years. He always felt lucky he didn't have to live under the specter of the Klan as much as his father did. Troubles with the Klan had started when his father, Sam Sr., ran for public office. Sam Sr. had worked for Ed Baylor, who had been the Sheriff for twenty years. Over time, Ed had become fairly obese, weighing in at over three hundred pounds. Towards the end of his career, Ed would delegate most of the fieldwork to his deputies, of which Sam Sr. had become the most trusted. Ed recognized talent, and Sam Sr. stood out from the other people who sought careers in law enforcement because they didn't want to do manual labor in the factory or fields. When Ed was set to retire, he knew he could pick his replacement. Even though Sheriff's were elected, an endorsement from the outgoing Sheriff usually meant an easy victory. This was not the case with Sam Sr., who was black, while the other deputies were white. Ed took Sam Sr. aside and said he was ready to support him if he decided to run. He warned Sam Sr. there were people who would never accept a black Sheriff.

Of course, both of them knew that the one person who would fight the most against Sam's candidacy was Cecil Millar. Cecil made many public announcements supporting the white deputy, Pat Hurlston, who was running against Sam Sr. Both Ed and Sam Sr. knew Cecil had many times the money and people resources than either of them put together, and Sam Sr. did not have the support in the town to run against the Klan. Ed advised Sam Sr. to enlist the help of Matt Clark. Clark was considered a progressive individual who did not believe race should determine the next Sheriff of Pope's Mills. Clark did not want the next Sheriff to be controlled by the Klan and heartily endorsed Sam Sr. Clark allowed Sam Sr. to have access to the plant for several meetings with the workers. At the meetings, Sam Sr. spoke humbly about his time working the fields, living the life of the sharecropper, and that he understood the people in Pope's Mills better than Hurston.

On Election Day, the pressure was intense for the voters in Pope's Mills. Initially, many people did not vote since Cecil had two Klansman standing outside of the middle school writing down the names of the blacks entering into the polls. Ed went to the polling place and saw telltale bulges in the back of their pants. A search turned up two Colt handguns. In Kentucky, it is legal to carry concealed weapons; however, it is a felony to have firearms on school property. After a small scuffle, the Klansmen were arrested, allowing the employees of Pope Paper to vote Sam Sr. into office.

***

Farms and woods occupy much of the land outside of Pope's Mills and that Friday morning, all the farmers were going about their business harvesting crops of corn, oblivious to the FBI operation being conducted in their area. Sattler and Jefferies made a tactical decision to try to interview Millar at his home, rather than in town. Sattler thought he would gain the cooperation of the community by keeping a low profile throughout the investigation; hauling away a longtime resident for questioning would be a public relations debacle. There was something ominous in the words of the Sheriff, and Agent Sattler was not going to take any chances. Two SUV's were positioned in the Millar driveway. There was a roadblock on Route 212 in case Cecil had somehow bypassed the entrance. The registration records at the state indicated that Millar had owned several Remington rifles and Lugar pistols. Both Sattler and Jefferies wore their Kevlar vests.

It took about ten minutes for the field people to set up, and Sattler and Jeffries drove up the long, winding driveway in their black, four-wheel drive SUV's to serve a search warrant on Millar. About halfway up, they encountered a metal gate with a large padlock. The gate was marked with a sign with large red letters "NO TRESSPASSING ALL VIOLATORS WILL BE SHOT." They were not informed about the gate, and Sattler agitatedly searched the back of the SUV for bolt cutters. He couldn't find them and phoned the other team members. After a five-minute delay, another SUV came from behind and an agent with bolt cutters took the lock off the gate. Sattler proceeded up the road. "Okay, when we get to the house I want Agent Jackson to cover the back door and Agent Blake to go to the barn and start searching there. Understood." All the other occupants nodded, "Yes sir."

The SUV made its way to the top of the ridge and was greeted by two German Shepherds barking noisily in a pen surrounded by a chain link fence. The dogs stood on their hind legs with their claws and teeth ripping at the fence in desperation. Sattler was the first person to leave the SUV, motioning the other agents to the back of the house and the barn. The rancher house with the white siding and red trim windows looked silent, as if there had been no activity there all morning. A van and a car were parked in the driveway adjacent to the house. Sattler put his hand on the hoods, which were cold to the touch.

There was no sign of the 1978 Ford Truck.

Sattler found this interesting since the house had been under surveillance for the past twenty-four hours. After making certain Jackson was at the rear entrance, Sattler strode up the concrete sidewalk to the house and rapped his hand on the solid-steel front door.

"Mr. Cecil Millar, I'm Special Agent Sattler from the FBI. We've got a warrant to search the premises." There was no answer. Sattler motioned to the other two agents to search the barn and garage in back of the house.

Blake stood at the entrance to the barn pulling at the iron handles of the massive, wooden front doors. With a groan, the front doors to the barn opened. The barn had no windows, and Blake was greeted by darkness. Blake heard an ignition turn and suddenly, two headlights shone in his face. The rear wheels of the Ford spun in place, and then the vehicle exploded forward, forcing Blake to jump out of the way. The red truck sped in front of the barn making a tight circle, spraying the FBI vehicles with mud. Rather than going down the driveway towards the road, the truck headed toward the woods in the rear of the property.

Sattler, initially surprised, got his bearings and ran back to the SUV, followed by Jefferies. Sattler started the ignition and pulled out after the red truck. Millar had a one-minute head start going down a dirt road partially obstructed by trees. Jefferies got on the telephone, "All units, we are in pursuit of a 1978 Red Ford Truck heading west on an unimproved road in the rear of the property." Sattler got onto the dirt road with his wheels spinning. He shifted the vehicle into four-wheel drive and gunned the engine. The wide chassis had little horizontal clearance between the road and the trees, and tree branches made a scraping noise against the sides of the vehicle. The SUV hit a deep rut sending notebooks and briefcases flying through the cabin. The thermos of hot coffee in the front seat holder jumped out and splattered onto Jefferies pants. "This road ain't worth shit!" he yelled at the top of the lungs in pain.

Sattler said, "The son of a bitch can't be too far ahead of us." The SUV accelerated up a rise, and Jefferies felt himself vibrated out of his seat. Sattler continued to gun the engine as the vehicle hit the crest of the hill and ahead, saw a clearing of small brush and grass. About one thousand feet to his right, he noticed the red Ford heading across the expanse. "We got him in the open now," Sattler said, as he turned to parallel the course of the truck.

The brush was getting thicker, but the SUV was able to match the pace set by the Ford. The road was practically nonexistent, and Jefferies felt the car knocking down the brush under his feet. Sattler said, "I think we've lost him again." Small trees were starting to appear in the path, and Sattler was swerving to avoid them. Jefferies turned on the GPS in the console and tried to get a fix on the SUV's location. The GPS screen showed them about one mile from Route 212 with all the other roads about five miles away. "I wonder where the asshole thinks he's going. There's nothing out here." Sattler looked at the screen for a second and in that time a large oak tree appeared in the path.

Jefferies pointed ahead and said, "Let me deal with the GPS. Just look where you're going." Sattler veered to the left of the tree almost putting the SUV on its side.

Jefferies, relieved the SUV did not roll over, said, "We must have lost Millar. Why don't we put the chopper in the air and see if we can spot him."

"We don't have time for the chopper, and I'm not giving up so easily." Sattler saw a red truck about one-hundred feet to the right in the trees. "We almost have him," he said under his breath as he pointed it out to Jefferies. He turned the wheel, sharply forcing Jefferies against the car door. The two vehicles were only twenty feet apart when they headed down the two parallel ruts in the road. The red Ford suddenly made a right hand turn into the brush, and the SUV kept its forward momentum. The trail abruptly ran out, and Sattler saw a vertical precipice jutting out over the river. Sattler hit the brakes hard sending the vehicle into mud two-feet deep.

Sattler tried putting the truck into reverse, rocking the large chassis back and forth. After a few minutes, the SUV was hopelessly stuck. The engine was beginning to overheat and Jefferies said, "It's no use. Let me see if I can help." Getting out of the vehicle, mud up to ankles, Jefferies started to push as Sattler hit the reverse. Jefferies was out of breath; his pants encrusted with mud as he rested against the side of the SUV.

There was a faint sound of a vehicle from behind. Sattler looked in the rearview mirror, wondering if it was the red Ford truck as the backup team of agents appeared. Sattler got out saying, "Did you see where he went?" The other agent shook is head no as he exited his SUV that looked immaculately clean compared with Sattler's SUV. Sattler said, "I think I left him in some shrubs about two-hundred feet back. The agent went back to the SUV to continue the pursuit when Sattler said, "Let me drive, I know where he is."

After everyone piled into the only working SUV, Sattler headed back on the trail towards the Millar residence. The SUV stopped, and Sattler looked into the brush to see if he could spot any tracks. He got out. There was silence save for a Mockingbird in the tree making a rustling noise. Across the brush, the mockingbird's mate responded to the first call. Sattler walked further into the dense vegetation and saw the truck tracks. Suddenly, the sound of an engine roared and the red truck bolted from its hiding place. Running back into the SUV, Sattler floored the gas, spinning the wheels against the grass, and jerked forward. "Good," he said excitedly, "He's going back towards the house. We'll get the other units and surround him." Jefferies contacted the other agents. The red truck darted between two red trees in front of them. The sudden move did not surprise Sattler and he turned the vehicle to follow the truck. Jefferies said, "I don't think we have enough room…" He was not able to finish his sentence as the SUV sped through the trees with a crash as both of the side mirrors were torn off. The SUV slid down the steep, slippery forty-five-degree incline. Jefferies saw brush scrape against the window and put his head between his knees, thinking Sattler was going to overturn the vehicle. Remarkably, Sattler turned the wheel to compensate, straightening out the SUV without sliding.

Sattler said, "He's running out of places to go. In front of us is the river."

There was a small clearing on the bank, and Sattler saw the river running swiftly within its channel. The river was about forty feet wide, muddy from a previous evening's rainfall. The red truck paused momentarily and then started to cross, the surface of the water reaching the top of the Ford's tires. The Ford made steady progress to the other bank. Sattler said, "If he can make it, so can we."

Jefferies responded, "Wait a minute, maybe we should see if we can pick him up on the other side."

Sattler had already made the decision to cross. The black SUV tentatively made it onto the gravel stream bottom. It advanced the middle where the bottom of the channel could not be seen. Sattler slowed the SUV to a crawl. The SUV was two thirds of the way across when the front wheels dropped into a deep hole in the creek bottom. Water came up to the engine and the vehicle stalled. Sattler's face became red with anger as he got out of the SUV and watched the Ford as it disappeared up the bank across the river.

***

While Agents Sattler and Jefferies were engaged in their pursuit, Sam was in his office receiving complaints from townspeople about the FBI roadblock on Route 212. Route 212 was a major road out of town; the roadblock meant a detour of approximately twenty minutes for people traveling to Gottlieb

Heights. By nine o'clock, everyone in town had heard about the FBI trying to question Cecil and there was rampant speculation about his involvement with the blowing up of the dam. Even though most people thought Cecil was an ignorant bigot, the consensus in the barber and beauty shops, where everything of importance in town was discussed, was that he was not up to the task.

Sam asked himself about how long it takes for the FBI to pick up someone for questioning. It had been two hours and Sam thought, "Cecil is up to his usual bullshit." Deputy Travis was in the office doing some filing and Sam asked, "Doesn't Cecil have a brother who lives in Larue County?"

"Yes, I believe he does," Deputy Travis said without looking up from his filling. "Why are you asking?"

"Oh, I'm just curious, that's all. Feel like taking a break from your work and going for a drive with me?"

"I supoose. What for?"

"Grab your hat, I will tell you on the way over." Sam let Travis drive and told him of his simple plan involving a level of play-acting.

It took forty minutes for them to bypass the FBI roadblock and arrive at a driveway off County Road 313. The driveway was quite innocuous looking with a metal mailbox labeled "Millar." Sam quickly got out of the car and studied the layout of the property. As he hoped, the garage was out of visual range from the house.

Travis slowly walked up the gravel driveway toward the two story wooden frame house. Chickens were running around the front yard as a hound dog napped on the front porch. Travis knocked on the front door and a man of about fifty, with graying hair and wearing a dirty t-shirt, appeared.

"Are you Cecil Millar?" the deputy said in a very loud voice.

"No, I'm not. I'm his brother, Owen. What's the beef?" the man said curtly.

"No beef. We've got two tickets to the Sheriff's Ball for him."

"He's not here," Owen responded.

"You sure? We tried to deliver the tickets to him but he wasn't home so we thought he'd be here."

"That's a whole lot of effort just to drop off tickets," Owen said suspiciously.

"The Sheriff's Ball comes once a year and we wanted to make sure that he came. He's very popular back in Pope's Mills."

"Why don't you just send him the tickets?"

The deputy took off his hat and scratched his head. "Now that's a good idea. We'll try that. Thanks for the suggestion. Can I use the phone in your house? My cell phone is dead and I need to call someone."

Millar snapped, "I've got no phone. Now, if you'll leave, I've a lot of chores around here and I can't spend my time screwing around."

Travis had distracted Millar long enough and it was time to leave. The deputy tipped his hat to the man officiously. "Thanks for talking with me." Travis walked back to the car and drove away as Owen stared.

Two minutes after the Sheriff's car vacated the property, another small, gray-haired man left the house by the back door. The man ran into the garage, got into a red, 1978 Ford Truck and thrust the key into the ignition. Nothing happened. The man turned the key again: nothing. Cursing, he went out to the cab. Propping up the hood, he found was a set of disconnected engine wires.

He felt a tapping on his shoulder.

There was Sam standing over him with a smile on his face holding the distributor cap. "Looking for this Cecil?" he asked as Millar's face turned ashen.

***

As expected, Agents Sattler and Jefferies were in a bad mood having spent the morning retrieving the two black SUV's that became casualties of the chase with Millar. At about eleven a.m. he received a message from Sam to come over to the municipal building. As Sattler came into Sam's office, he announced impatiently, "I hope this is important. I've got a lot to do this afternoon."

Sam got up from his desk. "Walk over to the jail with me. I want to introduce you to an old friend of mine."

Sattler followed as Sam walked to a small, windowless brick building in back of the Town Hall. The building was an old garage converted to a jail during Prohibition when moon-shiners would periodically get arrested. It was a very modest jail: three cells and enough space for six people. Sam inserted a large, steel key into the thick metal front door and swung it open. In the last of the three cells, the Klansman rested peacefully on a cot. Sam said in mock formality, "Agent Sattler, I would like you to meet Cecil Millar. He's all yours; my gift to you."

Millar stood at the bars of the cell. "I see, Sam, you have improved on your family's status in town. Your father was a *servant boy* waiting on Clark, hand and foot, wiping his ass, and now you've become *messenger boy* for the FBI."

Sam laughed, "Cecil, I'm glad we've finally found lodging for you equal to your *status in town*."

Sattler turned to Sam and said, "Thank you, Sheriff. We've got questions for Mr. Millar.

Cecil said, "Pleased to meet you, Agent Sattler. I didn't know I'd have a FBI escort on my daily drive. I hope you boys enjoyed yourselves as much as I did."

Sattler gave an intense gaze to Cecil, surprised how an elderly man of such small stature eluded them. "Mr. Millar, I've got six agents right now searching your property for any explosives or equipment related to the manufacture of explosives. Everything depends on you. I told them to search your property by the square inch if they have to, so I hope you get accustomed to your new surroundings. You may be here a while. You cooperate and we might be able to speed things up."

Cecil sat back on the bed and chewed on a toothpick he retrieved from his pocket. Turning his back to Sattler, he said, "Go ahead, mister fucking big-time FBI agent. Search until next year. I've got nothing to hide. You folks from the Beltway think you know everything. You have no any idea what goes on 'round here. A few Negroes get killed and everybody comes down here on a holy crusade tellin' us how and when to do things. Before the government sold itself out to the Negroes and the Jews, we all had a moral Christian upbringing. No one worried about terrorists, guns, or explosives. There was a natural order to things. All of us knew our place in society and we never had any trouble. The government comes in here polluting everyone's mind and no wonder someone blows up a dam. Frankly, I'm surprised it hadn't happened sooner."

Sam said, "You know, I've must have heard that talk fifty times. Don't misunderstand me, I don't hate you for what you say; I take real pity on you. You remind me of a mutt I found one day wandering around a junkyard; I begged my father to adopt it. But we found out why it was abandoned. The dog had no sense in the world, and, left to his own devices, choked to death eating his own shit. I'm simply dumbfounded you haven't choked to death on all the crap you spew out during the course of a day."

A coy smile appeared on Cecil's face.

Sam said, "I'm glad you find all of this funny."

"No, I don't find this funny. I think it's real sad when an enemy of the people puts a Knight of the Christian faith in jail. I'm just thinkin' about the twenty million-dollar lawsuit I'm going file against the FBI and the Town of Pope's Mills for false imprisonment. I know a few lawyers lickin' their chops for their chance to do this."

Sattler responded, "Your lawyers are certainly going to be busy. I think they'll first be defending you against all the criminal conspiracy charges when we find explosive residue on the bed of your truck. You know, we have a witness who saw your truck on the dam before it exploded. Tell us who you hired to place the bombs and maybe we can put you in a minimal security institution to spend the rest of your natural life."

Cecil said in a defiant voice, "You got goose egg. Nothing. I'm not going to help you out on your fishin' trip."

"Have it your way then." Sattler threw up his hands as he started to walk out of the jail.

Sam followed him and turned around to Cecil and said before leaving, "Take my advice—don't eat all your dinner. There are rats the size of small dogs that come around here at night and they get angry when they don't get fed." Sam then closed the metal door with a force that vibrated the small building.

The two men walked halfway back to the municipal building and sat down at a brown picnic table in the back that served as a lunch area. Sattler said, "Congratulations, Sheriff, looks like you have succeeded in embarrassing me again. I bet an informant in your office tipped off Millar to our operation."

Sam said, "I told no one about your interest in Millar. No one alerted him regarding your warrant. The fact is, people can spot your black SUV's from a mile away. I'd say Cecil probably had enough lead-time to pack an overnight bag before trying to escape in the pickup. He has done this before. A few years ago, someone from the IRS tried to serve him with some papers. That guy got stuck one-hundred feet from his house. I'd take it as an accomplishment you got as far as the river."

Sattler didn't take too much solace in the comment. "You could've told us about his evasiveness."

"I tried, but you were too interested in apprehending him yourself. I'm not trying to embarrass you. I promise I won't mention my involvement to the press. You can take full credit for the jailing of Millar."

"Okay, why the generosity? What's your interest in this, other than your relationship to the Stewarts?"

"It's my community and I just want to be involved. I'll be content to work under your direction and take any shit-task you want to hand out. But, I want to be in the loop and know what is going on."

Sattler said tentatively, "I'll have to think about it."

Sam looked at Sattler in the eye and said, "Let's be honest. We don't like each other. But that doesn't mean I can't work for you. I can psychologically deal with working for a boss whom I dislike." Sam paused. "Believe me, Agent Sattler, I've got plenty experience doing just that."

CHAPTER 7

Sam began to frequent the Collins Hotel for breakfast and dinner after being absent for days working on the investigation. It was Friday night and the restaurant was unusually crowded. Sam was looking forward to dinner this evening. The special was his favorite: roast turkey with stuffing, biscuits and gravy. He sat on his stool at the counter drinking his Coke, watching people chatting.

Down at the end of the counter was Bob Dickey from the River Authority reading the menu. Sam remembered seeing a River Authority car in town. Periodically, Dickey would ask Sam a few questions about any observations he may have had prior to the explosions, trying to finish his own report. Sam could see the bags under Dickey's eyes and deduced the man was under great pressure. Out of the corner of his eye, Sam saw Joseph enter the restaurant. Joseph stood at the perimeter of the dinning room waiting for the next seat. The man sitting next to Dickey left, and Joseph was seated in the empty spot. Joseph recognized Dickey from a Dams conference in Knoxville and introduced himself.

Sam turned around and flirted with the young black waitress behind the counter. The waitress had a small waist and a large chest that projected through her blue uniform. Sam said, "My, that's a nice ring you've got there."

The waitress replied, "Oh, it's nothing…just one of those cheap stones"

Sam said, looking into her eyes, "You must have beautiful hands then because the ring looks like it cost thousands of dollars."

Thelma, working behind the counter, gave Sam an angry "she's too young for you" look as Sam quickly tried to finish the conversation. "My name's Sam…maybe we can get together and talk sometime."

The waitress responded, "I'm home from college and my boyfriend is taking me back next week, so I don't know if we'd have the time. But thanks for the comment about the ring. I'm sure he'll appreciate it."

Sam saw Thelma laugh at his failed pickup line; he turned his attention to the conversation between Joseph and Dickey, which was beginning to intensify. Sam overheard Dickey saying heatedly, "Are you implying that most dams in the state are unsafe?"

Joseph thought for a moment. "No, I didn't say that. All I meant was, if there were a significant rainfall like the one in 1972, many of the structures would not be able to withstand the storm."

Sam watched as Dickey's facial muscles tense and his arm movements become more exaggerated. "We live in the real world, not academia. I have to maintain seventy dams on a limited budget and personnel."

Joseph said, "The issue here is not the difference between the 'real world,' as you put it, and the 'academic arena.' Americans have become lazy, taking for granted the safety of the dams that have been built. In countries like Japan, France and Germany, they take better care of their infrastructure."

Dickey's voice was becoming more agitated. "If they have better maintenance, it's because of American money from all the products they've been able to unload on our markets."

"The problem is not with the global trade imbalance, it's with resource allocation. We waste a great deal of our own tax dollars on frivolous spending projects that have little economic benefit, except to reward one's political patronage. If we spent the money wisely, we would not have the magnitude of the problems that currently plague us."

"Are you telling me we're mismanaging the dams in the state."

"Well, I do have a couple of suggestions…"

Dickey's face became a solid red as he finally erupted, "I've had enough of you, you ignorant, arrogant son of a bitch. I'm not going let some fucking asshole tell me how to run things." Dickey punched Joseph in the chest, knocking the wind out of him. Joseph fell out of his seat, landing on the floor and covered with the salad from his dinner plate. Dickey rose and picked Joseph up by the collar, like some kind of puppet. Joseph had little recourse but to squirm his legs. Having a height advantage of six inches and outweighing Joseph by over eighty pounds, Dickey had little problem lifting him off the floor. Joseph seemed more shocked than injured. Dickey, not finished, dragged Joseph through the dining area and pinned him against the wall.

Sam was able to get out of his chair quickly enough to restrain Dickey by the shoulders as he held Joseph. "Don't we have enough trouble around here? I've seen ten year olds act more maturely." Dickey settled down as Sam held him and finally released his grip on Joseph.

"I've made my point, Sheriff. Just keep him away from me," Dickey said as he walked back to his chair.

There was complete silence in the restaurant as everyone turned around to watch the fight. Sam said, "Okay folks, show's over for tonight." Sam looked over to Joseph and asked, "Are you alright?"

Joseph examined his disheveled clothes. "Yes, I am fine. I think I need a new shirt though."

Sam called over to Thelma, "Looks like I have to take a rain-check on the turkey dinner." Thelma nodded as Sam took Joseph by the arm and walked him outside to the squad car. Sam opened the passenger seat door and said, "Please, accompany me."

Joseph had a puzzled look on his face as he settled into the front seat. "Am I being arrested? I am sorry about the trouble. I didn't realize he would react that strongly to criticism."

Sam got in beside him. "I'm on leave and not Sheriff anymore so I've got no authority to arrest anyone. Anyhow, if I'd arrested everyone who said the wrong thing to the wrong person in this town, we'd need a prison that could hold three thousand inmates…including myself. I guess Dickey has been under a lot of stress, like all of us, for the past few days. I wouldn't take it personally. You were very lucky I was there. I wouldn't want to see you get hurt."

"I am sorry. I think I need to do some more Karate practice."

"Yes, you can definitely use some more practice. Do me a favor and try not to get it while I'm around. I've got enough problems already."

Sam made a left turn from Main Street and proceeded north on County Route 212. They passed dairy farms with cows in the pastures lazily eating hay. The heat of the day began to ease, and Joseph rolled down the window. The smell of manure filled the car. Joseph looked at the farms with their rolling green fields and said, "Where're you taking me? We passed town about five minutes ago."

"I'm taking you back to my house. I thought you could use a good meal since you were interrupted during dinner."

"I appreciate that, but it is not necessary."

"No problem, I need the company. You'd be doing me the favor."

"Well then, by all means, I would love to visit. I thought you gave an excellent eulogy." Joseph looked over at Sam. "You even spoke it without crying."

Sam smiled, "You're quite the spy. I should've realized you were listening to me practice."

"How long did you know them?" Joseph asked.

"I've known Charlie ever since I was a kid, so it must be about twenty five years. I didn't become friendly with him until I was in college."

"You were not friends when you were young?

"We were rivals. We competed for everything…spots on the football team, women, anything you can name. I thought he was jealous of me because my father was Sheriff and his father was only a school custodian. He thought he could outperform me on the football field and we both competed for a receiver slot on the varsity football team. I must have worked out all summer, running five miles a day, throwing the football, and catching. One of the happiest days of my life was when I beat him out for the varsity team. The day after I won, I saw him after school. Charlie came up to me and said it was a waste of time for him to go out since it was a 'foregone conclusion' that I would get the position. I looked at him funny. I was really proud, and I thought I had finally beaten him fair and square. He simply looked back at me and said my father was 'the white man's nigger and everything was fixed.'"

Joseph heard epithets such as "Camel Jockey" used to describe Arabs and understood the hurt Sam must have felt hearing a slur being used to describe his own father.

Sam continued his story, "I'm not sensitive about the term 'nigger;' I've heard it thousands of times. That didn't bother me as much as I thought that Charlie should be the last person who could judge my father since his family didn't contribute as much to Pope's Mills as my father. He overcame many obstacles and gained the respect of a lot people to get his position. I could've walked away, but instead I just got angry and hit him on the jaw. I have to give Charlie credit; he knew how to take a punch and immediately came back with a fist to my stomach. Some people saw us and broke us up. While they were doing that, Charlie got one of his hands free, hitting me in the nose and breaking it. My nose never healed properly. You can see a little bump here." Sam pointed to a small irregularity on the bridge of his nose.

"I wouldn't have noticed it unless you told me about it," Joseph said politely.

"Thank you. You don't expect me to believe that?" Sam smiled.

"So, how was it that you became friends?"

"We never spoke again during high school. Charlie changed to track and field and I stayed in football. He became quite good in the hurdles.. We both got scholarships to Kentucky State University. One day we accidentally met after practice and started talking. Back in Pope's Mills, we were rivals, but at the university, we were outsiders. All the differences we had in high school seemed trivial. We realized we needed to be friends to survive college. We wound up getting an apartment and started meeting women together. I introduced him to Eve; she was in one of my English classes." Sam eyes seemed fixed ahead as he momentarily went into a daydream and then broke out of it asking, "How about you? Are you married?"

"I am too busy working to find a wife. I do not have enough time for a family."

"My personal feeling is everyone should get married once, and if you find that special someone…twice."

Joseph did not get the joke and wanted to get off the subject of marriage and relationships. He turned quiet, gazing at the sun setting in the fields.

Sam noticed Joseph's shyness and said, "You don't mind if I talk to you about your personal life"

"I don't mind," Joseph said, "there is not a whole lot to talk about. I am curious why you are telling me the details about your own life?"

"Now, that's an interesting question. I see it as a process of elimination. Spending most of my life in Pope's Mills, I could always talk to people about their families and their problems. That all changed when I became Sheriff. Now that I'm the authority figure in town, they cannot speak to me without fear of getting into trouble. I'd walk up to people gossiping in the street and their conversation would immediately end. Conversely, there's no one in town who I can trust to keep information to themselves. I have no family to speak of, so it comes down to you, a professor who will return to college once everything is over."

"I feel honored I can be your 'confidant.' It does seem to me you are one of the few people involved in the investigation not driven by ego, or the need for publicity."

"You must be taking about George Sattler?"

Joseph nodded.

"They're always going to be men like him. The best thing you can do is stay away from them. There's no way he'll allow you to win. Now, Mike Jefferies, the ATF agent who works for him, he's not quite all that bad once you get to know him."

"The one question I do have is about your attitude towards Cecil Millar. He is an enemy who has sworn to destroy you, and you do nothing about it. You are clearly in a position to force him out of town."

"You have to remember, I'm a Sheriff who happens to be black— I'm not a black Sheriff."

"I am afraid I don't see the distinction."

"The people of Pope's Mills have given me the job based on the trust that I will treat everyone in a fair and equitable manner. I'm not here to be some kind of social activist trying to change people's attitudes about race that have been formulated over the past decades. My only job, and it's a simple one, is to keep the streets safe."

Joseph was now beginning to understand the conflicting emotions and feelings that drove Sam's personality. Sam was not simply another dumb jock using his muscle to keep order. He understood ethics and social responsibility of his position; subjects not taught in school. Joseph felt embarrassed he did not initially trust him.

The two-lane road became completely dark with only the headlights from the cars illuminating the asphalt. Sam became quiet, reflecting on the moment. He slowed the squad car by an opening in the trees that lined the road. Sam turned the car into the opening, which led to a dirt road. They drove on the road for two hundred feet before it ended at the front yard of a two-story farm house with decorative wood shutters adorned with carved roosters. There was a long, wooden chair on the covered porch. Sam turned off the ignition and left the car; and Joseph followed as Sam strode up the wooden stairs, unlocking the front door.

Sam flicked a switch and the living room filled with light. Much to Joseph's surprise, the room was tastefully decorated. There was a wallpaper border of a pasture scene on top of the wall that had the same color scheme as the flowered-cloth couch. Sam went to the kitchen and foraged for food in the refrigerator. He then looked in the freezer and found a package of hamburger and a plastic sack of frozen vegetables. He called from the kitchen, "I can have the burgers defrosted in about fifteen minutes. I hope that's good enough for you because that's all I have."

"Hamburgers will be fine, thanks. This place is quite a distance from Pope's Mills. How did you come upon it?"

"Actually, it's my father's. He bought it from Matt Clark. Clark always had trouble finding reliable tenants for the property, so he unloaded it for cheap. I think of if as some sort of reward for his help with Reverend Adamson."

Joseph remembered overhearing the name in the restaurant. He made a mental note to ask about it later. "Is your father still alive?"

"He died one night working in his office in the municipal building. They found him in the morning face down on the desk. The doctor said it was a massive heart attack. He died instantaneously and there wasn't anything anyone could have done to save him. That's what I call loyalty, dying on the job with 'your boots on.' At the time, I was closest to knowing the duties of the office, and that's when I took over. It was difficult at first but I made the job my own."

Sam grilled the burgers expertly on a gas grill. They quietly ate supper at the picnic table outside on the porch. After dinner, Sam sipped a beer while looking at the gray haze in the sky that formed the Milky Way.

Joseph sat beside him. "Something tells me there are more things you want to talk about other than your friends and your divorce."

Sam took a swig of his beer. "You're a very perceptive individual. In recent days, my life's been turned upside down and I've had many feelings of helplessness. I'm not used to that. I'm the person who everyone relies on to be in control."

"Everyone has those thoughts, especially at critical times in their lives. I felt that way when my father died."

"You don't know everything that has happened…I could've saved them," Sam said with resignation. "I was up there on the road to the dam when the explosives were placed. I did nothing. I was more concerned about my problems with the Mayor and the Town Council than I was with thinking about what was going on around me."

Joseph said, "Thinking that must be a huge burden. It is not rational to be going on this 'guilt trip.' You can't be everywhere at one time. Maybe you have too high of an expectation for yourself. It seems that you are consumed with being an authority figure. Let's say you were there and confronted them. They would have killed you too, and then we would be investigating your death."

Sam leaned back in his seat. "Perhaps you're right. All I know is, its going to take a while for me to resolve it in my mind. I'm taking some responsibility by helping out on the investigation. How did they rope you in?"

Joseph told Sam about his initial meeting with the FBI, and how they virtually blackmailed him with the loss of his green card. Sam listened sympathetically. He put a false military tone to his voice, "I'm sorry you got drafted for this duty, recruit. It looks like they've put your balls in a vice. I hope your 'tour of duty' goes without incident—other than what has happened tonight." Sam already decided to have a private chat with Dickey about his behavior at the restaurant. "I'll do my best to make things easier for you," he said.

The air became cooler with the breeze picking up. Sam said, "I'm sorry I don't feel like taking you back to town. You have your choice of sleeping arrangements: the couch inside or the porch out here. It can be pretty nice outside; it's still early in the year and the mosquitoes aren't too tough."

"Well, I prefer to be out here. It would be just like sleeping in the courtyard during summer nights in my house in Jounieh."

Sam said, "Good choice, I've slept out here on many nights. I'll bring you a pillow and a blanket."

"Before you do, please tell me about the Reverend Jake Adamson. I've heard the name mentioned a few times since I have come to town."

Sam was surprised Joseph had heard the name and tried to downplay what occurred. "It's a long story and it's over and done with. The FBI had already investigated the incident. Jefferies showed me the report. I have to admit they've done a thorough job. They've interviewed everyone involved and determined it bears no relationship to the dam."

Joseph checked his watch. It was a quarter to nine. "It's still relatively early so you might humor me and tell me what happened."

Sam knew he would be answering questions about it eventually and decided to acquiesce. "This is a two-beer tale." Sam ducked back into the house, returning with a six pack. Opening the first bottle, he proceeded to tell the story of the Reverend. Joseph sat on the bench in contemplative silence, listening as long-distant people and events were remembered.

CHAPTER 8

Every place has a golden time when everyone is fat and happy, and Pope's Mills is no exception. In spring of 1994, the success of town's economy could not have been better seen than at the Antioch Baptist Church, where two weeks before Easter people were dressed in brightly colored outfits and wearing their fanciest jewelry. The pews of the church were crowded with worshipers and the blades in the wooden ceiling fans could not dissipate the heat of their bodies.

Theresa Clark sat in the back of the church with her father. She wore a white dress with a navy blue sash across the waist and a matching hat. Even though she was only sixteen years old, she had her mother's fashion sense. She was the only child of the wealthiest man in town and felt an obligation to look the role. Fifteen minutes into the mass, Theresa could feel the perspiration clinging to her dress. She got up from her seat to seek refuge in the basement Bible-study room, where it was ten degrees cooler. In the large open area, a class was in progress. Theresa grabbed a seat next to her friend Sue Ann, a high school friend who got the job of assisting the classes. The week's Bible passage was the story of Noah. The class was filled with ten year olds sitting on the carpeted floor, craning their necks to hear what the teacher was saying.

The teacher, a man in his mid-twenties with blonde, short-cropped hair, light blue eyes, and tall muscular build, spoke quietly about the generations of the the Bible's holy men. Suddenly the man boomed the words in a deep voice as he read from the Bible cradled in his hands, "And the Eternal saw that the wickedness of man was great in the earth, and that every imagination of his thoughts of his heart was only evil continually... And the Eternal said, 'I will blot out the man whom I have created from the face of the ground.'"

The children snapped to attention as if hit by a bolt of lightning. The man, standing on the ladder set up in the front of the class, told the story of Noah. As he read, he acted it out, including the forty days of rain and the "deluge of waters" as he continued to climb the latter until he reaching the ceiling.

Sue Ann leaned over to Theresa, "Isn't he terrific?"

"He seems to be more interesting than the Deacon," Theresa observed.

"The Deacon is on a pilgrimage to the Middle East, and this guy Jake Adamson is his temporary replacement. In my book, the Deacon is a withered old fart. They can forget about him. He puts me asleep. This new guy's cute."

Theresa said, "Now we get to the real reason why you like him."

"You can't tell me he's not a hunk."

"I try to think of other things while I'm in church."

Sue Ann started to giggle. "Sure you do, 'Miss Holier Than Thou.'"

Sitting on the table, Jake started to ask questions of the audience. "Why do you suppose the lord used water to punish the evil people in the world?"

One boy raised his hand. "He used water because a large volcano would be too messy."

Jake leaned back, stroked his chin, and gave the answer his full consideration, "I think you're on the right track. Why do you wash your hands with water?"

"I wash them to get them clean," responded the boy.

"The lord used water to cleanse the world of the evil. Water is a major part of our Holy Scriptures. It's used twice in the book of Exodus when Moses changes the water to blood and also when he parts the Red Sea and drowns the Egyptians." The church bell rang signaling the services were over in the upstairs chapel. Jake put out his hands. "May the Lord bless you in your coming and going and all of you have a healthy and happy week. Amen."

The children scattered, running up the stairs to the sunlight and to the waiting parents, while Jake collected his books from the table. Sue Ann got up, took Theresa by the hand, and led her up to the desk. Sue Ann said, "It was a great class today. You really seem to be reaching the children."

"Thank you. I try my best to make the Bible come alive for them," Jake responded.

"I would like you to meet my friend," Sue Ann said shyly.

Jake gave a glance over to Theresa, examining the features of her face and looking directly into her eyes. "Oh yes, you must be Theresa. You are Mrs. Lillian Clark's daughter."

Theresa opened her mouth in astonishment, "How do you know my mother? Ever since she had her stroke, she never sees anyone."

"I knew her when she was working as a volunteer coordinator for the City of Louisville. I was a student at the seminary and worked on some of the local food drives she organized. I met you when you were twelve years old, when she brought you to the food distribution warehouse. Don't you remember me?"

Theresa shook her head.

"I remember you and, of course, your mother. She had a boundless energy and taught me that anything is possible. She must have given out a thousand meals to the homeless, with little or no resources. I was told about her stroke and she's in my prayers."

"Thank you Jake. I will have to tell my mother about you when I get home."

Jake extended his hand. I live on the Fliecher farm outside of town. Fliecher has a son who is mute, so I help with the harvesting and the chores when I'm not working in the mill. Anytime you need help with anything you can ask me, okay?"

Theresa smiled nervously at the offer, then realized Jake's sincerity and shook his hand. "Alright, sure,"she said.

Matt Clark appeared from the stairs and walked over to the group. "Theresa, come, we're late for lunch. He saw Jake and said, "I heard we had a new teacher." He held out his hand to Jake, who gave it a firm shake. "I hear you're very knowledgeable about the Bible."

"If you want to call it 'knowledge,' I call it 'faith.' All the answers to the problems of the world lie within the Bible...if you possess the faith to find them."

Clark decided to press to the central question, "I'm curious how a man like you is working in the middle of Kentucky."

Jake thought it presumptuous for Clark to question his motives. He hesitated for a second and then spoke in a deliberate voice, "I went into the seminary because I thought I could help people. A few years ago when I graduated, I was put into a fairly poor parish in Louisville to work for a minister who had been there for twenty years. I had a lot of ideas as to how to make things better for the poor, but the priest kept me mired in church bureaucracy—attending meetings and writing proposals. After about a year of being frustrated, I decided to leave the priesthood and set out to experience more of the real world."

"I'm still curious why you picked Pope's Mills to live?"

"I grew up in Campbellsville, which is only forty-five minutes away, and I heard the plant needed workers. I don't know what draws someone to a place. I guess you can say it's a combination of things. I suppose I like the simplicity of life here. The first time I came, I saw the Kendall River and, being an avid fisherman, I got out of the car and within five minutes had caught an eight-pound catfish. Everyone seemed friendly and smiled. The town just seemed to welcome me."

Clark still was not completely satisfied with the answer but decided to drop the issue. "I'm glad you're helping out here. I think this church is essential to the survival of the community; I donate a significant amount of money and sit on its board of trustees. If you have any ideas about any improvements, you can bring them up to me and I will be happy to have them considered by the board. I warn you the same bureaucracy you hated in Louisville is present here in Pope's Mills. I would venture to say the church runs the same way it had when it was founded eighty years ago. Change is a very slow process around here."

***

The next day, Jake wore large headphones to create his own quiet world as he was dwarfed by the large metal press transforming layers of cellulose to fiberboard. Even though Jake was in the middle of the factory floor with workers attending machines on each side of him, he felt a sense of isolation. No one had even tried to talk to him since he started work a month before. Finishing the batch of fiberboard, he turned around to find a barrel-chested black man standing behind him.

"Nice day, Mr. Adamson."

Arnold always began his conversations with "Nice Day." Arnold's happy disposition was a result of his mother drinking during her pregnancy, which led to his mild retardation. Arnold had the mental capacity of a ten year old. Jake would take time to speak to Arnold, while other people at the plant disassociated themselves from him.

Jake took off his headphones and said loudly over the clackity-clack of the press, "Yes, it is Arnold. How do you feel today?"

"I feel good. I found a pretty flower beside the road. Want to see it?"

"Yes, I do."

Arnold took a newspaper from his jacket and unrolled it revealing a yellow daffodil. "Ain't it pretty?"

"Yes it is Arnold. You're one of the few people I know who can see the beauty around us. You should take it back home and keep it in a safe place."

Jake heard heavy footsteps on the concrete floor. Craig Bromel, the floor supervisor, appeared. Balding and in his early thirties, Bromel was Jake's height but about forty pounds heavier. His five-day growth of beard and oil stained jeans with red suspenders gave him a "rough" quality that made it easy for him to coerce employees. He could get them to do tasks they wouldn't normally do. As Arnold was looking at Jake, Bromel tapped Arnold on the shoulder. Arnold was startled and dropped the flower on the ground. Bromel pointed at the wash pail filled with dirty water. "How many times have I asked you not to leave the bucket in the middle of the corridor? We're required to keep the area clear. If someone tripped over it, the company would be liable."

Arnold did not understand what Bromel said, but the tone of his voice was harsh. Looking away Arnold voiced, "I am sorry, sir."

Jake said, "It is not his fault. I distracted him from his work. Anyway, the pail was only there for a few seconds."

"Stay out of this, Adamson," Bromel snapped. "He's been working here for five years and we need to keep hammering these things into him—or he'll forget everything." As Craig walked away, he stepped on Arnold's flower, crushing it under his heel. He bent over, scooping up the petals and dropping the dirty mop water as tears fell down his cheeks. Jake said, "It's alright, together after work we will find another flower for you to keep." Looking out of the corner of his eye, Jake saw Craig go to the next machine and was smiling as he had a conversation with a short brunette woman. Craig hugged the woman and kept on walking down the corridor.

After two months in Pope's Mills, Jake knew everyone in the factory by name. The only person who kept silent was the petite brunette at the adjacent station. One day, he noticed she wasn't at the machine. It was five to seven in the morning and it was plant rules that all employees be at their stations by seven o'clock or risk getting docked an hour of pay. By sheer observation, Jake knew the operation of the machinery around him and, at the top of the hour, started the conveyor, feeding the paper to be bound. Jake had enough skill to operate both stations at one time. Craig was on his morning inspection and noticed the station was unoccupied. Impatiently, he turned to Jake saying, "Where's Anna?"

Jake threw up his hands.

Anna bounded up the corridor saying, "Don't have a heart attack, I'm coming."

Craig had a scowl on his face. "You get *me* into trouble when you aren't here on time."

"Don't act pissed because I'm a few minutes late. The world won't end. I had was some car trouble. Anyhow, I called you twice and I couldn't reach you, so I had to bum a ride from my sister."

Craig shook his head and went about his rounds. Anna threw a smile at Jake and started working. Later in the morning, Jake was eating his baloney sandwich in the lunchroom when he looked up to find Anna sitting across from him. Anna said, "I want to thank you, Reverend, for covering for me this morning."

"It was nothing. I'd already forgotten about it. I didn't want to see you get docked."

"Craig wouldn't have docked me, but it was very considerate of you to do that. I've known him for years; he seems like a pecker-head, but he's a pussycat on the inside."

"By the way, I like being called Jake. I'm an ordained minister but not a 'Reverend'. It's more an honorary title."

"Oops, I'm sorry. Everyone around here calls you 'Reverend.' I thought you knew."

"No, I didn't. I don't mind as long as it's a nickname. I just don't want any special treatment because of my training."

Anna laughed. "Don't worry. Everyone gets the same 'special' treatment around here: crappy and lousy, but this job helps me make ends meet until I get my break as a singer."

Jake said, "That's great. We could use you in the church choir."

"My main talent is Country, not Gospel Music, but I'm sure I can sing with the right person in the lead."

"Come around to the church and I'll introduce you to the choir director."

"I will. The choir singing may help me develop my voice."

Jake was pleasantly surprised when she kept to her word and showed up at the practice. Anna had a well-developed voice, even though she claimed she never had any formal training. The choir director was pleased and assigned her the mezzo-soprano part.

Jake's life developed a rhythm between working, Bible study, and Sunday school classes. After teaching, he would go out to the Collins Hotel for brunch with Anna. Anna would have the fruit salad and coffee, while Jake would order the chicken and gravy with a side stack of pancakes. Anna would talk about the songs she was writing, while Jake would discuss his senior citizens Bible study classes.

Everything seemed to be going well when a month later, Anna arrived late for the choir and seemed distracted throughout her performance, her voice wobbling and hoarse. Jake could see that her demeanor had become very sullen. When they had lunch together, she became taciturn, looking away from the table, not touching her fruit salad.

Jake asked, "Is there any problem I can help you with?"

Anna responded mechanically, "Everything's alright."

"Right now, you'd be chewing my ear off about all the songs you're writing."

"I haven't written anything new. I'm practicing my current material," she said in a low voice.

"Sounds good, I'd love to hear it."

"Not now, maybe sometime later."

"Of course, I didn't mean now. I thought later this week you can come over to the farm, or I can hear the songs at your house."

Anna glared at him, "If you really want to know about problems, I could tell you about some of your own. Why do you find the need to get involved in everyone's life? Everything would be better off if you minded your own business."

Jake realized that what triggered the comment was his offer to come over her house. "All I wanted to do was to listen to your music. I thought that would make you happy after all our discussions. I did not want to pry into your personal life."

Anna looked at her watch. "I hope you don't mind. I've go a lot to do at home," she said as she abruptly left the restaurant.

After that Sunday, Jake noticed changes to her everyday habits. Anna stopped talking to him at the factory, and Craig became more belligerent to him. Even though Craig had a wife and a baby boy, he had been dating Anna for years. Craig objected to her participation in church activities, and saw Jake as a threat. Jake felt powerless but understood Anna's warning not to interfere. Somehow, he found it difficult to sever his connection to her. They had become very close, and ignoring her would be like cutting off a hand. Jake pretended not to pay any attention, while keeping an eye on her during work.

It had been a few weeks and the tension was easing slightly. Summer was quickly approaching and everyone looked forward to a long Independence Day weekend, when the plant would close. At noon, the lunchroom was a place of quiet celebration as workers brought in pies and cakes to share. Jake had finished his sandwich and was eating his cake when he saw Anna enter. He was aghast when he noticed a black and blue mark on her cheek. Her jaw looked puffy, making her oval face unsymmetrical. He quietly ate lunch and then approached Anna, "Good day Anna. What's that terrible mark on your jaw?"

"I walked into a kitchen cabinet," Anna said abruptly.

"The cabinet must have a mean left hook," Jake responded in a deadpan voice.

Anna went back to eating her lunch trying to disregard his comment.

Jake asked, "How long have you been sleeping with him? Is the relationship worth all this pain?"

"I told you, it's none of your god-damned business. You act so superior to everyone. If you ever took your nose out of the Bible, you would understand what it takes to live here."

"I don't think it's in the job description to sleep with the boss. I'm not talking about the Bible. Remember, I'm your friend. Every day you stay with him, you're losing your self-respect. You are such a vital person, and all this nonsense is draining the energy from your life. Just remember, you will never accomplish any of your dreams of being a singer as long as you stay with him."

Anna had no response. She walked over to the table of pies and started to talk to the women sitting at the adjacent table.

Jake left the lunchroom, and started work for the afternoon. Anna occupied her station with an expressionless look on her face. Jake had hoped he helped change her mind about Craig. When it was time to leave, Jake walked out to his dented Chevy Nova in the parking lot. A long line of cars waited to leave the gate. Jake stood at his car, waiting for the traffic to clear. Across the lot he noticed Anna having a heated discussion with Craig.

"I'm not going with you,." Anna protested.

"Get in the fucking car. I have the weekend planned, and you are not spoiling it." Bromel stood about ten feet in front of Anna, positioning himself to block any move she made.

Jake approached and asked tersely, "Is there anything I can help with?"

Craig said, "Stay out of this, Adamson. This is between me and Anna."

Jake put himself between Bromel and Anna. "Okay, I'll go when you move out of the way and allow the lady to do what she wants."

"Look, you snot-nose son of a bitch. Clear out or I'll knock you back to your car."

"You're certainly brave when it comes to intimidating retarded people and women half your size. You're not so tough. Back in my old parish in Louisville, I dealt with men who could wipe the floor with someone like you."

"Okay, you asked for it asshole." Craig made a fist and swung towards Jake's face. Jake saw the punch coming and tried to side step it. He was a bit slow and it connected with his lip. Jake lost his balance, going down to the ground on one knee. Stunned, he wiped the blood from his lip onto his hand.

Craig stood over Jake and said with bravado, "Looks like you bleed like the rest of us."

Jake knew he had no chance of defending himself while Craig was standing over him, so, while kneeling, he threw his fist into Craig's midsection. Craig stumbled back a few feet, allowing Jake to get up from the ground. Jake stood with a boxer's stance and started to move away from the car where Anna was standing. Craig lunged with another punch. The punch was slower, and Jake had time to feign to his left and connect his right hand to Craig's jaw. The blow had no impact, and Craig came back with a left to Jake's shoulder. Jake noticed Craig was covering his face, leaving his midsection open again. He moved in, taking another punch to the arm, and, with all his strength, hit Craig in the solar plexus. Craig fell to the ground, doubled over in pain.

Anna ran over to Jake. "Are you alright? Did he hurt you?"

"I'll survive." Jake said, his lip bloody.

Anna looked over to Craig, "Looks like he got what he deserved."

"He's not hurt. I just knocked the wind out of him. Let's take his advice and get out of here."

Jake sped out of the nearly empty lot and took Anna back to the house she shared with Craig. They did not have much time since Craig would be quick to follow. Jake was amazed at the speed in which Anna packed her clothes. After she threw them in the back seat of the car, Jake drove Anna to her sister's house, where she took shelter behind closed doors.

Word spread quickly about the fight; some people seemed sympathetic while others avoided speaking to him. Jake got the management reaction when he arrived to the entrance of the mill the next Tuesday. He was directed to the personnel office and informed he was terminated and issued his last paycheck. Jake went to the church that night to teach Bible study. Finding out it was cancelled indefinitely; Jake realized everything he had worked for during the past few months had fallen apart.

***

Jake didn't see Anna again until September. Jake had come to town for supplies and was breezing up and down the isles of the supermarket, filling his cart with canned vegetables. From a distance, he spotted a petite brunette in an apron. As Jake approached her, his heart raced. Anna gave a look of recognition and walked over, hugged him and rested her head on his chest.

"Oh, it's so nice to see you. I thought you'd left," she said.

"I didn't leave, I'm a full time hand on the Fliecher farm, now."

She looked in admiration at Jake and took in his sun-bleached, blonde hair and his dark, tanned skin. "I see farm work agrees with you. As for me, I didn't hang around the factory too long. I lasted a week after you belted Craig. I knew the manager of this market, and he needed another cashier."

"Looks like you have traded up," Jake commented.

Anna said, "I've been back to the Antioch Church. There're a whole lot of people asking about you."

"I would have come back to the church, but I didn't think anyone wanted to see me." He smiled and said, "Hey look, the farm is only twenty minutes away so why don't you come and visit me? I'll cook dinner."

Anna laughed, "I remember how you cook." She hesitated for a moment and then said, "Okay, you've got a deal; one condition...*I'll* cook the dinner."

That night, Anna showed up wearing blue jeans and a denim shirt at Jake's, ready to do kitchen work. Jake introduced her to Lew Fliecher, the owner of the farm. Lew was a tall, rail thin man in his mid-fifties with a reddish complexion. He seemed pleased to have company for dinner, especially that of a pretty young woman. Other than Jake, his only companionship was his developmentally challenged son in his twenties, Cylus, who never spoke. Cylus stood silently in the sparsely furnished living room and stared at Anna from under his tuft of uncombed, dark hair. On a tour of the first floor, Jake proudly showed her where he had put up new drywall and an electrical fixture in the downstairs bedroom.

After a round of lemonade, she cooked roasted chicken, biscuits, and gravy for the men. During dinner, Lew entertained her with the story of how he met Jake. He had caught him trespassing, fishing the trout stream on the farm. Lew said jokingly that Jake was the "most talented fisherman he knew at the end of the sixteen gauge shotgun." Jake added that he had to share the sixteen-inch, brown trout with Lew and Cylus or risk being shot. All of them laughed. Lew spoke about Jake's handyman skills in maintaining the house. Jake started talking about taking odd jobs as a plasterer and carpenter to earn extra money.

After dinner, the men sat on the living room couch and sang gospel tunes as Anna played piano. Even Cylus, who hardly ever seemed happy, broke out with a smile. After Lew and Cylus went up to bed, Jake sat on the sofa as Anna sat next to him, putting her arms around his neck.

Jake said, "I admire your stamina. Thanks for helping with the dishes."

"I don't know about you, but I was raised in a house where you had to finish the dishes before going to bed."

"I've been living alone for a while and have become *undomesticated*," Jake said.

"You throw a nice party. How many bedrooms does this house have?"

Jake reacted with surprise, "Why are you asking?"

"I don't feel like navigating these roads at this time of the night. I just may have to stay here."

"I have a bedroom on the first floor and Cylus, the second. I can sleep on the couch tonight," Jake offered.

Anna put her hands on Jake's muscled chest. "Don't I have a say in this matter?" She leaned over, looking into Jake's eyes and kissing him on the lips. The kiss was soft and Anna leaned back satisfied. "You're a good kisser for a former minister. I think you have some natural talent. I'm glad you left the church. It's a shame to see such talent go to waste."

Jake responded in kind, "I've always loved you—from the first time we met on the floor of the mill." Anna lifted up his shirt and started kissing his stomach as Jake embraced her, breathing softly on her neck. Anna suddenly broke the embrace and stood up, slipping off her tight-fitting, blue jeans. She took off her shirt slowly, button by button, revealing an hourglass figure. Jumping back on the couch, Anna aggressively put her legs around Jake's waist, almost making it difficult for him to breathe. Jake slid his hands beneath her underwear, massaging her buttocks. She kissed him more fiercely as she said, "Yes, we definitely need more time to talk about the sleeping arrangements."

***

Anna became a perennial guest at Fliecher Farm, cooking meals and helping out with the chores. Eventually, Anna started inviting people from the Antioch Baptist Church to dinners. The farm was transitioned from a place of solitude and desolation to one of weekly gatherings and forums. Anna would arrange for the food, while Jake organized the meetings. The gatherings often consisted of a sing-a-long after dinner followed by a discussion of current events and Bible study.

Theresa Clark heard second-hand from a member of the church about the meetings. She knew her father would forbid her from going so she made up a story of going over a friend's house for dinner. Then she would get a ride from Sue Ann. Jake was pleased he attracted younger people to his gatherings and spoke with them about his ethics and the need for community service. Jake had noted that Theresa seemed to take after her mother with regard to her attitude about volunteering. At Jake's urging, Theresa began helping out at the hospital. Theresa returned to the farm whenever she could break away from her chores at the house, and from her work at the hospital. Jake reciprocated Theresa's trust by giving her a pendant with a gold-plated cross. Theresa would always make it a point to wear the necklace whenever she visited.

During the meetings, there were many discussions about home repairs. Using the contacts he made from the church, Jake traveled regularly into town to make general home repairs. All the money he earned went toward his personal ministry. There was a lot of business for Jake so he took on Cylus and Arnold as assistants. Jake couldn't have asked for two more reliable people. They consistently performed their tasks without question.

One of Jake's new clients was a landlord on Main Street who had managed several storefronts. One of the stores, empty for a number of years, had extensive water damage in the ceiling and walls from pipes bursting in the winter. Jake noticed that even though the store needed cosmetic repairs, the wood floor, brick masonry, and roof were still in good shape. The restoration of the plaster walls and ceiling was a long, arduous job, especially after working during the day on the farm. One night, Jake was nearly limp with exhaustion. He sat down to take a break and for a second and took in the large front room filled with benches and a lectern. He realized his former church was immaterial. Jake thought to himself that if he had a way of generating income, it did not matter what the church thought about his activities. Jake then understood why the images had appeared to him; he had to create his own mission in town.

Jake soon learned that it would take all his business skills to establish this mission. He was able to negotiate a cheap lease with the owner of the store, and, with the help of the members of his group, rehabilitated the structure. Jake owed his success to a combination of sheer luck…and knowledge of local businesses. A church in a neighboring town had recently undergone its own rehabilitation, a process that included getting rid of its old, wooden pews. The pews just needed to be sanded and a coat of polyurethane applied. A restaurant in town was going out of business, and Jake made an offer for the large, commercial grade, gas stove. Jake also made arrangements with the local grocery to collect all the unsold fruits and vegetables that would have been thrown out. Local farmers also came by, laden with imperfect corn and tomatoes.

After a couple of weeks, the ministry had taken shape and finally Jake realized his dream of helping people directly, without going through the bureaucracy of a church. Jake decided to name his mission "The Shadybrook Outreach Mission" after the stream on the farm he took refuge in during hot days. To him, it was symbolic of the mission to provide shelter for people in trouble. He painted a wooden sign and proudly hung it in front of the building. There was no shortage of hungry people and the mission drew people from the surrounding areas. The needy would walk an hour to get to town. Jake made a generous offer to give rides so they could travel back to their homes. Anyone without a roof for the night slept in the kitchen by the stove.

Anna had been very supportive of Jake and had worked side by side with him to build the mission. Jake's love for her grew, and he became dependent on her for help. Jake could tell by Anna's behavior that she was becoming distracted and preoccupied with some sort of problem. One night, Jake decided to have other people take over the ministry and scheduled a dinner with Anna back at the farm. Anna set the table and cooked chicken just like the times they had when they worked on the farm together. Over dinner Jake asked, "Is anything bothering you? I think everything is going very well for us. You have been so important in my life, helping me set up the mission. I just want to say I could not have done it without you. "

"Thank you, Jake. I have never met anyone so dynamic. I wish you all the best in the future."

"It is 'our future,'" Jake corrected Anna.

"I've been meaning to tell you something. I thought you would have noticed by now…I've been pregnant for two months."

Jake's jaw dropped. He regained his composure and then leaned over to kiss her. "That is such great news. You didn't have to keep it a secret. It doesn't matter. I'm willing to take responsibility. I've also wanted to tell you what's been on my mind for all these months we worked together; I would like for us to be husband and wife."

Anna smiled and held Jake's hand. "I love you too Jake and it is very sweet of you to propose." She paused, becoming more serious, "To be honest, I don't know whose baby it is. My failure in life has been my weakness for men."

"I don't care whether the baby is mine or not. I'll raise it as if it's my own."

"I know you would and you'd be a great father. But that's not the issue. I've stayed up many nights trying to figure out what to do next. I've decided to leave Pope's Mills. I cannot raise a baby here."

Jake, becoming distraught, said pleadingly, "You should reconsider your decision. You have so many friends here. You can't just pull up stakes and leave."

"Remember six months ago when I was living with Craig Bromel. You told me I would never accomplish any of my goals as long as I stayed with him. You were right. There are too many ghosts in this town for me, and I will never have any career in music if I remain here. I know you're in love with this place and here lay your future, whatever it is. My future is someplace else and fairly soon, we will have to go our separate ways."

A week later, Jake helped Anna load her belongings into her car and watched her drive away. For the first time in his life he felt a sense of loss. Not only did he lose the soul mate that he had shared his life for the past few months, but also a piece of his future. The baby would be the empty vessel in which he could fill with his feelings like his own. Now, any chance of having a family was out of reach. Jake emotionally compensated by working sixteen-hour days. Arnold and Cylus became full time employees of the ministry. It was not uncommon for fifty people to show up for a meal and a Bible reading.

One day, Theresa came by to view the mission. It was before dinner and the room was filled by men with haggard faces as they lined up around the perimeter of the sanctuary for dinner. Jake glimpsed Theresa and walked over, putting his arms around her shoulders and giving her a kiss on the forehead, "So, you stopped by for some of my home cooking?" he asked playfully.

"I've already had something to eat. When you invited me over here you said it was important. Remember?"

"Oh yes, I did." Jake laughed. "There is so much going on, I kinda forgot about the invite. I thought you would want to help out."

"I heard about Anna. I'm terribly sorry about her leaving and I know you're one short. Sure, I can pitch in a little, but I can't do it all the time. My step-father complains he doesn't see me enough as it is."

Jake found an apron hanging on a hook and tied it onto Theresa's waist. "I work fast and have already found some replacements," he said as he led Theresa through the men to the metal counter. There stood a high school boy with un-combed, dark brown hair and a thin build. Theresa immediately recognized his from homeroom. "You see, I met this scraggly looking thing from the Antioch Church." Jake put his arms playfully around the boy's neck and then swiftly put him into a head lock.

The boy protested, "I'm trying to serve dinner here."

"Don't be a stranger, Evan. Say hello to Theresa," Jake said, turning the boy's head directly towards Theresa.

"Howdy there, Theresa," Evan said, nearly choking.

Theresa waved back and then started to ladle the thick fish chowder from the large stainless steel pot into the men's bowls. Jake joined in and had the men fed in less than thirty minutes. Jake made the after dinner service short so he could get Theresa back to her house by eight, ensuring that Clark would not ask any questions.

A reporter showed up for one of the meetings and took pictures of the people who ran the ministry. Shortly after, there was a large article in the Gazette about Jake's operation. The press had the effect of drawing more attention to the ministry. Health inspectors regularly stopped by from the county to inspect the kitchen. Jake attributed the inspections to the enemies he made within the town. He began take out his frustrations now on the government; his daily sermons became more critical of local politics.

Jake saw a subtle change in the way he was treated by the townspeople. Some remained friendly, while others became cold and indifferent, as if Pope's Mills had been split in two. The local grocery that had been giving him their old fruits and vegetables was suddenly selling out, or was consistently out of stock. It was becoming more difficult to put meals on the table, but somehow Jake managed to make things work even with more limited resources. One morning, Jake saw a crack in the front window where someone had thrown a bottle. Now he was concerned about the safety of the people in the mission, and started to keep a shotgun in the office under the desk.

***

When it arrived, it seemed like an ordinary piece of mail. So ordinary it remained unopened for a week. It was a notice that the Town Council had determined the mission was in violation of community zoning. The date of the hearing in the Town Council was set for the next week. The letter said the ministry would be able to present witnesses in its defense. Jake did not take the matter seriously, thinking he would just make some token improvements to the building to keep the Council at bay. After all, he was running a charitable organization benefiting the community. Some people thought he should have hired an attorney, but in Jake's mind that was overkill.

The meeting was held in the high school auditorium. Jake arrived with thirty people from the mission, not knowing what to expect. The members of the Council included the newly elected Mayor Williams, who sat on the stage behind a large oak table. Jake looked proudly at the audience. He had made a lot of friends in Pope's Mills. The back door to the auditorium opened and Theresa Clark walked in. Jake nodded to her.

Mayor Williams banged the gavel on the table as the Council secretary sat next to him, preparing to take notes. "I call this hearing to order for Zoning Case #389 of the Shadybrook Outreach Mission." The Mayor looked over towards Jake, who sat on the stage opposite from the Council. "I see, Mr. Adamson, you've brought no legal representation. I hope you understand this is a legally binding hearing."

Jake stood up. "Yes, I do. I thought I could come to an accommodation with the Council without an attorney."

Williams turned to the secretary. "Okay, let it be noted that you have waived legal representation," Williams said. "Are you aware of the complaint against you?"

"The letter said we were non-compliant with the existing zoning," Jake said, trying to sound innocent.

"The space you are occupying is zoned commercial and there is evidence that you are using it for industrial or institutional purposes with regard to the mission," Williams retorted.

"We do sell various services to the people of Pope's Mills. We have a tax number with the Commonwealth of Kentucky. I have all the records with me."

"All of us on the Council understand. This community has three churches and they all are located on land that is zoned for institutional use. I don't see what entitles you to an exception to this?"

The people in the audience booed the question. Jake made a gesture to try to quiet them down. "I don't want to be treated any differently. But in other places in the state, I have noted long-running missions in the commercial district."

"What other communities do is no business of mine. The sole purpose of this hearing is to determine if your operation is compliant with the zoning of Pope's Mills. Do you have a home improvement license for the repairs you are performing?" Williams asked, ignoring the mood of the audience.

"I don't see how the question is pertinent. We keep tax records of all the income and the disbursement of salaries."

"I take that as a 'no' then. I was only trying to help, Jake. If you had a business license, we could possibly have said the mission serves as a commercial operation. It seems you have no legal basis to be where you are. You're asking the Council to believe the mission is a benefit to the town. "

Jake was starting to get annoyed. "It's obviously a blessing for the community."

There were a few people who voiced from the audience, "Amen. You tell them Jake."

The town solicitor, Wayne Cauldill, got up from his seat. "I've got some questions for Mr. Adamson." Wayne wore a blue and white pinstriped suit, his oily, dark hair meticulously combed back on his scalp. With sweat forming on his brow from the stage lights, he said, "We've done some research on you. They're some things in your background that we need clarified."

"I thought this hearing was about the mission. I did not expect to be put on trial here," Jake responded, taken by surprise.

Wayne put his hands on his pinstriped suit jacket and leisurely grabbed his lapels. "You're appearing as a witness in a hearing and we're entitled to question your background. Of course, you're not obligated to answer any of the questions. However, any question you don't answer would be considered in the final decision."

Jake felt trapped and stood there helplessly in front of the Council. "I've got nothing to hide."

The solicitor continued, "Good. Some of the information I'll be using is from the Gazette article published a couple of weeks ago. I assume that you have seen it and that the information is correct?"

"Yes, I've seen it. It's more or less truthful."

"The article stated you attended the Baptist Seminary in Louisville, but when we checked, there was no such person as Jake Adamson having graduated."

There was dead silence in the room. Jake hesitated then spoke, "There's a simple explanation. 'Jacob Adamson' is the name on my birth certificate. My father left my mother before I was born, and I became an orphan at age five after my mother died from kidney disease. My adopted family's name was 'Brown' and my father called me 'Jack' rather than 'Jake.' I attended the seminary under the name of 'Jack Brown.'"

Cauldill pressed on with the questioning. "Your name, however, was changed back to Jake Adamson after you left the ministry in 1989. The article inferred you left voluntarily. Is there anything you want to add?"

"I was frustrated by church politics."

"Wasn't there another reason? A woman named Cynthia Burroughs had brought a suit against the church saying that you had fathered her son. I've got a clipping here in my folder from a newspaper about a 'Jack Brown' being mentioned in the suit." Wayne held up the folder in front of the audience. "The suit was settled out of court for an undisclosed sum. But the church was ready to hold disciplinary hearings with the possible result of removing your minister's license. Didn't you change your name back to Jake Adamson because of all the publicity in the papers?"

Jake looked back at the people in the audience. Some were state of shock; others were enraged and were hollering at him to get off the stage. Williams made a token gesture of banging the gavel again. "I'll have order! Or else I'll call the Sheriff and have the auditorium cleared." Williams tried to be serious but held back a smile, pleased the audience had turned against Jake.

"There was no basis for the suit. Cynthia was a methadone addict who became emotionally attached to me. She was insisting I council her daily and she was constantly intruding in on my important church duties. I eventually referred her to a psychiatrist. She took it personally that I refused to see her and decided to get even by falsely accusing me. I forgave her. She needed the money from the settlement to fund her drug and psychiatrist treatments."

"Isn't it true that you have fathered a baby here out of wedlock? The woman has subsequently left town."

Jake turned red in the face. He yelled at the Council, "Now that's a damned cheap shot! It's complete hearsay! You've got no authority to question my personal affairs. I've done nothing illegal."

Wayne stood at the lectern waiting to put the final knife in the carcass. "I'm not arguing the legality of your actions. All I'm saying is that there's an established pattern to your behavior. Now you want to run an organization in town that would put you in contact with many women." Wayne turned to the Mayor. "I've got no more questions."

Mayor Williams said, "Thank you, Mr. Cauldill. Jake, is there anything you want to present on your behalf?"

Jake stood silent for a minute trying to calm himself after making the critical mistake of getting upset in front of the Town Council. Jake wanted to storm out of the meeting. Instead, he looked back into the audience at the people from the mission. All of them seemed to be in disbelief over the disclosures. He owed them an explanation and a reason for them to believe in the mission again. Jake faced the audience, turning his back to the Council. "Yes, I do. I just want to compliment Mr. Cauldill on the job he's done insulting my character, insinuating that I'm some type of sociopath interested in making woman pregnant and then abandoning them. I'm not going to give any credibility to the statements by responding with any details. I'll humbly admit that I'm like anybody else on this earth, and I've made some mistakes. I've come here to start life anew and to make a difference. I'm not going to talk about how many meals I've served since starting the mission, or the number of people I've helped. You folks on the Council are good at digging deep in the past to find the negatives, but you ignore the present and the testimony of your neighbors. Everybody in town is concerned about putting food on the table and clothes on their backs. I'm not against that. But it seems that even with three churches in town, everyone is worshipping money and worrying where the next dollar will come from. I see the spiritual balance sheet. There are aged, poor, and destitute in need of assistance in their daily lives. Please allow me to continue to help the people of this town and to maintain the balance sheet on the positive side…"

Mayor Williams stood up from his seat, interrupting, "Thank you, Mr. Adamson. I think we've gotten enough information to make our decision. We will retire to make our judgment." He banged the gavel on the oak table.

"I'm not finished! You said you would hear me out," Jake said, red in the face, pointing his finger at the Mayor.

"The hearing's over, Mr. Adamson…"

"But I haven't finished presenting my case…"

The members of the council stood up, put their papers in their briefcases, ignoring the people who sat aghast in the auditorium. They walked away from the stage as Jake yelled after them. "You will not pass judgment on me, but I assure you the Almighty will judge you for who you are. It says in the Bible, Job 10, 'You bring new witnesses against me and increase your anger towards me; your forces come against me wave upon wave.' but mind you, I'll have my day in court…"

Jake saw Theresa get up and walk quickly toward the door. He sprinted out of the room, trying to avoid the people in the auditorium. He caught up to Theresa in the middle of the school corridor. Theresa said angrily, "I trusted you and after the performance you put on at the paper company, I defended you to everyone, but you kept things from me. I feel like such an idiot. Why didn't you tell me about what happened to you in Louisville? All along you were just using me to gain influence."

"What happened back in Louisville is all politics. I pissed off some of the hierarchy of the church and they decided to blow the incident out of proportion. That's who released the story to the papers." Jake saw a tear run down Theresa's face. He put his hands on Theresa's shoulders, trying to comfort her. "Theresa, you are going to have to tune everything out and listen to your own inner voice. Everything I've ever told you came from my heart. Whatever happens to me now is in the hands of the Lord. All I can ask you to do is not to care what is going on with me, and to work hard to reach your potential."

Theresa grabbed Jake's wrists and pushed them off her shoulder. "Keep your hands off of me! I'm not playing your god-dammed games anymore!" she shrieked as everyone in the corridor stopped talking. She walked down the hall, stopping after twenty feet. She lifted the gold pendant with the cross from around her neck and threw it at Jake. It landed at his feet and he stooped to pick it up. Theresa yelled down the hall, "You can keep your 'fools gold!' Stay away from me; I don't want to see you again!" she said as she trod down the hall, slamming the door behind her.

Two days after the meeting, Jake received a certified letter stating the Council found him in violation of the zoning and he was to vacate the premises. Jake realized the decision to evict him had been made before the hearing. The disappointment was that no one from town spoke out to defend him. He decided that he would remain. The town would have to close the building itself.

The mission remained open for one week. Jake arrived one morning and saw Arnold and Cylus waiting outside the mission doors along with a group of people waiting to eat breakfast. The doors were padlocked with a large "No Trespassing" sign. He announced to the group, "We're allowed to retrieve our personal effects inside." He spotted a one foot diameter piece of concrete on the road. Breaking the lock with the concrete, Jake went into the building, followed by the rest of the people.

Sheriff Sam Sr. had been expected trouble and rounded up the part-time deputies to control the crowd. As Jake exited the building with a box of books, Sam Sr. was waiting outside. Sam Sr. and a deputy shoved Jake against the brick wall and cuffed his wrists. "The building has been marked. You are now trespassing," he said. Out of the corner of his eye, Jake noticed Cylus struggling with the deputies. One of the deputies hit Cylus across the legs with a nightstick, bringing him down on his knees. Jake yelled, "You don't need to hurt him. He's harmless." As he wrenched out of Sam's grip to help Cylus, a deputy tackled Jake and a scuffle ensued. It took the Sheriff and the deputies ten minutes to gain control.

That day, ten people were arrested. The small, paneled hearing room in the municipal building was filled with defendants and onlookers for the trial. All the defendants pleaded guilty except for Jake, who tried to be his own attorney. After a thirty-minute trial, Jake was found guilty of criminal trespass and resisting arrest. Given the limited space in the jail, the judge sentenced everyone to two nights. Jake received the full penalty of one week for the trespass and two weeks for resisting arrest.

Jake served his time without complaint and returned to the Fliecher farm. Later that winter, old man Fliecher got sick and died of pneumonia; the property was left to Cylus. Jake took over management of the farm and began to raise soybeans. Everything turned peaceful in Pope's Mills and Jake was not seen in town again.

***

About a year after the incident with Jake Adamson, Sam Sr. was filling out paperwork in his office so he could leave for the day. The telephone rang on his desk. It was Matt Clark. He was frantic because Theresa never returned home from school. Sam Sr. tried to calm him, asking the usual questions about whether she could be with friends or acquaintances. Clark started listing the people he had called. Sam Sr. said, "This is a small place, I'll get a group of people together and we'll find her."

That night Sam Sr. and the four deputies crisscrossed the town, but to no avail. It was as if she dropped off the face of the earth. Morning came, and Sam Sr. started calling up sheriffs in neighboring communities. He was also interviewing classmates who said she had left school that day alone. Sam Sr. notified the state police. After three days of a statewide search, they reported no leads in Theresa's disappearance.

The break in the case came at an unexpected location: the supermarket. Sam Sr. was in the front of the store paying for a quick dinner from the deli counter when he overheard a conversation between the manager and the delivery boy. The manager was walking past the delivery box for the Fliecher farm when he spotted a can of feminine hygiene spray. He said to the boy, "Looks like this got in here by mistake. They don't order this stuff from us."

The boy said, "It's no mistake. Jake specifically asked for it."

The manager scratched his head as he picked up the can "Its three guys out there. I wonder what they would use it for?"

Sam Sr. stared at the box and finally realized the whereabouts of Theresa Clark.

Sam Sr. got a deputy to obtain a search warrant from the judge while he headed over to the Fliecher farm. Sam Sr. parked down the road where he would be out of view. Sam Sr. could see Cylus in the tractor plowing the field, but could not locate Jake or Arnold. Sam Sr. kept an eye on the farm while the other deputies arrived. He pointed to toward the main house. "I bet they're holding her there."

Sam Sr. went to the back door and kicked it in, disintegrating the wood. The sudden crash terrified Arnold, who was mopping the floor in the kitchen. Screaming, arms waving, he ran head-first into the deputy coming in through the front door. Sam Sr. did a quick search of the first floor, entering the master bedroom where he saw someone asleep in the queen size bed.

It was Theresa.

Jake exited from the bathroom next to the bedroom. "What the hell is going on here?" he asked.

Sam Sr. got into the hallway and struck Jake squarely on the jaw, knocking him to the floor. "I'll make sure you go away for a long time, you sick son of a bitch!"

CHAPTER 9

"Jake was transferred to a jail in Gottlieb Heights, the county seat, where he was arraigned on the federal charge of kidnapping," Sam said as he sipped his beer and looked forlornly at the stars. "Kidnapping wasn't the only charge he faced. He also was up on a series of state charges." Sam hesitated for a moment, and then took another couple of sips. The next words were difficult to utter, but he eventually got the courage and said, "They took Theresa to the hospital for a physical…there was evidence that she had been sexually molested."

Joseph looked back at Sam with a look of sadness and disgust. Joseph thought back to the prayer for help Theresa had posted on the wall of her closet, and everything came into perspective. Sex had always been a taboo issue in Arab cultures. His parents never spoke about it and never showed any public affection. The Arab concept of honor or "wajh" was directly related to sex, with families often suffering dishonor due to the conduct of a daughter or a sister. The sexual purity of a woman, described as an "ird," was something that Arabs thought of as growing within a woman as she matured, and, once lost due to a sexual offense, could not be regained. Being in a small town, Joseph wondered about the stigma others had attached to the molestation.

Sam said, "We're not used to dealing with sex crimes in Pope's Mills and the entire community was in shock and disbelief. My father took the affidavit from Theresa himself. Her story was that she was walking home alone from school."

"Don't kids usually walk home in groups?" Joseph asked.

"Pope's Mills is a town where everyone trusts each other and doesn't worry about violent crime. Up to that point, we didn't think we had to guard our children. Unknown to Theresa, Jake had trailed her in his car and when she was halfway home, out of view of any houses, he pulled up to her. He offered her a ride to her father's house, but wound up taking her back to the farm where he held her prisoner for three days. Jake had come on to her several times while she was there. She would not voluntarily have relations with him, so he handcuffed her to his bed, stripped her of all her clothes, and then he violently abused her. The lower portion of her body was covered with bruises. There were marks where her wrists bled from the handcuffs. She did her best to escape, but it was no contest. Jake was a much bigger man, and he controlled her easily. It was all fairly graphic and my father would only talk about it in vague terms.

Joseph asked, "What about the other two people who occupied the buildings? What were they doing while this was happening?"

"Apparently, very little. Arnold was the only person who shared the main house with Jake. Remember, he had a mind of a ten year old. He didn't know what was going on. Cylus was mute and in a world of his own. He still doesn't communicate with anyone."

"Did the case ever reach trial?"

"This time, Jake hired an attorney, a public defender out of Louisville. At the arraignment, Jake pleaded not guilty to the charges. He was claiming it was some type of 'Government set-up.'" Sam laughed and shook his head. "'Government set-up'—bullshit. They had him cold. However, the public defender did have some talent. At the preliminary hearing, he was able to argue the pre-trial publicity in the area precluded a fair trail and was able to get it moved to Xavier, a town located about one hundred miles north of Lexington. As it turned out, all the legal maneuvering didn't really matter. About two weeks after he was in jail, Jake got severely depressed. Personally, I don't blame him. I'd be depressed if I was facing over one hundred and fifty years in jail on various criminal charges. They found him one morning hanging from a bed sheet in his cell. In my opinion, he did everyone a favor. It would've been a tragedy to have Theresa cross-examined in open court and make her relive everything that happened."

Joseph inquired, "What ever happened to Cylus and Arnold?"

"Arnold was taken to a group home. About a year later, he had a bad fall and died of a brain hemorrhage. Cylus is locked away in Burwood Hospital, a mental asylum about forty miles away from here. As I said, the FBI did a thorough job researching the entire episode. Everybody directly connected with Jake is dead or locked away someplace…"

"And what about Theresa? Whatever happened to her?"

"She has the most tragic story of the group. Six months after she finished high school, she was traveling out in Arizona when she got into a head on collision with a truck. She died instantly."

Joseph decided to take a devils advocate position. "What do you think drove him to kidnapping? It doesn't make any sense to me. He seemed to behaving rationally up to that point."

"People can be very adept at covering up their own psychotic behavior. I'm not trained as a psychiatrist; I had only had one abnormal psych course in college. The cause of his behavior could have been anything, and I'd only be only spitting in the wind trying to figure it out. You have to remember, he came from a broken family. Maybe he was sexually abused when he was with his foster father. I read a study once that said abused children have a tendency to be molesters when they grow up. Maybe all the charitable work he was doing was some sort of cover for his true intentions—his need for controlling people—especially women. The molestation was possibly his way of staking claim to her."

"Why Theresa?"

"Why *not* Theresa? She was young and fairly vulnerable to suggestion. Theresa's father was the richest man in town. By kidnapping her, he thought he could be a father figure that would place him in a position of power. Putting the situation into its proper context, Jake was in charge of a religious cult and wanted the unquestioning obedience of everyone in the group. At one time, Theresa was an active part of the group who finally realized it was all a deception and had wanted to leave. That upset Jake, who had tried to get her back. When he failed, he resorted to violence."

Still skeptical Joseph said, "A 'cult'...I think that is an exaggeration. To me a 'cult' is simply a unified group that has practices outside the beliefs of society. Jake's actions opening a mission were within Christian practice."

Sam countered, "Cults are helmed by charismatic leaders who persuade their followers to follow *their* rules. I heard that Jake insisted everyone who lived with him have a cross tattooed on the back of their hands; because it says in Deuteronomy 'You should love the Lord your God...which you should teach diligently to your children ...and should bind them for a sign on your hand.' So he paid for five people to get cross tattoos in a parlor in Gottlieb Heights."

"You still haven't given me an iron-clad argument that Jake was crazy. I don't think anything you have told me so far would hold up in a court of law."

Taking a final gulp of beer, Sam said, "There is one last thing I didn't tell you. Towards the end, Jake was fairly delusional. They searched his cell after the suicide and found a bunch of writing on a legal pad. He had termed himself a 'messiah' and said that he would be 'resurrected to bring justice to the world.' Now, if that isn't crazy, then I don't know what is."

"Did anyone take what he wrote seriously?" Joseph asked.

Somewhat intoxicated, Sam put down the last beer and said to Joseph sarcastically, "Yeah, all of us in town are still waiting for the 'resurrection' to happen."

CHAPTER 10

It had been four days since the FBI released Cecil Millar from custody. The investigation was at a standstill. There was a marked tension in Pope's Mills as to whom the next suspect would be. In a log cabin outside of town, Dutton Anderson lay in bed, oblivious to the FBI and everything else associated with the investigation. Looking at the afternoon sunlight recede through the bedroom window, he rolled over, watching the woman next to him as her stomach slowly rose up and down. She suddenly lifted herself up, leaning over him, picking up the bottle of twelve-year-old bourbon on the adjacent nightstand. She poured the light amber-colored liquid into a yellow-flowered, paper cup.

"This completely defeats the purpose of drinking twelve-year-old Bourbon, having it in a paper cup," Beth scoffed.

In a deadpan voice Dutton said, "It's only appropriate. The paper came from the factory in town and I'm going to recycle the cup. So don't worry."

Beth didn't find Dutton's facetiousness amusing. The ice had melted and she had to resort to drinking the Bourbon straight. She would have smoked a cigarette, but took the last one an hour ago. Though slightly over forty, she did not look a day past thirty, even though her skin was starting to develop brown age spots from sunbathing. Her hair had been dyed blonde, a symptom of a woman trying to relive her youth. Beth still admired her own firm body. The breasts were beginning to sag a little but everything else was tanned and in place. After the daily health club visits in Gottlieb Heights, she felt she should be admired. Men were put on this earth to be dominated and her trophy's naked body lay next to her in bed, staring ahead. Beth looked at the clock on the wall as it turned five. "Oh shit, I lost track of time. I need to get home and make dinner. My husband is a lazy asshole incapable of even putting a hot dog in the microwave." She said as she quickly began putting on her underwear and bra.

Dutton heard the sound of cars pull up outside and then a loud knock on the front door. He slowly got out of bed saying, "I wonder who the fuck that could be." Beth stood motionless, a worried look on her face. "Keep cool. Whoever it is, I'll get rid of them," Dutton reassured her and with one jerk of his arms put on his pants. He reached for his shirt that was thrown over the chair and went downstairs to the front door. The knock turned to banging and Dutton hastily opened the door and stepped out into the sunlight in his wrinkled corduroy shirt and faded jeans. He squinted as he put his hand to his forehead, trying to focus his bleary eyes on the four men standing inches away.

Taking out his badge from his suit jacket and flashing it towards the open door, Sattler announced, "FBI. Agents Sattler and Jefferies. We need to ask you few questions. Mind if we step inside?"

"Yes… I do…I'm in the middle of something right now…," Dutton responded. But the two agents gave him a hard stare. Dutton reluctantly held the door open as they walked into the cabin with Sam and Joseph both lagging a bit behind.

Sattler said, "I'm sure you recognize Sheriff Sam Johnson and this is Dr. Hamiz. He serves as our consultant in this case."

Dutton said, "Yes, I've had the pleasure of meeting Dr. Hamiz." Sattler and Jefferies eyed Joseph suspiciously when Dutton added, "We spoke over a cup of coffee at the Collins." He moved into his small kitchen adjacent to the living room and started to fumble through his pots in his sink. He found a stainless steel teakettle, filled it with water and placed it on the small, white-porcelain gas stove. "Anybody want some green tea? It's organic."

Every one declined, except for Joseph who said, "If it's caffeinated, I could use some." As everyone stood watching Dutton, Joseph moved through the living room with its torn cloth sofa surrounded by bookcases filled with chemistry and physics books. He started to nervously thumb through them when he noted an entire bookshelf devoted to water resources, including a book on the design of small dams by the Corps of Engineers. Jefferies took notice. He walked over and started to search the bookcase.

Sattler handed Dutton a folded photocopy of a newspaper article from his suit jacket pocket. Dutton gave it a cursory look and handed it back to Sattler, "Yes, I wrote the letter. I did it nearly two years ago. It's a kinda funny, after I wrote it I got no response from anyone and now I get a visit from the FBI and the local sheriff."

Sattler watched as Dutton went into the kitchen cabinet looking for cups. He said, "You came to Pope's Mills eight years ago to teach high school. You're thirty six years old and single. We have records of you serving a year in Danbury for possession of coke."

"Big deal. Everybody in town knows I've got a rap sheet. It's ancient history. I've stayed clean. I don't tolerate any drugs in my classes. You ask Sam. About a year ago, I told him about one of the kids doing crack."

Sam nodded, "I remember. But we're not talking drugs this time."

Sattler read from the photocopy, "You wrote, and I'm quoting here, 'The dam has become an albatross around the neck of the community. Every year we loose valuable fishery habitat and we cannot afford to have it remain. For our children's sake, we must decide to remove it altogether. The embankment can be removed quickly and inexpensively through the use of dynamite or high powered explosives.' Shall I read on?"

"I meant it as constructive criticism. I'm an environmentalist, not a terrorist. I didn't intend for someone to blow it up."

Jefferies took a dusty cardboard box from underneath the bookshelf and pulled up the flaps covering the contents. He quickly motioned to Sattler to come over. "You ought to see this...," he said.

Sattler peered into the box and smiled. It was filled with newspaper clippings and photographs of the dam. He picked up a handful of papers and showed them to Dutton.

Dutton turned red, as he stammered, "That's... my personal archive...*You can't do that...*"

Sattler pulled an envelope out of his suit jacket and threw it on coffee table. "I'm sorry, a federal judge disagrees with you. I forgot to mention that we've got a warrant to search the premises. *We can do anything we want.* If I were you, I'd come clean."

"You think since I'm an ex-con, I would blow up the dam?"

"We generally think in terms of motive and opportunity. You seem to be the self- righteous type, and maybe you felt like you were making some sort of environmental statement. Having a general background in chemistry and electronics, you could have taught yourself about bomb construction. You probably met people in the joint who could have given you the finer points of creating explosives for the proper effect. This cabin is located away from town and you could have fabricated the explosives without drawing any attention to yourself."

Dutton said, "Yes, while I was in jail I did meet guys who told me about creating explosives out of lawn fertilizer and dish liquid. I consider myself a resourceful person and given enough time I could've built some good devices. But I spent my time in prison doing something constructive: getting a degree in teaching. Anyhow, how stupid do you think I am? If I were planning to blow up a dam, would I be sending a letter to the editor beforehand? It's a close-knit community. I knew the child and parents who were killed. I may have trafficked in drugs, but I'm not a murderer."

Jefferies added. "Maybe you didn't intend on killing anyone. The day it happened was a church picnic. You knew everyone living along River Road would be there. You thought no one would be home, and that no one would die."

Dutton seemed to be entertained. "You guys have come up with a really good theory. I'm genuinely impressed. I hope you did not waste a whole lot of time thinking of it. Because there is one big problem: I couldn't have done it."

"Why not?"

"Because I was with someone the day it happened."

"Okay, tell us who."

"I don't want her name mixed up with this. You must promise me that you'll keep everything confidential."

"I can assure you, we make it our policy not to release to the public any information regarding a pending investigation," Sattler said in an assured voice.

Beth appeared on the upstairs landing feeling there was no more point in sitting in the bedroom trying to avoid being discovered. "Is there anything I can do for y'all?" she called down to the people in the living room where everyone seemed startled, including Sam.

Sam, somewhat embarrassed, looked up and said, "Beth, I never thought we would see each other under these circumstances. Why don't you come on down and join us?"

Beth walked down the steps and took a seat in the rocking chair opposite the sofa where everyone was seated. "I was upstairs and heard everything. I can corroborate everything Dutton said."

Sattler stood up and said, "Who the hell are you?"

The woman responded, "My name is Beth Williams… I'm the wife of the Mayor."

***

It was high noon when Joseph walked down Poplar Street on the way to Christine's Pub. Maybe it was a guilty conscience, but he sensed tension everywhere he went after the questioning of Dutton and Beth the previous evening. They were unceremoniously hustled into two separate SUV's and questioned for five hours at the library before being released at ten pm. The FBI had promised to keep everything quiet. However, by mid- morning, their affair had become common knowledge and was the source of widespread rumor and speculation.

Joseph missed Sam. Sam was involved with meetings with the FBI, and today he would have to eat lunch alone. Joseph felt awkward going to an unfamiliar place for lunch. Ever since the incident with Dickey, he was forbidden from entering the Collins Hotel. He had heard from Sam that Thelma would allow him back only if he paid a retainer against any future damages. Sam made arrangements with the owner-proprietor of Christine's, Dwight O'Connor, to keep a spot saved for him at the bar. Sam asked Dwight to watch over Joseph and to keep him out of any arguments the likes of which had gotten him in trouble over at the Collins.

As Joseph walked in front of a dirty laundromat window, he noted the wanted poster for Suspect No. 1. The poster was the culmination of hundreds of man-hours of effort from the FBI. The FBI had sent out a team of agents to look at the videotapes of the store cameras along Main Street; they were looking for the 1978 Ford pickup. They were able to find it in a portion of a videotape from a gas station surveillance camera. Unfortunately, the glare from the afternoon sun obscured the driver's face. After two days in an imaging lab, they developed the most probable face of the man in the car and merged it with the description given by Tommy Armstrong. It was a non-descript man in his late twenties with a thin face, squat nose, a crew cut, and small, wire-rim glasses. Much to Sattler's disappointment, no one had identified the person in the poster to collect the quarter-million dollar reward.

Joseph concentrated on the poster for a moment then noted people briskly stepping around him on the sidewalk. Feeling out of place and in the way, he quickly walked down the street toward Christine's. As Joseph crossed Poplar a few feet from the bar, a stout man in a gray hat and jagged scar on the lower part of his cheek eyed him. The man stepped out in front of him before he was about to enter and said, "You're working with the FBI aren't you?"

Joseph said, "Yes. I am. Is there anything I can help you with?"

The man spat on the ground in front of Joseph. "You and your friends should stop harassing the people around here. Cecil Milar and Dutton Anderson are good, taxpaying citizens. They didn't deserve the treatment they got."

"I was not involved in their arrests. I just do tech support," Joseph said, trying to be relaxed and non-confrontational.

"Maybe you should be supporting them from someplace else."

"Alright, I will tell them when I get back to the library," Joseph said in vain, trying to escape.

Another man in a black bowler hat, trimmed black beard, and dark glasses approached. He spoke directly to the man with the scar. "Whatever happened to hospitality here? I don't care what the FBI does; you don't speak to folk like that. This is no place or time to talk politics. Why don't you step aside and let him get his lunch?"

"Hey man, are you the guardian of civility?" the man with the scar asked.

"No, but I know people, and I know how to choose my battles. If you wanna fight, you'd be takin' on the both of us. Buddy, sounds like your beef is with the FBI, not this man."

The man with the scar turned around and disappeared down the street. Joseph felt relief not getting into another scuffle and said, "Thank you for helping me out. I would like to show you my appreciation by buying you a drink."

"You don't owe me nothin', but I wouldn't mind gettin'some re'freshment."

Joseph quickly went through the door and grabbed a stool by the bar. Dwight, a squat, muscular ex-marine sergeant with a crew cut and eagle tattoos on both of his thick arms worked behind the bar. The four big-screen TV's showing ESPN and CNN hung strategically so that one didn't miss a play while getting a beer. A smoky haze hung about the tin ceiling as people lit their cigars and pipes and amicably chatted with each other. Dwight was a hunter and several stuffed owls and a deer heads adorned the area above the bar. Pictures of Dwight posing with the bucks he had killed hung prominently on the wall. Back issues of the magazine *Guns and Ammo* sat on the bar for anyone to leaf through. Joseph could see where people cut out ads.

Dwight saw Joseph sit down and politely went over to him. "So what will it be today, friend? We've got pork barbecue and turkey sandwiches."

Joseph sat back, thinking about the blandness of the food and said, "I'll just take the chili."

Dwight said, "I see you're a connoisseur of fine chili. I think I still have some from yesterday. I'll put in some more Tabasco, the way you like it." The man with the black bowler hat hung up his black leather coat and sat next to him. Joseph motioned to Dwight to get two beers.

"Drink up, and thanks again for speaking for me back there," Joseph said appreciatively. He was often accused of being in his own world, and wanted to be friendly to a stranger who had just helped him out.

The man, still wearing the black bowler hat, said, "My mom and pop taught me to be courteous and polite to folks; I hate seeing someone treated badly."

"I still think people are very nice around here with only a couple of exceptions."

The bowler man held out his hand. "Name's Clifford. Everyone calls me 'Cliff' after 'Cliff Robertson,' the actor."

"My name is Joseph Hamiz. Sometimes my students call me "sneeze" behind my back— the lab where I work is so cold and damp it aggravates my allergies. It also rhymes with my last name."

Cliff chuckled, "I know, good buddy, how it feels. When I was young, I had such nasty allergies, I went two times a week to the doc." Cliff started to tentatively sip his beer while looking at the menu stained with chili and barbecue sauce. "So, you with the feds helpin' with the investigation?"

"Yes, you could call it that. I serve as a consultant. "

"A consultant, huh?" Cliff said with a "hillbilly accent" difficult for Joseph to understand. "What a fancy name. I wish I went to college to become one of those."

"All it means is that I answer their questions."

"How they doin' in their investigatin'? I hear bits and pieces 'bout it over the radio and TV. Hear they call out the State Police and National Guard to give 'em roun' the clock protection. I know there's a lot of 'em cause every time I look I see one of 'em. Must take lot of money to protect 'em all."

"They just want to make sure that what happened here doesn't repeat itself in another part of the state."

"I hear they talkin' to folks around town."

"They have conducted several hundred interviews. I don't remember the exact number. They have a general description of the two people involved, and a half-blurred photo of someone taken through a truck window. I think they are still searching for a motive."

"Good buddy, to me motive's simple: people stop believing in Gawd and start worshiping Gov'ment. Gov'ment comes here buildn' these beautiful shinnin' structures to hold back the water. They bend down and prostrate themselves in front the material the Gov'ment created. Only Gawd's perfect— and man's limited in what he can do, and everythin' he do fails. Joseph, you read the Bible?"

"I have read it when I was in an elementary school run by Jesuits. It was so long ago, I don't remember much."

"Nice to hear that you got a proper education."

Joseph scratched his head and smiled. "The only thing I remember from elementary school is the song 'Amazing Grace.'"

Cliff took a sip of beer and said, "Oh, yeah, it's one of my fav'rit hymns."

"I remember one day in fifth grade, I was in science class, and they had to clear the building because of a bomb threat. They put us in this large, underground shelter. It was an awful place, dark and damp. A hundred kids were down there. Everyone was scared and miserable. A boy started to cry and his sobs echoed through the walls. My science teacher suddenly stood up and started singing "Amazing Grace." All the kids joined in, and the boy stopped crying. Now, whenever I'm under stress, the words to that song come to mind."

"Good buddy, Holy Bible is a way of life for me. It has a lot to say about things goin' on today. One of my fav'rit passages from Isaiah goes somethin' like this:

'Strengthen the feeble hands,
Steady the knees that give way;
say to those with fearful hearts,
Be strong, do not fear;
your God will come,
He will come with vengeance;
with divine retribution
He will come to save you.
Then will the eyes of the blind be opened
and the ears of the deaf unstopped.'"

"I am sorry, but are you saying the bombing of a dam and the murder of innocent people is an act of God? That it is all part of God's plan?" Joseph asked, incredulously.

"No, I'm not. I feel deeply 'bout the family and the child. Their deaths a terrible, terrible waste. But think about it this way, how'd you be if you spent your entire life in front of a loaded gun?"

"Are you comparing a dam to 'a loaded gun?'"

"Listen up, good buddy, and tell me if you agree. Suppose you take a gun, somethin' out of the ol' west and cock it. All that's keepin' the gun from firin' is the trigger. There's a spring keepin' the trigger from strikin' the bullet. Now, over time, the trigger get rusty and the spring breaks…the bullet fire. Hey look good buddy, it's goin' to happen. It's the same way with a dam. All that's holdin' the water back is the embankment and once it breaks you got fifty feet of water comin' on top of you. It's the family's fault they livin' downstream. They mislead by the Gov'ment."

"The dam was safe. I reviewed all the records."

"I am not talkin' records. Records can be faked. I believe in this country and all its people, but I wouldn't trust what the Gov'ment says at face value."

"The dam was needed so they could bring business into the town. There are over two thousand people who depend on the paper industry to live."

The bar was getting crowded with people from the mill. Cliff leaned over and said, "You right, good buddy, paper mill been important to the town. Don't disagree with you there. But, good buddy, in the gen'ral scheme of things it changed nothin.' What if the paper mill didn't locate in Pope's Mills? Pope's

Mills would still be a farm town and some other burg would've got the mill. Am I right or what? The three hundred people would be workin' someplace else, and someone else would have got rich other than Stan Pope and Matt Clark."

The steaming bowl of chili arrived on the bar. Joseph put his nose over it, inhaling the spices. Cliff made a face. "Whew, that chili smells strong enough to peel paint off the wall."

"Ever since my allergies started up, I have liked spicy food. It also helps keeps my sinuses clear," Joseph explained.

Suddenly, the bar became quiet as the TV screen filled with the picture of the suspect in the bombing of the dam. The announcer gave a description of the red truck, and he gave the eight hundred-phone number to call with any information.

"It is a shame the only national publicity Pope's Mills gets is because of this." Joseph commented.

"Looks like the FBI's got a tough job. I wish 'em good huntin.' Good buddy, there's lot of hidin' places in ol' Kentuck,'" Cliff said with resignation as he put some bills on the bar. "I've got to get back to work but I changed my mind, I want to get the tab for lunch."

Joseph protested, "I want to pay. It was my pleasure."

"No. I insist. It is not everyday that I meet an educated fella like yourself." Cliff put some money on the bar then left as quickly as he appeared on the scene.

As Cliff exited the saloon, he walked down Poplar Street hearing the muffled sounds of bluegrass music. It was a lazy stride and he was in no rush to reach his destination. Cliff looked at ease, not wanting to draw any attention. He watched as the people went in and out of the supermarket and saw them busily hauling rakes and hoes and other gardening equipment from the hardware store. He had been in Pope's Mills on dozens of occasions, but no one recognized him. Another face during a time when there were many outsiders in town would not make a difference. He walked a couple of blocks to the edge of business district where there was an empty Veterans of Foreign Wars building. The two story, white brick structure had not been used in years and had broken windows. A faded yellow Chevy Camaro was waiting for him in the parking lot in the rear of the building. Cliff got into the car, not paying any attention to the man in passenger seat. Both of them were silent as the Camaro sped out of town. Cliff made an effort to keep pace with the other cars, maintaining the speed limit, but also keeping his distance from other vehicles on the road.

About fifteen miles from town Cliff pulled the Camaro over into the entrance of an abandoned farmhouse. Cliff's beard itched him. He gave a firm tug at the base and the beard came away from his face. He took a bottle of rubbing alcohol from under the seat to clean away the remainder from his jaw and cheek. Taking off the latex that covered his nose and removing the sunglasses completed the transformation. He looked about five years younger and his face much thinner.

The stout man with a scar on his cheek sitting in the passenger seat patiently waited for Cliff to take off his makeup. "Did you get the info?" he asked.

"The FBI's being predictable; they haven't any idea what's going on," Cliff said without the heavy hillbilly accent. "We should proceed with our plans."

Both of the men became quiet again. Cliff methodically packed the makeup into a paper bag on the front seat. He pulled out of the farmhouse lot and directed the car towards Route 68. The car proceeded onto the highway, merged into the afternoon traffic, then disappeared out of sight.

PART TWO

CHAPTER 11

The old, metallic face stared back; a constant gaze that did not change with time, which was exactly what Jesse liked. Even though the large, pink body with its tail fins had seen many years of wear; it still had a sleek, flamboyant, aerodynamic quality. The guts of the beast were spread out on the floor in an almost random fashion amongst the wrenches, pliers, and the hammers. Its body fluids slowly dripped onto Jesse's hands and into the pores of the skin. Replacing the four-barrel carburetor of a Cadillac Deville convertible with a 325 horsepower engine that displaced 390 cubic inches was a larger-than-life task.

Jesse took a break, sipped a Pepsi, and gazed at the piercing green eyes of a 1950's pinup on the garage wall. The red-headed girl, sitting on a jet blue Corvette, denim shirt tied around her waist, was symbolic of a bygone era when Richmond's Car Care lot was filled with cars waiting for service. The garage had been filled with pinup posters when it was purchased in 1968. Two years after Jesse's father bought the gas station, the state constructed a new Route 23 to Gottlieb's Heights. The new road bypassed the station, making business drop off, permanently.

Suddenly, Jesse saw a extended hand holding a shinny colt pistol and said, "Oh my lord! It's a robber! All the money's in the cash register. Just take it and don't hurt my child. He's the only thing I have."

The colt pistol did not move.

A boy, wearing a cowboy hat and holding the pistol, stood in the middle of the garage. With a black kerchief tied around his mouth, he said, "You're not suppos'd to give up that easy."

Leaning over into the cavernous engine compartment and using a metal torchlight, Jesse said, "Sorry Toby, I don't have the time to play victim today. I'm in the middle of replacing this carburetor. If I don't get it done by five when Ms. Furgeson gets back, no one will get dinner tonight. You can help me out and hold the light on the engine." Taking the boy's hand, Jesse pointed it onto the vacant spot that held the carburetor.

"What's for dinner tonight?" Toby asked curiously.

"Meatloaf," Jesse said dryly.

"Yuuggh! We had that last night!" The meatloaf had been overdone, burnt with a black crust— the thin tomato sauce that covered it could not hide the charcoal taste.

"Toby, you know we don't have an unlimited food budget. Look, I'm not the most perfect cook, but if you're good and help me eat it up, I'll grill up some frankfurters for you tomorrow. Why don't you play with your toys while I finish this up?"

"I wanna go over to Howard's house and play his new baseball video game."

"His house is clear across town. I don't have the time to drop you there."

He removed the kerchief covering his mouth revealing two missing front teeth. Toby had a head of curly red hair, a face of freckles, and a fair complexion that resembled his mother's. Toby, being stubborn, said with a pleading voice, "I haven't played a video game in a week and you promised if I was good you would take me over to play."

"I said, I don't have the time!"

"Okay, I can walk it."

Jesse was tired of fighting with Toby. "I don't have time to discuss it with you. They're predicting thunderstorms for this afternoon. I don't want to see you walking back in that weather. You have to grow up a little and understand that I can't keep all my promises. You'll have to stick around here and play with Ralph." Part sheep dog and part cocker spaniel, Ralph was a companion for Toby and served as a guard dog for the gas station.

"Oh, I never get to do anything. I'll just go over to Jimmy Parson's house and see what he's doin'." Toby pointed towards the adjoining property, Jimmy's Appliance Repairs, a white bungalow with blue shutters, surrounded by a wooden, six-foot privacy fence. Ralph, of course, was not deterred by the fence and entered the yard on a regular basis. Toby would chase Ralph through the property as Jimmy, a bachelor in his mid-forties with a thick handlebar mustache, watched a baseball game in the rear, screened-in porch. Jimmy seemed amused with the intrusion. Toby was well known and liked in the neighborhood. Jesse didn't mind him playing with any of the neighbors, except for Jimmy. Jesse simply did not trust him. On the surface, he appeared very friendly and cordial, but everything else was a mystery. Hardly anyone appeared going into the house with appliances needing repair. Jesse's fears were confirmed after a neighbor confided that Jimmy was the son a bookmaker in Lexington. This was not a concern until one day Jesse noticed Toby playing with a pair of dice. When asked where he had gotten them, Toby said they were from Jimmy and that afternoon, he was taught how to shoot craps. Jesse decided that Toby would not spend any more time with Jimmy.

"I told you to leave Mr. Parson alone," Jesse said, deciding to leave the discussion of gambling for later.

Toby began to whine, "Can I go out with Ralph and get some frogs in the ravine?" The ravine drained the runoff from limestone cliffs that rimmed the outskirts of the town. To most people, it was an earthen ditch fifteen- to twenty-feet deep, but, for a seven year old, it was a canyon in the western wilderness. Up the slope were two large, silver-painted metal tanks holding the water supply for the town. One of them had the name "Gottlieb" painted onto it and the other, "Heights."

"Don't you have enough frogs in your collection?"

"When I went to feed Frankie this morning, he was gone." Frankie was the large bullfrog Toby had housed in a shoe box in the office for the past week, annoying Jesse with his mating call.

"Oh Shi...Shoot," Jesse said, making a concerted effort to hold back the curse word in front of Toby. "You need to keep better track of your critters. I'm operating a business here." After having been bent over the engine for the past hour, Jesse stepped out from under the hood of the car, revealing a feminine figure in her mid-twenties with tight fitting blue jeans and a head of reddish-brown, closely-cropped hair, slightly curly. She had a fair complexion with green eyes that contrasted with the streaks of brown dirt from the Cadillac. She pursed her lips together and gave Toby and intense, motherly look. Toby looked back with equal sincerity. Realizing it was the least amount of trouble that he could get into for the afternoon, Jesse said, in a rather exasperated voice, "Just go then. I want you out of there at the first sign of thunder. You know how quickly the ravine fills with water after it rains. I don't want to have to send a posse after you."

"Yes Sheriff Ma'am," Toby saluted as he walked out of the garage. He unleashed the dog and sprinted towards the trees and shrubs at the perimeter of the gas station lot. Toby followed Ralph closely, both disappearing down the slope.

Jesse's maternal instinct forced her to go outside to watch Toby run across the lot. She was used to seeing him play close by while she did her repairs. It was a natural progression that he was becoming more self-reliant as he got older. Jesse was afraid Toby had his father's spirit for independence. She remembered throwing Keith's TV and stereo out the window after finding him bent over in mid-thrust with a former high school cheerleader. That was four years ago. She had yet to collect a dime in monthly childcare payments from him.

The afternoon air was becoming dense with humidity as Jesse surveyed the gas station lot. There was a spider web of cracks in the concrete pavement that needed to be patched, big enough to have weeds growing through it. The building itself held up well for being sixty years old. The yellow paint was peeling from the red "Richmond's Car Repair" sign atop of the service bays. Some of the asphalt tiles in the pitched roof needed replacing as well as the gutters for the downspouts. Of course, there was no money to do any of these things. At the end of the month, Jesse had barely enough for the apartment rent.

Drive-in business was fairly light for a Friday afternoon, and, hopefully, she would have the time to finish the carburetor job. She was about to go back into the garage when a late-model, white Thunderbird pulled into the lot. The driver, an elderly black man, got out looking at a map. "I'm looking for the Federal Building...must pay some tax today so they don't foreclose on my house."

Jesse had given directions to the Federal Building about five hundred times and said, in a bored voice, "You passed it. You're on Old Route 23. You need to turn around and go back on the Route 23 that goes through town and then make a left on High Street, go up two lights, and make another left onto Federal Street."

The man still looked confused and she pointed to where he was on the map. "You see, you are now between the Federal Building and Simmons River. You are very close. Actually, you are just one thousand feet away." She pointed up the hill at the gray concrete building in the distance with its circular, marble-faced columns looking like a Greek temple. "You could walk it but since there's no direct route, you're going to have a five-minute ride." The man tipped his hat and drove off.

The breeze started to pick up. Jesse could sense a storm was coming. Gottlieb's Heights was located between two limestone ridges, between which the Simmons River flowed. The ridges, several hundred feet high, had a tendency to channel thunderstorms into the town. The river was about one hundreds yards away and ten feet in depth at its deepest areas.

Jesse went back inside to continue her work on the carburetor. Hearing the sound of another vehicle entering into the lot, she stood up and saw a yellow pickup truck pull alongside the pump— a black tarp tightly covered the truck's cargo. A thin, tall man wearing dark sunglasses and a baseball cap left the truck and took in the surroundings; it appeared as if he were seeing Gottlieb Heights for the first time. He retrieved a red, plastic, ten-gallon gas tank from the passenger seat and silently started filling it from the pump.

Jesse continued her work, trying not to make any eye contact. The truck was riding close to the ground, and Jesse quickly observed that the truck had to be carrying its full load. Jesse also noticed that the 1978 Ford had recently been painted yellow. Whoever did it performed a sloppy job and got paint over the rectangular headlights. The new paint was rather thin on the hood and she could see it covered the original color of red. She knew the automotive body shops in town. No one in Gottlieb Heights would have been guilty of such poor craftsmanship. It was definitely an amateur job done by the truck's owner, she assumed.

Having a second sense about people, Jesse could see out of the corner of her eye the man staring at her as she worked. Over the years, many men had stopped into the station, looking her over and visually undressing her. She had long grown accustomed to this treatment, since most men she knew were preoccupied with sex. However, this man was different; his stare was unfriendly and hard, as if he were condescending to her.

The pump made a clicking sound as the tank finished filling and the baseball capped man walked back to the truck, maintaining his gaze. Jesse strode over to the truck and announced, "That'll be twenty dollars, please." The man looked forward and she nearly expected him to drive off without paying. Taking a wad of bills out of the top pocket of his silver-gray work shirt, he peeled a twenty-dollar bill from a roll of cash and unceremoniously handed it to her. He then gunned the engine out of the lot.

***

The yellow truck traveled through the commercial district with its requisite dollar store, pharmacy, and antique shop selling oak chairs to the tourists. People were running through the crosswalks, busy with their Friday afternoon errands. The road was lined with a number of law offices that serviced the Federal Building. The driver looked out of the window with disdain at the trappings of government. He leaned out of the window and spat on the ground. The truck sped through the light for the road leading to the Federal Building and then turned left several blocks ahead onto a residential street lined with colonial and ranch homes for the wealthy residents of town. The street went back toward the hills for a few blocks before terminating on a cul-de-sac. An access road off the cul-de-sac had a sign reading, "Gottlieb Heights Municipal Property—No Trespassing." The road had a gate comprised of an eight-foot high, rusted, chain link fence that rolled into place over the access road and was secured with two padlocks. The gate, usually closed to any traffic, was inexplicably open. The truck went through the gate, slowly traveling up the winding road to the ridge.

The truck stopped on the road about one hundred feet from its destination, and the man got out to hike through the woods. The trees were dense, but thinner toward the edges of the ridge. The baseball-capped man walked within ten feet of the edge of the rocky slope and looked down at the valley. The sun had dropped to the level of the cliffs on the other side, shining into the man's eyes. The Federal Building was one hundred feet below, glittering in the sunlight. Above him were two, massive, circular tanks painted in battleship silver-gray. Between the tanks was a windowless pump building with a set of painted iron pipes leading down the slope towards town. There was a thump-de-thump sound coming from the building like a heart beating.

A middle-aged man with thinning gray hair and oil-stained, blue coveralls appeared from the tank area. On the man's shirt was a sewn on patch reading "Water Department" and below it embroidered "Tom." Tom approached from behind as the baseball-capped man was putting his hands over his eyes to cover the glare. Tom announced in an official sounding voice, "Hello, I'm the caretaker. May I inquire to what your business is? This is a town facility. No one's allowed up here. There's a sign down the hill."

In a folksy style, the man with the baseball cap responded, "Really nice view you have from up here. You see the entire valley. I was admiring the scenery so much I must have missed the sign. I was looking for the entrance to the state park."

"The state park is about twenty miles west of here. You're way lost."

"I was going to hunt some deer and do some fishing."

"Hunting is not allowed. No firearms allowed." The caretaker went on to say in a possessive voice, "I want no one putting holes in *my* tanks. The steel plate is only half an inch thick. Some people think they're cute and fire guns at the tanks to make them leak, and it's me that has to fix 'em."

A second man with long dark hair appeared in the brush behind the caretaker. The baseball-capped man played for time. "No need to worry, friend. I have no plans to fire any guns up here. But you do have some huge tanks."

The caretaker looked up in admiration. "Yes, they are one of the largest water storage facilities in the area. Both of them are two hundred feet in diameter and thirty-feet high, each having the capacity to hold approximately seven million gallons." The caretaker hesitated for a moment seeing that the man had a silver-gray cap with matching shirt and pants. He scratched his head and said, "That's sure some strange outfit you have on. You're clothes are the same colors as the tanks."

"You know something, you're right. I never noticed that."

"I bet if you would stand beside them, no one would see you," The caretaker observed, oblivious to the dark haired man that now stood only a couple of steps behind him.

"I guess that's the nature of camouflage."

The caretaker scratched his head and laughed. "Why would anyone want to camouflage themselves with these tanks?"

In one, seemingly effortless and fluid motion, the long-haired man put left his arm across the caretaker's shoulders and with his right hand, grabbed the caretaker's chin, twisting his head violently. An audible snap was heard and the caretaker fell lifelessly to the ground. "Looks like he'll never find out," the longhaired man said in an unemotional voice.

The tall man with the baseball cap stood there with his mouth open, amazed at the swiftness with which the caretaker's neck was broken.

"What are you staring at?" the man with the longhair said in a casual manner, as if nothing had happened.

"I've never seen a man killed before."

"Henry, it's simple; you just need to know where to apply the leverage," the longhaired man said as he stood behind the body now laying on the grass in a contorted position.

"I swear, I didn't see him coming. He approached me from behind and started asking all these stupid questions."

"With the way you were tromping though these woods, I'm surprised the whole town isn't up here asking questions. You're fifteen minutes late."

"I was getting some gas in town," Henry said in a nonchalant voice.

"You are an idiot. I told you to get everything done before you hit the road. You're going to upset my timing."

Henry bent over and started to drag the caretaker's body to the bushes.

"Don't waste your time with him. The water will wash him away. Get your ass moving. I want the truck here in two minutes so we can start offloading it. I want everything placed inside the hour…or I'll break your neck, too."

***

Jesse scanned the ravine but saw no signs of activity. Finally, she yelled at the top of her lungs "*TOBY!*" There was no response. She yelled louder, "*TOBY get your butt up here. Now!*"

She heard the sound of feet scraping dirt. Toby finally appeared fifty feet from his mother. "Here I am mom," he said, as he scrambled up the slope.

"What did I tell ya about getting out of there?"

"You said to get out after I heard thunder, and I didn't hear any thunder."

"You know what I meant, young man," Jesse admonished. "You need to learn to follow directions. I'm only trying to keep you out of danger."

"Yes ma'am." Toby stood there on the concrete pad with his tee shirt and blue jeans plastered with mud from the ravine. "Look what I got." He then proceeded to show his mother a large, box turtle he found.

Jesse looked at the turtle curiously. "He's handsome, but I don't think he wants to be part of your zoo. Why don't you put him back where you found him? He is going to be much happier in his home."

"Oh mom. Can I just keep him for a few days?" Toby begged.

"We can talk about it later. What am I going to do with you? I can start a dirt pile with your clothes. Better get inside, it's starting to rain. How did you get covered with mud? Toby looked back at his mom and shrugged. "Okay, come with me and I'll get you cleaned up," she said, leading him back by his hand to the red bricked building.

As Toby entered the gas station, he quickly put the turtle on the floor of the office, and, while his mother was taking off his shirt, it started its long trek back to the ravine.

* * *

Henry looked down at the ground like a spider suspended in midair. Climbing always made him feel free and in control of his destiny. He put his right foot in a rope loop to steady himself against the cold steel of the water tank. With his free hand, he reached into the knapsack attached to his stomach, pulled out a gray disk and stuck it to the smooth surface of the tower. There were five more modules that needed to be placed on top of the tank. The ropes were slippery with rain, making his task even more dangerous. Henry heard a boom out in the distance and looked across to the figure in a harness on the second tank in the midst of placing a disk. "Oh shit, I hope it isn't thunder."

The long-haired man leaned back in his harness, took off his hat, and lifted his head up to the sky, letting the water soak his face. "Isn't the rain beautiful? It says in Samuel 'I will call upon the Lord to send thunder and rain, and you will realize what an evil thing you did in the eyes of the Lord.'" He looked down with satisfaction as the runoff from the hill filled the ravine.

Henry showed a note of apprehension. "It is neither the rain nor the thunder I'm concerned with. If the lightnin' should hit the tank, it'll set off the explosives; and we'll both be history."

"By my reckoning, the center the storm is still about fifty miles away, and if you stop complaining, you will have finished your task well ahead of that," the longhaired man responded, still gazing at the sky.

Henry climbed to the top of the tank and rappelled to another location. The explosives had been placed in a doorway pattern on both of the tanks. He climbed back to the ground, viewing his work with self gratification. "I would love to be here when the tanks go up and get a look at their faces in the Federal Building."

"No, we're going to be in the next county by that time," said the longhaired man as he rappelled down to the ground. "The authorities will be quick to set up road blocks, and I want to be off the main routes by then."

Henry followed the other man as he walked down the access road to a point where it split and a small trail went into the woods. After walking a few paces on the trail, they reached a yellow Camaro parked under a bush. The longhaired man maneuvered the car carefully onto the access road. Proceeding slowly, stealthily, down the road, the Camaro eventually reached the wide, residential street. The longhaired man quickly got out of the car, rolling the gate closed and replacing the padlocks. Henry turned around in the front seat. The rain falling on the back window obscured the view of the tanks, and Henry was confident that nobody would notice that anything had ever happened on top of the ridge.

*** *** ***

It was a typical Friday afternoon with workers sporadically leaving the Federal Building to go to their cars, the weekend awaiting them. Bernie Jones, a paunchy, middle-aged man with a razor cut, sat at his small, gray metal table beyond the glass wall of the atrium. He looked out over the entrance, staring anxiously at his watch. Time was not passing quickly enough. It was fifty minutes after three and there were another forty minutes left to his shift. By his visual gauge, the parking lot was half full, which meant there were still a significant number of people in the courthouse for that time of day. Being a guard, he knew most of the people who worked there. As people filed out, he held the glass door for them and tipped his hat out of general courtesy. He spotted two secretaries, a blonde and redhead, dressed in mid-length skirts and low cut blouses, carrying two large potted umbrella plants that had partially turned brown. Bernie had had his eye on Nancy and Barbara for the past two months; they could always be seen leaving the building together. Seeing his opportunity, he said, "Have a nice weekend girls. What nice plants you got there."

Nancy, the redhead with the long legs, said, "They were dying at our desks and need some serious care."

Bernie saw the growing intensity of the rain, "Sorry to hear that. Can I help you carry them back to your car?"

Nancy, the smaller woman with short, blonde hair and powerfully built arms responded, "That is nice of you to offer, but we can handle this ourselves."

"Are you sure? It will only take me a minute, and I don't think there will be a terrorist attack on the building during that time." He opened the glass door for them and started to walk them out to the parking lot. "So, do you two live around here?" he asked casually, trying to not seem too obvious in his interest.

"We share an apartment in town," Barbara said.

"Oh, I live about five minutes outside of Gottlieb on Route 35. On Fridays I usually grab a cold one at O'Casey's, if you're both interested."

Nancy quickly responded, "*We* will think about it, but I think *we* have other plans for the weekend."

The guard got the intended message and shook his head in disgust. He watched the women chat amicably as they walked back to their brown Nissan.

* * *

Jesse looked at Toby as he put on his clean jeans. She felt proud that she was always prepared with a spare change of clothes for him at the station. The jeans were nearly too small and the boy strained to put them on. Fairly soon, she would have to buy him new clothes and wondered where the money would come from. Business was still light for a Friday and Jesse decided she would take advantage of it and close early.

"Did you like exploring the ravine?" she asked, as he finished putting on his shirt.

"Sure did, Mom. You know I like that stuff."

"You're certainly brave and fearless." She suddenly leaned over, grabbed Toby around the waist and kissed the boy on the forehead.

Toby made a grimace, straining out of his mother's grip. "I'm getting too old for that, mom."

"I spent all this time cleaning you up, I might as well check out my job. You're never too old to be kissed by your mother." Toby started playing with his metal trucks on the office floor and Jesse could tell he was becoming melancholy. She went down on her knees to grab the truck out of his hands to get his attention. "I was thinking that I ought to bring you by the Baptist Church and have you join up with the Cub Scout Troop."

"That would be okay…I guess," Toby said hesitatingly.

"I thought that you liked exploring. There you would go out on hikes and overnight trips."

"I want to do that mom, but…"

"But what…"

"I talk to Billy down the street, and his father takes him to the meetings."

"So, that doesn't mean I can't do it."

"His father also goes on the trips with him."

Jesse stroked her chin thoughtfully. "I've gone camping before. I think we have a tent somewhere." As Toby started to walk away, she bent over and grabbed him by the belt loop, looking him squarely in the eyes. "Are you tellin' me I would embarrass you by going to the meetings? That's silly. I bet not many 'men' can do what I do."

Toby looked back with a blank stare.

She continued to say, "Okay, how many 'men' have single handedly put V8 engines in their Mustangs and the same day put on chrome dual exhausts?"

Toby shrugged his shoulders, "I don't know, Mom."

"You're damn right you don't know. No man I know. I was doing that before any of them even got a license to drive. They were ridin' their bicycles down the street when I was working on engines. So remember, I can do anything and everything a man can do. "

"Yes, Mom, but it ain't the same as having a father there."

Her son could be as disagreeable and stubborn as she. But Jesse understood Toby's needs, and no matter what she did, she could not be everything to him. "I know it's sometimes tough for you to grow up without a man around the house. I just had a bad experience with your father, and you cannot expect me to get emotionally attached to someone else so soon. Adult relationships don't work that way."

"When I talk to Jimmy next door, he says you are the most beautiful woman on the block and should be married."

"Oh, he says that? I thought I asked you not to speak to him."

"I can't help it. Sometimes he's in his front yard when I walk by and he always asks about how you're doing."

"I'm flattered he's interested in me, but it ain't mutual. I don't want you to speak to him about me, understand?" Toby nodded in bewilderment. "It's difficult for me to explain to you but I simply don't trust him— you cannot trust everyone you meet. Trust has to be earned. I wish this world was different." Jesse turned from her son, knowing that as Toby grew older, she would have to have more of these conversations with him. The streaks of rain hit the large pane windows, forming diagonal patterns. Jesse remembered the work she needed to do outside before closing. "Why don't you play with your toys while I take care of some paperwork and do some housekeeping?"

Jesse walked outside in the middle of the rainstorm and started to clean up the paper and the bottles that had accumulated on the lot throughout the day. She had worked hard on the Cadillac, and the cold rain felt good on her skin. Locking up the two gas pumps, she was about to get back inside to finish closing when she heard the staccato of a series of explosions from above, followed by a "whooshing" sound. She gazed up towards the top of the cliffs and saw the tank labeled "Heights" surrounded by a billowing cloud of white smoke, water cascading out. The ground shook as a twenty-foot wall of water rumbled down the rocky slope. The second tank exploded inward, sending a second tower of smoke upward, both of the waves heading downward towards the Federal Building. The front of the wave hit the Federal Building parking lot, upending cars in its path. The cars tumbled over, rolling as if they were metal toys on a playground.

***

Bernie Jones sat back in his chair, chatting with his supervisor. When he heard the explosions, he initially interpreted them to be thunder. Then, hearing the dull impacts of metal against metal, he sprinted outside the glass atrium as the wall of water tossed cars as it traversed the lot. He stood on the marble steps and watched as the wave threw a blue truck past him. It crashed into the atrium window. As the window disintegrated, a jagged piece of glass dropped down, slicing into the upper part of his neck and nearly decapitating him. The truck slid to a rest, upside down on the atrium carpet.

The main body of the wave slammed against the courthouse, sending a wall of murky water into the first floor. Panicked workers filled the entry hall only to find no means of exit. An elevator arrived at the ground floor and as the doors opened, water rushed in. A woman wearing a blue pantsuit jumped back as the bottom of the elevator filled with debris from the first floor. She quickly walked out, cursing that her clothes were ruined and was greeted by the truck turned over onto its hood in the lobby. She looked at it with her mouth wide open, as if it were a sculpture on display, and then put her hands over her mouth and gasped as Bernie's lifeless body floated nearby.

Further down the Federal Building lot, Nancy turned the key in the ignition of her Nissan and the car came to life. She started to back out of her spot and inexplicably felt the car rise off the ground as people screamed from other parts of the lot. The edge of the wave jolted the side of the car against the adjacent light pole; there was a loud crash as the pole toppled onto the car's hood. Barbara shrieked as she saw Nancy unconscious in the driver's seat. She quickly tried to exit through the passenger door. As the water poured into the window, she saw a silver Chevette boosted off the ground and thrown in an arc towards the Nissan. The front of the Chevette made a glancing blow into the side of the car as Barbara gasped relief. She then turned, momentarily putting her arms on Nancy's shoulders, trying to revive her friend. As she was looking into Nancy's eyes, she saw the grill of a large Ford truck smash through the windshield.

***

All Jesse could do was stand in front of the station to watch the carnage. Frozen in terror, she stared as the flood-wave traveled down the ravine, picking up cars from the Federal Building parking lot, sending them into the building's marble columns. After the third impact, one of the columns buckled, collapsing the front of the building. She was brought out of her trance when she heard Toby screaming from the station, "What's happening Mom!"

Realizing she couldn't outrun the wave coming down toward her, Jesse ran back and grabbed Toby yelling, "Get back in the station, Toby. All hell's broke lose out here!" She quickly took Toby into a cinderblock storage room used for parts and set him on the ground. She looked around for Ralph and found him cowering in one of service bays. Jesse picked up the dog and dived into the storage room, closing the door behind her. She put Toby's head between his knees and covered him with her body.

The wave cascaded down to the station, picking up cars from the Federal Building parking lot as it moved down the ravine. It seemed like an eternity, waiting, surrounded by blackness as Jesse sat in the dark closet waiting for it to hit. Toby felt his mother's heart beating through her work shirt. Picking his head up from his knees, he said, "Mom, what're we waiting for?"

Jesse stroked his head, putting it back between his knees and said, "Hush up! I want to hear what is going on outside."

Toby said, "I hear nothing..."

At that point, Jesse felt a crash as water rushed into the back of the building, accompanied by the sound of engine parts flying from the shelves onto the floor. Jesse covered her head with her hands, deflecting the impact of the oil filters falling on her. There was a large explosion as the sheet glass in the front office shattered. Both Toby and Jesse let out a scream, only to be muffled by the sound of car bodies crashing against the rear of the building. A pickup truck was thrown into the garage door of one of the service bays, splintering it into glass and wood shards. Now there was a constant bombardment of cars against the bricks of the building as if undergoing shelling by some enemy. Jesse felt each vibration throughout her body. She continued to clutch onto Toby, making certain he did not move. Suddenly, the impacts stopped and Jesse leaned up against the wall in relief. She sighed as she said, "I think it's all over now. We'll be okay." She stood up, brushing the debris off her clothes.

Another wave crashed into the building, causing Jesse to fall back to the floor. There was a groaning sound coming from the ceiling as an entire section of the roof ripped away. She looked up and saw the ceiling tiles fall down, followed by wood and roof shingles. Water poured in from a gaping hole in the roof. Jesse took Toby's hand, "This place is not safe anymore. Let's move."

She tried to open the door, but it would not budge; there was something obstructing it from the outside. She threw her body up against it, feeling it give only slightly. Toby imitated his mother and started hitting the door with his tiny arms. Jesse said, "Don't do that honey, you'll hurt yourself." Feeling around in the darkness, she located a stepladder amongst the boxes of auto parts. "Toby, stay away from the door. Mommy's going to break it down." Wielding the stepladder over her head, she swung in an arc, disintegrating the top half of the wood. A second swing took out the bottom half. Jesse stumbled out into the debris of the station. The big oak desk in the center of her office had been overturned and driven against the wall. The remainder of the office had been turned into a jumbled, soaking mass of papers and glass shards.

Toby ran out of the closet and starting exploring the ruins of the building. "Looks like a tornado came and hit this place," he yelled out. Jesse caught him by the arm, and sat him down in a corner of the garage not occupied by debris. "I don't want you budging from this spot. I don't want you walking around in this stuff. It can hurt you laying on the ground as much as it can coming down on top of you."

"Mom, I can help you…," Toby whined.

"You can help by staying put."

Still somewhat in shock, she stumbled out of the garage and saw the wreckage from of cars and trucks washed from the Federal Building. A pickup truck lay on its side, the windows smashed onto the concrete. In another part of the parking area, a car was upside down, facing up like a turtle helplessly on its back. Hoods and fenders of assorted sizes were resting against the pumps, on display as if the station had become some grotesque flea market.

Jesse heard the sirens and alarms of emergency vehicles racing towards the Federal Building. The wind was picking up and the rain stung her face, obstructing her sight. She could vaguely see that the entrance had been damaged; to what extent, she did not know. Jesse scanned the neighborhood and was relieved there was no appreciable damage to the neighboring houses down the road. The fifty-foot bridge traversing the ravine had been washed out, leaving a dark chasm filled with water and debris.

Jesse walked over to the ravine where there were cars resting in the mud that covered the bottom. Cars that were not being discharged downstream teetered on the edge of the downward slope. She looked down, trying to see if there was anyone trapped inside any of them. She called out, "Is there anyone down there?" There was no response.

She started to walk back to the shelter of the station when she heard the sound of a car approaching. A black Lincoln was cruising down the highway, oblivious to the dangers that lay ahead. Jesse ran out to the center of the road, waving her arms wildly and screaming. Rain or shine, most cars traveling Route 23 go about fifty, and there were no immediate sign of the car slowing. She screamed, "Stop, the bridge is out! Stop. Goddamit!" It was too late and about ten feet from the bridge she heard the Lincoln slam on its brakes. The car started to skid, and then, as it approached the bridge abutments, launched into space and crashing into the wall of the ravine.

She ran to the concrete abutment and could see the Lincoln wedged between two other sedans at the bottom of the channel. The front of the car was crushed like an accordion, the windshield smashed. "Oh, shit" she said, as she raced back into the service station office to grab the first aid kit and flashlight.

Jesse quickly ducked into the garage where Toby was sitting in the corner holding Ralph. She led the boy to the front of the windowless office, clear of glass and debris. "Now listen to me carefully, Toby, I have an important job for you. You stay put here with Ralph, and if you see any emergency vehicles tell them I'm down in the ravine rendering assistance. Under no circumstances are you to budge from your spot." She ran back out to the ravine and disappeared down the slope.

Toby stood in the office, hearing police car sirens in the distance. He was thinking about the adventures to be had on the outside. Throughout all the commotion, he was going to be stranded in an office. Even Ralph was getting impatient and beginning to squirm against his grip. Toby dropped the dog to the floor and Ralph proceeded to run circles around him. After a minute, Ralph stood on his hind legs and looked back with a playful glance. Toby said, "I know you hate being cooped up in here as much as I do, but mom says I have to be a look out." Ralph seemed to understand what Toby was saying and obediently sat on the floor.

There were a few moments of near silence the only sound was the rain tapping on the roof. Water quickly began to accumulate where the roof was sagging, and suddenly, a five-foot section fell to the floor in a service bay with a crash. The building shook, causing a large, metal box of tools to drop to the ground, spilling its contents and making a noise many decibels louder than the ceiling falling. Ralph, terrified and confused, jumped through the empty window frame, running across the lot to the trees on the other side of the road. Toby screamed, "Come back here Ralph!" as he chased the dog across the lot and into the rainy dusk.

***

Joseph displayed a PowerPoint slide on the white wall of the conference room, grabbed the Styrofoam cup coffee on the oak conference table, and nervously took a sip. He continued speaking in a monotone, "Using the National Weather Service Dam Breach model, we were able to replicate the field run data from the high water marks noted on the Kendall."

A group of fifteen people had gathered to hear the preliminary report on his re-creation of the events surrounding the Kendall River dam bombing. Sattler wearily thumbed through the thirty-page document as he sat next to Joseph. He flicked his wrist to look at his watch. Joseph had been speaking for only ten minutes but it already seemed like thirty. Breaking into the monologue, he said, "I think we have enough information now." Sam sat across from Joseph and politely pretended to listen as he reviewed the previous days contact reports from the state police. He gave a "thumbs up" sign and Joseph looked back and smiled.

Jefferies, deep in thought, said, "I find your discussion fairly enlightening. In summary, you are saying that the entire event lasted about forty-three minutes."

Joseph went to his portable computer and brought back the slide showing the time graph. "Yes, when I was running my scenarios, the duration varied from roughly thirty-five to fifty minutes. But I am relatively confidant that it lasted forty-three minutes, give or take five minutes. In all honesty, I wasn't as exact as I should have been; I was rushed in taking the field measurements."

A gruff sounding voice at the end of conference table tersely chimed in, "We have not as of yet finished reducing the data for the Cromwell Creek Dam, upstream of the Kendall Creek Dam. How then could you know the inflow to Kendall Creek?" Everyone looked back at Bob Dickey sitting in the dark.

Joseph continued to look down at his portable computer and put up on the wall the graph for daily inflow for the previous year. "I assumed it's equivalent to the inflow for April of last year you published."

Dickey responded, "Did you adjust for precipitation? We had more rain last year."

"I didn't think it was needed…"

"I think it throws serious questions about the validity of what you did," Dicky commented.

Sattler turned and said to Dickey, "I appreciate your comments, and you will have time to respond to the report in writing, but I am satisfied that Dr. Hamiz has confirmed our chronology of events on that date. Sattler decided to change the topic. "Maybe we should discuss the progress with the surveillance of the existing dams."

Jefferies said, "We've been coordinating with the National Guard. We've got over two hundred people doing twenty-four hour surveillance on the list of the fifty high-hazard dams given to us by Dr. Hamiz. Over the four day period, we noted no unusual activity at any of the structures."

Dickey tried to give the appearance of cooperation. "The state has also sent fifty people to our facilities. We are working around the clock to help the FBI."

Jefferies added, "We have contacted authorities in neighboring states of Ohio, Tennessee, Illinois, Indiana and Missouri, and they have stepped up their own security…"

Sattler's mobile phone rang. He answered the call. His face became ashen as he spoke a couple of words and hung up. "That was the state police barracks near Gottlieb's Heights. There have been a series of explosions in Gottlieb. Someone has blown up the water tanks there. The front entrance to the Federal Building has been destroyed. The state emergency response team has mobilized and it will arrive there in about fifteen minutes." With Sattler's announcement, the room became quiet. Everyone who had been relaxing around the table now sat at attention.

"Using the local roads it's going to take us thirty minutes to get there. That's without traffic," Agent Jefferies said.

Sattler got on the phone and was in immediate contact with the landing field. He had a brief conversation and then announced, "Okay, I've just ordered the helicopter from the airport. It will be here in ten minutes."

Everyone got up from the table and started to gather their field clothes. Dickey asked Sattler, "I know I need to be there, I've been cleared to be on an emergency response team. Could I get a lift?"

"We are not a taxi service, but just as long as we share information, I've no problem with giving you a ride. I don't want any more bullshit from you," Sattler responded.

"No problem, we aim to please." Dickey said. As he left, he shot back an annoyed look back at Joseph.

Joseph followed Sam to the back of the mansion where a large expanse of green grass served as a helipad. They saw the helicopter approach from the distance. Sam said, "I've known the Sheriff in Gottlieb, Rick Woods, for about ten years, ever since high school. I'm going to help out an old friend. You've got no stake in this, so I suggest that you stay back here, mind the fort, and run your computer models."

"You are wrong, Sam. I also have 'a stake.' My life in this country is on the line here. Contrary to the opinion of my colleagues' back at Kentucky Institute of Technology, I do go out in the field from time to time. Anyway, I have been staring at statistics for the past four days, and I need some fresh air."

Sam nodded, "I hope you've got some experience with disaster scenes. The town is probably a mess. It's not a place for a casual observer to take a tour. My advice is that you hang close to me. I'll make sure nothing happens to you."

A crowd of people gathered on the back porch, including Sattler, Dickey, Jefferies, and two other field agents. The helicopter hovered for a couple of moments before setting down on the soft grass. Jefferies and the two field agents rushed past the group and opened the passenger door. Dickey followed. Sam looked at Joseph, "You can still change your mind. I'll not think any less of you." He then walked steadily toward the helicopter, bent over as he climbed in and fastened his seat belt. The pilot, wearing Kaki pants, yellow jacket and dark sunglasses, climbed out his door, reading a weather chart. Sattler looked over his shoulder, pretending to know what the chart meant.

The pilot said, "They're experiencing some severe thunderstorms, including reports of hail to the west of Gottlieb. If we leave now, we can duck underneath them. If we stand here any longer, we'll be pressing our luck."

"Okay, let's leave now then," Sattler said in an eager voice.

Joseph stood on the fieldstone patio assessing his options, not knowing what to do. Sattler looked back at him, and finally said, "Well, what are you waiting for, an engraved invitation?"

Joseph walked up to the helicopter and hesitantly got in, taking a seat next to Sattler. Sattler reached over Joseph and slammed the door. The pilot pivoted the control stick and the helicopter jerked upward. Joseph saw the ground recede beneath him and gazed out the window as the helicopter traversed the Kendall River, which resembled a silver ribbon as it snaked back and forth through the valley. Joseph looked through the front window and saw the bank of dark, gray clouds that loomed ahead.

Sam glanced at the light, pullover coat that Joseph wore and said, "Is that all the foul-weather gear you have? You're going to get soaked." Joseph simply shrugged in response as Dickey snickered from across the seat.

The pilot turned around and said, "You guys better tighten your belts. We have a fairly choppy ride ahead of us," and the helicopter banked into the clouds.

CHAPTER 12

Jesse slipped down the steep mud bank that formed the side of the ravine into a landscape of cars. She stopped short of a small Honda sedan that had rolled over, resting sideways in the channel. Shinning her flashlight in the window, she saw the empty front seat. She rested her hand on the roof of the car as her legs sank up to her calves in the dark, brown ooze. The water pressed her legs together making standing up a far greater effort than she had expected. Reaching for a car antenna, she was able to maintain her balance as she unstuck her right foot and put her weight onto the left, feeling her body sink even deeper in the muck. Jesse maneuvered herself towards the abutment where she remembered seeing the Continental leap from the road. At this rate, she realized she would never reach the car.

Having no intention of becoming a permanent addition to the bottom of the ravine, she decided to adopt a different strategy. She grabbed the top of a van door, and with all her strength, was able to free both her legs and swing them up, one by one, onto the hood of the car. She then stood up on the hood of the van and spotted the roof of the Continental about twenty-five feet ahead, downstream of the bridge abutment. Jesse made a slight crouch and jumped, her feet landing squarely onto the hood of the adjacent sedan. She chose her next stepping stone: a small brown station wagon. This time, the hood was curved down and her landing was not as perfect; she fell on her hands, dropping the white, plastic first aid kit. The kit slid down the hood, nearly falling into the mud before she reached over and grabbed it. The metal was slippery as she climbed onto the roof and then onto the trunk— she had trouble maintaining her footing. Finally, five feet from the car, she eased herself back into the mud and the water. Since she entered the gully, the water had risen about six inches and was now above her knees.

Jesse heard a woman moaning and shinned the light into the Continental. The windshield was cracked, but she could plainly see that a dark haired woman in her fifties, with a circular contusion on her forehead, was barely conscious. The gray haired man in the driver's seat looked pale, breathing laboriously. Jesse recognized the couple. They were the Warrens, managers of the Gottlieb Shop and Bag, a small grocery store located on the outskirts of the town. The Warrens represented the upper class in Gottlieb, and neither Jesse, nor her parents, socialized with them.

The rain continued to sheet down. Jesse was soaked to her skin. She tried the passenger door. It was locked. Mrs. Warren, in the front seat, looked too much in shock to respond to any directions. Jesse would have to find a way into the Lincoln. She had years of practice getting into locked cars. Many times, it was as simple as manipulating a wire coat hanger through the rubber window gasket seal. She did not have the time or a hanger, so she surveyed the area near the car for any rocks, but did not see any on the bank. A few chunks of concrete were on the ground near the abutment. Jesse leaned over, nearly losing her footing, and snatched the concrete. She swung the mass into the passenger window and it bounced off. The second time she put more muscle into her swing, and the window cracked. Again, she hit the widow; this time it disintegrated into small pieces.

The window breaking completely surprised Mrs. Warren, and she made a high pitched scream. Jesse got into the back seat. "It's okay. I'm here to help."

Mrs. Warren spoke in a semi-conscious state, "Where am I?"

Jesse looked over the front seat and noticed splotches of red on the dashboard and the windshield. Poking her head up front, she could see in detail the woman's injuries. The dashboard had mashed her leg below the knee; the jagged white bone sticking out of the skin. The sight of such a major injury did not shock her. She had had a compound fracture of her left arm when she fell out of a tree at the age of thirteen.

"You've landed in the ditch. You've hit your head a little on the windshield, but you'll be okay. You've lost some blood from your leg. It's badly broke," Jesse observed.

"How is he? I don't hear him."

"I don't know how badly your husband is injured." She glanced over to the unconscious silver haired man in a gray trench coat. "He appears to be breathing though."

"You take care of him first."

"Why don't you let me decide who I help first?" Jesse opened the first aid kit and found only gauze and some antiseptic, no strong fabric. Reaching behind her, she tugged hard and ripped off the collar from her shirt.

"What are you doing?" Mrs. Warren said, eyeing Jesse wearily.

"I'm making a tourniquet to put on your leg." Jesse looked around the car and found a yellow mechanical pencil. "This may hurt a bit, but it will control the bleeding." She tied the fabric around the broken leg and inserted the pencil into the knot. She twisted the pencil and the woman grimaced. "You can keep pressure on that yourself while I help out your husband."

She felt the man's neck but could not feel a pulse. She would have to try something more drastic. Jesse reached over Mr. Warren and found the lever for the car seat. She flipped the lever, but the power seat did not adjust. Gently, she pushed his head back and without hesitation pinched his nose as she put her mouth over his and exhaled into his lungs. For over ten minutes she tried to breathe life into the unconscious man. Exhausted, she raised her head and realized that Mr. Warren's body had become cold. She rested her hand on his leg and felt a warm sticky substance ooze over her fingers. She looked at her hand; it was covered with blood. She was too busy trying to resuscitate Mr. Warren to notice the pool of blood under the seat. She reached around and felt that a metal reinforcing bar from the bridge had broken through the door and the seat, going upward into Mr. Warren's abdomen. The impact of the car against the abutment had been so severe; the man had been impaled as he sat. She checked him one last time, shinning the light into his face. The pupils did not react. The dead man stared back at her with a surprised look; she gently closed his eyes.

Jesse decided she needed to the leave the car, not having the luxury to sit and wait for help. There were no sounds from the outside other than the rain falling on the roof and hood. This had concerned her. Hadn't the emergency personnel come, or maybe they were in the other locations. Jesse knew that she would have to get the woman out soon, or else she would loose her, too.

•

The pilot's description, "a choppy ride," turned out to be an understatement. The helicopter dropped drastically several times in response to pressure fronts. Joseph got motion sickness easily and was bent over most of the trip, feeling like puking, clutching an airsickness bag. He could see Dickey smiling at him and was determined not to give him the satisfaction of throwing up. After an eternity, Joseph saw the town of Gottlieb approach from his side window. Gottlieb was about three times the size of Pope's Mills, as it occupied a plateau on the Simmons River Valley. The first thing Joseph noticed through the curtain of rain was the array of lights on the towers of the chemical companies that lined the river. The town looked surreal in the dusk, like some city in a fairy tale.

The helicopter banked to the left where it hovered above the two gray disks on a ridge, fire trucks and emergency vehicles below it. The tanks looked intact from directly above, and Sattler asked, "Do you think you can get down a little so we can view them from the sides?"

The pilot responded, "I will try, but I don't know how long I can hold it."

The helicopter dived, the rear of the machine waving back and forth trying to steady itself in the wind. The constant movement brought back Joseph's motion sickness. The pilot flipped a switch in the cockpit, and two giant floodlights illuminated the scene. Everyone stared ahead in awe at the two gapping holes; the one-half inch, steel plate ripped apart like the cardboard of a milk carton, the edges blackened. The tanks were completely emptied, and Joseph could see their empty interiors glowing in the floodlights.

Bob Dickey interrupted the silence, "Oh shit, the sides look nearly gone."

Sattler said dryly, "It looks like they did a rather efficient job here, just like Pope's Mills."

The heart of the Gottlieb water system had been completely destroyed. The pump house took the full force of the failure and was disintegrated. A rectangular brick foundation was all that remained. The piping that went up the ridge into the pumps looked like tangled spaghetti.

Sattler spoke to the pilot through his headphones, "We've seen enough up here. Let's get down to the Federal Building to get a closer look."

The pilot obediently rotated the helicopter one hundred and eighty degrees and flew toward the Federal Building complex where the parking lot was filled with fire trucks and ambulances. Three of the four columns holding the rear entrance had been cut in half. The steel overhang, disconnected from the building, had dropped to the ground and lay intact in front of the entrance. In recent years, large boulders had been added to the perimeter of the building to guard against someone with a truck filled with explosives from ramming the structure. A red SUV was caught on a boulder as the flood receded, displaying it like a trophy.

Overhead, Sattler could see that the emergency efforts concentrated in two areas: the front entrance to the building and the rear of the parking lot where there was a concentration of overturned cars. Ambulances at both locations collected the injured and speed out of the lot. A state police car acted as a checkpoint controlling the movement in and out. The helicopter hovered over the building for about five minutes at which point Sattler said, "We've accomplished enough up here, we need to land to look at things first hand."

The pilot shook his head. "It doesn't look like there's enough room on the parking lot with everyone down there. We're going to find with a secondary site."

The helicopter started circling, shinning the spotlight on the areas surrounding the parking lot. The light illuminated the front of the gas station and the washed out bridge. Sattler said, "We've been circling the road for a couple of minutes, and with the bridge out, I haven't noticed any traffic. Do you think we can chance it?"

The pilot looked nervously at the power lines situated halfway between the roadway and the river, "I don't know. It looks tight. If I land on top of the high-tension lines, we're fried. But then, the only other site in the area is the Airpark and that's fifteen minutes from here." He hesitated for a moment and said, "Oh, what the fuck, I've landed in far worst spots in Nam, and on top of that, I didn't know if Charlie was going come out and shoot my butt off with AK-47's as I was coming down. I got so accustomed to sitting on my helmet there's a permanent indentation in my ass."

Sattler and the rest of the agents laughed along with the pilot as Joseph put his head between his legs, assuming the worst. The helicopter began an agonizingly long decent. Watching out of the window on the opposite side of the pilot, Sattler said, "You are doing great. You have about fifty-foot clearance with the line."

The pilot replied, "We're not out of this yet." There was a sudden gust of wind toward the river and the helicopter lurched sideways with the tips of the rotors straying a mere ten feet from the electric lines. Everyone in the passenger compartment drew a heavy breath. The pilot brought the helicopter back toward the center of the road and said, "See what I mean. No need to worry. I've got things under control," as the skids hit the blacktop of the roadway.

Joseph took off his seatbelt as Sattler leaned over and opened the door. Ducking under the swinging blades, Joseph got out, grateful to be putting his feet back on solid ground. Sattler turned to Jefferies, "I would like you to be my lookout in the air and help me coordinate. I know there's only about fifteen minutes of daylight left, but I would like for you to see if you can spot the red Ford from the air. Jefferies switched his position and climbed into the front seat opposite the pilot as everyone else exited the helicopter.

Sam pulled a fluorescent yellow poncho out of his jacket and offered it to Joseph, who politely refused it, pulling up the collar on his pullover in a futile attempt to shield from the rain. "In this deluge, you're going get chilled to the bone. You might as well take it. I'm a big guy and have a lot of my own natural insulation. It takes much nastier weather than this to make me uncomfortable." Joseph smiled gratefully and took the poncho fitted for Sam, large enough to make him feel like a balloon.

Before lifting off, the pilot said to Sattler, "I can't guarantee I can stay up for any extended time. Looks like I'll be flying one hundred feet above the tree tops to avoid the wind." The pilot started the engine and the helicopter hovered a few feet about the road and then rose out of sight in the downpour.

"Let's split up," Sattler spoke to Sam. "I'm going to take Dickey and the two other agents. We'll go over to the Federal Building. I've got a feeling that's where they need the help." He glanced at Joseph who was nervously trying to shake off the cold rain pounding on his poncho. "Sam, why don't you take Joseph and check out the nearby buildings and houses for any victims. If anything comes up, we can keep in touch by cell. Okay, let's move," he said as he jogged through the wet grass and brush up the hill toward the parking lot.

Sam knew he had been left out, snubbed. Not minding being assigned the most mundane aspect of the field effort, Sam nodded to Joseph, "Okay, you ready to shove off?" Sam looked over toward the windowless shell of a service station and trotted with Joseph in tow across the parking lot filled with wrecked cars. Sam went through the entrance without hesitation, while Joseph stood outside in awe of the damage created by the wave. When Joseph finally entered, the acrid smell of decay greeted him. Joseph noticed a large piece of cardboard in the middle of the office. It was the poster of the red haired, 1950's pinup girl. He picked up the poster, examining it with amusement. Joseph lifted his head and saw Sam staring at him.

"We're not here to go through other people's belongings," Sam chastised as if he were talking to a child. Embarrassed, Joseph set it back down on the floor. He walked with Sam through the remnants of the roof and ceiling as Sam yelled, "Is anyone there?" After receiving no response, Sam said, "This place checks out. Most likely the occupants weren't here when it happened, or were able to get to a place of safety."

Sam went out to the parking lot, shinning his flashlight in the ravine and noted that the cars were up to their hoods in water and mud. Spot checking the passenger compartments, he didn't detect any movement. Sam was not optimistic that anyone trapped inside the cars would still be alive. He would have preferred to go down in the ravine, but figured it was too dangerous to try to find any victims. He drew his cell phone out of his pocket and quickly tapped out a number. "There are about twenty cars washed into the ditch here. You need to send a few wreckers to see if any of them can be pulled out. There still may be some people down there," he said.

Over the background of ambulances sirens and people shouting, Sattler said, "You need to hold on. All emergency equipment is occupied. Maybe in twenty minutes something will be available. Call me then," and abruptly hung up.

Sam turned to Joseph in frustration, "He said to 'hold on.' I would say the asshole is good at holdin' onto his pecker. I think we should move on and not hang out here like a pair of idiots. Let's see what else needs to be done."

The dusk quickly turned to darkness. Sam noticed the streetlights along the road begin to light, casting an eerie glow over the confetti of tree limbs that covered the asphalt. Sam surveyed the adjoining neighborhood along the road and pointed to some houses. "I need to get across the ravine to see if everything is alright. Let's walk towards the river and find a convenient place to across."

Crossing the highway with Sam, Joseph noted that a Chevy Impala had impacted a thirty-foot high wooden power pole, nearly shearing it in half at its base. Sam warned, "This is dangerous; we got to keep people away from here until it's repaired. There are fifteen thousand-volt supply lines at the top of the pole. I wouldn't want to think about what would happen if it came down."

As they followed the ravine, the vegetation became denser. Joseph could feel the briars ripping apart the plastic of his poncho. Sam barreled through the brush and found that the gully became much wider and shallower. "I think we can cross here." Sam waded in the water up to his thighs and lifted himself to the opposite bank. Off toward the river, Joseph heard a dog barking and a child's voice. Sam said, "I wonder who the hell that could be out in this storm. Why don't you go and check it out, while I go ahead and make sure everybody is all right over here."

Hiking over to the riverbank, Joseph stood on the edge, looking at the water tumbling over the rocks in the channel. The river had risen to the top of its banks. Even though he was one hundred feet from the main part of the river, there was a still a heavy current toward the bank. .

Joseph looked upstream and saw a pear-shaped island of tall, river elms in the outer part of the channel, majestically rocking back and forth in the wind as if swaying to some dance rhythm. A boy's voice carried downstream from the island. "Get over here Ralph; I'm sick of chasing you," the boy said as he ran behind the dog, which effortlessly eluded his pursuit. The dog would periodically sit down and let the boy catch up to within a few feet and then sprint off again through the trees. Both the boy and the dog seemed to enjoy the game, even with the rain coming down in sheets. Joseph watched for a few minutes and then decided it was time to interrupt them. He yelled out, "Hey, little boy."

Toby ignored him and continued chasing Ralph.

Joseph took off his hood and yelled louder, "Hey, little boy. Perhaps you should come to this side. It is dangerous to be out there." Even though a mere fifteen feet separated them, Toby was still too busy with Ralph to concern himself with anyone on the opposite bank.

A hissing and crackling sound could be heard from the overhead electrical poles. Joseph looked up and saw the wooden power pole that had been hit by a car leaning over at an obtuse angle to the ground. In the wind, the wet leaves of the tree adjacent to the pole periodically brushed against the exposed wires of the transformer, creating a blue arc of electricity. Joseph could swear that just a few minutes before, the pole was nearly vertical.

While examining the pole, Joseph heard the child's voice call out from behind him. "Who are you?" The boy and dog, soaked from the rain, stopped playing the game of keep away and were both curiously examining him from across the water.

Joseph looked over and repeated exasperatedly, "Hey, little boy with the dog—you should come over to this bank."

The boy looked over toward him and said, "Who are you? I don't remember seeing you around here."

"It doesn't matter where I am from. Why don't you come over here with your dog?"

"I think I will stay over here. My mother told me not to talk to strangers."

"That's a good rule, but you know sometimes rules are not meant to be followed. I am with the FBI. We just landed at the gas station."

"That must have been cool. Was that a helicopter that I heard? I thought…" Toby stopped in mid-sentence and looked quizzically at Joseph's face. "You don't look like you're from the FBI. You look like you come from some foreign country. Can you show me a badge?"

"I do not have a badge. I just have this tag they put on my jacket."

"Okay, let me see it," Toby said eagerly.

"I have to take off my poncho to do that."

"So take it off."

"Well, I will get wet." Joseph reluctantly lifted the yellow poncho over his head, and put it on the ground as the rain soaked his clothes and skin.

The boy focused his eyes on the label. "It doesn't look like anything."

The paper inside Joseph's plastic badge had become drenched. He said in an apologetic voice, "It used to be an ID. All the ink has washed off of it. It is not designed to be used in the rain."

"Then, I'm not going cross," Toby declared.

The river had risen within a few feet of Toby. Joseph stepped back upon realizing he was in water up to his ankles. Separated twenty feet from the boy, every passing minute the distance between himself and the boy widened.

.

Agent Sattler spoke into his small, digital voice recorder as he watched a group of volunteers. Many were still dressed in their office clothes, drenched to their skin, loading the injured onto gurneys and into ambulances. Sattler noted most of the injuries were cuts from shattered glass, broken collarbones, broken and sprained arms, most the result of furniture being overturned and file cabinets falling. Sattler spoke to the rescue personnel and got an unofficial count of twenty people having been taken to local hospitals. However, he needed a more authoritative report from the officer in charge of the scene. Down the parking lot, he saw a clean-cut, tall, gray-haired man in his late forties wearing a fluorescent yellow raincoat and talking on his portable phone. "...checked Mid County General Hospital and their emergency room are beyond capacity. We'll have to start taking them to Shepard's Memorial over in Pollard County."

Approaching the sheriff, Sattler produced his badge from underneath his raincoat and immediately asked about acquiring a list of eyewitnesses. Rick Woods was a no-nonsense individual who understood the changing dynamics of managing an emergency situation and the priorities that go along with it. A longtime tobacco chewer, Woods had a talent for spitting tobacco juice from his mouth to any specific spot within a ten foot radius. He casually spat two inches from Sattler's shoes and said, "Mister, we're having enough trouble getting them out of the building, let alone compiling a list. We usually do that after we get the victims to the hospitals. If you and your people want to start a list, that's fine with me, but just keep out of our way."

Sattler said in a conciliatory manner, "We'll make sure we won't interfere with your recovery efforts. Is there any way we can help out?"

"Yes, maybe if you could get about five backhoes and a team of people with chain saws. With this thunderstorm, the resources of Gottlieb are strained to the limit. The state sent us some people, but they're down in the parking lot cutting people out of cars."

A call came in on Woods' radio. After muttering a few words into the microphone, Woods walked quickly toward the rear of the lot with Sattler following a few feet behind. A deputy was watching anxiously as a jaws-of-life pulled apart a truck and two cars. It was a tangled mess, difficult for Woods to tell where the truck started and the two cars ended. The deputy put his head into the remnants of one of the cars that Woods could tell was once a Nissan Sentra. The front end of the truck landed on part of the roof, diagonally entering into the passenger compartment through the windshield. Woods poked his head into the Sentra's passenger compartment, finding the seat covered with blood and glass. The faces of the victims were smashed to an indistinguishable pulp. From a cursory inspection of the corpses, he could tell they were women. He could feel a knot form in his stomach. Over the years, Woods had been to many scenes of automobile accidents, but was still not desensitized to seeing the victims. An ambulance came. The attendants quickly pulled out the bodies and put them onto stretchers.

The deputy handed Woods a plain, brown leather purse stained with blood, "We found this in the car."

Woods shuffled through the purse and his face turned to sorrow. "Don't call her father," he said, "I will do it personally." He turned to Sattler, "Her name was Nancy Aldera. We went to high school together. I went out with her sister. Her companion is most likely Barbara Park. They were two of the nicest people you'd ever want to meet," the sheriff said, as the rain channeled off of his hat.

Another deputy walked by announcing, "I just got the weather report. The center of the thunderstorms is still ten miles to the west. We've got thirty more minutes of this mess."

"I pray to the lord I can make it through days like today," Woods responded. He spoke to Sattler, "I hope you're satisfied now. You've got two names for your list. Remember, I'm in charge here. Keep your people out of my way. If you don't mind, I've got more victims to locate." He then briskly walked away.

* * *

Everything became quiet in the Continental; only the muffled pattering of raindrops sounded on the car's roof. Jesse listened to the semi-conscious breathing of Mrs. Warren. Applying mouth-to-mouth resuscitation to the woman's husband drained her of energy. For a few minutes, she sat in the back seat thinking about her next move. She leaned up front, breaking the silence. "How do you feel? I still need you to keep pressure on your tourniquet. I may have heard someone outside a little while ago, but they aren't there anymore, so I'm going to pull you out of the car myself."

Mrs. Warren spoke in a pained voice, "How's my husband, Herbert? I haven't heard anything from him."

Jesse did not know how to tell Mrs. Warren her husband had died in the seat next to her and so blurted out the first thing that came to mind. "He's…. unconscious. I did everything I could do to help him."

Mrs. Warren stared ahead, a tear rolling down her face. She said, "You don't need to lie to me. He's dead isn't he?"

Jesse nodded. The woman let out a howl of pain followed by sobbing. Jesse took the woman's hand, holding it for a couple of minutes as she calmed down. "We need to keep our heads about us. We've got to get out of the car. I think I've enough strength to pull you out."

"I…I don't want to leave here without him," Mrs. Warren said as she outstretched her hand towards the body reclining in the front seat.

"I'm not going to leave your husband here. I promise I'll get him pulled out after I take care of you. I'm going to need to open your car door. You may get a little wet."

Jesse leaned over, pulled the latch on the front passenger door, and felt the mechanism unlocking. The door would not budge. She muttered, "Oh, shit," as she moved over to the back door. Wedging her body in the backseat and pressing her weight against the door with her feet, it still did not budge. She glanced out of the passenger window; the mud had flowed to the base of the glass. She was pushing against the mud flow but figured she might as well have been pressing against concrete. This definitely complicated her plan to drag Mrs. Warren out of the car. Exasperated, Jesse said, "I'm sorry, I'm going to have to leave through the window and get help. I'll be back in five minutes at the most."

"Please, don't leave me alone to die," the woman pleaded and started to sob again.

"You aren't going to die. Everything will be okay. Trust me."

The old woman looked over towards Jesse, barely able to keep to her eyes open. Jesse grasped her hand again and felt it becoming cold, a sign that Mrs. Warren was getting weaker and going deeper into shock. Jesse took off her coat and put it over the woman. "You need to keep awake. You hear me, you need to keep conscious."

"I will do my best. I wish I had your strength."

"You'll do fine." Jesse went over to the window and she felt the wind blow past the car. A pickup truck perched at the top of the gully above the Continental suddenly shifted its position. Jesse did not see the truck, but heard the groan from above. The wind flipped the truck into the gully. There was a boom as the roof of the truck hit the roof of the car. All the unbroken windows of the Lincoln shattered, and the roof instantaneously lowered by a foot. Jesse ducked, covering her head as she was sprayed with broken glass from all directions. She slowly picked up her head. After brushing off the glass, she shined her flashlight up front. In the glow of the light, she saw Mrs. Warren open her mouth in one continual scream. Jesse felt trapped in a nightmare.

***

Joseph found himself standing helplessly on the riverbank, watching the boy on the island playing fetch with his dog. Joseph never felt himself an authority figure, especially when dealing with children, and waited for Sam.

After all, Sam, would get more respect from the boy, having had experience dealing with children

The dog, stick hanging from its mouth, ran to the shore and the boy followed. The boy hesitated at the water's edge and then started to cross. At that moment, something seemed wrong and Joseph felt a sense of impending danger. "Maybe you shouldn't do that."

The boy stopped in his tracks. "Why not? I'm finished playing on the island."

"It may not be safe to cross. The water has gotten deep. I would say it is three feet high."

"I've swam in ten feet of water."

"That was probably in a swimming pool. I don't want the current to wash you downstream."

"Now you want me to stay here. Make up your mind."

"Before, there was only a little water between us. Just stay put until someone gets you." Joseph heard a rustling in the bushes behind him. He turned around expecting to find Sam, but instead saw a man in his early forties with a large, handlebar mustache.

The boy called out, happy to see someone he knew, "Hey Mr. Parson, how ya doin'?"

Parson yelled back, "What's all commotion out here. Hey there, Toby? What are you doing?"

"I came to find Ralph."

"Does your mother know where you are?"

"She's out saving someone that fell into the ditch with a car."

"Uh huh. We better get you back to the gas station. We don't want her to worry about you."

Parson waded into the water. "How about taking a piggy back ride to land?"

Toby smiled and said, "That sounds real cool, Mr. Parson."

Joseph smelled the ozone from the transformer and said in a concerned voice, "Be careful, there are a lot of sparking electrical wires. I do not trust electricity."

"Cool your heels mister. No need to worry. I know what I'm doing. I've walked across this river plenty of times."

Parson took off his sneakers and slowly entered the water, his body sinking a few inches in the mud as Joseph looked on nervously. Stepping carefully with both arms out, trying to maintain his balance, Parson put one foot in front of the other as he lowered himself into the muddy river bottom. Parson was waist deep in the current, midway between the shore and the island, when Joseph heard the utility pole crack. The pole fell towards the water, seemingly in slow motion. Joseph yelled at the top of his lungs, "GET OUT OF THE WATER!" Startled, Toby reflexively jumped back onto the island. Parson looked up at the pole swinging down, unable to move from his spot. As the transformer hit the water, he screamed as all the life left his body. He became rigid and his clothes began to smoke. His face turned black and his hair started to burn. Finally, his body landed face first into the water. The river took on an eerie, smoky haze, with a nauseating smell of burnt flesh.

Toby's face became white as he watched the entire scene. He held onto Ralph and began to shake uncontrollably. Joseph stood back from the river's edge and saw the boy go into a near catatonic state. Trying to control the situation as best he could, he nervously said, "My name is Joseph and Toby, I won't let anything happen to you."

The boy continued to look forward with a blank expression.

"Toby, listen to me. You're going to have to hold on....," Joseph unconsciously used the term 'hold on' and thought what an idiot he was for saying the same banal phase the FBI used and followed it with something nearly as stupid, "...and make sure that neither yourself nor your dog go near the water."

With tears falling from his eyes, Toby muttered, "His name is Ralph."

"Okay, both you and Ralph sit tight and the sheriff will be right over. I'm certain he will figure out a way to get you off the island."

Both Toby and Joseph stood across from each other watching the river slowly rise. Toby stared at the ground, slowly petting Ralph and talking to himself, "...I want to go home...Mom... Where are you...I need you...go home where it's safe..."

Joseph asked, "Where is your mother?"

"....in the gully...."

"What gully? We didn't see anyone in the gully."

"...in the gully...," Toby repeated.

Joseph could not make sense out of anything that Toby said. It was a relief when Sam came running out of the trees. Nearly out of breath, he said, "I heard screaming. Is everything alright?"

Joseph said, "No, it isn't. Someone named 'Parson' just got electrocuted standing in the water, and I just stood by and watched it happen." Joseph pointed to the body in the river, to the boy on the other side, and then directed Sam's attention to the street lamps. "Look, the lights are still on around us. The lines are down but somehow there is a connection being maintained. There must be ten thousand volts going through the water."

Sam, horrified, said, "We got to get the power shut off before someone else gets fried."

"Well, when is that going to happen?"

"Don't look at me, man. I know as much as you do. I don't have a crystal ball in front of me telling me when things are goin' to be done. I haven't seen any electric company crews around. I assume on a night like this, they're being spread thin."

Joseph started brainstorming ideas. "With situations like this, doesn't the fire department usually come down and get the boy out with a long ladder."

"I wish they could. I was also up and down the road and there are impassable fallen limbs everywhere. With the bridge out, the fire department cannot get anything over here. Anyhow, with the metal ladders they have, there would be a hazard." Sam stood there holding his hands up for a moment in the rain. "Do you feel that? The storm is letting up and the winds are dying down. We can probably get the chopper back in the air and get a harness around him and to lift him out. He then called Sattler and filled him in on the particulars. After a few minutes, he got off the phone. "He agreed with me and is sending the helicopter. It will be here in five to ten minutes."

Joseph walked over towards the edge of the water and said, "Toby, just hang in there. We are sending in a helicopter to pick you up."

Sam chimed in, "I know you're scared. We will help you. Listen to the man in the helicopter and do exactly what he tells you."

Toby got up looking skyward for the helicopter as the rain washed the tears from his face. At that moment, Joseph felt complete empathy for the boy. Many times in his life he had felt frightened, alone, and separated from everyone else. Now there was a completely helpless child trying to survive. Toby's fate was his future.

Within a few minutes, Joseph heard the sound of the helicopter and then Sattler's voice in the distance. Sattler came over from the Federal Building along with Dickey and was talking on his phone with Jefferies in the helicopter, coordinating the rescue. "The boy is on the south side of the island. Do you have a visual?"

The helicopter turned on its searchlights and illuminated the trees with an intense circle of white light. The spotlight ran along the shoreline until Toby and Ralph were at its center. Toby turned away when the light shone in his face. He gripped Ralph close to his chest as the dog squirmed and barked.

Jefferies said, "We have him. Do you think he can move another ten feet from the trees? They're going to obstruct the line."

Sattler yelled over to Toby, "You need to move over to get in the clear."

Toby shuffled his feet over towards the river so that there were only a few feet of clearance between him and the water. Sattler called back, "We moved him as much as we can. It's all up to you folks now."

Jefferies went to the back of the helicopter and opened the door. With the wind in his face, he attached the rescue harness to the end of the rope, coiled in a spool in the rear of the cabin. He quickly unwound the rope as it descended down toward Toby. As the rope reached a point about five feet above the boy, the spool became empty. Jefferies spoke into his headphone, "We need to get lower."

The pilot nodded and the helicopter floated down. Now the rescue harness was dangling above the river. Jefferies said, "Now we're out of position. We need to move about twenty feet to the north. The pilot looked down as he maneuvered the stick. The nylon harness was only two feet above Toby. Sam yelled over the noise of the rotors, "You are going to jump for it, Toby." Toby leapt but was only able to touch the gray fabric with the tips of his fingers. Sam said, "You're going to have to let go of Ralph." Toby put the dog down and it cowered at his feet. With the next leap, Toby got a momentary hold of the harness before it slipped out of his wet fingers. There was a sudden gust of wind and the helicopter gained about ten feet in elevation. Toby stared toward the clouds, waiting for the helicopter to make another try. The helicopter hovered for a second, and as it went down again, the harness disappeared in a group of elm trees.

"Oh shit," Jefferies said, "I was afraid of that. We're stuck on a tree." He got down on his knees and tried to jerk the rope free, with no success. The pilot said, "Let me see if I can break us loose." He maneuvered the machine up and noticed that the engine was running high on the rpm's. As the helicopter pulled the rope, it became more entangled in the tree. After a minute, the engine started to redline and the pilot spoke into his headphone, "We need to abort. Disengage the line." Jefferies looked down at the metal reel but could not see the release mechanism.

The pilot tersely said, "Sometime today, please, we're going down." Jefferies took out his pocketknife and started sawing at the nylon rope. The pilot, impatient with Jefferies, leaned over and pressed a red button on the reel explosively disengaging the line. The frayed remains fell at Toby's feet as the helicopter banked back toward the airport.

As the helicopter retreated from sight, Toby cried out, "Come back! Come back…" He went down to his knees and started wailing.

Sattler tried to calm the boy, "The helicopter will return. It just needs a new rope." He reached for his phone and called his contact at the power company. Joseph was within earshot of the conversation he gauged as unsuccessful as the helicopter rescue attempt. He overheard Sattler shouting over the phone, "I don't care how many *fucking* hospitals are on the local grid. You need to shut off the power." After an animated, five-minute discussion, Sattler hung up in frustration and announced, "The nearest substation is two miles away and the crews are trying to gain access through the downed trees. It's probably going to be another half hour before the roads are cleared and everything coordinated with the hospitals."

The boy continued crying as a line of five people all started shouting to him at once. This only made him more inconsolable.

Over the raised voices Sam heard singing:

"Amazing grace. How sweet the sound"

Sam turned around and saw that it was Joseph. He shot Joseph and angry glance and was about to yell at him to shut up; instead, he silently stood there trying to understand the rationale behind Joseph's behavior. For a moment, he listened and found the singing melodic and soothing. Sam gave a quick glance over to Toby, who had stopped crying and had taken his hands off his face. Unconsciously, Sam started to sing along in his baritone voice,

"T'was the Grace that taught

My heart to fear,

And Grace, my fears relieved,

How precious did that Grace appear

The hour I first believed"

Toby stood up, smiled, wiped the tears out his eyes, and forgot about everything that was happening around him.

Joseph looked over to Toby, "I won't let anything happen to you 'my brother.'"

Toby said, "I know you will figure somethin'. Please, make it quick, Mr. Joseph."

Sam went over to Joseph and put his hand on his shoulder, "You surprise me. I would have never thought of doing that." Sam turned up the palms of his hands and noted that the rain had ceased. "Not only did you make a child happy, you also made it stop raining. Now all we have to do is wait for the power company to pull the switch and then rescue him."

Joseph looked over to the river, and noted a few large rocks in the center that had been visible were now were covered with water. "I think your celebration is premature. The river is still rising."

Sam asked, "How's that possible?"

"The storm was moving from west to east, and now it's raining on the upstream areas in the watershed. That is how. It is obvious that the Simmons River has not yet crested. Not only that, we may not have the half an hour it will take to turn off the power before it overtops the island. Judging by the rate the river has been rising, I think we have perhaps twenty minutes...at most. We cannot depend on the power company to solve our problem..."

Sam was out of options, "Okay then, what's your idea?"

Joseph said, "I think we are going to have to find something to span the water."

Sam looked at the twenty feet that separated the boy from the people on the bank of the creek and said, "You're going to be hard pressed to find anything to bridge the distance."

Joseph anxiously glanced around the island, thinking that there must be a better place to try to cross the water. He gave a thin smile when he saw that further downstream, a large three-foot diameter tree, partially felled by beavers, was leaning into the river with some of its trunk not yet submerged. He announced proudly, "We don't need to span the entire twenty feet. All we have to do is get onto the tree. I would say maybe ten feet."

"You are the man to do this. But I wouldn't want to speculate how much loading the tree can take."

"My estimate is that the boy is all of eighty to one hundred pounds. If he lay on the trunk, we can distribute his weight."

Something told Sam that Joseph was right, and he could not rely on anyone else to save the boy's life. Not wanting to be an observer anymore, he said, "Okay lets' go. I don't want to see anybody else get killed, especially not another child." He gave a serious look over to Joseph and then started to run down the riverbank toward the residential neighborhood.

As he started to trot after Sam, Joseph called over to Toby, "We need to get something, and we will be back in a few minutes. Until then, these other men will take care of you."

They heard Toby's call back, "Where're you going?"

Joseph yelled, "I don't know. When we come back I promise I will come over to get you."

"Please hurry," Toby said, his voice trailing down the river after them.

***

There is always a way out, Jesse thought, as she ran her fingers around the frames of the rear windows that been smashed down to mere slits. She had been brought up to believe in God; and perhaps it was divine intervention that delayed her exit from the car. She was seconds from climbing out of the window, and if she had, she would have been crushed in the window frame. The interior of the car was now the pitch black of a tomb. Pressing the button on the metal flashlight, she focused the beam to the front of the car where the broken glass on the dashboard sparkled like diamonds. She held the light on the front for a few seconds and noticed it getting dimmer. Climbing into the front, she took her arm and, with a quick sweep, removed the broken glass from the top of the dashboard. Getting a firm grip on the seat, she tried maneuvering her legs out of the windshield. She felt the remnants of the glass cut into her shins, but undeterred, pushed further. Blood ran down her leg. She grimaced as she pushed harder. The space left between the top of the dashboard and the opening around the windshield was only about a foot. Gritting her teeth, she tried pushing the rest of her torso through the opening, but the pain in her ribs was unbearable. She needed only a few more inches of clearance. After a couple of deep breaths she pulled herself out. Tired and frustrated she collapsed down in the back seat. She moved her feet, and felt them sheathed in a cold layer of liquid mud. She went over to the doors and put her hands on the openings that were once the windows and could feel the steady flow of the brown ooze coming in from the ravine. The car was quickly filling with mud. She screamed at the top of her lungs "Goddam. Son of a bitch. Motherfucker."

Mrs. Warren stirred uncomfortably in the front seat and said in a low voice, "Why don't you stop doing that. You are making my ears hurt. Cursing at it won't help. Admit it, we are both trapped at the bottom of a ravine and if anyone were out there they would probably not hear you. Why don't you give up and accept that we're both going to die. I'm not afraid to meet my maker."

"Look, I still have a child I want to raise, and I don't want to think about leaving this life. I want you to keep talking, but I don't want you to say that shit. Why don't you talk about something else— anything other than death? Maybe something pleasant?"

"I remember when Herbert and I went on a vacation to the Bahamas. We'd never taken a vacation before. Up to that point, we had been consumed with running the store and putting our two kids through college. We spent the whole day on the beach drinking Rum Runners…in the evening they had a big fireworks display that lit the sky…"

Jesse smiled. "That's funny. It reminds me of when I was a kid and my parents used to take me to the Fourth of July fireworks displays. They used to shoot fireworks out of a mortar. Being a kid, I was quite impressed with the way they fired the sparklers which lit the sky. My father would never let me buy any fireworks so I decided I could improvise my own. We would sell some of the roadside flares. I took one and lit it and then with my slingshot fired it into the air.

"Your parents must have loved you for that."

"It actually worked fairly well. The flare went up fifty feet. The only problem is that it landed in a garbage bin, and my father had to call the fire department to put out the fire. I lost my allowance for about six months…" At that moment, an idea hit Jesse. Jesse realized their main challenge was to get noticed by rescuers. "I'm just curious; do you have a flare in the car?"

"I don't know. Herbert did all the car maintenance. But I vaguely remember one time we got a flat and he put flares out in the road. The toolkit is in the trunk. I'm afraid if you find one and lit it no one would see it."

"Not if I fired it out of the window." Jesse said.

***

It had been ten years since Sam played football. He felt every bit of it as he became winded after running two blocks down the road. Sam learned over, trying to catch his breath and wheezed, "I'm so tired, I don't even remember what we're looking for."

Joseph, who was surprisingly not as winded, stopped in his tracks and said, "Something that is non-conductive. It should be made out of wood or rubber: a large wood ladder or something like that."

Sam scanned the modest, two-story wood frame houses adjacent to the road. "Okay, something about fifteen feet long, non-conductive, and can hold a man. I was never very good at scavenger hunts."

"Scavenger hunts?"

"I'm surprised that you never heard of them. It's one of those games you play when you're a child…you're given a list of things to find in a certain amount of time. "

"I was never very good at games. So I hope what we are doing doesn't become one."

Sam nodded, "Amen, friend. Amen to that."

They continued to run together down the road, both of them cold and soaked to the skin. Everything was quiet in the neighborhood with the exception of a dog barking. Sam ran a hundred feet and stopped. "I'm not spotting anything remotely resembling a ladder or any long wooden object. I think our problem is that we're looking at the front of the houses rather than the backyards where people would be more apt to store wood." He pointed to a concrete entrance on the left-hand side of the road and proceeded to run down an alley. "It looks mighty suspicious two people going through an alley at this time in the evening, but it's the only thing we can do."

The lights turned on in the house directly ahead of them and Joseph said, "We had better move fast. I don't want people mistaking us for trespassers and shooting us."

"We are trespassing. I've seen your people skills, so let me deal with the property owners. Knowing the sheriff here, I can explain my way out of anything."

They approached a brick garage. Sam looked around the perimeter and, resting against a window, was an old wooden ladder roughly ten feet high. Sam picked it up and brought it back in the alley for Joseph to examine.

"It's white pine," Joseph observed.

"So what?"

"It's a soft wood. It will never hold the weight of a man; and look at it, it is falling apart."

"You didn't say what kind of wood you wanted. We may not find anything better."

Joseph wandered onto the closely-clipped grass yard, looking around, trying to get ideas for what to use. The dark plastic drain hose at the end of gutter caught his attention. Joseph went over and pulled it out. "I think we can use this for support and possibly floatation." The backyard of the next house had a laundry line supported by two, circular metal posts. "Sam, do you have a penknife?" Sam tossed him a small Boy Scout knife, and Joseph awkwardly crossed through the evergreen hedge separating the properties and cut a fifty-foot piece of nylon cord." He went back to Sam, dragging the cord through the hedge. "Clothes line to tie together the wood…when we find it. How are we for time?"

"It's already been seven minutes. I don't see anything else matching your criteria. The alley terminated one hundred feet ahead at the road. "We're running out of houses. It seems your idea did not work out. " Sam said.

"I have not given up yet," Joseph said stubbornly as he jogged ahead. Sam, surprised by the brazenness of the comment, sped up his pace to catch up to Joseph.

At the end of the alley was a wooden Cape Cod house. There were two floodlights illuminating the rear of the house, which had a four-foot high picket fence with a sign, "BEWARE OF DOG." In the glow of the lights, Sam could see a beautifully landscaped yard with red flowering azalea bushes and pear trees. One corner of the property had a mound that was terraced like a fancy wedding cake with various types of flowering plants. Sam noted, "That's a really nicely maintained garden. My ex-wife was a gardener, and she always pestered me to do landscaping like that."

Joseph eyed the property and got elated. "That's it! Look at what's creating the terraces."

"I don't see what you're talking about." He then examined the mound more carefully and at the base were black wooden pieces of wood, ten-feet long, with a square section of about eight inches.

"Don't they look like railroad ties? That will definitely support a man's weight," Joseph said excitedly.

The picket fence did not bother Sam since traversing obstacles was part of the job. He had chased suspects over barbed wire fences and received several cuts. Sam's major concern was the occupants of the house. There was a dim light on the second floor, but there was no time to knock on the door and explain everything. Sam said, "Okay then, let's get the ties and go." He quickly climbed over the fence and waited for Joseph. "Okay, your turn. I can give you a boost if you need some help."

Joseph stood there frozen on the other side of the fence. "I can't go into the yard. It has a dog."

Somewhat exasperated, Sam said, "Now, after all this bullshit we've gone through, you're going to tell me you're afraid of dogs?"

"I had a bad experience with them when I was in Beirut," Joseph said embarrassed.

"I bet there is no dog here. The property owner probably put up the sign to scare people away."

There was suddenly a loud barking coming from the front of the house. Both men looked towards the front, expecting to be confronted by a large animal. The barking got closer, and there was the sound of a heavy dog chain clanking.

Sam stared ahead expecting the worst. When the dog came out of the darkness, Sam nearly collapsed on the fence laughing. It was a small, white terrier, slightly larger than a cat he once kept in his garage.

Still laughing, Sam said, "Wow, what a vicious beast we have here." He turned to Joseph, "Don't worry, I'm good at making friends with dogs," and bent down extending his hand for the dog to sniff. Instead, it lunged for Sam's pants and sank its teeth into Sam's calf. Sam gave a cry of pain as he shook his leg, trying to extricate it. The animal fiercely stayed attached as Sam danced with it across the yard.

The light in the kitchen came on, and a middle-aged lady walked out of the house with a baseball bat in her hands, "I don't know who you are but you better leave before I call the police."

Sam, standing up on one leg, announced, "I am Sheriff Johnson from Pope's Mills and we need wood from your yard for a police emergency."

The woman gave an angry face and started to go back into the house to make the phone call.

Joseph shouted in a pleading voice, "I know you don't believe us. We need the wood to save a small boy down at the river. His name is Toby and likes to be sung to."

The woman stopped at the doorway and then turned around facing the men, "I've baby-sat for him. Is he in trouble?"

"Yes, he is in serious trouble, and if we take any longer, he may not survive. We don't have time to explain in detail, but I am begging you to trust us."

"This has to be the strangest thing that has happened to in the thirty years since I came to this town." She hesitated for a moment. "Alright, pile the wood in the truck, and I'll take you down to the river."

Sam said modestly, "Before I do that, can you do me a one big favor, and remove your dog from my leg?"

The woman made a whistling sound, and the dog came running into her arms. She lifted the dog with both hands, kissing the terrier on the mouth. "Poor Prudence, did that big man hurt you?"

Sam was embarrassed but was too proud to admit it. He saw Joseph standing at the fence, smiling at the entertainment. He said in a gruff voice, "Joseph, you better get your butt over here, we have wood to load." With the dog safely secured, Joseph climbed over the fence, and helped Sam remove the railroad ties. The woman got her pickup truck from the driveway, and both of the men laboriously loaded it with wood. The three of them proceeded to pile into the front seat for the trip to the river.

Joseph gave Sam a bemused look and as the truck went down the road and said, "By the way, I do fine with people if given a chance."

* * *

The plush back seat had become a sea of mud. Jesse moved around trying to feel the edges of the seat to pull the upholstery from its backing. The fabric was stronger than she estimated. The mud made every movement a serious effort and trying to fight off its cold chill sapped Jesse's energy. She tried to stay optimistic to not think about the serious possibility of being buried alive.

"I can barely move," Mrs. Warren said.

"That's good; it will keep your leg immobilized. Just hang in there. I'm going to try to reach your trunk."

"How are you going to do that? The seat is fixed, and it doesn't fold down like some of the seats in the new cars."

"I know that." Jesse said impatiently. "I'm familiar with a 1990 Lincoln Continental."

"I don't see how you're going to get to my trunk?

"If the seat won't move, I'm going to have to go through it."

"Through my seat? I don't understand."

"Your flare must be in a tool box. Most people don't use one very often, and hopefully your husband kept it towards the back of the trunk. All I need to do is cut a large enough hole through the seat to get to the box. I have a fairly large pocketknife and I think I can get it done with that."

Jesse took out her red-enameled knife with three-inch serrated bade, put her hand out through the mud, and started sawing through the seat. She winced as her hand was cut by the springs. The knife hit the soft portion of the cushion and Jesse started pulling out the foam seat backing.

"How you doing?" Mrs. Warren inquired.

"I'm getting there, though it is tougher than I thought. Remember, try to think pleasant thoughts," Jesse said, busy working at the seat.

"The mud is actually starting to feel good." Mrs. Warren said, closing her eyes and grimacing.

"Just pretend that you are taking a mud bath at a premium spa."

"You're the character everyone says you are."

"I never take myself too seriously," Jesse responded. "I'm not making enough progress. I'm going to need to speed things up a little." Jesse switched positions and started to kick at the area she had been sawing and felt the seat starting to give. Jesse groaned as she tried to put all the stamina and strength she had into the kicks. On the third try, she felt her foot go into the trunk. "Okay, I'm through. Now all I need to do is get the box."

She reached down and tried to poke her hand through. "I don't feel anything. Are you sure your husband kept a kit?"

"Well…I am as certain as any…any…thing else. He is…was…a cautious man and always wanted to be prepared," Mrs. Warren said in speech half-slurred, showing the signs of hypothermia and blood loss.

"I'm just going to have to be a little more aggressive." Jesse took off her shirt and tied one sleeve around her arm and the other around the plastic handle at the ceiling. Taking two deep breaths she put her head in the thick brown liquid.

After thirty seconds, she came back up covered with mud, her face nearly blue. She gasped for air. It was a minute before she recovered enough to speak.

"Well…well, did you get it?" Warren said anxiously.

"I think so…." Jesse pulled a gray, oblong metal box out from under the mud. "I got it!" She anxiously opened the box and went through the contents that included a hammer, wrenches, pliers, and an assortment of Philips Head screwdrivers. She breathed a sigh of relief when she found, under all the tools, a flare.

With the most import item in hand, all Jesse needed now was a slingshot. She put her hand through the mud one more time and felt under the seat. Grimacing, she pulled out a spring. Foraging through the tool kit for something to use as a slingshot base, she immediately eliminated most of the items as being too small. The pliers, though, had large handles that flared apart. Jesse carefully attached the spring to the ends of the plier handles. Pulling on the spring, it quickly snapped back with a "twang." Satisfied with her creation, Jesse sat in front of the window with the slingshot in her right hand and quickly yanked on in the flare-wire her left hand to ignite it. The wire was corroded and peeled off in her fingers. "Goddam this fucking piece of crap! How old is this thing?"

"What…what…is the problem?"

"The igniter doesn't work. I need a lighter. Jesse put her hands in her blue jeans that were covered with mud. "Oh shit, I don't have one on me. Now I wish I smoked."

"Herbert smoked pipes...may...may...be he put one here." Mrs. Warren opened the glove compartment and fumbled with the items. "I...I found it," she announced.

"Oh good, you found the lighter."

Mrs. Warren sat there holding a pair of blue glasses. "Now I...I...know where my reading glasses are. I searched the h...house for them for hours..."

"*The lighter, remember, the lighter....,*" Jesse said hysterically as the mud started to come up toward her neck.

"Here it is," she said as she passed back the monogrammed lighter to Jesse.

Jesse flipped open the lighter and flicked the flint with her thumb. The lighter sparked but with no flame. She flicked it again with the same result. "Come on, come on, goddammit work!"

"It's prob...ably flooded, you...you...will have to wait...wait for a minute to let it clear out."

"*We don't have a minute.*"

"Some...some...times my husband used to blow on it."

Jesse pursed her lips together and started blowing on the lighter. Before she tried the flint again, she mumbled, "I've come this far. I am not going to let this lighter fuck me up." She rotated the gray flint again and this time, a small orange flame came out."

She put the flame to the top of flare and smelled the paper as it started to burn. Unexpectedly, there was an eruption of sparks. It came so abruptly that she nearly dropped the flare into the mud. Smoke filled the car, and she heard Mrs. Warren cough. Jesse knew that she would have to quickly fling it out of the window, and hope that it cleared the pickup truck had landed on top of them. She put the flare inside the slingshot and pointed it out the window. Pulling the spring to its limit, she released it. Jesse looked through the slit, but could not immediately see where it landed.

Jesse spent the longest five minutes of her life watching the mud rise closer to the roof of the car. She tied to think about some of the happier moments in her life: the delivery room at the hospital, holding Toby for the first time, watching him walk his first steps.

Mrs. Warren said in a low voice, "Looks...looks...like every...thing was in vain. It...it was a good try though."

With the mud up to her chin, Jesse started banging on the ceiling of the car with all her might, screaming.

"I told you...you...that you were wasting time with that f..f..flare. There... there...is no one out there to see it."

Finally losing her patience, Jesse said what she wanted to say ever since she entered the Lincoln, "Why don't you shut the fuck up. All you've done is tell me I'm wasting my time. If we're going to die, I would rather it be in silence without hearing some old bitch telling me everything was for nothing!"

Mrs. Warren sat there with her mouth open, completely stunned.

Jesse heard voices from above and then felt the pickup truck on the roof move. Maybe it was her imagination. She wondered if this would be the last feeling she would have. The next noise was the rasping sound of metal scraping against metal. Jesse looked out the window as a man's face appeared in the crack, "Keep your heads down, we're going to cut off the top." Jesse saw the blade go through the roof and watched as it snipped in a circle. There were footsteps, and the roof of the car was peeled back like a tin can lid. Jesse thought she had died and gone to heaven. There were the nondescript figures of firemen above her—all wearing long coats and resembling angels. After the darkness she experienced for the past hour, she could barely keep her eyes open when she looked up at the spotlights shinning on the car.

***

Agent Sattler stood across from Toby who had stayed quiet since the departure of Sam and Joseph. The other six men that gathered around Sattler called out to the boy, but were unable to get any response. Toby gazed ahead in his own world. The water was six inches below Toby's feet and slowly rising. Sattler stayed on his cell phone talking to his contact at the electric company, getting updates on the progress with the power shutdown. He whispered to another agent, "The crews are making progress, but may take another twenty minutes to access the substation. Send back the helicopter; we're going it give it another try."

The agent responded, "The 'copter went back to the Gottlieb Airpark for refueling. It will be here in about thirty minutes."

Sattler said, "This is getting damn tight...too tight for comfort."

Voices could be heard down the river. Joseph was taking the lead with two pieces of railroad ties stuck under one arm, dragging a length of plastic tubing with the other. Sam was in the back, breathing heavily. "Slow down, I don't want to lose it all in the river."

Joseph looked ahead, "We are nearly there; only another hundred feet to go." He trotted past Toby and dropped the wood unceremoniously on the riverbank across from the downed tree.

Toby perked up, "You came back, Mr. Joseph."

Joseph smiled and said, "We won't leave until we get you, my brother."

Sattler hung up the mobile phone and dashed over to Sam. "Where were you and what do the hell do you think you're doing?"

"We went on a scavenger hunt, and we're going to build a bridge with the wood we found. You can stand there like an asshole and question us, or you can help put this thing together. It's your choice."

"I've got the situation well under control."

Sam glared at Sattler, "I see. The water is just below the boy's feet, and you're stubborn enough to wait until he's nearly electrocuted to explore any other options."

While Sam and Sattler continued their argument, Joseph laid the wood boards side by side and started to tie them together. He bent over awkwardly, and, with little success, tried to wrap the cord around the pieces. The wood was wet and slippery and the knots he tied would not hold. Joseph took to lifting the pieces to his chest only to find the wet railroad ties slipping out his hands. He then felt another pair of larger hands steadying the pieces. "You will never get it done like that, you need to lash them together while they're on the ground." It was Bob Dickey standing next to him. "I made a raft when I was a Boy Scout. You hold the wood while I tie." Joseph decided not to argue and held the wood in his hand as Dickey firmly crisscrossed the rope. Joseph brought over the corrugated, plastic drainage-pipe that would serve as the base, and Dickey quickly attached the sections of the pipe to the "bridge." The finished structure was little more than a composite-beam a foot and a half wide and about twelve feet in length.

Joseph realized he had just one chance to drop it in place at the proper location. If the wood fell into the water, everything would be lost. Glancing over to the fallen tree, Joseph found a spot were the trunk and two main branches met, forming a natural cradle. Both Dickey and he lifted up one end and pointed the other into the notch. The wet wood was difficult to maneuver and balance. Joseph felt the muscles in his back strain as he shifted the bridge over the notch. The end moved back and forth. Finally, when it was a couple of inches from the cradle, they dropped the piece in place, making first a "thud" and then a "creaking" sound as the weight of the bridge was transferred to the branches. Joseph and Dickey anchored the other end in the firm clay of the riverbank.

Sam and Sattler stopped talking when they saw the completed bridge. Sattler stared at the bridge and was immediately skeptical. "This thing you created doesn't even look like it will hold the boy, let alone a man."

Joseph snapped back, "I'm certain it will support someone crawling across on his stomach."

Sam was more of a realist about the rescue. "We cannot ask Toby to come across on this thing alone."

"I will have to get him then," Joseph said.

"No, I can't allow you to do it. Why are you taking the risk?"

"Toby trusts me and everybody else here seems to scare him. Look at yourself. You weigh over two hundred pounds. I don't know if the bridge could withstand all the stress you would put on it. I weigh only one hundred and forty pounds."

"You're not going!" Sam said emphatically.

Sattler interrupted the exchange, "I'm still in charge here. We're still waiting for the chopper to come back. If the situation changes, *I* will decide what will be done and who will do it."

***

Jesse sat in the back of the fire department ambulance. She now wore a bright orange shirt with solid black letters "GOTTLIEB FIRE DEPARTMENT" printed on the back. She tried to forget about being pulled from the car wearing only a bra and blue jeans. She was covered from the top of her head to her feet in mud that itched and that was quickly drying on her face, forming a cake. Jesse began scraping off the mud as the attendant used a scissors to cut away the bottom part of the legs on Jesse's good jeans. The heavy-set, lethargic woman assistant said in a reassuring voice, "Don't worry about that, we'll get you cleaned up at the hospital. My mother always told me to wear clean underwear if you have to go to there. You need not worry about it, honey. I've treated much filthier people. I've had heart attack victims shit in their pants." She briefly examined Jesse's legs. "You've got some deep lacerations on your arms and legs from the broken glass, a couple will require stitches. You're very lucky. In another couple of minutes, you would've been a goner. Did you get a Tetanus shot recently? Because if you haven't, you'll need one…"

The attendant continued to ramble on and Jesse closed her eyes, shutting out the woman's voice to relax. There was something missing. Anxiety stricken, Jesse asked, "Have you seen my son, Toby?"

"'Fraid not." The attendant said as she wrapped a blood pressure cuff around Jesse's arm.

"He's seven, has freckles, and red hair."

"He sounds cute. But I'm sorry, I've not seen him."

Jesse took off the cuff. "You'll have to help me later. I need to find him."

"You can't do that. You're hurt and need medical attention…," The attendant said as Jesse ran from the ambulance and into the garage.

"*TOBY, TOBY. Where are you, baby?*" Her voice reverberated through the building. She walked outside, stopping the fireman and asking them frantically,

"Have you seen my son? All of them shrugged their heads, walking away. With each person she stopped, the question became louder and more desperate.

Down toward the river she noticed a set of lights and a crowd of people. There were wrecking trucks in the road alongside the bridge with chains attached to the cars. Jesse walked up to one of the operators and pointed to the lights, "What's going on down there?" The operator kept his concentration on the chain as the winch slowly moved a truck out of the gully and then he said in a casual voice, "I heard on the radio they're trying to rescue a boy and a dog from an island in the river."

Jesse stood in the street, erupting in fear and anxiety, "*Oh no, my god!*" She raced toward the river crying out. "*TOBY! Where are you?*"

Toby, who had been standing on the island crying, yelled back, "I'm here mom!"

She approached the crowd and was about go into the water when Sattler stopped her. "Let go of me, you fucking jerk!" she yelled.

The agent held her to the ground, "Sorry, I can't let you go any further, there is a downed-electric line. You'll get electrocuted."

Still on the ground, she extended her arm toward Toby. "*I want my son!*"

Ralph, sitting at attention on the bank, broke away from Toby and scampered across the rough, wood bridge. Joseph nervously backed off when he saw the dog running across. The dog continued down the bank, moving through the people, and jumped on Jesse. Sattler loosened his grip as she cuddled the dog, tears in her eyes.

Everyone on the bank was so distracted by Ralph's appearance that no one noticed Toby walk from the tree branches onto the bridge. Joseph yelled out to him, "Do not do that! You need to go on your stomach!" Toby dropped to his knees, jiggling the bridge as he moved across. Without hesitation, Joseph dropped down on his stomach and onto the wet planks, keeping Toby in sight. About one foot below him, the water was charged with electricity that felt like ants crawling over his body.

The boy crawled to the middle of the bridge but then suddenly stopped. "I'm scared," he said.

"I am too. Just stay there; I will come to get you," Joseph said, keeping his eyes on Toby.

Sam was only a few feet away, on his knees, arms extended, calling to Joseph, "Keep cool. You're doing fine. Keep your eyes forward. Don't look down."

The bridge creaked and shifted slightly, the knots straining as Joseph held out his hand. "Take my hand my brother. I am going to pull you back."

Toby was motionless. "I don't know…"

"I have kept all my promises to you; haven't I? We have to move quickly. I promise I will sing to you after I bring you back."

Toby smiled, extending his hand. "My mom sings better." Joseph took the small hand and began to gently pull. They were only three feet from the shore when the clotheslines holding the bridge together started to snap. Jesse screamed. The middle of the bridge collapsed. Toby's feet dipped towards the river, dangling one inch above the water. Joseph winced from the pain in his shoulder. His grip stayed firm, though, keeping the boy from backsliding into the water. Without thinking, Sam leaned over Joseph and lifted Toby by the collar through the air with his massive hands. There was an expression of happiness and surprise on Toby's face as he was placed on the soft clay. Seeing Toby out of danger, Sam grabbed one of Joseph's shoulders and yanked him face down onto the riverbank, as the remainder of the bridge, hissing and smoking, sank into the river.

The assembled crowd began to loudly clap and holler. Jesse ran to Toby and held him in one long embrace. "Never ever do that to me again! Understand!" she said, as tears came down her cheeks in brown rivulets.

Toby finished hugging his mother and looked up into her face. "Mom you look like a big mud pie. I bet you can start a big dirt pile with your clothes." Jesse laughed and everyone else around her broke up laughing.

Sam came over to Joseph who was still on the ground. He extended his hand to lift him up. "You did it, man."

Joseph stood up, mud on the tip of his nose. "I guess I can breathe now."

"Now you can," Sam said with a beaming smile.

The crowd surrounded Joseph. They shook his hand and patted him on the shoulder.

Jesse yelled out, "I want to meet the man who helped my son."

As she spoke, the entire town was plunged into darkness. Joseph stood on the bank saying, "Now they decide to turn off the power…"

CHAPTER 13

The short, balding man spoke in a serious monotone voice as he directed the small, red dot of light from the laser pointer to the three dimensional molecule rear-projected on the wide, white screen of the conference room, recessed in the dark walnut wall paneling. The room, located in the Federal Building below ground level, had dark blotches from the water damage caused by the flooding. The agents sat around the conference table, absorbed in the precise, technical details of bomb making. Dr. Dan Schelling was on assignment for the past week from the FBI Explosives Unit headquartered in Quantico, Virginia. Schelling, a veteran of several major investigations, including the bombing of the World Trade Center in 1993, and the Nairobi and Dar es Salaam embassies in 1998, was an expert on Improvised Explosive Devices, and had a reputation for being thorough and meticulous in his field work. He stood in front of the conference table and continued his presentation, "We were able to find a sample metal fragment approximately fifty-feet northwest of the tanks. It is labeled AE-1 in the photograph found on page seven of your folders." There was a massive sound of shuffling papers as everyone in the room turned to the page. "The fragment had a substantial amount of the residual explosive charge. Using gas chromatograph analysis, we determined the base charge, composed of nitrocellulose with nitroglycerine, increased the blast energy. These are fairly common explosives, found in the construction of many pipe bombs."

Sattler rubbed his bloodshot eyes. Sitting across from Sattler around the conference table, Sam wrote notes on his legal pad. He noticed the signs of exhaustion in Sattler's behavior— reduced hand/eye coordination and slowed speech. The four hours of sleep a night over the past two weeks began to take its toll. Overall, the investigation was becoming a public relations embarrassment for the FBI. The bombing was featured on the three major networks. The press emphasized in the reports that the second bombing occurred in the town next to Pope's Mills, virtually under the nose of the FBI. The next day, in a high level meeting with the Bureau Chiefs from Washington, it was decided Sattler would be replaced if there were no significant progress.

Drawing a sip from his mug of coffee, Sattler asked, "Are you saying the people responsible here are different than the people involved in the Pope's Mills dam collapse?"

"Quite to the contrary, there are quite a few similarities."

"Educate me then. In Pope's Mills the base explosive was RDX, right?"

Schelling put down the pointer and faced the agents assembled. "The device used in Pope's Mills also had a TNT precursor. But in both instances, we found traces of Dibutyl Phthalate and Methyl Centralite used to plasticize and stabilize the base explosive, respectively. I would say there is a one in a million probability that two people creating explosives would have used exactly the same additives down to their specific chemical structures. Our conclusion is that these agents came from the same lab."

"What about the truck. Did you find any residuals there?"

"The truck was in the water for a period of time and the evidence obtained from it is not as easy to analyze as the metal from the tanks. Yes, we performed some preliminary chemical tests of the metal and found micro traces of nitroglycerin. It's likely the truck was used to carry the explosives. We'll have more information on that at a later date."

Jefferies took over the questioning, "Does anything you have found match any profiles we have on file?"

"Over the two weeks since Pope's Mills, we've done an extensive search through our database looking for any matches. Of course, there've been similar explosives used, but nothing with the same chemical composition. We know many bombers have "signatures:" they build the same type of bombs or have similar targets. In this case, two water supply systems have been attacked. The fact that we cannot match any existing profiles leads us to believe Pope's Mill and Gottlieb Heights may be the first times the bomber has attempted anything. The perpetrators may be "new on the block" but I'm impressed with the level of knowledge involved in the construction of the devices. Whoever was responsible did his research. Obviously, the bomber selected what he felt was the most appropriate explosive for the job. My gut instinct and my twenty years of experience tells me that a target like Pope's Mills was chosen well in advance."

Sattler said, "The advanced target selection confirms our thinking. Thank you, and please keep us posted as to your progress." As Schelling sat down at the conference table, Sattler turned to Jeffries. "I've read your interview report with Ms. Richmond with great interest."

Jeffries nodded. "She says a man stopped at her service station about an hour before the explosion with a yellow 1978 Ford Truck. The Ford Truck matches the one we found in the gully. We later did an analysis on the metal and determined the truck had been red, meaning it was most likely the same truck used in Pope's Mills. Anyhow, she spent a few minutes with the man and we got a good description. A sketch artist produced this shot." Jefferies projected the computer-animated image on the large screen. It was a man in his mid-twenties to early thirties, baseball cap, a thin face, and blue eyes.

"Now, can you show us the enhanced photo from Pope's Mills?" Sattler asked.

Jefferies pressed a couple of buttons on his laptop and the image changed to the photograph of the man in the red truck. Sattler examined the features of the face for a moment and then said, "Can you show us a side by side for comparison?"

Sattler stood up smiling in satisfaction. "It definitely matches the photo we got of the man in the truck from Pope's Mills. Have we got a fingerprint crew dusting the truck?"

Jefferies responded, "We started doing that yesterday. We got a few partials. We tried matching them in our database and came up with nothing."

"Have you got a vehicle ID number from the wreckage of the truck?"

"Yes, we both got a license plate and vehicle number. We tracked the vehicle number to a truck stolen from a Louisville suburb about a month ago. The license plate was taken from another red ford truck of similar vintage also in the Louisville area. It was switched with the plate of the stolen truck in an apparent attempt to confuse the local police. I would say it worked. Anyway, who would care about the theft of an older vehicle? I'm afraid it's another dead end."

Sattler reviewed the report again. "I see no mention of the second suspect. Did Ms. Richmond see anyone else in the truck?"

"No. Do you think this time Suspect Number One acted alone?"

Sattler hesitated for a moment. "I don't think so. Maybe this time Suspect Number Two cased out the area prior to the planting of the explosives."

Jefferies looked through his paperwork saying, "I believe Agent Conway has something with regard to that."

A young agent, a recent academy graduate, stood up. "Actually, the information came to us in a background check of Tom Owens, the maintenance man found in the gully." Conway launched into a description of Owens, one of the half dozen maintenance people working for the Gottlieb Heights Water Department. Interviews with his co-workers revealed he followed the same daily routine of doing maintenance on the machinery in the town water treatment facility in the morning and after getting an Italian sub at the local farm store and then moving on to the tank farm on the hill. Bank records indicated that on this particular Friday, he deviated slightly from the routine and made a withdrawal from an ATM in town.

Sattler interrupted the agent's description of the last hours of Tom Owens life, "I appreciate all the homework you did. Can you just 'cut to the chase' and tell us how this relates to Suspect Number Two?"

Conway projected a videotape onto the screen. "This is the tape we got from the bank machine. At first glance we saw nothing unusual. But I would like to draw your attention to the upper right-hand corner of the frame. We have blown it up here. There is a yellow Camaro that slows down as it passes behind Owens and then speeds up as it exits." The image changed to a convenience store. "We also got the tape from the farm store surveillance system. There are two cameras in the store, including one that monitors the front cash registers." The tape showed a man in a Water Department shirt standing at the counter. "You can see in the street behind the store window a yellow Camaro pulling into a parking spot as Owens pays for the sub. He was obviously followed. We sent the tape from the bank to the Special Photographic Division and got an image of the face of the driver." Conway projected the face of a man in his late twenties with long, dark hair and brown eyes.

Sattler stood up from his chair and hit his hand on the table in an effort to keep the agents motivated. "We should put ourselves in the shoes of the bombers. The tank site was protected by a chain link fence. I could break through the fence, but I wouldn't want the maintenance man to walk in on me while I was planting the explosives and alert the police. It would make sense that I follow him to the site to make certain he was dead before I did anything. So you think this man may be Suspect Number Two?" Sattler asked, looking around the table at the other agents.

Jefferies said, "Our analysts have reviewed it and found it matches the general description of the shorter man the boy saw on the dam in Pope's Mills."

"So does five percent of the male population in the Commonwealth of Kentucky," Sattler said sarcastically. "We need something else to tie the man in the Camaro to the bombings other than him trailing Owens before he died. We need to canvas the city with the photo and see if anyone recognizes the face." He turned to Jefferies, "Did you interview the homeowners who live in the vicinity of the tanks? A local—or someone—must have seen one of the suspects before the tanks blew."

"We interviewed about a hundred people and maybe a half dozen thought they *may have* noticed two people in the vicinity of the tanks. We got no specific descriptions, just people saying they looked up and briefly saw two figures on the walls of the tank. You have to realize, the tanks are partially screened by trees and even if it were a bright, sunny day, I think we would have trouble finding eyewitnesses. In this case, it was raining and people were staying indoors."

"Keep working on it," Sattler said, at the limit of his patience.

Sattler leaned back in his chair, closing his eyes in an effort to relax. "I think what is hampering us is that we still do not have a handle on the motive. No doubt water is being used as some sort of weapon of mass destruction. In Pope's Mills, the target of the dam break is not clear. Here in Gottlieb Heights, I could say definitely that it was the Federal Building. I wonder if anyone has given it any consideration."

"I know what we could eliminate as the motive," Jefferies said. "We have not received any extortion notes from the bombers…at least not so far. So we know the motive is not money. No terrorist groups have come forward to take responsibility, so, most likely, the bombers have no political agenda. The only other major reason left is 'revenge.' Seeing how badly the Federal Building was damaged, I would say it was someone trying to avenge himself with the government. Now, that's a big area. There've been many groups promising vengeance with the government. We'd only broken the surface when we interviewed Cecil Millar with the Klan; there are plenty of organizations out there with similar agendas."

One of agents rose, "Maybe not an organization but a person with an accomplice or two, someone with a bone to pick with both Pope's Mills and Gottlieb Heights."

"We went by that assumption when we initially investigated Pope's Mills. We found nothing. What you are really hinting at is that both communities may share something in common. I think once we discover what that is, we will be all that much closer to the identity of the suspects." The meeting ran over three hours and Sattler could see that everyone around the table was becoming restless. "One last thing I want to mention before we break. Last time we all met in Pope's Mills, I asked why water is being used. The people doing this obviously have access to explosives, or can fabricate them. Why not simply use the explosives to destroy the targets. Maybe water has some sort of symbolic importance."

Jefferies started running through a list of items, "To most people, water symbolizes life, water is a dream symbol for birth, and children are baptized in water …"

Something clicked in Sattler's mind. "Maybe someone is associating some sort of religious significance with this event. Maybe we're dealing with some type of cult. Why don't you take a couple of agents to see if there are any cults operating in this area?"

Jefferies smiled uncomfortably, "I will make that priorities number fifty two and fifty three."

"I know you are working sixteen hour days. But you understand the pressure we're under. I am sure you will find the time."

Everyone got up to leave as Sam gathered his papers in front of him, ready to work the tip line. Sattler called him back, "Perhaps you want to stick around. I was going to call Dr. Hamiz down to see what he has to say about the tanks. He seems much less nervous when you are around." Sattler was not blind to the friendship that developed between Sam and Joseph, and he was going to use it for its maximum benefit.

Sam sat back down and nodded at Joseph as he timidly opened the oak door to the room, computer in hand. Joseph searched the receptacles around the conference table and finally, after a few minutes, found an outlet to connect the display port of his computer to the conference room screen. Sattler waited for Joseph to set up and then asked in a low-key manner, "So tell us what you've got."

"I followed the same procedure I used in Pope's Mills. I went to the town engineer's office and I got the plans for the water supply system. The system operation is really quite straightforward in principle. It is based on the concept there is less water demand during the day when people are away from home working, than in the evening or the morning when they are back in their houses using their dishwashers, flushing toilets, and taking showers. So during the day, water is pumped from the water treatment plant into storage so it can be discharged to the customers in the evening. This would lead me to believe that at four-thirty in the afternoon, when the tanks were blown up, they were most likely at peak capacity."

Jefferies chimed in, "The time was chosen because four-thirty was when most people were leaving the Federal Building for the day, and the loss of life would be maximized."

There was awkward silence in the room. Sattler looked though paperwork when he said, "Do you have any additional information for us?"

Joseph pulled up his notes from the computer screen. There was a profile showing the maximum elevation of the wave along the gully. "I developed a mathematical simulation of the tank break and was able to confirm the results from the water marks on the Federal Building. Initially, I was not able to match the observed water levels. The results were ten feet lower than the watermarks. It was readily apparent that I was not maximizing the elevation. I reviewed all my assumptions, which included the tanks being blown at the same time. I was only able to match the water levels when I lagged the failures. I did a number of simulations, and found that to match the damage that was observed, the tanks must have been blown about fifty seconds apart."

Jefferies said, "Fifty seconds difference, huh. Now that is interesting—that the bomber knew to do that. Jefferies turned to Sattler, "What he says makes sense. Some witnesses did report hearing the explosions in two groups."

Sattler lifted his head from the papers, "It doesn't surprise me the bomber had some engineering training."

"That sounds like an understatement. Looks like the perpetrator had done a lot of work in the area," Jefferies retorted.

Sattler said, "It was part of our initial psychological profile. We may want to do another database search of graduate schools when we have more information. Dr. Hamiz, we appreciate your insights. Even though the bomber has switched tactics, I still think we need you doing your work on dams. We may still be at risk regarding those structures."

Joseph collected his notes, putting them neatly into a thick manila folder, and placing them in their spot in his briefcase. Before closing the case, he took out another folder labeled "Newspaper." He quickly slid the folder to Sam who asked, "What's this?"

"I thought that you would find it amusing. It is a copy of the front pages of the *Pope's Mills Gazette* on April 17th, the day the dam collapsed, and the *Gottlieb Heights Herald Times* for May 2nd, when the tanks were blown."

Jefferies was confused, "I don't understand what these newspaper headlines have to do with our investigation?"

Sam reviewed the articles. "They're not recent. They're ten years old."

Joseph went around the table and looked over Sam's shoulder. "After you told me the story about Jake Adamson, I thought I would check the newspaper archives. I overheard that Adamson's arrest occurred on the same date the dam was blown up, and I thought it might be interesting to pull the newspaper." There was a large article on page one about the arrest, with a large black and white photograph of him in handcuffs surrounded by the sheriff and deputies. The article had the usual details regarding the arrest, including a dramatic description of Sam Sr. breaking down the door of the farmhouse and the background information regarding Jake's earlier arrest for trespassing and disorderly conduct.

Moving to the upper copy, Joseph said, "Now here's the article from May 2nd." The *Herald Times* had a smaller color photograph of Jake in an orange jumpsuit, being led into the recently completed Federal Courthouse. "What fascinated me was that the preliminary hearing was held on the same date the tanks were blown."

Sam scratched his head, "Yes, now that you mention it, it is an interesting coincidence. It would answer a lot of questions as to why Pope's Mills and Gottlieb Heights were the targets of the bomber, especially the Federal Building here."

"I think that's all it is: a 'coincidence,'" Sattler said, "We went down this road when we did our Pope's Mills investigation. There is nothing that would lead us to believe anybody associated with the affair would be responsible for the simple reason that everyone close to Adamson is dead. While I appreciate the thought, I don't like the idea of anyone wasting time, especially when we are under pressure from the public. My advice to you, Dr. Hamiz, is to concentrate on the areas of your expertise, and let us think about the possible motive."

"Sorry sir," Joseph said, bowing in deference. "I thought I was helping out." Joseph closed up his briefcase and quickly walked out of the conference room.

Sam stood up out of his seat and gave Sattler a hostile stare. "Now that you mention it," he said, his voice dripping with sarcasm, "I should go back to my 'area of expertise,' which happens to be the phone tip line. Excuse me...*Sir.*" Notes in hand, Sam strode out of the room, slamming the oak door behind him. Sam's departure left Jefferies sitting around the teak conference table alone with Sattler, who had gone back to reviewing reports on his notebook.

Jefferies picked up the copies of the newspaper articles that were on the conference table. He mused out loud, "What if Hamiz is right and the answer to this thing is right in front of us?"

***

When Joseph came back to the makeshift office on the third floor, he saw Sam with headphones, taking notes on a legal pad at a long folding table. The furnishings, sparse even by government standards, included two surplus metal desks with scratched gray tops lining a bare white wall and three green, rusted file cabinets on the other wall. The folding table sat squarely in the center of the room.

Joseph turned on the computer and was about to do database work when he was interrupted by a soft knocking on the wooden office door. For an office conducting a government investigation, there were few formalities; usually people came through the office unannounced. Joseph tentatively opened the door a few inches and saw a curly haired, red-headed woman wearing tight fitting jeans, and a crisp, gray work shirt.

"Hello there," she said in a low voice, smiling.

There was an air of familiarity in her voice and Joseph stood in the door, staring ahead and trying to place her. "Do I know you from someplace?"

"I'm Jesse... you know...Toby's mother."

"I am sorry, I did not recognize you."

Jesse laughed. "I was covered in mud, wasn't I? I clean up well."

"I heard they rescued you from a car. I hope you are okay."

"I feel fine except for a few stitches they gave me at the hospital. I feel like the rag doll my mother gave me when I was five years old, with stuffing coming out. May I come in? I was talking to one of the FBI agents in the building, and I thought I should stop by. I wanted to meet you to thank you in person for saving my son's life."

Joseph realized he was blocking the doorway and stepped aside, allowing Jesse to walk in. "In all honesty, I felt obligated," he said. "I don't know what I would do if something happened to him. He seemed like such a nice boy."

"He really is sweet. Even though he likes to argue with people too much—but that's common for his age. He's playing video games at a friend's house as we speak. I came up here to mention that Gottlieb Heights is having a dinner tomorrow tonight at the Moose Hall for all the people who helped out in the emergency. If you want, you can come as my guest."

Joseph thought for a moment, "Thank you, but the FBI is making extensive demands for my time. I need to run some calculations."

Somewhat taken aback, Jesse said, "Maybe on Sunday the three of us can get together for dinner, and you can see Toby again."

"I don't know where I am going to be on Sunday. But I will keep that in mind," Joseph said tentatively.

Embarrassed about being rejected twice, Jesse's demeanor changed from warm to cold. "Alright then, I see you're busy. I should let you get your work done. She got up and officiously shook Joseph's hand. "I just want to thank you again." She walked away, her footsteps resonating down the corridor.

Sam saw her trot off. *"Are you goddamed crazy, man.* If a woman like that came up to me and asked about dinner, I'd go in a heartbeat."

Joseph started tapping at the computer, bringing data up onto his screen. "I have good reason for not wanting to get involved with a local. I know nothing about her, except that she fixes cars in a garage. So, I would sit there trying to speak about topics she would not understand, and she would probably talk about cars. I can not think of a more miserable way to spend an evening."

"So you think that she's beneath you? She does not merit your time because she does not have a doctorate or some advanced degree from a university?"

"I am not saying that. I am merely observing that we have nothing in common." Joseph thought that Sam did not understand the mores that he had grown up with. It was not a matter of superiority or inferiority. Everyone deserved courtesy, respect, and politeness. One simply did not interact with people outside of one's social status. His parents consorted with people in academia because they themselves had met at a university. People who went to college did not socialize with people who had no formal education. He was expected, one day, to marry into a family that had the same values as his parents. This ensured continuity from generation to generation.

"Nobody is asking you to become romantically involved with the woman. It was an invitation to be social, to meet other people, to have dinner and talk."

"One thing my father had always noted was that Americans are pretentious about everything. They can speak at great length about nothing. To talk to someone just to be social is a waste of time—and disrespectful."

Sam was disappointed and annoyed that Joseph was distancing himself from others, and that his callous, sometimes arrogant attitude had not changed in light of recent events. He leaned over the table and said gruffly, "I know now why you're not married. You understand everything about science and numbers, and nothing about people. I don't know anything about Jesse. For all intents and purposes she could be someone with an elementary school education who can barely read or write, but I'm certain, given your background, she would have volumes of knowledge about the life you've been missing."

***

Jesse watched from the front table as the crowd shuffled back and forth on the bright yellow linoleum floor. With over two hundred people in attendance, the hall was at near-capacity. The room was beginning to get hot, even though all of the windows and doors were open to the evening breeze. Jesse stood by one of the doors in one of the only two dresses she owned, letting the cool air wash over her. The buffet dinner was late and people who already had had five beers from the open bar were talking loudly, the sound echoing in the metal-sided building that resembled a small aircraft hanger. All the big events in Gottlieb Heights took place in the Moose Hall, from weddings, proms, to town festivals. The band was setting up on the stage behind her, and Jesse looked on as the musicians fumbled with their guitars, basses, and banjos.

Jesse cup was getting low on beer and people were periodically coming by to offer a refill. Jesse would politely refuse them. She did not like getting drunk, although, this night she was thinking of breaking that rule. She hated being the center of attention and figured the alcohol would lower her anxiety. There were fifteen people sitting at the front table, including the mayor, the head of the city council, and the police and fire department staff. Initially, they all gave their greetings and then politely engaged in their own conversation.

Occasionally, people would come over to kiss her, including some men she did not remember, many of them saying, "We're very proud of you." One of them was Steve Duggin, her high school shop teacher who liked to dress up in a white cowboy hat and tall, brown leather boots. She found this amusing since Steve was born in Amherst, Mass, and Kentucky was the farthest west he had traveled. In high school, he was a mentor who taught her the finer points of engines. He hugged her for a minute, running his hands along her lower back towards her buttocks. She smiled politely as she pushed him away. Out of general courtesy, Jesse chatted with him, commenting on how well he looked. When she first met him, he was in his late thirties, had muscular arms and chest. Now, in his early forties, he had tints of gray in his thinning hair and his stomach was paunchier. As Duggin spoke about his personal life, Jesse asked herself whether or not he was trying to pick her up, and how silly and vain it was a for man to date a woman that was nearly twenty years younger.

As people were starting to sit down, Joseph, who standing in line for soda, looked to the front and saw Jesse involved in her conversation with Duggin. He decided not to introduce himself. He had entered the hall ten minutes before and was still situating himself. The front table was first to be called to get their food at the buffet table. As Jesse got up, she noticed Joseph and gave a faint smile. Joseph had his back turned to her, and he was oblivious to her gaze. With a glass of Coke in his hand, he scouted out a nearly empty table towards the back. It quickly filled with people. Joseph tried finding someone who was familiar to him in the crowd. Even someone like Agent Sattler or Jefferies from the FBI would have been a welcome relief. His worst fear, spending time with an entire room of strangers, was becoming true.

Being towards the back, Joseph's table was the last to be called. He filled his plate with ham, chicken, and a salad of greens. When he came back to the table, a man with a medium-length, salt and pepper beard and yellowed teeth sat next to him with a plate full of wings covered with barbecue sauce. After a dozen chicken wings, he extended his chicken grease and barbecue sauce covered hand out to Joseph, "Hi. My name is Ned," he said as he took a swig of beer. Joseph introduced himself, gingerly shaking Ned's hand. Sauce on his hands from Ned, Joseph took a handkerchief from his pants pocket and wiped off his fingers. Ned apologized, "I'm sorry. They have not invented a neat way of eating wings. I don't believe I've seen you around town. I'm one of the volunteer firemen. Are you from one the companies in the area?"

"No, I am afraid I am not. I am here with the FBI."

Ned went back to devouring the wings; appearing intimidated when he heard "FBI." Joseph continued to eat and was halfway through his dinner when Mayor Sheppard got up to speak. Joseph noticed that Sheppard looked a good ten years younger than Mayor Williams of Pope's Mills and presented a more professional public persona. Most people would have called him a "yuppie." He was wearing a tan suede sports jacket with matching colored trousers. He introduced everyone at the head table, and then launched into his formal remarks. "I generally don't make speeches at these dinners, but I have a few brief announcements I want to make. First of all, I would like to thank the firemen, policemen, and the EMT's for their quick response to the emergency. We owe them our lives." Everyone stood as the room broke into spontaneous applause. The Mayor continued, "Secondly, I want to thank Beverly Warren for picking up the cost of the food for this meal. She did this out of her gratitude to everyone who helped out. She suffered the loss of her husband, Herbert, who was a good friend of ours. Beverly is resting in the hospital on her way to recovery, and she needs our love and support in her hour of grief."

Sheppard paused for a moment and turned his head toward Jesse, as if to make a dramatic gesture. "With everyone pitching in, I do not like to single out anyone in particular. However, I do want to mention one person who is sitting at this table with us tonight…Jesse Richmond. It was her bravery and perseverance that saved Beverly's life. Her determined, fighting spirit is an example to all of us." There was another round of clapping and whistling. Jesse sat there, blushing. She modestly stood up and acknowledged the crowd. "Her business received major damage as a result of the bombing. She has little insurance, and I am starting a fund to make the necessary repairs so she can get back on her feet again. There are also a few contractors who volunteered their services to help out. I just want to say that no one is alone in this community. What impacts *one* of us affects *all* of us. Together, we will make it through this difficult time. In a few minutes the band will play some music. We will clear the floor and I hope people can stay for some entertainment, and drop some money in the jar."

Joseph continued to eat and was planning to make an exit from the hall in a few minutes. He wanted to allow Jesse to show her gratitude, but he felt like a stranger and did not to become involved in her affairs. When he stood up with his empty plate, ready to leave, he saw Ned standing and pointing his finger at him. "Now I know who you are. I saw you on TV. You were the fella that saved the boy down at the river."

"Yes, I was one of the people who helped." Joseph wondered how many people recognized him from television. When Joseph was identified as one of Toby's rescuers, all he could say to the reporter, in a stiff voice, was how happy he was Toby was alright. Now Joseph wondered if when he got back to the university, would be incessantly questioned about his role.

"They say you're from Lebanon. Is that Lebanon, Pennsylvania or Lebanon, Indiana?"

"That is Lebanon, the country."

Ned laughed, chicken bone in mouth. "Now I feel stupid. Isn't that somewhere around Greece?

"It is on the northern border of Israel in the Middle East. It has some very rugged mountain terrain, very similar to what you find here in Kentucky. The mountain region was home to many feudal warlords who all vied for control of the government during the civil war."

"So who rules there now?"

"You mean what kind of government?"

"Isn't there a King Farruk or something like that?"

"Lebanon is a democracy—actually, a republic. The head of the government is elected by the legislature. There is a National Assembly that has one hundred and twenty-eight seats." Joseph scratched his head, "At least, I think that is the correct number. There are political parties just as in America, except they are more motivated by religious and clan issues than political ideology."

"So, that's why there was a civil war, because of the clans?"

"Yes, I suppose you could say that, but it is difficult to give a brief and accurate answer to a question that spans decades, if not centuries. The war could be quite simply described as a seminal conflict between Christians and Muslims, between which there have been previous battles in the 1800s and 1900s. However, this is a great oversimplification since Lebanon can claim itself to be home to several minority groups including Christians, Druze, Shias, and Jews. Some ascribe the war to part of the class struggle between rich Christians and the Moslem poor. These internal conflicts existed before the war flared up in 1975, but until that point Lebanon had a democratic system that was unique to other Arab countries in the Middle East…"

Jesse noticed Joseph was beginning to lecture Ned and strolled over, "Maybe Dr. Hamiz will finish answering your questions later. Do you mind if I borrow him for a while?"

"No problem, little lady," Ned said, tipping his hat to Jesse and sitting back down to his food.

"I thought I would rescue you from answering questions all night," Jesse said apologetically. "I know it's impolite to ask so many but pay no mind to him; he's just curious about you."

Joseph said rigidly, "No, I am not offended. I got a full education about the United States when I was in elementary school in Lebanon, and I noted a long time ago Americans do not receive a similar education about Arab countries."

"I guess we have a gap we need to bridge between our cultures," Jesse responded. "I thought that coming here to dinner tonight would allow you to learn about us a little."

"In the twenty years I have been in this country, I traveled all around the East and West Coasts."

"Uh, huh. I'm glad I'm dealing with an expert," Jesse smiled politely.

The band finished setting up their instruments. The lead musician picked up his fiddle and country western music echoed though the hall. People got up from their chairs and began dancing. Jesse nudged Joseph on the elbow, "Perhaps you want to be a gentleman and do me the courtesy of a dance?"

Joseph shyly followed Jesse onto the dance floor where there was a line forming. Staring down at the floor, Joseph tried to match the steps, stepping on the feet of the woman next to him. "I am sorry, the footwork looked simple."

The woman smiled back, "No problem, honey, we all have to learn sometime."

Jesse saw Joseph getting increasingly frustrated. He stepped on the woman's foot again. This time she moved to another position in line. Thankfully, the line dance was over and the band started playing swing-style music. Jesse grabbed Joseph's arm and started twisting her hips. He stayed stationary, not knowing how to react. Duggan saw his opportunity and came over, "Can I break in?"

Humbled enough; Joseph lifted his hands, "By all means." Duggan took over, clasping Jesse's hands and whispering into her ear.

The salted meats made Joseph thirsty. Not readily finding another soda, he took a bottle of beer from the steel tub on the floor, and started to drink. Jesse and Duggan were dancing within inches of one another. Joseph watched them for a moment and then decided to leave the hall. He found a bench outside the front entrance, and sipped on the beer under the clouded nighttime sky. The lot had a surreal, eerie illumination with the grills and hoods of the cars shinning in the light of the full moon. The beer felt good going down his throat, and Joseph closed his eyes and relaxed. He was halfway through the beer when heard footsteps behind him. "Mind if I join you," the voice said.

Jesse sat next to him. Surprised, Joseph turned to her. "I thought you were going to dance with your friend."

"Oh, he is just an old acquaintance, nothing more. I came out here because I was concerned you weren't having a good time."

"I just needed some air. That is all. I do not do very well with large crowds of people."

"Me neither. I consider myself a socially shy person."

"I saw you talking to a many men, and I was worried a boyfriend would be offended if he saw us dancing."

"None of them are my boyfriend. As a matter of fact, I'm not seeing anyone at the present time. All the men around here remind me of my ex-husband; a lot of them just want to get inside your pants. When I was young, I made the mistake of obliging one of them. I don't plan on making the same mistake twice. Anyhow, I didn't come out here to talk about men. To be honest, I wanted to apologize for what went on in there. I don't blame you for being mad."

"Mad about what? I am a poor dancer."

"Not that. The way the Mayor treated you."

"I don't understand."

"You risked your life and he gave it no mention during his introduction. I find it unforgivable to treat foreigners that way."

"Oh, I am used to that. I didn't come for recognition. I prefer he did not say anything. I would have been embarrassed."

"Then why did you come?"

"I came because you asked me. I thought it was rude to refuse your invitation."

"So you did it just to be polite?" Jesse pretended to be offended.

"No, I also came here because…"

"Because …why?"

"I realize that I gave you bad impression after our conversation at the Federal Building. I thought we could talk a little more," Joseph said nervously.

"So, what do you want to talk about?" Jesse responded playfully.

"I am curious about one thing…maybe you can answer this question. Why do you repair cars? That's a strange profession for a woman."

"Yes, not too many women work on cars. The obvious answer would be I took it up because my father fixed cars. Time goes fast when you are working on a car and I would be completely bored if I had a desk job somewhere. An engine is something you can feel and touch. And it's not entirely physical work; there is a mental component. It's like being a doctor, having a list of symptoms and trying to find a problem."

"'A doctor: isn't that an exaggeration?"

"No, not at all. People have skin, a brain, circulatory system, sweat glands that keep you cool, and lungs that take in air. Cars have roughly the same parts: a metal body, computers, water, oil and gas pumps, radiators, and carburetors."

Joseph thought for a moment, "I see your point. I am sorry I do not think mechanically."

"When you really think about it, most everything we do involves a car, so I look at myself as someone who performs an essential service." Jesse stood from her seat. "I'm a little hyper. Mind if we walk a little." As Joseph looked up, his eyes caught Jesse's. The parking lot lights illuminated her body through her sheer, flowered dress. Joseph sat back admiring the silhouette. Her legs were short, but in good proportion to her hips. Her waist curved in delicately, and her breasts were nicely rounded. As she strolled down a row of cars, hoods gleaming in the moonlight, she called back, "Are you coming, or are you going to vegetate on the bench all night?"

Joseph snapped out of his dream and joined her.

"This place reminds me of happier more innocent times. I used to come up here when I was a kid with my parents. We used to listen to country music together and then go to the dances. After I first got married to Keith, nearly every Friday night, we used go out to the movies, get some ice cream, and park in a spot right down there." She pointed to a parking spot at the end of row. "It was in one of those red Chevy Impala convertibles. We were in the back seat, top down, on a clear warm night in July, during which you could see all the stars in the sky. Come to think of it, I have cars in my blood. My parents told me I was conceived in a Buick Roadster; my mother gave birth to me in a yellow Thunderbird; and I nearly died a few days ago in a Continental. Judging how my life has turned out, I will probably die in a car, but now I hope it will be peacefully, at a ripe old age."

Joseph didn't want to hear anymore about death and asked, "How is Toby? I missed him tonight. I thought you would bring him."

"You think *I'm* hyper. He's worse. He would be running around creating trouble. He's with a baby-sitter. I think you've met her, Mrs. Buxley—she lives down the road; you borrowed some wood from her. You and the sheriff made quite the impression."

"Oh, the woman with the Terrier dog," Joseph said with some anxiety in his voice.

"Toby has been talking about you for the past couple of days, 'the mysterious man' who saved his life."

"I am not very mysterious." Joseph shrugged his head.

"I've explained why I work on cars. How did you get involved with dams?"

"Lebanon is a land of forests and mountains, and has more sources of water than other Middle Eastern countries, but water supply is still a source of conflict. I have always dreamed of creating water systems for people, so they could develop the land." Jesse seemed bored with the explanation and Joseph smiled and said. "Okay, the real reason I took it up was Jack Nicholson."

Jesse perked up, "Jack Nicholson, the actor? You're loosing me."

"*Chinatown* was one of my father's favorite movies. He must have seen it about twenty times. That movie is about building a dam for Los Angeles in the 1940's. Dams were always on my mind. I worked for the Pennsylvania Department of Environmental Protection in their Dam Safety Division when I was a student at Penn State. I have been working with dams ever since."

"I'm sure working in for the university goes a long way toward your dreams."

"I wish I could be so confident. Sometimes I think I am just passing the time." Joseph became quiet and reflective. Strains of country music could be heard from the building. Jesse moved her hips according to the beat as Joseph looked on curiously.

"Lemme show you how to line dance," Jesse said as she grabbed Joseph's hand.

"This is a parking lot."

"So what?"

"I have never danced before in a parking lot."

"Looks like you haven't done very much dancing, period. This is just as good a place as any. It's really very simple. Just watch me."

She stepped her right foot forward and then rocked back on her left, keeping pace with the music. Joseph looked down at her feet and copied her movement. Her toe grazing the asphalt, she crossed her left foot over to the right side. Joseph clumsily stepped over to the right. Jesse grabbed his shoulder, steadying him, and said, "Do it gently with your foot just touching the ground, like you are walking on air." Joseph repeated the motion, this time sliding his foot, making a "swishing" sound on the asphalt. Jesse grimaced and then laughed, "You look like a wounded steer. Relax a little, just think of yourself with a bunch of beautiful women who are all smiling at you, and you're in heaven." Joseph grinned and then, in slow motion, moved the tip of his foot across the hard surface. Jesse made a one-quarter turn right, and then, while swinging her hips, swept her booted toe out towards the left side and placed her hands on Joseph's hips. He did not seem to notice that they moved in unison. "See you have it," she announced proudly.

Just as Joseph was getting into the rhythm, the music stopped and the band began playing a ballad. He started to walk away. "This is a slow song. I am sure you do not want to dance to this one."

Jesse took both of Joseph's hands. "These are also simple. The man is supposed to hold the woman's right arm and put his right arm on her waist."

"Be careful. I do not want to step on your feet," Joseph said nervously.

"Don't worry, I will watch out for you. There is nothin' to it; you feel what your partner is doing and follow her." Jesse gazed into Joseph's blue eyes. "They always play the slow tunes towards the end of the dance. By that time, you have selected the girl you want to hang with for the rest of the evening. If you're lucky, the woman would be tired and put her head on your shoulder like this." Jesse slowly placed her head down, resting it besides Joseph's head. She began to whisper in his ear, "You both move as one and as she looks up into your eyes, you can feel everything your partner feels."

The music stopped again but Jesse continued to hold Joseph in her arms. "You see that's all there is to know about dancing. The real secret is, all you need is a good partner."

Chapter 14

T he Clark mansion was quiet; the only sound was a single FBI agent downstairs answering the phone. A new crop of agents had been added to the investigation and were occupying the FBI offices in the Gottleib Federal Building. Joseph had moved back to Pope's Mills in order to meet their space needs. He did not argue. He relished the idea of doing his work in relative quiet and solitude, not having the problem of Sattler or Jefferies looking over his shoulder, offering their comments.

He missed seeing Jesse. She had come over to the Gottlieb Federal Building office twice with cookies and donuts she had bought from the bakery in the center of town. She would hang over Joseph's shoulder, and ask questions about the work. All during the visits, Sam would be sitting back in his chair smiling. As Joseph checked his watch, he realized that it was about this time every afternoon that she brought food.

Joseph put away the set of blue prints, and wrote a few items on a sheet of paper for the database. As he did, he saw the box of paper from Dutton Anderson about the Kendall River. Needing a diversion from the routine of reviewing blueprints, he upended the box onto the oak desk. Joseph surmised Dutton did a thorough job researching the dam, nearly to the point of obsession, and had even collected hundreds of pages of water quality data for the Kendal River downstream. There were old Corps of Engineers planning studies from before the dam was constructed, pictures of the site before building had started and of the dam during construction. Joseph quickly thumbed through the pictures, having seen them before. He quickly lost interest and was about to put the material back into the box when he laid his hands on a packet of material labeled "Clark," wrapped in a rubber band.

The packet was a collection of biographical information taken from newspaper articles, press releases, pamphlets, and the Internet. From the information, it appeared that Clark embodied the "American Dream" of growing up on a small farm in rural Stockdale, Ohio and then becoming a multi-millionaire industrialist in Kentucky. Clark, born in 1919, was a product of the Depression. Spending his childhood and adolescence in relative poverty framed Clark's attitude toward work throughout his life. Excelling at science and math in high school, he went on scholarship to Purdue University where he majored in Civil Engineering and graduated in the top ten-percent of the class in 1940. After marrying a childhood sweetheart, he returned to Stockdale and was drafted into the Army, only to be rejected because he was nearly blind in his right eye. Still wanting to help his country, he got a job with the Louisville District Corps of Engineers in the Office of Planning. After spending two years working in planning for levees and miscellaneous small projects, he was named project manager and was given the responsibility for the design and construction of the dams. Working long hours at the Corps, his marriage unraveled. But he had the fortune of having been placed in charge of a group of engineers and geologists who designed the dam in Pope's Mills and then another on the Raccoon, a tributary to the Ohio River in Cummings, Ohio.

The Cummings Dam was what Clark deemed the "project of a lifetime," a one hundred and sixty-feet high gravity dam and power house with five turbines capable of creating power for fifty thousand people. The lake created by the dam was also used for recreational boating, and there was a five hundred acre park adjoining the lake complete with nature trails. The design would later win the regional Civil Engineering Achievement award for 1961. Joseph looked through the packet of information and found one of the publicity stills taken for a local newspaper. Situated between two hills that formed a constriction in the river, the grayish concrete structure had columns projecting from the curved concrete surface, making it look like a fortress. As an architectural embellishment, it had two square towers jutting out on either end of the dam, completing the castle-like appearance.

It was the Cummings Dam project that capped Clark's career at the Corps after nearly twenty years of service. After working with the Corps, Clark joined Farwell and Johnson, a modest sized design firm in Louisville with a staff of one-hundred people. He served as a Vice President, managing modest water projects in Illinois, Ohio, and Kentucky. After three years with the design firm, he became partners with Thomas Pope, speculating in real estate and development ventures. When Pope died in 1973, he became sole owner of the company, which ran the paper mill operation in Pope's Mills.

Joseph reclined in his chair having spent the better part of an hour reviewing the biographical information. He still did not see the connection between Clark's career and the destruction of the dam in Pope's Mills, or of the water tanks in Gottlieb. Joseph could only speculate as to why Dutton did the research on Clark. Joseph remembered that when he first met Dutton at the Collins Hotel, he had left the option open of speaking again. That was before the FBI arrested him. Maybe Dutton had changed his mind about cooperating. It was just about five o'clock in the afternoon, and Joseph decided to chance it and drive up to Dutton's cabin.

As Joseph drove on the private dirt road, he saw the blue pickup truck packed with moving boxes on a ten-foot long trailer. Dutton was in front, dressed in blue jean overalls, piling boxes into the trailer. He noticed Joseph pull up in his K-car and smiled. He put down the box and walked up to the car door. "Hello my friend, dropping by to say goodbye to me."

Joseph seemed surprised, "I never knew that you were leaving. Where are you going?"

Dutton scratched his head, "That's a funny question. I have not figured that out yet. I was fired yesterday, and I decided not to stick around to become some fungus on a rock. I plan on leaving tomorrow, but I have a few minutes to spare if you want to talk. Why don't you come in?" Dutton opened the door and walked back to the cabin. Joseph followed a few steps behind, breathing heavily, carrying the square box of records in his arms.

The interior of the cabin that seemed closed in on his first visit was now larger, with much of the furniture on the first floor having been moved. As Joseph entered, he almost tripped over the boxes of books and clothes on the floor, causing him to drop the record box, nearly spilling all the contents on the floor. Amused by the display of clumsiness, Dutton said, "I didn't need the records back. I am only going to throw them out, but I appreciate the thought."

"I was going to ask you a few questions about them," Joseph said trying to catch his breath.

"Before you do, I can see you need a break," Dutton said. He went to the refrigerator, pulled out a beer and threw it over to Joseph, who almost missed it in the dim light. "All the tea is packed. I'm sorry that this is the only beverage I can offer." He took a cigarette out of his pocket, and with a flick of a kitchen match, lit the tip. Dutton alternately took sips of beer and drags of the cigarette. "I used to care if I smoked in here, but now, given the circumstances, I don't give a fuck. Maybe I will start a fire and burn this place down. It ought to take all of ten minutes."

"You really don't mean that. So did they tell you why they were terminating you?"

"Other than screwing the Mayor's wife," Dutton laughed, "The reason quoted to me was that I had engaged in 'improper moral behavior,' whatever that means. I heard the Mayor had his hand in it. After the FBI interview, word must have leaked out about my affair with Beth. I never thought the FBI would keep quiet about it anyhow. Williams controls the school board, and it was the board that demanded my principal fire me."

"That is a shame. You seemed like a knowledgeable person who took great interest in his job," Joseph said, trying not to appear sorry for Dutton.

"Thank you, but I suppose I got myself into it. I guess if I really wanted to stay here, I wouldn't have let his wife come on to me. It is hard for me to deny, especially when the FBI walks in on us."

"I still have a few questions about the box of material," Joseph said earnestly.

"Ah hah...so, you are here to soak me for information before I leave— not because I am such a nice guy," Dutton playfully retorted with a smirk on his face.

"Well..." Joseph paused trying to be polite, "...yes. I suppose you could say that."

Dutton relaxed on a box. "Seriously, I'm glad you found the time to look through the records."

"It was a lot of information and quite frankly, I was overwhelmed by it." Joseph reached down into the stack of records and found a one-inch thick ream of paper covered with columns of numbers. "For example, this water quality data..."

"Collecting the information started with my students mentioning to me that their parents and friends were getting sick with various types of skin and intestinal cancers. I was floored when the State Department of Heath and Human Services in Frankford told me the cancer rate for Pope's Mills was approximately twenty percent higher than the other towns in the county."

"And you thought it all had to do with the concentration of PCB's and mercury in the river water, all byproducts of paper processing," Joseph said, looking at the table of numbers.

"...among other nasty things that they didn't even test for. Yes, I had mentioned it at a couple of Town Council meetings. They all ignored me. That turkey, Mayor Williams, just sat there with a vacant look in his eyes."

"Is that when you started researching Pope Paper? I saw your file on Matt Clark."

"Oh him," Dutton said in a condescending voice.

"How can you have a negative opinion about someone you had never met?"

"I don't hate him. Actually, I'm quite envious of someone who had such a good thing. From what I understand, he was a real golden boy; he could do nothing wrong. I came here in 1997, about four years after he died and people were still talking about him as if he was still running the place. People in this area are fairly clannish; so I asked myself, how could someone born in a small town in Ohio, a world away from Pope's Mills, gain so much influence?"

"Reading the file, I surmised that somehow he had met Thomas Pope, the son of the founder of the community," Joseph said sipping his beer.

"It is a bit more interesting than that," Dutton said, giving a mischievous smile. "To gain any insight on the matter, you really have to know a little local history. If you look at aerial photographs in the library, in the 1930's this town had only a general store and a couple of houses on the main road. The rest was all farmland, and if you stood on Poplar Street where the municipal building is, you would see only corn and alfalfa fields clear to the horizon. Thomas Pope owned about five thousand acres of farmland, which is not very valuable by itself. So good old Thomas was by no means a pauper, but he was not as rich as someone who had commercial land or who had ownership of a business making some sort of product."

Joseph broke in, "I still do not see the connection. I know Thomas Pope and Matt Clark became partners many years after the paper business was established."

"Be patient for a minute and let me continue developing the timeline. There was not much industrial growth in Kentucky in the 1930's, and in general, things did not start to happen until people started to return from World War II in 1943 and 1944. People were coming back from the war and having babies, and there was a significant demand for new housing. So say you're Thomas Pope, seeing all this happen. Everyone around you is making money hand over fist, building new factories to create the construction materials; and here you are sitting on five thousand acres of practically worthless farmland. There were two things that could add a great deal to the land value…it fronted the Kendall River, and it had a railroad. I would have loved to have been with Pope when he thought of building a paper plant. He probably saw a train carrying wood pulp going through town. Paper and cardboard are critical components of any construction material, and even better, once the building boom is over, you can make other types of products. When you think about it, Pope had all the ingredients necessary to create a fledgling paper industry …land, a supply of cheap labor from the farms, and a railroad to get the products to market. All he lacked was…"

"Water," Joseph called out loud.

"You get a gold star. I see you're catching on. Paper processing requires millions of gallons of water per day, well exceeding the flow of the river at certain times of the year. You need to recognize the Kendall was a modest size stream, nowhere near the base flow of the Ohio River, where many heavy industries are located. The lack of a steady supply of water was not insurmountable. Pope did not exist in a vacuum, and I am certain he heard about the Corps of Engineers building dams in the area. All he had to do was somehow get a dam built on the Kendall River in close proximity to town. All his water supply needs would have been met. I'm sure he thought long and hard about the 'problem' before coming up with the solution."

"Enlist the help of someone at the Corps of Engineers."

"You see…you knew what I was going to say. The real genius of the whole plan was selecting Clark. Clark was part of the planning group, and he was young, aggressive, and intelligent. He was particularly vulnerable to any offer since he was in the midst of a divorce at the time. There was a club in Louisville where engineers got together and had dinner, and perhaps that's where Pope met Clark. Clark was a prominent member of the club. You saw the announcement in the bulletin that Clark was named Engineer of the Year for 1955."

"Everything you have said is complete conjecture. You have no proof of any of this," Joseph broke in.

"Nothing that would stand up in a court of law, but there is evidence you've glossed over. Do you have the old photographs you got from Armstrong, the ones taken at the dam site during construction?"

"Yes I do." Joseph went into the cardboard box at his feet and pulled out the leather-bound album.

Dutton thumbed through the book and came to a photograph of Clark and Pope standing at the site, looking at construction plans as a steam-driven bulldozer moved dirt. "Okay what do you see here?" He asked.

"A bulldozer compacting the clay core for the dam," Joseph answered.

"That's the engineering answer. You really don't see what is happening in the photo?"

"Okay, I give up. Why don't you stop speaking in riddles and tell me."

"Look how close they're standing to one another while holding the plans."

"So what?"

"Two people who did not know each other would maintain a much larger body distance, and it's not just this photo. There are several other photos in the library that look just like this one."

"I did not realize it was a crime for two people to become friends while working on a project."

"I would find it unusual that someone working for the federal government, doing engineering studies, would be on such good terms with a local official. I figured he would have been more impartial. But you're not getting the overall picture. Let's say that you are Clark. You have been working for the Corps for ten years, and, in 1953, making, at most, a salary of about two thousand dollars a year. Maybe that's enough for a small house in Louisville, a modest car, and nothing else. That small amount money would have been decreased significantly with the divorce. You're a bright, young person who saw a lifetime of eating baloney sandwiches through no fault of your own. Then there's a great stroke of luck and you meet someone who offered to help hire a lawyer to clear up the divorce, and then give you a yearly salary of ten thousand dollars, a king's ransom in those days. All you had to do was get the Corps to build the dam on the site. You're a senior member of the planning division and you could slant the studies to make Pope's Mills the best place for it."

"I doubt any *one* person within the Corps of Engineers had the influence to sway the decision like that. The final choice was made at the highest levels."

"Yes, I'm sure Pope bought off a politician or two to ensure the deal, but Clark was the man on the inside, and that was a highly valuable commodity."

"Clark did not work with Pope for several years after he left the Corps."

"Yes, both Pope and Clark were skillful at covering their tracks. It would have been fairly obvious there was some sort of collusion if Clark would've worked for Pope right after he quit the Corps of Engineers. That's why he became a vice president at a local engineering firm for a couple of years. People have a short memory about a lot of things."

"Just for argument's sake, I will concede that you are right about Clark. How does that translate into a motive for the bombing? Why would anybody care after fifty years how Pope got the dam built?"

"To me, the dam is symbolic of how everyone in this town has been screwed over by the Pope Paper Company, and it all started with bribery and back-room deals. Not everyone has a college education like you, but people aren't dumb. The way I reason it, I'm not the first person to figure this out. Actually, there are probably a whole lot of people around here who have known this," Dutton said in a voice that was becoming more enraged. Taken over by anger and frustration, he pointed a finger into space. "I would say nearly everyone in this town has a motive for blowing up the dam, and because I'm an outsider with a prison record, I get singled out to be investigated by the FBI." Dutton put down his beer and grinned, "Oh hell, I can go on forever. You need to forgive me. I seem to get in these moods."

"I understand. I get angry myself at the number of innocent people who have died in these bombings."

Dutton started chucking to himself. "I get mad at what happens to me. But still, I'm human and can appreciate the irony of the situation. I sell five hundred dollars of coke. I get a two-year prison term at the federal pen in Danville, while Clark, engaged in a conflict of interest and violating all the ethical guidelines in the book, he gets to live in a mansion on the hill and die a multi-millionaire. That's what I call...fairness."

Chapter 15

Toby kicked the red and white soccer ball down the length of the grass field, dribbling it from foot to foot, showing great speed and agility for a seven year old. As he neared the two rocks that delineated the goal, he swung his leg back, ready to take a shot. Joseph ran towards him from behind, laboriously trying to block the ball. He put his foot ahead of Toby's leg, trying to kick the ball away. He was one half second late, and the ball bounced into the goal. Off balance and exhausted, Joseph fell face-down to the grass and lay there motionless while Toby jumped up and down in an impromptu celebration. Joseph rolled over onto his back, still breathing hard, as Toby stood above him. "I lead you now six to two. It's your turn to try to get a goal."

Joseph looked up at the cloudless blue sky and wearily shaded his eyes. "Do you think you can allow your vanquished opponent a few moments rest?"

Toby stood above Joseph, looking down at him curiously. "You're the one who challenged me."

"I try to forget that," Joseph said, as he tried to catch his breath.

"I thought you said you played soccer when you were young."

"I did, when I was growing up in Lebanon. I was a much better player."

"My mother can beat me. When we play she usually outscores me ten to five."

"Maybe she should be playing rather than me," Joseph said in a low voice.

"I heard that!" Jesse called out from down the field. "I have my job. Remember, I'm setting up the lunch for you both."

"I can do that, seems like a less strenuous activity," Joseph offered.

Jesse took the plastic tablecloth out of the trunk of the blue Taurus and spread it onto the picnic table. He was about to return to the car to get the Styrofoam cooler with the food. "It's a beautiful day. Why don't you do another point while I finish setting up? It will help you get into shape."

Joseph slowly got up on one knee, stood up, and said to Toby, "Since it looks like I am not going to get any sympathy around here, I am just going to have to beat you."

Toby clinched the muscles in his jaw and concentrated as Joseph kicked the leather ball slowly down the field. With a burst of speed, he went in front of Joseph and stole it.

This time, Joseph backtracked, and with both hands outstretched, covered the area of the goal. Toby kicked the ball into the air. Joseph grabbed it. "Not this time, brother," Joseph said. Toby ran up and with an upward motion of his fist knocked the ball out of Joseph's hands. As Joseph chased it, Toby threw both his hands around Joseph's legs, tackling him to the ground.

"That's illegal! You can't do that!" Joseph yelled.

"Who said we are playing by the rules?" Toby replied as he climbed onto Joseph's back, pushing him face down to the grass. Toby put his hands around Joseph's neck, briefly putting him in a chokehold; then got up, pursuing the ball and effortlessly kicking it into the goal. He raised his arms in victory and chanted, "I win! I win!"

Jesse announced, "Lunch's ready. Break time." Joseph, covered with grass, lethargically stood up and limped over to the picnic table. Jesse glanced over to Joseph standing next to the table with a pouting expression on his face, hair mussed, blades of grass covering his white, button down shirt and gray slacks. In the midst of laughter, she said, "Joseph, you look like shit."

Joseph found no humor in the comment and continued to look defeated. Jesse took her hands and started to clear the grass off his shirt. "It's your fault you showed up for a picnic in slacks and a button down shirt. Looks like you are going to have to change your clothes before going back to work."

"I usually play soccer standing up. I didn't expect to be rolling around in the grass with a seven-year-old boy."

"Seven-year-old boys are largely unpredictable," Jesse said.

"Does he usually play that rough?" Joseph said, examining the grass stains on his pants.

"No, he's generally shy with people. He must like you."

"Then I am glad he does not hate me. I would really be in bad shape then." Joseph smiled as he sat next to Toby, who was already ravenously eating a chicken breast. Taking a leg and thigh from the pile of chicken in the middle of the table, Joseph started to scan the area with a worried look on his face. Jesse was in the middle of drinking her ice tea when she put the glass down to run to the car. She quickly returned carrying her purse. After a searching for a minute she found a bottle with red fluid. "I almost forgot, I made a last minute purchase of Tabasco sauce at the convenience store. I couldn't get a larger size, so don't use it all up on the chicken."

Relieved, Joseph loosened the top and poured half the bottle on his chicken.

Taking a bite out of her wing, Jesse noted sarcastically, "You don't need to thank me."

Joseph put down his drumstick. "Oh, I am sorry. I was completely remiss. Thank you for everything. It was quite nice of you to buy lunch. What is the occasion?"

Jesse said, "I wanted to get away from the station. I was sick of dealing with the building contractors. I don't want to sound ungrateful for their help, but they want to build things with cheaper materials than what I had in the original building. Anyhow, I don't want to get into a detailed discussion about it. I thought you needed a break, too, and that you wanted to get together with Toby. How do you like the park? There's a stream about one-hundred yards towards the trees. Don't you hear it?"

Joseph heard the sound of water cascading over rocks. "Yes, I do. I think there is also a dam that crosses the stream about two hundred yards upstream." Searching his memory for a moment he added, "It is a twenty-foot high concrete dam constructed by the state in the mid-nineteen eighties and has a drainage area of ten square miles."

Jesse said, "We can walk to it if you want? I am sure Toby would go with you. He likes to hike and explore."

Joseph's voice turned terse. "So that is why you took me here, to look at a dam? I get enough of dams fourteen hours a day. I just want to be back to college teaching, and be free of this. Don't take that the wrong way; I don't want to be away from you. You are the only positive thing that has happened to me in a long time."

"So I am only a 'positive' thing, not a 'good' thing, or the 'best' thing that has happened," Jesse said teasingly.

"You know, I have a theory about all of this," Joseph said between mouthfuls of chicken.

"So tell me about it. What's your theory?"

"Everything is somehow connected with the minister who committed suicide ten years ago. The timing of the bombings coincides to his arrest and trial."

"Are you talking about that guy, Adamson?" Jesse leaned back in reflection. "I remember him vaguely. He was the nutcase who kidnapped and raped a young woman. You honestly think the bombings are related to his arrest and death?"

"It was not 'raped'…I think 'molested,'" Joseph corrected her. "I do not have enough information to say either way at this time, whether or not the bombings are related to Jake Adamson, but I still think it is a valid theory. I am disappointed no one at the FBI wants to pursue it. I do not even know if Sam really thinks it is viable."

"If I were you, I wouldn't let anyone bully me or keep me from giving my opinion. I'd stick to my guns."

"How about if I explain to you that…"

Jesse put her arms affectionately around Joseph's shoulders. "I think you're cute when you're serious."

Joseph felt taken aback. "You are not going to listen to me?"

"Do me a favor. It's too nice of a day to rehash recent events; it makes me depressed and angry. I see the real issue here is getting you the respect you deserve. Do you have any other facts to back up your theory, other than it being some sort of coincidence?"

"No…"

"You're the scientist. Isn't it basic scientific principal that you have to validate theories by finding some sort of evidence to support them? It looks like you still have some work ahead of you."

"Yes. The problem is that I don't have access to the FBI case files, and given Agent Sattler's initial response, I don't think I can go and ask him for his help."

"You're limiting your sources of potential information. I'm sure there are other places to find out about this guy 'Reverend Adamson' other than the FBI files; it's just that you aren't thinking. Everyone who has walked on this God's green Earth has left some sort of paper trail in multiple locations. You just need to figure out which ones to tap."

Toby, who had been eating contentedly, quickly finished his chicken and, after washing it down with a Coke, let out a long, loud belch. Embarrassed, Jesse leaned over the table. "I told you never to do that!"

"I saw it in *Ben Hur*. It is rude not to croak when you are eating food with an Arab," Toby said innocently.

"You know better! Now apologize, and if you're done, you can take your soccer ball and go practice in the field. I'll be watching, so don't go to far away."

"Oh, Mom. I wanted to walk the stream. Mr. Joseph, I'm sorry for what I did. Do you want to go with me?"

"Give us a few moments peace and do as I say," Jesse said as she took a forkful of coleslaw.

Toby grabbed the ball and kicked it up high into the air. Ralph, sunning himself by the picnic table, suddenly made a dash for the moving object with Toby racing from behind.

Jesse turned to Joseph. "Now tell me what else is bothering you, other than the investigation."

"Nothing else is bothering me," Joseph said defensively.

"I see you pouting. There's something stuck in your gut. You might as well let it out."

"I look around at the trees, the grass, and feel like I don't belong here. I feel like a stranger, that I am intruding."

"I thought if I got you away from work you would relax. My parents used to take me here for picnics when I was a little girl. Isn't it pretty?"

"Yes, it is beautiful," Joseph said mechanically, looking at the oak trees.

"If you say everything is beautiful, then why don't you sound happy?" Jesse asked.

Joseph had a serious look on his face and waited for Toby to be out of earshot. Letting the words slip out he said, "I hope you did not take me here out of a sense of obligation, because of what I did for Toby."

Jesse gave Joseph a hard stare. "Is that what you think? That I've been seeing you because I want to repay you for saving my son's life. That's bullshit. I see you as an intelligent, sensitive human being. I thought you were different than the typical asshole I meet around here. Maybe I've been gravely mistaken."

"Maybe you have." Joseph picked up a biscuit and practically swallowed it whole. Jesse seemed taciturn as she slowly swirled her coleslaw around the plastic plate. Joseph finally broke the silence, "You asked me, and I gave you an honest answer. It would also be truthful to say that I appreciate everything you have done for me. Over the past few days, you have made my life worthwhile. I just feel insecure. People know nothing about me; they just see me as an Arab from Lebanon. The reason you feel so comfortable having a picnic in this park is that you have lived here all your life. You expect me to have lunch in a strange place and within a half hour feel like I am home. I am sorry Jesse; it does not work that way."

"Is Lebanon 'home' for you?"

"It used to be. But I don't think I can go back there. I am used to living in the United States, but I have never lived anywhere here for more than two years because my father liked to relocate around the country. We even moved when I was in the middle of my senior year in high school. I only knew a handful of people when I was a teenager."

"So, you did all of this because of your father? Who was he?"

"He was a lot of things. He was a teacher, a musician, a politician, and unfortunately, to some people back in Lebanon, he was also a traitor, a betrayer of trust."

"He's your father; knowing you, I just believe the stuff about him being a traitor," Jesse said with a sad look on her face.

Joseph understood that Jesse simply wanted to make conversation, but some things were beyond polite discussion. He simply wanted to forget what had happened in Lebanon. He sat on the grass watching Toby dribble the soccer ball down the field. But how can one forget part of one's childhood. He closed his eyes, and, for a moment, he felt he was back there.

***

The temperature was over one-hundred degrees on that summer day. The heat surrounded and encapsulated everything, but Joseph did his best to ignore it, as he dribbled his barely used, red and white soccer ball in the street outside of their white-washed, stucco house in Jounieh. The house had a flat roof and tall, pointed-arch windows that denoted an Islamic influence in the architecture. The stained glass windows, usually open on a blistering, hot day to allow for air circulation, were conspicuously closed. Joseph heard a voice calling him as kicked the soccer ball around his mother's prized fig tree in the front yard. He did not pay any attention to the tree as he continued to kick the ball. A woman with red-tinted, black hair appeared at the wrought iron gate which was decorated with metal fig leaves and led back to the courtyard. She called out, "I said only a ten-minute break, and now it is fifteen minutes. Time to get back to your schoolwork. You don't want to keep your math tutor, Mr. Bachir, waiting."

"Mother, can't I practice for a while?" pleaded Joseph. He followed his mother back to the large, square courtyard, leaving the ball on the manicured grass and returning to the austere wooden chair and desk under the red-clay shingled roof. There, a husky, bearded man wearing black stood in front of a chalkboard. Bachir had once studied to be a priest and wore a large silver cross on his neck that glowed in the afternoon sun. In one single motion, he drew a circle in thick, white chalk. "Today, we continue the study of the geometry of conic figures. As we said the last time we met, the circle is the locus of all points in a plane equidistant from a single point." He put two heavy chalk points on the outside of the circle and painstakingly labeled them "A" and "B" and continued lecturing "The length of arc A-B is equal to the central angle divided by one-hundred and eighty degrees times the value…"

Joseph looked away to the other white-washed stucco houses that glowed in the distance and framed the city that jutted out from below. During the past two weeks, there was tension in the house. Joseph's mother, Hespah, would have long discussions with his father, Abraim, in their bedroom. They would always talk politics in the bedroom, the only place besides the study where there was any privacy. To Abraim, Hespah was his ultimate confidant, and his sounding board. No decisions about the family were made without her consent. During the past week, he would get frustrated with her arguments and would walk out, slamming the door. Later, Joseph would find them in the courtyard, sitting on a bench holding hands as if nothing happened.

At four o'clock, Joseph had completed the lesson and Bachir was about to leave when Joseph reminded him of his promise to practice soccer with him at the end of the day. Bachir smiled and shrugged his shoulders. "Okay, I will play with you for a few minutes."

Joseph hurried back to the front yard. He set the ball on his shoe and started to bounce it on top of his feet in the front yard, where the cement driveway formed a semi-circle. "See what I can do," he said, showing off for the tutor.

The sound of Abraim's black Mercedes Benz broke Joseph's concentration. The car drove up to the home, stopping a few feet from the entrance. His father, a short, thin man with curly graying hair got out of the driver's seat. . His mother opened the door, as if on cue. A man in his twenties, stone-faced and wearing a white turban, exited from the passenger side. He opened the rear door for a taller man in late-middle age with a white beard and turban. Joseph had never seen the visitors before, but out of habit looked away since he was always taught never to stare at strangers. They both exuded a formality that was unlike other guests his father brought to the house. The guests were smiling, but both seemed nervous. Abraim shot a concerned look toward Joseph; he did not expect to see the tutor with his son so late in the day.

Joseph stopped playing and watched his mother at the door, in a silk blueprint dress, receive the visitors. "This is my beautiful wife, Hespah," Abraim announced, as the visitors arrived at the ornate front door decorated with a red and purple rectangular pattern.

Joseph's mother gracefully extended her thin hand. "*Bayti baytak* (My home is your home),"and continued in Arabic. "If there is anything I can do to make you comfortable, please ask. I have some mint tea, and if you are hungry I have some freshly baked bread and humus for you."

Both of the visitors bowed and the taller bearded man said in response, "I am honored to be here. I brought an arrangement of flowers for your lovely home." He said, offering a wicker basket covered in plain brown wrapping paper. Abraim looked in the direction of the tutor.

As Abraim escorted the visitors into the house, he whispered a few words to Hespah, still standing in the doorway. Hespah quickly approached Bachir, who had picked up his briefcase, ready to leave. "Time has lost me," She said politely, "I apologize for not being a better host. Since I cannot offer you a ride, can I at least give you your taxi fare back to Beirut?"

"No, thank you. I didn't mean to stay this late, but I wanted to fulfill my promise to your son to practice some soccer. You will find his assignments on the chalkboard in the courtyard," Bachir explained.

"I will make sure he does them," she said as she put her arms around Joseph and kissed him on the cheek. Bachir hurriedly strode down the hill towards the main road. Hespah took Joseph into the house and sat him down on the leather sofa in the living room.

In the vase on the coffee table was the expensive arrangement of roses and orchids the visitor brought. "So show me what you learned in school today," she said, opening his math books. Joseph could tell that she was making pretence not to care about the meeting between the men in the study. His mother always conveyed an air of dignity, but this time she seemed extremely distracted. Joseph wanted to ask who the visitors were, but knew it was not his place to question what his parents did. He started to thumb through his notes, showing his mother the various geometric shapes and explaining their properties. As he did, she nodded, half-listening to what he was saying, half-trying to hear the conversation in the study. She stroked his back and said, "You have been very good during this difficult time. I just want you to know that no matter what happens, you have been a good boy, and you make both of us proud."

As his mother departed for the bedroom, Joseph heard the conversation in Arabic behind the closed doors. She came back wearing the red satin dress she only wore on formal occasions. She checked her watch and went to the kitchen where Alvira had been busily cooking. He overheard her mother say, "Thank you for all the cooking. You can go now."

Alvira responded, "Are you sure? I can help you set the table."

"No, thank you. I have Yousef to help me with that." As Joseph began to quietly set the table, his father and the two visitors exited the study. They were chatting amicably, his father's arms stretched around both his guests' shoulders—all three of them were smiling. Joseph stood at attention as his father finally brought the guests over to him. The tall bearded guest went down to a crouch, looked into Joseph's face as if to make a detailed examination of all its features, and shook his hand with a solid grip. "Hello, my name is Siddiq Al-Rafai. Are you the famous Yousef Hamiz, the mathematician?"

"I don't know if I know mathematics," Joseph said, nervously transfixed by Al-Rafai's pale blue eyes.

Al-Rafai smiled back. "Mathematics is very important. If I knew more of mathematics and less of politics, my life would be a lot happier. There are a lot of famous Arab mathematicians like al-Khuwarizmi and Ibn Khaldn who made their contribution to the world culture."

He did not know any of the people that were mentioned.

Al- Rafai said, still crouching position, "You do not know them? I had to learn about them when I was in school. They did work with numerical progressions."

A faint smile came to Joseph, "...like 1,3,5,7, 9..."

"Yes, but more complex...things that gave me a headache when I thought of them. You will soon discover that a lot of things in life are a progression. Maybe when you grow up you will be wise and understand them better than me. I am a rather simple person, but it seems to me we are always at the end of a progression of events for which we are not responsible, over which we mostly have no control." He called over the other man. "I want to introduce you to my son, Alexander; he is my eldest, the same as you."

Alexander was less formal than his father. As he held out his hand he said, "I saw you playing soccer when we came in. Perhaps we can play after dinner."

Joseph didn't know how to respond and looked up at his father. Abraim said, "You have to excuse him. My son can be reticent at times, but would be honored to play with Alexander. I see that my wife has some food on the table; come and let us speak over dinner."

The centerpiece of the table was a large casserole dish of Taboli. Taboli, a salad made from parsley and tomatoes and cracked wheat, was the favorite of Abraim's, and he passed it over to al-Rafai to get the first helping.

There was a plate of pita bread to his right. Al-Rafai uncovered the bread, still warm from the oven, and savored its yeasty aroma. He ripped the top piece in half and ceremoniously passed the rest over to his son. He put the salad inside the pita and ate it as a sandwich. "This is delicious, my compliments to your wife."

Abraim laughed, "Hespah doesn't come close to our stove, our maid Alvira does the cooking during the week. On the weekends, when she is resting, I do the cooking, and my son helps me in the kitchen." Abraim reached over to Hespah who was sitting at his side and held her hand. "Her job in the household is to raise Yousef and personally oversees his education. She also serves as my closest political advisor; she knows the other members of the Council better than I do."

Al-Rafai leaned over toward Hespah. "I have always wanted to know what the Council is thinking. So how do you accomplish this feat?"

"It is very simple. I play Mah Jong with their wives over tea once a week," Hespah said, while eating the minute amount of salad on her plate.

"Politics and Mah Jong, an interesting combination."

Hespah interjected, "But we talk better things than politics. That's what men speak. We talk about our families."

"Oh, you do? Abraim, you have a very smart and beautiful wife, who knows how to listen—a talent hard to find in a woman. My wife, Sorah, also shares this talent. She is the head of my household, a job in which she is very proficient. She is very worldly, and is the one who suggested I send Alexander to get his MBA in the United States."

Hespah, who seemed initially nervous, was finally beginning to relax. She went to the kitchen and brought back Bitinjan mah Hommous, a stew made from eggplant and chick peas, Shawarma, sliced barbequed lamb marinated in special spices, and a plate of Shish Kabob. They were laid out on the mahogany table in fine china platters decorated with blue flowers. Through the dinner conversation, Joseph stayed silent, but noted that al-Rafai's inquisitive eyes never seemed to stop moving, looking everywhere around the table. A couple of times their eyes met and al-Rafai gave him a wink.

Seeing that everyone had finished their meals, Hespah cleared off the table. Abraim folded his hands across his stomach. "Ah, now is my favorite time: coffee and desert. Allow me to show you my pride and joy." Walking over to the oblong, carved wooden buffet that rested against the wall, he removed the embroidered cover from an espresso machine sheathed in silver. Next to it sat an oval platter with six translucent, demitasse cups arranged in a circle. The surface of the machine was immaculately polished, its metal skin glowing in the dining room light. A large pressure dial dominated the face, along with two curved silver arms. Everyone watched intently as Abraim worked the knobs like a wizard bringin the machine to life. After a few silent minutes, it snorted stream from the main spout. Like a magician with quick and deft movements, Abraim adjusted another knob and a steaming, golden-brown liquid exuded from the chrome orifice into a cup.

Hespah came out of the kitchen bearing a silver tray of baklava and ice cream. Joseph thought it truly must have been a special occasion with two of father's favorite desserts on the table. Joseph could smell the honey and butter from the pastry, but waited patiently as Al-Rafai and Alexander were served first. Joseph took the portions offered and then dug into the frozen concoction, light on the milk and cream but heavy with sugar, savoring its stringy, taffy-like texture. He alternated it with bites of the crunchy, nutty tasting Baklava.

Satisfied from the meal, Al-Rafai sat back in his chair and lit a cigar. "I am happy that two people from opposing points of view can find an area of agreement. We both want a government where a Muslim and Christian can achieve equality in a free capitalist society. I was a man with four sons and three daughters. Two months ago, I buried a son who was blown up by a car bomb in East Beirut. I have now lost two of my four sons and one of my daughters since this war began. All I see is war and killing around me. Last week, I saw a group of fellow Muslims hack the body of a young man to pieces so they could dump them on the street and blame the Christian Phalange Militia. I cannot believe I have been living with this insanity for ten years."

Abraim nodded in agreement. "Yes, we have all lost friends and relatives. But we are all optimistic that this conflict will come to an end. Beirut can be the French Riviera of the Middle East again. People are going to want to travel here to do their banking business. They will all need a place to stay. Your idea, to build a new hotel in downtown Beirut, is a solid one. I have seen firsthand the remains of the hotel district, now a collection of bombed out shells of buildings. As you know, all the buildings have been looted; they have even stolen the toilets. I made the mistake of taking Yousef with me when I went there, and Hespah didn't forgive me for a week."

Hespah chimed in, "That was not an intelligent thing to do."

Abraim smiled back at his wife. "I know it was not. I did not realize how much the district had become a haven for packs of dogs made homeless by the war. They must have smelled the food I had in the car, and when Youself and I got out for a better look at the buildings, a pack of six dogs surrounded us, barking and growling. We were both lucky we were only twenty feet away from the car when they lunged at us. A German Shepherd clamped onto my son's blue jeans. I tried kicking at him, but he was fairly aggressive and started to attack me." Abraim pulled his leg out from under the table and showed the hole in the fine, tooled leather of his boot. "You see, the dog bit through the leather. If he would have gone any further and broken the skin, I would have needed a rabies shot." Abraim looked over to Joseph and reassuringly stroked his arm. "My brave son is still traumatized by the incident; he jumps now whenever a dog barks at him from behind a fence."

"Yes, both of our families have taken physical risks on this business venture," Al-Rafai said as he glanced at Alexander who was listening intently. "I usually travel with six bodyguards, but today I come in friendship with my oldest son as my sole protection. We have to trust each other for this arrangement to work. We will share the risks and both reap the benefits. I promise when the hotel opens, I will allow members of the Hamiz family be part of the management team, and open hiring to Christians, Maronites, Shias, Sunnis, Nasserites, and Palestinians. I am going to be generous and let everyone gain from the venture."

Abraim leaned over the table and looked at Al-Rafai intently. "So, we all have an agreement, in principal, to be partners. I will provide you the banking connections for the financing. There are going to be people who don't want this war to end. There are going to be fanatics on both sides who do not want us to go through with this business arrangement. I still have political associates who believe that the only lawful government for Lebanon is a Christian government where Moslems are second class citizens. I have searched my conscience, and I cannot believe that."

Al-Rafai smiled as he relaxed his hands on the table. "My belief is that the truth reveals itself through the righteous. The only hope I possess for the future is partnerships such as this hotel venture. I will only do business with people who will cooperate with us."

Alexander looked over towards Joseph who seemed bored at the political conversation and gave a tug on his shirt. "How about that soccer game we agreed on?"

Joseph, eager to escape from the dinning room table, quickly collected his soccer ball, while Alexander, dressed in a dark brown jacket, matching brown pants, and black wing tipped shoes, waited for him outside. After a few minutes of frustration trying to run circles around Alexander, Joseph tried kicking the ball away, only to be blocked by Alexander who effortlessly kept it away from him. Alexander picked up the ball. "Maybe I should show you how to dribble the ball so your opponent can't get to it." He put the ball back on the ground and moved it around gracefully with the front tips of his feet. He handed the ball over to Joseph, "Now try."

Placing it on his right foot, Joseph tried the same motion but couldn't control it. Alexander quickly kicked it away again. "No, just do little movements with your foot. You're trying too hard."

Joseph put the ball back on the ground, this time moving the ball much more slowly and deliberately. Alexander looked down at Joseph's feet, nodding in satisfaction as Joseph practiced, "Yes, you seem to be getting it. Now practice that, and next time we meet, I will show you how to kick the ball farther."

"You are pretty good, Alexander. I wish someday I could be as good a soccer player as you."

"You will, Yousef. You will," Alexander reassured him. "I have had years of practice. I played when I went to Dartmouth; made the second team."

"You went to Dartmouth?" Joseph said, surprised.

"Yes, I have undergraduate and graduate degrees in Business Administration from there. My father wanted someone in the family who could run his business affairs for him."

"I want to learn more about the United States."

"I can tell you that most of the U.S. cities aren't like Beirut. You can relax even in one of the largest cities in the world, New York City, and not worry about being shot or blown up. I could not, however, face traveling on the Subway. Even an adventurous man such as myself has limits."

It was getting toward eight-thirty in the evening and the yard started to get dark. Joseph could see his father at the door with his mother and Al-Rafai. Al-Rafai gently kissed his mother's hand, "It has been a pleasure. I hope soon you enjoy my wife's cooking. I don't know if she can make tabouli as well as your maid does. You will have to get your maid to divulge to her the recipe."

Yousef could tell his mother was falling under Al-Rafai's spell. She gave a broad smile as she playfully quipped, "She has her secrets. But I will consider doing it."

Al-Rafai called to his son, "Come, Alexander, we must leave, we have a dangerous journey ahead of us." Everyone present knew traveling at night was risky, especially for a Muslim in the Catholic controlled areas of Beirut.

"My father is calling me," Alexander said as he shook Joseph's hand. "I am sorry; I will have to teach you soccer some other time. Maybe, I can find you some other kids your age to play with. They may not be Christian, though."

"That would be fine," Joseph said, as Alexander walked back to the car and opened the rear door for his father. Abraim got into the car and slowly drove down the hill.

That night, Hespah quietly stayed in the kitchen cleaning the dishes, slowly wiping each plate and gently putting it back in the cupboard. She looked anxiously out the front windows, awaiting Abraim's return. She was visibly relieved when he came back two hours later. They stayed up, amicably chatting and reading in the living room. At ten-thirty, Joseph went to bed but was awakened at midnight, bothered by a dream. Thirsty, he went to the kitchen to get some water. As he drank, he noticed the door to his father's study was open. He went to close it and found the arched, double doors that led to the courtyard swung wide open. He was about to close them when the saw the outline of a figure sitting in his father's stuffed leather chair behind the desk, illuminated by the moonlight. His heart leapt, but then was comforted when he saw there were wisps of smoke coming from the chair, escaping to the open air of the courtyard. Joseph fumbled through the dark, found the switch on the wall, and flicked it on.

His father turned around, angrily taking the pipe out of his mouth. He said sharply, "Turn off the light; I don't want to wake your mother. She needs her sleep. She had a stressful day."

"I am sorry, father," Joseph said as he turned the light off, returning the room to its moonlit illumination.

"What are you doing up, Yousef?"

"I had a bad dream, father."

"Come here and sit with me. I couldn't sleep either." Joseph took a small oak captain's chair from it resting place along the bookshelf and pulled it alongside his father. Joseph closed his eyes and rested his head on his father's arm. Abraim put the hand carved wooden pipe back into his mouth. He always smoked when he was alone in the library. "So how did you like Alexander?" he asked.

"He was nice. He offered to teach me to play soccer. When I first saw him get out of the car, I thought that he was just a local tough that was hired to be a bodyguard. I did not know he was college-educated in the states."

"Today, you have learned one of your most important lessons of life; people often are not what they initially appear to be. When I first met him in the central market with his father, he seemed the same way to me, but as we spoke, he appeared to be quite knowledgeable about running a business."

"He was funny about some things. It was ninety-five degrees out but he kept wearing his coat."

Abraim laughed at the innocence of his son. "That's because he had a shoulder holster under his coat with a forty caliber automatic pistol."

"You mean he kills people?" Joseph asked incredulously.

"I am sure he is ready to defend his father's life, which may mean killing people. You have to understand that even though he is a cordial person and a college graduate, he is nevertheless a product of growing up in the streets of Beirut. You have been lucky all your life. So far, we have been able to shelter you from the war. But if it goes any longer, you may have to carry a gun to protect yourself."

"I am frightened of guns."

"I would never suggest that lightly. Buying you a gun is far from the solution to the problem, but I do think about your safety all the time. That is one of the reasons I am giving serious consideration to sending you to the United States to go to high school. I have some friends there, and I have made some preliminary contacts with the U.S. State Department for you to obtain a Green Card."

"Will you and mother be there with me?"

"I don't know if we will all be there. Then again, you may not have to travel abroad. Lots of things are up in the air at this point. If my business arrangements turn out the way I expect them, I am optimistic that we will be staying here for a long time. Because of moderates like Al-Rafai, there is a possibility we can have peace, and you will be able to spend the rest of your life here, if you so desire. But then things can always go wrong, and one needs contingency plans."

"I want to be here in this house in Jounieh with you and mother," Joseph said, tears rolling down his face.

Abraim stood up to comfort him, and took him outside by the hand to the fresh air of the courtyard and the evening breeze. "I know you do, but a lot of things are beyond my control. I feel bad for you being born here in this culture that supports war and violence. A few years ago, I believed that the only government for Lebanon should be Christian because that is what your grandfather held true. He met a lot of great people of the church including Daniel Bliss and William Dodge, who came over here and taught the New Testament. Ever since that time, our lives have been intimately connected with the church, along with our family banking businesses that have given millions of dollars to church-run projects such as orphanages, hospices, and shelters."

Still deep in thought, Abraim walked slowly across the brick patio. He looked over toward the mobile chalkboard on which there was a large circle in thick white chalk that glowed in the moonlight. "It is quite appropriate you are learning about circles. It appears that we all seem to be trapped here in this 'closed circle' of violence and revenge." He slowly traced his finger around the circle as he spoke. "A few weeks ago, I was traveling down to Beirut to get some things from my office at the university. I drove down a side street that paralleled Rue Clemceau. Blocking my way was a ripped apart, burned out baby carriage. I quickly got out and moved it to the side of the road. When I came back to the car, I discovered blood on my steering wheel. I was shocked to see my hands covered with blood. As it turned out, a few hundred feet ahead in the road there were several ambulances parked in front of a house where a Christian member of the Council was visiting a friend. I found out from a policeman at the scene that a bomb placed under a car had prematurely exploded, killing a mother and baby as they walked past. Their blood was literally on my hands. Later in the day, I found out that the Christians had retaliated for the bombing by gunning down a Moslem cleric." Abraim finished tracing the rest of the figure; taking his finger off the board where he started. Every time we embark on a course of violence, we always find ourselves at the beginning, never having solved any of our problems.

"I realized that I could no longer isolate myself from the war. Soon after, I saw Al-Rafai in the Commodore Hotel, while I was meeting a colleague for afternoon tea. He was a formidable presence, and I was frightened of him as you were frightened of Alexander. A few years back, I had met him in the marketplace. He accused our family of being war profiteers, people who financed the militant Christian militia groups, and being that, we had made ourselves targets for murder. I took the statement as being an implied threat. Even though I categorically denied the charge, he didn't seem convinced, and since the first meeting, I was always wary of him. However, this time he beckoned me over to his table. Instead of threatening me, he offered me some lamb from his plate and for a few tense minutes, I looked across at him, making idle conversation. I didn't know what to say to him, and then out of politeness I asked about his family. He took out his wallet and told me that he had seven children, and now was left with three after fighting with the Christians. I felt humbled that I could not show him a photograph of your brother, who we lost at birth. We had both lost children as a result of the fighting, and as we kept on speaking, I discovered that we were both fathers who cared deeply about our families. He spoke about the concept of 'Tawhid'; how we are at one with God, and being that, we all have responsibility toward each other as if brothers. If he would have told me this a few years ago, I would have thought it to be posturing. But now, I do believe him and trust what he says. Tonight, we have made our covenant."

Abraim sat down on the bench, cradling Joseph's head in his arms and leaning over to kiss him on the forehead. "We speak our endless platitudes in the Council about ending the fighting, and resolving our differences. But the real lesson I have learned is that peace does not begin between nations; it starts with two people. You need to understand I usually don't have business discussions with other people in the room as I did today. You are going on your thirteenth birthday and quickly becoming an adult. You already understand we are a family of wealth. But wealth and possessions are just temporary, and given the conflict at hand, our financial status can change at any time. The legacy I want to leave you is not one of wealth or influence. It is what I did today. I made peace with a sworn enemy."

That night, Joseph feel into a deep, dreamless sleep in the courtyard as his head rested in his father's lap. He recalled now as the last good sleep he have for a long time.

***

Joseph opened his eyes again as his thoughts turned back to the present. He had recited the story of the events of that day to Jesse, who sat attentively listening under the branches of a box elm tree, slowly sipping a Coke.

She asked in a quiet voice, "Whatever happened to Al-Rafai?"

"My father set up another meeting with him at the Commodore Hotel. It was the only location they could meet, a neutral zone where no hostile action would take place by either the Christians or the Muslims. The meeting was scheduled to take place at three in afternoon. My father waited in the lobby till five, but no one came. Finally, he overheard on the television news that Al-Rafai and his son were machined-gunned to death about two blocks away from the hotel, while sitting at a traffic light."

"Was he killed by members of his clan for cooperating?"

"Eyewitnesses reported that the gunmen wore the uniforms of the Christian Phalangist Militia. They somehow knew of the meeting, and had a car ready for him on the route to the Hotel. My father knew he was going to be hunted by both sides. Al-Rafai's family believed my father's overtures were simply a set-up to get the head of their clan killed, and wanted vengeance. Likewise, the Christians wanted to kill my father for being a traitor. I was just getting back from school when my mother told me I had fifteen minutes to pack my clothes. She filled two large trunks with whatever household items she could lay her hands on. We escaped with the clothes on our back, but that is about it. We departed the house in a taxi, and spent the next two weeks in a secluded dormitory of the University while my father made arrangements to leave the country. A few days later, after Al-Rafai's murder, we heard that members of the Christian Phalanges came by and burned our house to the ground. No one came to fight the fire. The people in the neighborhood were too scared to do anything, so they simply left the house to burn to the foundation stones. In Lebanon, revenge was swift and certain." As Joseph finished the story, his eyes became wet with tears. Embarrassed, he hid his face from her.

"I'm sorry. I didn't mean to make you feel sad," Jesse said, as she put her arm around him.

Joseph stood up and walked away, too proud to accept Jesse's sympathy. "All through the years, my father never spoke about how the Christian militia could have discovered his business plans. Then one day I realized that only one person could have done it. It was Bashir who disclosed al-Rafai's visit to my house and, from listening in on conversations, knew the time and place of my father's meeting at the Commodore. We were all betrayed by my mentor, my teacher, the man who ate meals at our dinner table, and the man my father had trusted. Bashir believed that he was an upright, righteous man who walked with God, but instead was possessed by excessive and irrational zeal for revenge. Perhaps I shouldn't be blaming the entire thing on Bashir. My father was a man of determination, always trying to find a middle-ground to resolve conflict, and I think that given time, he would have offered some solutions. But ultimately, it was fanaticism that clouded people's minds, and that had made our life in Lebanon a closed circle."

CHAPTER 16

The darkness of the Clark mansion basement started to close in on Joseph as he sat at the oak table surrounded by cardboard boxes in various degrees of disintegration. The newspaper archive room measured twenty by forty feet, and underlay most of the first floor of the mansion. A single, florescent fixture flickered as it cast its dim, bluish light. Feeling a sneeze coming on, Joseph pulled a white handkerchief out of his pocket. The feeling went away as he put another stack of newspapers on the table. When he did, he exploded with a massive sneeze that nearly shook the papers off the table.

The basement was familiar territory for him, having been there the week before to find the article about Jake Adamson's arrest. The haphazard arrangement of the records in the boxes on the floor did not intimidate him. Last time, it took him nearly four hours to find what he needed. It was eight o'clock in the evening and Joseph had hoped to do today's research more efficiently. He did not intend on spending the entire night in the basement. The ceiling creaked as an FBI agent walked across the wood floor above him. There were some irrational fears that crept into his mind—fears of being in a dark room, alone, in the middle of the night—but he reminded himself that the mansion was the safest place in town, and returned to his reading.

The arrest occurred sometime in April of that year. He had hoped he would find an article about Adamson that was written before the arrest. There was no index of stories. It would be a process of trial and error reviewing all the individual papers. He was about to put a paper back into the box when he spotted thcin small type:

"Shadybrook Mission, 64 Poplar Street, Pope's Mills. Services daily at 6:00 PM. Donations of food and clothing accepted."

The ad meant that the mission must have already been in operation, and he would have to go back earlier to find the newspaper article about the opening. He folded the paper neatly into the box and proceeded to look for the newspapers for 1994. As he lifted the cardboard box, there was a rustling of papers as a black mouse flew out its hiding place and scurried across the floor. Startled, Joseph dropped the box onto the floor, spilling its contents. Breathing heavily, he bent over to pick up the papers now scattered over the discolored tiles. From behind, he thought he heard footsteps. He turned around to find only the darkness. He called out, "Is anyone there?" There was no answer and he returned to pilling the papers back into the box. Suddenly, an arm went across his neck, grabbing him into a chokehold. He made a muffled scream "Heeelllppp," and the arm relaxed.

Joseph looked behind him and saw Jesse laughing hysterically. Out of breath he protested, "That's not funny. You nearly scared me to death."

"Serves you right, asshole. Remember, you were supposed to meet me at Christine's for dinner at seven."

Joseph scratched his head. "Oh yes, I remember. What time is it now?"

"It's nearly nine o'clock. I did some detective work to find you here. The FBI agents recognized me and let me in."

"I am sorry. I guess the time passed by without me noticing."

"I forgive you. Since I had paid for a baby-sitter, I figured I might as well join you. I took the liberty of picking up some Chinese food," Jesse said, pulling four white take-out cartoons out of a paper bag from the restaurant.

"Good. I was getting hungry," Joseph said.

"Now that I'm here, may I ask what you're doing?"

"You suggested a couple of days ago I 'stick to my guns.' So I decided to research the Jake Adamson case myself."

"Ah huh. So that's why you're here in a damp hole that smells like shit—to do research into something that happened ten years ago."

"Yes, that is correct. There is nothing else I can really do. I do not have the resources of the FBI. You can not expect me to go door to door interviewing witnesses. So I figured I would do the next best thing and research it in the newspaper archives. Since Agent Sattler was fairly critical of the idea that there was any connection between Adamson and the bombings, I could not do the research during normal working hours. So here I am, stuck doing the work in the evening."

"That's interesting," Jesse said, playing along. She opened one of the white cartons and speared a piece of Mongolian beef with her fork. She then asked as she chewed, "Do you have any idea what you are looking for?"

"No, not really," Joseph said, putting another stack of newspapers on the table. "I am searching the records for any information that seems out of place."

"Like what?"

"I honestly don't know. The first bombing took place on April 17th, which was the anniversary of the arrest, and the second on May 2nd, the date of Jake's preliminary hearing in Gottlieb. The FBI says that any connection to the Adamson case is purely coincidental because everyone who was closely associated with him is dead or in a mental institution."

"They're probably right," Jesse chimed in.

"You were not such a naysayer back at the picnic."

"Well, I didn't expect you to be doing the research at nine o'clock at night," Jesse shot back.

"I do not believe in coincidences and my instinct tells me that they've missed someone; somebody who was close to Adamson but who did not receive much public attention."

Jesse said, "Why would that person wait ten years to do something? Isn't it a long time to hold a grudge?"

"Not in my book. Where I come from, conflicts can span generations, with the sons fighting the same wars their fathers did."

"You cannot consider what happened to Jake Adamson a 'conflict.' I remember hearing about it. It was a simple, open and shut kidnapping case."

"You have to step back and see the bigger picture. Before the kidnapping, Jake opened a mission, but the town subsequently closed it down. More importantly, the federal government prosecuted him for a crime for which he claimed innocence. I see both of those things as conflicts, and perhaps they were not resolved with Jake's death. Now someone else maybe is involved."

"Uh, huh," Jesse said, unconvinced. "So tonight, rather than sitting in a restaurant or a bar, having a nice steak on regular plates, I'm going to be eating food out of paper boxes in some shit-hole, reading about some fucked-in-the-head religious asshole, who had kidnapped and then sexually abused a sixteen-year-old girl?"

Joseph, amused, smiled and said, "In so many words...yes. I can give you a stack of papers and you can help if you want?"

"Just as long as I get out of here by midnight. Mrs. Buxley starts charging me double the hourly rate after that."

"You have a deal," Joseph said, extending his open hand. Jesse quickly gave it a firm shake. In a self-confident voice, Joseph said, "Alright, with both of us working, we will be able to get done in half the time."

Joseph divided the pile of papers in front of him, took half and slid the rest in front of Jesse. She quickly started flipping pages, scanning articles. Joseph looked over, amazed at the speed with which she was reading. She finished her stack well ahead of him, went into a box on the floor and brought out another. She flipped through the mildewed pages at a steady pace, all the while voraciously chewing her food. After an hour of steady research, she yelled, "Son of a bitch. I got it!" Pleased with herself, she passed the paper over to Joseph. It was the September 9th edition of the *Gazette*. Joseph gave the newspaper a cursory look. On the second was a headline, "New Mission Opens Downtown" along with a four-column article and a photograph of Jake, Cylus, and Arnold standing in front of the mission's large, storefront window. Jake was wearing a white shirt with a black tie, while Cylus and Arnold sported faded, blue work shirts and dungarees. All three were smiling and appeared fairly happy to be posing for a picture. Joseph gave the article a detailed examination and noted it contained some of the usual biographical information about Jake, and brief descriptions of Cylus and Arnold.

Jesse looked over Joseph's shoulder and commented, "I didn't realize Jake was such a handsome man. He's better looking than most of the men in Gottlieb— I would have gone out with him. It's too bad he was a fucked-up head case. And I cannot vouch for the rest of that crew, especially Cylus. Just from his picture I can tell that he was running on two out of six cylinders."

Joseph leaned back in his chair, digesting the article, disappointed it revealed nothing beyond what he heard from Sam. He scratched his head and turned to Jesse, "There is nothing here beyond the usual discussion. Maybe if we go back a few more months, there will be something else." Joseph was tired, but decided to press on. He stumbled over to a box on the floor, and spilled its contents onto the table.

Jesse flipped through the pages, now at a slower pace. Joseph sat back down, quietly absorbed in his reading. Jesse checked her watch and rubbed her eyes. She stopped and stared at Joseph. Joseph was too busy to notice that Jesse had moved her chair over and had started to massage his shoulders. Joseph eventually shook her off brusquely as she said, "Just trying to make you relaxed. You seem uptight. It's eleven on a Friday night and you're sharing a dark room with a beautiful, eligible woman and all you can do is read the newspaper. With most men I've met, I'd be fighting off their advances."

Joseph looked up from the newspaper. "Huh, what did you say?"

"I said this is a waste of time, and you're too stubborn to admit it," Jesse remarked, crossing her arms across her body.

"Perhaps you are right this time. I am going to look for another thirty minutes and follow your advice and give up." Joseph left his chair; this time going over to a spot of the basement where he had seen a file box with more newspaper records. He could not see in the dim light so he held the box up closer to the fixture. It was labeled in mildewed script. "Reporters Notes 9/92 to 12/92." The box was filled with spiral bound notebooks along with a three ring binder filled with negatives kept in cellophane pages. He dumped the contents onto the desk. "I think I may have found something. Why don't you look through the notebooks and see if you can find any of the notes on which the news story was based, while I sort through the negatives to see if they have any more photographs taken that day?"

"It's getting late. Do we have to do this tonight?" Jesse said rather sleepily.

"We might as well get this done so I can get this theory out of my head. You want me to stop mentioning it, don't you?"

Jesse reluctantly started sorting through the yellowed notebooks, while Joseph methodically took out the sheets of negatives and held them up to the light. After about twenty minutes, she announced, "I think I have found the notes, but they are in this weird handwriting that looks like Arabic and I can't read them. How about you?"

Joseph was closely inspecting a negative sheet. "I will take a look at it in a few minutes. I am comparing the negatives to the picture I saw in the paper. Nothing seems to match though."

"Maybe you're not choosing the right set of negatives."

"It is late. I may not be seeing things clearly. Why don't you try," Joseph said, passing a strip of black and white negatives over to Jesse. "I think I see a storefront window with a cross in some of the negatives. In other negatives, I see the words 'Shadybrook Mission.' My guess is it's from the story."

Jesse squinted to focus on the negatives. "You're missing things. I also spotted the word 'Shadybrook Mission' in the storefront window. Why do you say they do not match the picture in the paper?"

"Because I see four people standing in front of the window, rather the three mentioned in the article," Joseph said.

"Lemme see that," Jesse said, grabbing the negative back.

Joseph stood behind her, looking over her shoulder and pointing to the individual negative. Jesse said, "Looks like you know nothing about photography. This is the negative they used. When they printed the picture, they cropped the fourth person out. Anyhow, you see they only got part of him in the photo— only half of his face is showing."

"I wonder who it is?" Joseph asked out loud.

"Probably some bystander not associated with the mission," Jesse quickly responded.

"No, I don't think so," Joseph said, scanning the negative strip. He's in a couple of other pictures."

"Some people are embarrassed to have their pictures taken. My cousin, Nancy, for example, is a good-looking woman, but she had this thing about her chin. She thought it was too large and she hated to be in pictures. We would pose for family photos at Christmas, and she would step away from the group. Perhaps this person stepped out of the photo, but did not get far enough away so part of him was included in the shot."

Joseph nodded. "I agree. He intentionally tried to get out of the picture. This time, I don't think it was cosmetic. He definitely felt close enough to the other people to be there. It was a group photo that was obviously going to appear in a newspaper, and he walked away to avoid the publicity." Joseph examined the negative again. "From what I can tell, he is younger than the other people in the photo. We need to get the entire negative printed, but I would guess that he is only a teenager, possibly fifteen or sixteen years old. Maybe there is some mention of him in the reporter's notes."

Jesse handed Joseph the notebook. Joseph turned the brown mildewed pages. "The reason you can't read it is that it's written in shorthand. My father wrote all his notes that way." Joseph quickly scanned the paper. "The description is rather unspecific. But it says here that she saw a teen helping to serve the food. My bet is that it was probably the same person in the negative."

"Aren't you beating this thing to death? So what if some high school kid was doing community service by helping to feed the needy? You're talking like he was a member of some conspiracy."

"You need to remember that the picture was taken ten years ago, and the teenager is now in his mid-twenties. That matches the general description of one the men at the dam. It is too bad Cynthia did not get his name. Usually reporters get all the names in the room. Don't they?"

"I don't know. I'm too tired to do any more thinking," Jesse said, her head resting in her hands. "It's twelve-thirty. Can I go home now? I have to wake up at five-thirty in the morning to open the shop."

Joseph seemed elated. He leaned over and kissed Jesse on the forehead. "Don't look so sad. Now, all we have to do is connect a name with the face."

***

Jefferies stared anxiously at the partial image of a face on the computer monitor on the desk. "So you found the negative in a box of discarded newspaper records in the basement of this building?"

Joseph nodded.

Jefferies turned to his computer "It's funny. We have had over three hundred agents working the investigation and you may have found a piece of key evidence right under our noses. I looked over the report we did on Jake Adamson, and I see no mention of any teenagers. We were only investigating adults associated with the Adamson case. In all fairness, the report was done before we got the eyewitness account of the perpetrators on the dam. However, we should have revisited it once we found out the suspects were most likely teenagers at the time of Adamson's arrest."

Sam stood next Jefferies, watching the process of scanning the negative and loading the images onto the computer. "That sentiment's refreshing. I finally meet someone involved in the investigation who's not interested in covering his ass. But I wouldn't feel too guilty about missing the information about the boy. I reviewed your report and I found it fairly complete."

"Thank you, Sam. I apologize for all the shit you've gotten from Sattler over the course of the past three weeks. There's no reason why we should not have cooperated better from day one. You grew up here. Do you recognize this person?"

Sam concentrated on the image. "I'm really trying to remember but he doesn't look familiar. What may be hampering things is that we only have about sixty percent of his face. Is there any more you can get?"

Jefferies said, "No, there were only three negatives showing his face, and this one covered it the most. But we do have a solution. We can generate the rest of it using a program we have on our mainframe in Quantico. Just wait a minute while I gain access." Jefferies tapped a few keys on the computer and got a screen with the FBI insignia. He typed a password and got into the "Visual Recognition" program. "We got this software a few years ago. It is quite a significant improvement from previous programs that were two-dimensional and only recognized specific features such as chins or noses. This system uses three-dimensional modeling to match details using over nine hundred descriptors. Once an ID has been made, the system creates a surface that accounts for the pitch and yaw of the head."

"What about beards and mustaches?" Joseph asked.

Jefferies went on, "The system's quite robust and is not deceived by facial hair or by changes in hairstyle. Joseph, you are a math wizard and would be amused by this; it has a numerical algorithm that produces a wavelet for each image. It is this wavelet that allows for the model to search a database of over ten-million individuals per minute. But we're going to utilize it to create a three dimensional model of the face in the negative, and have it generate the remainder."

Jefferies put a white box around the image of the boy's head, cropping out the face. Jefferies typed in a command and a black mesh appeared over the face as if someone draped some sort of woven fabric over the boy. "Okay, I've generated a surface model. I'm going to ask it to extrapolate areas not shown; this may take a few moments."

The three of them watched on the monitor as the computer generated the rest of the face, node by node. Finally, after about a thirty-second delay, the computer displayed the full image. To Joseph, it was the face of an average looking teenage boy with no distinguishing features. The boy had a short haircut with both ears protruding slightly. He had a small mouth and a short, squat nose. Joseph saw the boy's black, piercing eyes gazing ahead, as if brooding.

Sam went up to the screen and gave the image a detailed examination. "I'm sorry, I still don't recognize the boy. It could be anybody."

Jefferies was fairly patient. "There's one more trick we can try. We can do an age progression on the photograph to see what he looks like today. We have a group of forensic artists back in Washington who do these studies in much more detail. But I have a tool that will allow me to make a first cut." He went into another menu. "This program predicts the structural changes in the face. I have to give the program a few initial assumptions," Jefferies said, busily working the keys. "The subject's age is a big one. What the hell...for now I am going to say he's sixteen. The computer morphed the image. The face became slightly wider, the distance between the eyes increased, and the hair became darker. "Okay, here is a first cut. Oh, I forgot, maybe I should ask the computer to remove the thick glasses the kid is wearing."

The computer took away the eyeglasses and now the face filled the screen. Sam looked at it quizzically. "It still doesn't ring a bell, and I have met nearly everyone in town."

Joseph asked, "Can you add facial hair to the image?"

Jefferies replied, "There are a lot of beards I can add. You tell me which one." Jefferies went to menu that showed about fifty varieties of mustaches and beards each one with its own nuance. Joseph pointed to a short, well-trimmed beard, and the computer placed it on the subject.

Joseph stroked his chin. "I feel as if I might have met someone like that around town. It has been three long weeks. I cannot place him. You are certain, Sam, you have never seen him?"

"Yes. I am," Sam said. "I find it funny that you may have come across him. Do you recall where? Perhaps we can ask some of the people where you were."

"I am sorry, I just cannot remember," Joseph said.

"That's okay, Joseph; all of us are fighting fatigue," Sam said.

Jefferies said in a resigned voice, "We're not are going to make any more progress with the photos unless we have an ID. We could greatly refine and improve the accuracy of the age progression if we knew what the boy's parents looked like. What were the boy's habits? Did he smoke? Did he have any sports injuries? This is where the computer models stop and the fieldwork begins. Maybe I can free up a couple of agents to canvas the area with both of the photographs and see if they can find out anything. It would even be better if the boy went to high school here and we can look for him in the yearbooks."

The mention of high school gave Sam an idea and he smiled, "Perhaps I can eliminate the fieldwork for you folks. There's a lady here who has met all the children who have gone to school in Pope's Mills. She is a bit elderly, but I'm quite certain she would love the company."

***

Sally Holiday put her knitting down and took a sip of her ice tea from a tall glass. Three of her dogs were sleeping at her feet in front of the chair-swing, enjoying a lazy afternoon on the front porch. The wind picked up as she also fell asleep. She awakened to sounds of the three dogs barking as an FBI SUV pulled up to the house. Sam and Joseph exited the vehicle, followed by Jeffries and Sattler. Sam steadily walked up the steps, stood on Sally's porch, and politely tipped his hat. Sally, wearing a white dress with faded purple flowers, looked older than sixty in the harsh light of the afternoon. The silver necklace with a deep-blue stone she wore around her neck clashed with the purple in her dress, drawing more attention to her outfit. "Good afternoon, Sally. I hope we did not startle you too much. You may have some information very important to the investigation. I hope you can give us some of your time to answer a few questions."

"Am I a suspect, an old lady like myself?"

Sam tipped his hat cordially. "I hate to disappoint you. But I'm afraid you're not on the list. I want to call upon your experience as a guidance counselor in the high school. You said to me that at one time or another, you've spoken to all the teenagers in Pope's Mills."

"That was about ten years ago, before I retired from the system. I haven't gotten out as much as I used to."

Sam gave a reassuring smile. "That's exactly the time period we're interested in."

"You know, Sheriff, I will do everything I can to help you."

Sam sat next to Sally on the porch swing and pulled out the picture of the boy, as Joseph, Sattler, and Jefferies looked on from the steps. As Sally contemplated the picture, her gray eyebrows narrowed and then opened wide in astonishment when she recognized the face. She then asked, "Where did you get this photo?"

"You know this person?" Sattler asked.

"Yes, I do," Sally responded. "I am not used to seeing a photo of him though. That's why I asked."

"It's a long story. We got it from the newspaper files," Sam said.

Sally slowly got up from the swing, and Sam put out his arm to help steady her. She said, "Why don't all of you come in and join me." Sam, Sattler, and Jefferies filed in behind her, while Joseph hung back on the porch. Sally turned around and asked, "What's wrong with your friend?"

"He's afraid of dogs," Sam responded.

"No need to be afraid of my babies, Joseph. I will make sure that they won't bother you."

When Joseph entered the living room, he nearly tripped over a pile of thirty-year old *Life* magazines. The entire house looked like a repository for paper. The living room was packed with memorabilia of all sorts: public service awards and citations from the mayor and the governor for teaching in the school system for forty years. Bookshelves of all sizes went around the perimeter of the room; every one crammed beyond capacity with notebooks and miscellaneous publications. In the center of the room sat a massive couch that had a ripped, brown slipcover coated with dog hair. At one end, there was a large brown hound dog sleeping with his legs over the edge. The dog had an ornate metal collar that read "BUTCH." Butch was snoring loudly, leaving a small pool of drool on the cover.

Beyond the living room was the dining room, seemingly long-abandoned for dining purposes and now filled with antique plates and knickknacks. Off the dinning area was a small kitchen stacked with pots and pans. Joseph was about to make his way to the kitchen to join everyone else when four barking dogs surrounded him. They pinned him to the back of the couch, all jumping and were clawing at his feet. Terrified, Joseph stood motionless.

Sally opened the refrigerator. "Can I offer you gentlemen anything? I've got milk, lemonade, ice tea, Coke?"

Jefferies said politely, "No thanks, ma'am. You said you knew the boy in the photograph?"

"I have some freshly-baked coffee cake. It never lasted very long when I brought it into school when I worked there as a counselor. Are you certain you gentlemen are not hungry? I know you all work long hours."

Sam knew she would talk forever unless someone took something she offered and he said, "I'll take a slice. You should all take one. It's the best coffee cake in the county."

Sally went into a cupboard and put four pieces of cake onto her fine china and served them to the group. "Sam knows I can't do much talking on an empty stomach. Well, back to business. We were talking about photos." She went over to one her bookshelves and pulled out a set of yearbooks. "If memory serves me correctly, I believe it is the 1993 Pope's Mill High School yearbook I'm interested in." For a minute, she thumbed through the pages. She went down the pages of pictures with her finger and came to an empty frame between photographs that had a name underneath. Yes now, I am sure that's him."

Sattler, with a mouthful of cake said, "I don't know what you mean. Did you find his photo in the yearbook?"

"He never had a picture in the yearbook. It's a good thing you folks came to me. You would have never gotten his name if you poked through school records, looking for photos. He's just one of those kids who never liked having his picture taken."

Joseph was still pinned against the sofa by the barking dogs. Sally looked over at him and said, "You really are afraid of dogs. Sam sometimes exaggerates about things. Come, my children, you can play outside while I talk to these gentlemen." Sally led them out the back door while Joseph sighed in relief.

When she came back, she saw her four guests eye her anxiously. Sally hesitated, milking the moment and said, "His name is Evan…Evan Young. He came to us when he was fourteen years old."

"He's not born in Pope's Mills?" Sattler asked.

Sally settled down on the sofa next to the hound dog. Softly petting Butch's head, she started telling the story. "No, he was born in Chicago. I have vivid memories of him. It was all very tragic. His father, Alfred, was a successful stockbroker. From the vague description I got of Alfred, I gather he was a rather brilliant man with a good mind for details. Evan and his parents lived in a nice house in Oak Forest, a bedroom community outside the city. I'm certain that, given Alfred's income and being an only child, Evan led a very privileged life and even went to a private school well-suited to his needs. One evening in late December, his parents went to a Christmas party at a posh hotel in the center of town. The hotel may have had fancy rooms, but a terrible electrical system. Sometime during dinner, there was an electrical fire in the kitchen that quickly spread to the ballroom. Five people died from smoke inhalation; two of the victims were his parents. So imagine yourself in the place of a twelve year old being put in the care of a baby-sitter, seeing your parents go out to a party, only to never come back. I would say it took whatever normal childhood he had away from him."

"Did he have any other family?" Sattler asked eagerly.

"That is the next part of the story. Alfred had a brother and a sister. The sister was single and lived somewhere in California, and the brother, named

Terry, was an accountant for the paper company. Evan's mother was an only child with no siblings. So through a process of elimination, Evan was left to live with Terry and Terry's wife, Sue—they had two boys of their own. Terry was about eight years older than Alfred, and his two boys had already finished high school and had gone to out-of-state colleges by the time Evan arrived.

"So it was Evan, his Uncle Terry, and his Aunt Sue living in their house?" Jefferies asked.

"Pretty much so. Why I remember Evan so well was because he was only fourteen years old and the richest person in town, except for Matt Clark."

"How do you figure that?" Sam was amazed Sally not only knew the social lives of the people in Pope's Mills, but also the sizes of their bank accounts.

"It's quite simple," Sally said modestly. "Terry hired an attorney who sued the hotel for wrongful death. From what I understand, the lawyer was able get a million dollars out of them. The parents had insurance policies and left a hefty estate. By my figuring, after the attorney, the family, and the government got their cuts, Evan came out with a couple million dollars. But he was only rich on paper. The Orphans Court left the money in trust for him until he reached the age of twenty one. Terry and Sue were given a stipend of a few thousand dollars a month for clothes and food for him, but that's about it."

"So you had many dealings with Evan as a school counselor during the time he was here. Was he happy? Did he have many friends?" Jefferies asked, while busily writing his notes on a legal pad.

"It was difficult for me to gauge if he was happy. He was very quiet. As a counselor, I found it difficult to reach him. He would only talk to you when he was asked a question and would respond only to the question and offered nothing else, as if he was being interrogated. I always felt he was holding something back from me. But then, sometimes that's normal behavior for a teen." Sally paused for a moment in thought. "Did he have many friends? I would say he was a loner. But given the situation he was in, I would not say that was unusual. Kids that grew up in town already had their social circles, their cliques. You all know that it is difficult for someone to go to new place to break into these groups and make friends. I think in general he was very bright, introverted, and shy."

Sattler asked, "Did he get along with his legal guardians?"

"Terry and Sue were nice, respectable church-going individuals. I don't think you can get a better class of people. They were in their mid-fifties when they got him, and they provided a nice home for Evan, but I never saw them together. I know which families are close around here when you see the parents with their kids on the playground or eating dinner at the Collins Hotel. Terry worked sixty-hour weeks at the mill, so he didn't have much time to raise Evan. Sue was a housewife involved in the Rotary, Bridge Club, and church work. I think both of them had their own daily rituals, and Evan was just someone who occupied their house. So I would not consider it a matter of love or hate, but more or less of Evan maintaining his own private life under their roof."

"So he did not have any friends and was not close to his uncle or aunt. You're saying that even though he stayed here for a number of years, no one knew him at all?" Jefferies said, with a note of doubt.

"No. I didn't say that. I was just getting to that part. Things changed a lot for Evan when Jake Adamson came to town. They probably met in the Antioch Catholic Church. They must have seen something in each other that clicked. On the surface, they had several things in common: they were both orphans, and they were both new to town. It was also a matter of timing. Jake's girlfriend, Anna, had just left him with what some people rumored to be his baby. Jake was flattened by what happened. He was ready for another relationship, just as long it did not involve a woman. I think that is what motivated him to take Evan under his wing. I would see them everywhere together, having something to eat at the Collins Hotel, or talking in the square. Jake even spent a few weekends taking Evan fishing in eastern Kentucky. I saw them leaving together in his Chevy Nova. They would pile their food and clothes in the back seat and take off. I think those were the happiest times for Evan when he was here."

Sally took a sip of tea and continued, "I noticed a big change in Evan around school. His friendship with Jake got him out of his shell. He became more social, and periodically I would see him speaking with classmates. The biggest thing I noticed was Evan's interest in religion. He would carry a copy of the New Testament to class. He was not one of the people who would proselytize you; he was very private about his beliefs. Overall, he had a symbiotic relationship with Jake; they both strengthened each other."

Joseph observed, "So you could say that Jake was a father figure to the boy?"

Butch woke up from his nap, making a howling noise. Sally petted him on his head. "Butch is the wise, old man around here. He's seen a lot of things through his weary eyes. He is definitely the king of the house, and he gets mad if he isn't periodically stroked…Joseph, they had a much deeper relationship than that. They were involved in all aspects of each other's life. Evan became intricately involved with the operation of the mission, helping out with the services and serving meals. He was dealt an emotional blow with all the problems that Jake encountered with the town. He was at the public meeting where Jake had his confrontation with the town's attorney. Evan was loyal to Jake and never believed all the things spread around Pope's Mills about him. Evan was also with Jake the day he tried to break into the mission and was in the melee with the sheriff and his deputies that day. Evan probably led a rather clean and virtuous life compared to a lot of teens around here who drink and do drugs, and being arrested and put into cuffs must have been a disturbing experience for him."

"Are you certain he was arrested? We saw the records and Evan was not listed?" Jefferies asked skeptically.

"That was because he was released without being charged. They called Terry at the plant and he picked Evan up at the sheriff's office. Anyhow, Evan was a juvenile, and he would have had to be tried separately from the others. Why go through the bother for a kid with a clean record, and whose only crime was to being friends with the wrong person? The sheriff probably figured that whatever punishment meted out at home would be ample enough."

"So how did Evan react to Jake being arrested?" Sattler asked.

"I tried talking to him about it, but he would not say anything. Given his relationship with Jake, he had a fairly stoic attitude. I never saw them together again in town. Evan closed himself off and retreated back in his own world."

"Did you think he knew anything about the kidnapping?" Jefferies inquired.

"Are you saying he may possibly have been part of some conspiracy? No, I don't think so; not to my knowledge. Jake never came to town. I am sure that Evan was told not to see him again, under any circumstances."

Joseph had been intently listening to the interview and interrupted with the question, "The kidnapping must have been a horrendous experience for you?"

"It was a terrible experience for everyone here," Sally snapped back.

"What I mean is that you knew Theresa. She was probably one of the kids you saw daily," Joseph elaborated.

Sally put her right hand on the necklace around her neck and started to fidget with it, moving it back and forth. "I saw her in the halls, but I never got a chance to speak to her. Before the kidnapping, she did not appear to need my help. After it happened, I suggested to her father she get professional counseling. I have a master's degree in counseling, but do not have a license. So, I would have felt awkward taking Theresa on as a client."

"That's a beautiful piece of jewelry there," Joseph said offhandedly. "Do you mind if I look at it?"

"Oh, this old thing; I've had it for years. It's cracked and gouged from all the wear and tear it's gotten."

Joseph, who was standing next to the sofa, went up to Sally and leaned over to give a detailed examination of the piece. It was a large, blue stone in an oval silver setting that hung from a thin silver strand. The stone had a crack going through the lower part of it and an off center white star. "My guess is that it's a cat's-eye. My father had many cat's-eye jewelry pieces," Joseph said.

He continued on with his previous line of questions, "Did she ever get the counseling?"

"I guess so. I made it a habit of not getting involved with Clark's affairs. He seemed rather sensitive when people did that, and I liked to keep my job. Poor Theresa, her life became crap. She was killed in that car accident while traveling in Arizona after she graduated high school. What a terrible tragedy. She was in the front seat of a car when it hit a pick up truck coming from the other direction. Everyone mourned her loss," Sally said as she continued to caress the necklace.

Joseph realized he was being led into a dead end. "Yes, I've heard that."

Sattler gave Joseph a tepid glance. "*We've all heard that.* I would like to get back onto the subject, if you don't mind."

"Oh, certainly," Joseph acquiesced.

"How was Evan affected by Jake's death?" Sattler asked.

"There are various reactions people have when close friends and relatives die suddenly. Most people show shock, then grief. They go to a funeral that gives them some type of closure with the loved one, and then finally experience some form of acceptance of what happened. From what I could tell, Evan did not grieve in the usual way. He did not take time off from school to go to Jake's funeral in Louisville. He just seemed more angry than anything else."

"Did he ever say with whom he was angry?"

"As I said before, he did not talk to anybody. Most of my assessment is really unscientific, but came from seeing his behavior and mannerisms in school. I've been working with teenagers for forty years. I know how to spot anger."

Sattler silently digested the information he was given. "You have been extremely helpful. Is there anything else you want to tell us?"

"Nothing much, the kidnapping happened towards the end of Evan's junior year of high school. The next year he stayed quiet. He left town to go to college soon afterwards."

"What were his plans for college?" Jefferies followed-up.

Sally sat back in the sofa and scratched Butch behind his ear. "I do recall he was good at math and science and got into Virginia Polytechnic Institute. I think he was interested in becoming an engineer."

The room became quiet, only the sound of excited dogs barking could be heard from the backyard. Evan matched the initial profile developed for bomber. Sattler was satisfied that finally, he was on the right track. He got up from the sofa and cleared off the cake crumbs from his pants. "We may be in contact with you to ask some more questions, if you don't mind."

"Anytime, Agent Sattler, I'm more than happy to talk to a handsome young man from the Bureau," Sally said in a motherly tone. Sally led the group out onto the porch and watched as they quickly traversed the steps down to the street. Looking down, she took the necklace off her neck and put the pendant in her hand, letting the silver chain fall towards the patio. Moving it in her hand, she noticed the star in the center glimmer in the afternoon sunlight. She sighed and closed her hand tightly around the pendant, holding it for a few moments as she watched them get into the SUV.

Sattler got into the front seat and immediately started giving directions to Jefferies. "I would like you to get a couple of agents and go over to the high school. I don't care that it's Saturday. I am sure Sam can get the building opened. I want all his high school records on my desk by tonight. I want to know the names of all his teachers, and I want them interviewed by tomorrow. I also want a couple of agents to go to VPI and get any college records. I want to know where he is right now, and what he's doing. Spare no resource. If you need the help of the state police—get it. I want a report on my desk regarding the activities of Evan Young on my desk by Monday morning. Understood?"

"Yes sir, I understand," Jefferies said, writing interview notes in a small pad.

Sally watched the SUV drive away, went back into the house, picked up the phone and dialed a number. She spoke excitedly into the receiver. "You will never believe who came here asking me questions…"

Chapter 17

Over the weekend, the life of Evan Young became the subject of a massive investigation by the FBI. By Monday morning, as promised, the report summarizing the weekend's efforts was on the library conference room table in front of Agent George Sattler. On Saturday night, Sattler was optimistic he would have Young in custody, being interviewed. Instead, the trail of his whereabouts ended at Virginia Polytechnic Institute. Young never finished his degree there, instead, he apparently deciding to leave the school in his junior year. His professors were mystified at the sudden withdrawal of an honor-roll student with a 3.7 grade point average. People there remembered him the same way Sally did: a brilliant, shy student who kept to himself. His only extracurricular activity was the Christian fellowship. The minister recalled that he always appeared to be very serious, and seemed depressed at the current state of events in the United States, criticizing the government as being immoral.

Up to that point in his life, Evan had left the usual paper trail. He had a driver's license, social security card, credit card, and a checking account at the local bank. The FBI pulled his driving record from the Division of Motor Vehicles. The driver's license expired ten years before: the checking account and the credit card were also gone upon Young's departure from the school. It was as if the person under the name of "Evan Young" had ceased to exist.

Sattler threw the report down onto the mahogany table. "This report I have in front of me asks more questions than it answers. I expected much more," Sattler said, his voice resonating with disappointment.

"I had a group of twenty agents covering it over the weekend. They worked on it non-stop," Jefferies explained.

"Did you try tracing the estate money?"

"Yes we did—two and a half million dollars of it, withdrawn in a series of ten cashier checks. We haven't been able to trace it. We even went to the IRS. Evan Young has not filed a tax return in ten years."

"He's probably living under some assumed name then. Have you done the age progression analysis on the driver's license photo?"

"There is some good news with regard to that. I have given it over to the people in Washington. They have the photos of Young's parents which allowed them to improve the accuracy of the computer age progression. We've done a comparison of the age progression photograph and the digitally enhanced photograph from the ATM machine in Gottlieb. The folks back in Washington say there is a ninety-percent probability the person in the two photographs are the same. I would say those are fairly good odds given that both photographs have been digitally enhanced."

"Ninety-percent is still not a hundred. My instinct, though, says that it is him, but we won't know that for certain until we get him in custody. He appears to have the money and the resources to plan and carry out these attacks. It now seems that the motive is simply revenge for the prosecution of Jake Adamson, who was a 'father figure.' He obviously believes for some reason that Adamson was innocent of the crimes he was accused, and that the government was responsible for his death."

Jefferies sat back in his chair. "I also find it interesting that Mr. Young was so taken with religion. You had mentioned that there was possibly some type of religious significance to these bombings since water was involved. This may not simply be 'revenge' but some form of 'biblical retribution.' The people we are dealing with are fairly fanatical, and may not want to be taken into custody alive."

Sattler thought for a moment and then commented, "You may be right about that. Let's develop a psychological profile of Evan given what we know about his childhood and adolescence. It may give us some insight as to what he will do next, and how to best get him into custody. In the meantime, we should distribute his photo to all the daily newspapers in the state. Someone is bound to recognize him. He cannot remain in hiding forever."

***

Jesse ran across the oak floor of the apartment hurriedly picking up model trucks and airplanes, putting them in her arms. "The place's a sty. Get off your butt and help. You live here too," she said with disgust to Toby, who was on the checkered cloth couch watching cartoons on the nineteen-inch color television.

"What's the big deal? It's only Joseph," Toby said, switching channels.

"This is the first time he has been over here. That's why. I don't want him to think that we live this way."

Toby sat up, turned his head, and looked at the general condition of the living room. Knowing any serious cleaning was a lost cause, Toby said, "It looks the same way as I remember it. This is how we live, Mom."

Jesse quickly walked over to the television and turned it off. Pulling Toby up by his arm she ordered tersely, "Clean off the table, while I vacuum."

Toby slowly grabbed the dirty cereal bowls off the table and went into the small kitchen nook to throw them into the sink already crowded with dishes. Toby went to the window, pulled the drapes, and looked down on the small, two-lane street filled with cars. A K-car approached, trailing a plume of dark smoke, as it slowed down and parallel parked inside a gap between two late-model sedans, looking like the odd car on the street. "I think he's here," Toby said, as Jesse continued cleaning. Toby pulled the vacuum cleaner plug from the wall. "*He's here, Mom!*" he yelled.

"You don't need to holler at me, honey. I hear you. Oh, shit. This place is not ready. Well, he'll have to make do with things the way they are," she said, throwing up her hands in futility.

In the meantime, Joseph stood outside the driver's side door in the middle of the road where two bags of groceries rested on the hot pavement. He stared ahead to what he thought was Jesse's red brick building. He thumbed nervously in his pocket for the paper on which he wrote the address. He checked it twice: "20 Thurmont Way, Apartment 2B." The front door opened, and Jesse and Toby appeared smiling. She walked across the street, threw her arms around him, and kissed him briefly on the lips. His blushed in surprise at the unexpected display of affection.

She peered over at the paper bags filled to the brim with cans of food and large, purple-black eggplants and said modestly, "Thanks for dinner. You shouldn't have gone through all the trouble." Jesse didn't know what to think, since no man she had ever known had bothered to buy groceries for dinner, including her ex-husband.

"You have been really nice to me buying me dinner and lunch. I thought this time I should make you dinner." Joseph did not want to admit he relished the idea of being in a kitchen to cook the Lebanese food he had sorely missed for the past few weeks.

Jesse picked up a bag of groceries and handed it over to Toby, who had been trailing behind. She sniffed the air. "Did you know your car burns oil?"

"I wouldn't doubt it. I don't have the time to look at it."

"When was the last time you changed the oil?"

"Sometime last year...I think, or maybe it was last winter. Who remembers when they last changed their oil?"

Jesse frowned and then laughed, "I do. You're supposed to change it every six months or three thousand miles. Give me the keys. I will pull it out back and do it for you, while you both make the dinner. That's a fair division of labor."

"You don't need to do that. I did not come here for you to do my work for me," Joseph said proudly.

"I insist. Give me the keys." Jesse stood in the middle of the street with her hand held out.

Toby tugged on Joseph's sleeve. "You had better do what she wants. You don't want to piss her off."

"Joseph, Toby speaks from experience. If you don't want find out how I am when I'm mad, I suggest you shut up and give me the goddamned keys."

Knowing that there was no other choice but to comply, Joseph put the set of keys in her hand. She quickly got into the driver's seat and closed the door, which popped right back open. She closed it harder. It popped open again. She called out the window, "After I get the engine squared away, I'm going to fix this pain in the ass door lock." She finally slammed the door, shaking the car. She thrust the key in the ignition, abruptly started the engine, and sped off down the street.

"That's my mom. Once she gets an idea in her head, she doesn't let go. It's like arguing with the wall." Toby shrugged. "Let's go upstairs. I'm starting to get hungry." As Toby swung open the front door to the apartment, Joseph put his hand over his mouth in astonishment, seeing the living room and kitchen in complete disarray. Toby did not pay any attention to Joseph; he simply upended the two grocery bags in front of the refrigerator and unloaded the contents. "So what are we going to have for dinner?"

"Lebanese chicken and rice and baba ghanouj," Joseph said, still trying to recover from the initial shock.

"Bubble Gum what?"

"It is mashed up eggplant with lemon juice, garlic, and spices. It is something we had before dinner when I was growing up. You will like it." Joseph surveyed the sink. "I cannot cook in this mess. So the first thing I need to do is clean the dishes. You can assist if you want."

Joseph ran the faucet, while Toby sat on dinette chair and asked reflectively, "Did you do a lot of things with your father?"

"We listened to music together, we used to play chess, and we cooked dinner together."

"Didn't your mother cook?"

"She came from a wealthy family. When she was young, she had a maid prepare her meals, so she never learned. Why are you asking?"

"My father left when I was a baby, and I wanted to know what growing up with a mother and father was like for you."

"I think most people have a special, unique relationship with their parents. I was also an only son. They were very protective and supportive of me, just like I know your mom is very protective of you."

"So, do you think my mother is good looking?" Toby asked innocently.

"You ask a lot of questions," Joseph said, scrubbing a pan.

"I always hear guys talk about her. They say that she's 'a babe' and I was curious what you think?"

"You certainly don't waste time asking personal questions. Yes, I think your mother is pretty. But that is not the sole reason why I like her."

"I find her difficult to figure, though. I've gone hunting with her. I have seen her crouch in cold wet leaves in freezing temperatures waiting hours for a deer to show. I didn't like it, I felt like shit. Ooops, I said a bad word…my mom doesn't like it when I swear, but I hear her do it all the time. My mom likes to curse a lot."

"Yes, I have noticed. She has quite a vocabulary."

"I have seen her lean over a car for an entire afternoon replacing engines and radiators and then come home with bruises and scratches and say nothing. But then, a couple of years ago, when my grandmother went into the hospital, she was standing in the living room with tears coming down her face. I asked her if she was crying, and she said that something was in her eyes. I know she was lying. She's very funny about those things."

"Yes, it is funny. She sees herself as physically tough, but then she is embarrassed by her feelings."

"Mr. Joseph, lemme show you something." Toby ran through the living room, and opened a closet door in his mother's bedroom. Joseph heard clothes move around on hangers and the "thraappt" of shoes falling to the floor. Toby appeared with a bow. Not a simple archery bow that Joseph shot during his youth, which was made from a piece of wood with a handle and a string, but a compound bow that looked like a piece of sculpture, a work of mechanical and materials engineering. It was about three-feet high and the curved end went up to Toby's chin. It had a polymer handle grip that conformed to the shape of a hand and two circular cams on the curved hardwood end used to control tension in the string. He picked up the bow and pretended to use the sight.

"My mother is strong. It takes forty pounds of pressure to pull back the string. You want to try it, Mr. Joseph?"

"No, thank you. I am up to my elbows in dirty dishes. I do not think your mother would like it if she saw you playing with it."

"I've seen her kill a whitetail deer from across a wide meadow. The deer was shot in the shoulder and my mother had to trail it nearly a mile before it died. It was a four-point buck that weighed over eighty pounds, and she dragged it over one-half mile to the road." Toby pointed to a small three by five inch picture on the wall, taken next to a pickup truck. "You see, that's my mom and the deer."

Not impressed, Joseph said, "I already knew your mother was a very determined person even before I found out that she killed a deer. Her resolve in difficult situations is one of the things I like about her. Now please put the bow away, it makes me nervous."

"Oh alright. You're no fun." Toby made a face and sheepishly walked back to his mother's bedroom.

Joseph was finally getting down to the bottom of the sink. He heard Ralph getting up from his nap. The dog scratched its chin with his hind leg ringing the small bells on his collar. Ralph leisurely went into the living room when he spied Joseph in the kitchen and curiously started to trot toward him. Joseph saw Ralph from the corner of his eye and grabbed a steel pan. "If you get within five feet of me, I swear to God I will knock you unconscious!" Ralph looked up innocently and sniffed the air, not knowing how to react. The standoff lasted about two minutes before Ralph decided to back down and make a tactical retreat into a corner of the living room.

After all the ingredients were assembled for the two dishes, Joseph stood back from the counter in admiration of his own culinary effort. It had been an hour since Jesse took the car for an oil change, and he wondered what was taking her so long. He wandered out the back door of the apartment and walked along the row of brick garages until he saw an open door and a light on. Jesse was one of the privileged few who were able to rent a garage in back of the building, where she kept her own personal car, a 1994 Ford Taurus that she had bought used. The Taurus was parked in the alley outside the garage. Joseph heard the clanking of tools and heavy breathing inside.

Joseph expected to find Jesse finishing up the oil change, but instead was greeted by valves spread on the floor, once part of the engine block. Jesse picked up her head. "Watch your step, there're parts on the floor. I don't want them scattered about."

Putting his head in his hands, Joseph said in a low voice, trying to control his temper, "All you said was that you were going to do an oil change. You did not mention taking apart the engine."

Jesse was not ready to concede anything. "That was quite a nice pile of steaming crap you handed me. It is a miracle your engine has not seized up on you while driving down the road. It is not an oil change you need. It is a complete engine overhaul. She picked up a cylinder off the ground. "Take a look at this. The metal is supposed to be free of residue but this one has a film of burnt oil. An oil change would be a band aid solution to a major problem. This thing is a rolling death trap."

"Can you have it fixed by tonight?" Joseph asked optimistically.

"No way, I need to work on it tomorrow." Jesse shrugged.

"I need it to get around. What do you suggest I do then? Hitchhike a ride to work?"

"Do not worry. I will drive you in the Taurus."

Joseph did not want to be seen being driven around by a woman and tried to be diplomatic and make up an excuse. "That is generous, but I want to take my chances with my own car."

"Oh, don't be a baby. If you can drive your piece of shit, then my car would be a limo." After an hour of working, Jesse started to feel hunger pangs. "How's dinner coming?"

"It is almost ready."

Jesse wiped her hands on a rag and turned off the light. "Screw your car and let's eat."

As it turned out, the dinner went more smoothly than the car repair. That night, Jesse and Toby sat at the small dinning table and were served by Joseph. Jesse looked inquisitively at a bowl of grayish, white mush. "What is this?" she asked, "Cold grits?"

"Instead of staring, why don't you try it?" Joseph said, as he came back with warm triangles of pita bread.

She dipped the bread into the mixture and cautiously took a bite. "Mmmm. This is real good. It has a tang to it. What do you call it again?"

"Baba Ghanouj. It is mashed, roasted eggplant with some sesame seed paste, lime juice, garlic, and pepper. Toby helped me make it."

Joseph saw Toby was already on his third piece of pita bread. "Hey, leave some room for the main course." Quite happy with himself, he added, "We still have chicken."

Between mouthfuls, Toby said to Jesse, "I like this cooking better than yours. Can we have this tomorrow?"

"You better watch what you say young man. I'm your mother and no matter who comes along, I still cook the best," Jesse admonished lightheartedly. She turned to Joseph. "I'm really impressed," Jesse said, putting down her napkin. "You're quite the chef, and you cleaned the kitchen for me. This is the first time I ever had a guy over and he left the apartment in a better condition than he found it. It almost makes me feel like celebrating. She left the table and got a bottle of white wine from the refrigerator and two wineglasses. "I've been keeping this in the fridge, waiting for the right occasion." She poured a glass for Joseph and then one for herself. "To friendship," she said as she clicked Joseph's glass. "We've grown close in a short time, and I hope we never loose that."

Joseph took a sip and clicked back, "May we all see peace and prosperity," was all that he could think in response.

For a brief moment, it seemed that there were only the two of them in the room. Joseph felt at ease sitting across from Jesse, who was coyly smiling at him.

Toby watched and declared in disgust, "If you two are going to kiss, I'm going to have to leave the table."

"If you're finished your meal, you can go and do your homework," she said, still gazing at Joseph.

"Yes maam," Toby saluted and ran off to his room with Ralph following.

"I'm sorry it's so difficult to have an adult conversation," Jesse said apologetically as Joseph started to bus the kitchen table. Jesse put on the radio and relaxed on the couch, drinking her wine. She turned on some soft music, took off her work shoes and put her tired feet on the coffee table. She motioned to Joseph, "You can come over here if you want. You do not need to clean off the table. I will do it in the morning."

"No, you are going to have a mess on your hands if I do not take care of this." Joseph moved around, noisily collecting the dishes and piling them in the sink, ignoring Jesse, who had picked up a newspaper from the floor and started to read. After a few minutes, Joseph returned wiping his hands. Jesse sat up and patted the seat next to her. "Come here, Joseph. Keep me company. I don't bite."

Joseph stepped over toward the sofa. Instead of sitting down, he moved toward the bookcase where he noticed a rolled-up pinup poster of the red-haired woman sitting on the Corvette—the same one he originally saw when he was at the gas station with Sam. Unrolling it slowly, he noted that the poster was wrinkled and faded from being wet, but still intact. "Hey, you kept the car poster from the garage."

"Oh, that old thing," Jesse said, taking a sip of wine. "My father thought it was amusing that the girl looked like me and he kept it over the years. He called it his 'Jesse' picture."

"I find the resemblance uncanny. You both have short, red hair, and the same build."

Jesse got up, snatched Joseph by the hand and made him sit down on the couch. "Stay here, there is something I want to show you," Jesse said as she dashed into her bedroom.

"So what do want me to do now?" Joseph asked impatiently.

"Shut up. I need a couple of minutes," said the muffled voice from the bedroom.

"What is it you are going to show me? I don't like surprises."

"Close your eyes," Jesse ordered.

"Why do I need to close my eyes?"

"I want you to get the full effect." There was a pause. Then the voice behind the door said, "Okay, I'm finished. Do you have your eyes shut?"

"Yes I do," Joseph said, crunching down his eyelids. "Now I am really curious."

The door to the bedroom opened and closed. "Okay, you can open them now."

Joseph wearily lifted his eyelids. Standing in front of the poster was Jesse dressed in the same red shirt tied around her waist and short cut jeans the same as the woman in the poster. Joseph opened his mouth in astonishment.

"How do I look? As a coincidence, I have the same clothes as the model. Does it look like I stepped out of the poster?"

"I never thought you were so beautiful," Joseph said.

Jesse sat next to Joseph on the couch and lightly put her fingers through his curly hair. "I'm a woman born into a man's world. People just want to see me as some type of tomboy grease-monkey mechanic who wants to be a man because I run my own business and sometimes I have to be tough with people to survive. I do not apologize for who I am. Just because I don't enter cakes in the county fair, or have flowered curtains on my windows, doesn't mean I'm not as feminine as any woman in town. I can be anybody you want me to be. How do you want to see me, Joseph? It's all up to you to decide."

"Well, I…I…really don't know," Joseph stammered.

"All I know is that you have changed my life, and you made everything worthwhile for me," Jesse said.

"I am at loss what to say…"

"You are not supposed to say anything. You're supposed to kiss me or do I need to show you how to do that." She put her arms around him, leaned over and pinned Joseph to the couch, while pressing her lips to his. Straddling him, she sat on his thighs and continued kissing him on the mouth. Joseph sat there blushing, not being able to move. As she finished kissing him, she put her hands on his chest, and started unbuttoning his shirt.

"What are you doing?" Joseph asked.

"I am making you more comfortable. You seem stiff. You need to relax," she said, while massaging his shoulders with her hands under his shirt.

"Oh I…I…I am comfortable. You don't need to do that," Joseph protested.

"Don't worry, I will show you what to do. Just let me do the driving," Jesse said, kissing Joseph's neck.

"Okay, just tell me where we are 'driving' to," Joseph said.

"You're cute," Jesse laughed.

The door to Toby's room swung open. Out of reflex, Jesse jumped off the couch. Toby felt as embarrassed as Jesse was. He quickly opened the door to the bathroom and seconds later, Jesse heard the sound of pee hitting the water of the toilet.

As Toby exited from the bathroom, Jesse said, "Hey, it's getting late and since it's a school-day tomorrow, I need you in bed young man. Say goodnight to Joseph and thank him for the meal."

Toby quickly walked over to the couch and shook Joseph's hand, "Thanks Mr. Joseph for letting me cook with you. Are you staying here tonight?" He asked anxiously.

Joseph was about to give a response when Jesse interrupted, "That's for Joseph to decide. Go to bed. I will be there shortly to tuck you in."

Finally she was able to relax. She brushed her teeth and took off her clothes, changing into a long tee-shirt that served as a nightee. She went over to the couch where Joseph was resting. "I made some room for you in my bed. You can sleep with me tonight if you want." Joseph did not respond. Jesse looked over to the couch and saw that Joseph was snoring steadily. "That's the story of my life; anybody I like is not interested in me," she said under her breath. She got a blanket from the closet and put it over the sleeping figure, flicked off the stereo, turned off the lights, and closed the door to her room.

***

A green Ford truck with the window open rode along a thin ribbon of road in the mountains. The driver wore a dirty, white cowboy hat and had an uneven beard. He held a beer in his left hand, tapping to the county music with his right. The early morning air was crisp and the hills surrounding the road were shrouded in fog. The truck maintained its speed, rounding a curve about five feet from the side of a mountain and skirting the shoulder of the road, spewing loose gravel. Taylor chugged the last of the fourth beer from the six pack and crushed the can in his fingers. Throwing it out the window, he reached for another. There was a red mail box on the side of the highway with the numbers "57" painted in black, marking an entrance onto a dirt road. The tires squealed as the truck turned left down a path just ten feet across and barely wide enough to fit the truck, kicking up a cloud of dust as it went. Taylor was in the middle of the fifth beer when he slammed on the brakes and stopped about six inches from a chain stretched across the path. Next to the chain was a sign, "NO

HUNTING NO TRESSPASSING." Taylor got out of the truck, still sipping the beer, and saying under his breath, "What the fuck is going on. He locked it." Taking out his key, he unlocked the large steel padlock and pulled the truck past the gate. Getting out of the car again, he stretched the heavy chain across the road, re-locked the padlock, and continued on his way. Finishing the beer, he continued for another five hundred feet, making a slight right turn onto a smaller dirt road and then accelerating up a hill to a plateau. Atop the hill stood a two-story, wood-frame house with a rectangular log structure on the right that served a bunkhouse, and a tall, white utility structure on the left that was as a garage and equipment storage area.

Taylor pulled up in front of the log cabin and was greeted by Carl Andrews, a heavyset man in his thirties with a jagged scar on his face caused by a fragmentation grenade. The grenade had been meant for his neighbor's dog that had crawled under a fence and had left a pile of excrement on the stairs of his house where Carl lived in Cynthiana, Kentucky. When he lobbed it over the fence, the grenade turned out to be defective and exploded prematurely in midair, the shrapnel imbedding itself in his neighbor's house, the wooden fence, and Carl's face, nearly tearing off part of his cheek. The stunned dog survived the encounter and was left with severe hearing loss. Carl, however, had to undergo several plastic surgeries to repair his face. Found guilty on charges of reckless endangerment and animal cruelty, Carl was sentenced to two years in county jail. Rather than dissuading Carl from the use of explosives, the incident piqued his interest. He left jail wanting to learn how better to control explosives. After he was released, he went from job to job as a laborer on a construction crew, and spent his money on manuals on refining the explosive properties of mixtures he found on the Internet and the "Anarchist's Cookbook."

Carl asked abruptly, "Did you get the newspaper?" Taylor was the messenger and "gofer" for the group and was beginning to regret his role. Taylor remembered Evan had always said that television news was nothing but "lies created by Government." Newspapers did not require any electronics, or any antenna or satellite receivers, that would call attention to the house, and was their only source of information from the outside world. Taylor would routinely pick up a newspaper on his bi-weekly trips to town for food and supplies.

Taylor asked Carl, "Why don't you make yourself useful and help me bring in the supplies? I've got some important information for Evan."

"Supplies aren't my responsibility. I help out plenty here," Carl's responded, while rocking in his chair.

Carl's brother, Randy, a tall man with a crew cut, heard the noise and out of curiosity came out looking sleepy; it was still early in the morning for him. Randy was the older, more level- headed and least belligerent of the two brothers, but still had a short temper that had landed him in jail on minor charges. Randy had less of an interest in explosives, having blown off the tip of his right pinky finger with a firecracker when he was ten years old. "Oh, let's give the little ass-wipe a break. He worked hard this morning. I can smell it on his breath." He grabbed a couple of the bags and brought them into the cabin. Carl, shaking his head, quickly followed suit.

Taylor went into the truck and grabbed the newspaper from the seat and was about to deliver it to the house, when he lifted his head and saw Evan standing next to the truck. Evan announced dryly, "You spent two hours in town on something that should have taken one."

"I got the newspaper you asked for. You should take a look at it. You've become front-page news. You see your photo is right there!"

Evan took a quick glance at the headline "FBI SEEKS MATERIAL WITNESS TO BOMBINGS" and then folded the newspaper in his hands. "So, I'm only a 'Material Witness' and not even a suspect. Now, I feel insulted," he quipped. "What the newspaper says doesn't concern me. It was an eventuality that they would talk to someone who remembered the relationship I had with Jake, and then get my driver's license photograph from the DMV. I wouldn't worry about it. If they knew where I was, they would be right here, now wouldn't they? Come talk with me for a few minutes. I have some things I want to speak to you about." Evan took a seat on one of the two chairs in front of the cabin and motioned for Taylor to take the other. Taylor hesitantly sat down, not knowing what to expect from Evan, and being careful not to make him angry. At times, he could be your best friend, and then, at the slightest provocation, would be was ready to kill you. Evan started out calmly, "I asked you to limit the time you were in town. You're one of our contacts with the outside and a very important part of our family here. I don't want you staying long enough for people to be suspicious, then we would all be in trouble."

Taylor started jabbering nervously, "Well…well…you know there was a long line of people at the food store, and I had to go to a couple of hardware stores to pick up the generator parts we needed."

"You were drinking. You don't hide it well," Evan said.

"I was thirsty and I had a couple of beers. Not a big deal."

"Do you remember when we met two years ago?" Evan asked.

"You bought me a sandwich," Taylor said, turning his face away from Evan's hard stare.

"Not quite the way I remember it. I stopped at a gas station along Route 150, outside of Danville. You came up to me and said you needed money for gas." Evan knew that Taylor remembered. It was one those stations by a barely-traveled road that had once been a farmhouse and had peeling white paint on its wooden siding. Inside, there was an old, gray-haired proprietor who had a hotplate behind the counter and sold pulled-pork barbecue sandwiches. There was a small red dinette set on the wooden floor in front of a ripped confederate flag that hung from the ceiling. "Your face was gaunt, and you looked like you hadn't eaten in days. After we sat down at the table, you wolfed down the sandwich and then I got you a second. I got you the food because if I gave you the money you would have bought beer and gotten drunk with it. You were broke and without any job. I invited you back here and gave you a roof over your head and a way to keep out of the gutter and be productive. Remember what I said when I hired you, and agreed to put you on?"

"You said as long as I was here, you expected me to be loyal. You valued that over everything else."

"Yes, but more importantly, I told you that I wanted you to keep sober. I did not want any drunks working for me. Up to now, you have kept your promise to me, and I'm grateful for that. Now you smell the same way you did when I had met you and that makes me upset."

"I'm not drunk," said Taylor. "I've not had any beer in a long time. I did not promise to give up alcohol because I was working for you. You do not control everything in my life."

"I do things for you and I create rules because you are more than an employee. I care about you, and these are not just empty words, I have shown you that many times. For example, back in February you got a nasty stomach virus. You had a one-hundred and four degree fever. I stayed up all night to cook you broth and give you liquids so that you wouldn't get dehydrated. After all of that, I drove out in one foot of snow on these mountain roads and got you medicine. You have made a commitment to live here, and while you do, you keep to the rules I establish. We have entered a critical time, and I need everyone here to have their wits about them and not be impaired with alcohol. Now go and help Henry with the wood for the fireplace. They are predicting temperatures in the low forties for tonight."

"Yes sir," Taylor said, relieved to be leaving.

Evan opened the door and walked into the cabin to find Carl and Randy on bunk beds reading a six-month-old *Time Magazine*. "How you guys doin'?" he said in a laid back voice. "Looks like they finally got to circulate my picture." He threw the newspaper on the top bunk where Carl was resting.

Carl read the article and gave a sigh, "Whew. Your travel ticket has been rescinded. Told you I have got good contacts in Pope's Mills, didn't I? Told you that I called my friend there and he said they visited Sally Holiday. They did not spend about an hour over there talking about the weather, either. Said they were talking about you. What a foursome they must have been: the bald, shrimp of an FBI agent with a napoleon complex, his lackey from the ATF, the big, black dumb-jock sheriff, and finally, rounding off the bunch, the Arab academic with his head up his ass."

"Yes, you told me several times." Carl did not have to repeat his statement. Evan almost had complete recall of everything said to him. He could recount month old conversations verbatim and had committed to memory multiple passages of *Moby Dick, Gone with the Wind*, and, most notably, the Old and New Testaments of the Holy Bible. He sat on the edge of the bed and started to lecture to Carl and Randy. "I don't blame her for giving them my name. She's a gullible, feeble, misguided woman who thought she could save the world by her work with children. She doesn't understand, like we do, that government is evil, and if something doesn't change, the United States will implode under the weight of its bloated and corrupt bureaucracy—just like that of ancient Rome two thousand years ago. The dark ages are swiftly coming upon us and ordinary people like us have little control over our fate. The government has sold itself out to the big corporations, the executives who only feel responsible to themselves but not to the people. The CEO's get fat off their million dollar bonuses, while millions of people go into poverty each year. The businesses that are supported by government have polluted God's earth, and our bodies are full of toxins that these businesses have created by the millions of tons. They poison the streams we fish and the water we drink. The water that surrounds us, that comprises ninety per cent of our bodies, that's part of God's creation and one of the holiest things we have, is being violated by this evil. I have seen healthy, good people waste away from cancer caused by these chemicals. None of these companies take responsibility for what they've done. They all sleaze away from it, taking refuge in our courts. The court system does not work. It benefits only the lawyers who use our laws to twist our basic, Christian truths. I have seen the guilty go free, while the martyred innocent are blamed and punished. It is the innocent that are reviled and hated, while the evil people who have put them into jail become our role models. It is the morally corrupt who've taken the power, who've got no love or compassion for their families. Sex has replaced love in our society. During a normal day, our children, our future, our next generation, see dozens of sex acts on television. Yes, television, the great god of the modern age— where the masses get their wisdom and where people defile each other sexually for money. It is government that pumps this pornography, disguised as entertainment, into our homes and pollutes our minds. No wonder that, when crime statistics are published, murder and rape are on the increase each year. That is why I limit the access to television, because that is how government controls our minds. The only way we can be truly free is to go back to the only truth in our society, the truth that lies within the Bible. With the Bible, we can fight the terrible, corrupt bureaucracy that has taken over our lives." Evan could have rambled on for another hour, but decided that he had made his key points. Carl and Randy sat on their bunk beds, mesmerized.

Carl said, "Speaking of evil, and the influence of the government, you want to hear about something else that will disgust you? The Arab guy that was mentioned as a hero, Joseph Hamiz, is seeing that girl, Jesse, over in Gottlieb. Ever since we blew up those tanks, they've been an item. He went to that dance with her, probably had his hand on her ass all throughout the evening. I spoke to someone who says he sees his K-car in font of her apartment constantly. I bet he is over there right now doing the horizontal mambo. Isn't that real sickening, or what?"

"I'm glad my good buddy, Joseph, found a girlfriend in the most unexpected place. He looked really lonely to me," Evan said, amused. "I thought we ought to discuss what we should be doing next."

"There are a couple of bridges I think we can demolish," Carl said eagerly.

"No. I have something major planned, and I do not want to waste the C4 on a minor bridge, but you may have just given me an idea. Hey Randy, did you finish fabricating those charges for me?"

"Yes, I did that yesterday."

"You have some leftover C4 then, with some spare timers and switches?"

"I believe so. Why?"

Evan sat back and with a smile on his face said, "The FBI has sent me a message via the press, and now, I would like you to give them my response."

***

It was only six in the morning when the agents departed from their hub at the library for their fieldwork in their black SUVs. Jesse pulled up in her blue Taurus, waited patiently as Joseph retrieved his briefcase and jacket from the backseat. Jesse leaned out the window and shouted to Joseph, who was walking away, "Call me when you want to be picked up in the evening."

Joseph met up with Sam who had just parked his patrol car down the driveway. Sam saw Jesse drive away and said with a grin, "I see you've found a ride to work."

"She has been working on my car for the past few days. She offered to give me a lift. That is all"

"Is that *really* all? I hear you have been living at her apartment for the past few days."

"Have you been spying on me, Sam?"

"No, but I hear things. There is no such thing as privacy here in Pope's Mills, Joseph. You should know that by now."

Joseph laughed nervously. "It may be difficult for you to believe, but there is nothing going on between us. I needed a place to cook, and they enjoy my meals. We are just friends. Remember, you told me I should be more social."

"Yes I did, but I didn't say to start living there, that's a tad more than socializing."

"All I do is sleep on the couch."

"Hey look, I don't care where you sleep. Whatever you do is your own business. My friendly advice is that I would not want to draw too much attention to myself until everything here gets resolved, and we get Evan Young in custody. You should be back at the Lakemount Hotel with the rest of the agents, but I understand why, after three weeks, you would want a break from that." Sam was at the front door of the mansion presenting his ID to the agent when he said, "By the way, Sattler wants to have a general strategy meeting with us this morning; I think he has a big assignment for you and Bob Dickey."

"Oh, my friend Mr. Dickey," Joseph frowned.

"I know he's a prick, but we still need his help. So just take his shit, be a professional, and get the work done."

"Yes, Sheriff," Joseph said and put his hand to head, saluting.

"Stop with the 'Sheriff' crap, Joseph. Just do it."

Joseph poked through his jacket, searching for his ID, and after a few minutes found it and trudged upstairs to his office in the mansion. When he got there, he found a set of plans for a dam outside of Xavier, Kentucky. Joseph searched his mind and recalled that Xavier was to be the location for the trial of Jake Adamson. There was a note attached from Sattler, "Be ready to discuss. Ten AM. Conference Room." So this was the "assignment" he was to be doing with Dickey, he thought. Joseph looked up Xavier on the Internet and got the generic description of the community. Xavier, a town of ten thousand people located about one-hundred miles north of Lexington, in the Bluegrass region of the state, was known primarily for horse breeding. But for Joseph, it was another little town in the middle of nowhere, whose claim to fame was that it had a little league team that came in third place for the past five years in the state finals. It also had a championship, eighteen-hole golf course on the outskirts that could be played for seventeen dollars during the weekday. The Chamber of Commerce calendar included the fishing derby in Braedon Creek, a tributary to the Ohio River, for the month of June.

The dam in question, located on the Braedon about ten miles outside of the center of town, was an earth dam that had a fifty-foot high embankment with an outlet structure that was a twenty-foot diameter concrete pipe through the fill. The dam was built by the community about thirty years ago, and the lack of funds on the municipal level for maintenance had forced the ownership to be transferred to the state, making it part of Dickey's jurisdiction. Joseph got an aerial map online and tried to locate any residential or commercial areas that would be damaged if the dam were blown. He found only trees, barns, and white picket fences. There was a two-lane state road about five miles downstream, but Joseph found it unlikely someone would demolish a dam just to flood out a road. Joseph thought he was missing something obvious and searched for it until the time of the meeting.

When Joseph entered the conference room, Sam, Sattler, and Dickey were already seated around the large table. Sattler said in a fake-genial voice, "Oh, there you are. Now we can start with the meeting. Pass Dr. Hamiz a cup of coffee." Joseph dumped the plans on the table and took the lukewarm coffee handed to him.

Sattler stood up from his seat and spoke, "Thanks in part to recent revelations, we've been able to make great strides in our investigation. It is only a matter of time before we locate Mr. Young, but in the meantime, we should keep an eye out for any potential targets. Yesterday, we got the psychological profile back on our suspect and it stated that we are dealing with an obsessive-compulsive individual bent on revenge. Personally, I could have told them that without any work, but I think, given the profile, we ought to be looking for someplace connected with Jake Adamson. The first town, Pope's Mills, is where he was arrested; the second incident on Gottlieb Heights is where Jake had his preliminary hearing. Naturally Xavier, the location of his trial, is going to be a future target. The trial date was set for September 23rd, but I don't think he will wait that long to try something. Jake died in the jail outside of Xavier, waiting for trial. I believe that, given the pattern that has been established, he is planning a bombing for May 20, the anniversary of Jake's death, a week from today. He has changed his targets to confuse us, but they are all related in some way to water. Given his interest in the Bible, I think he finds some religious significance associated with water. He will stick to that. That is why we have to mobilize and protect any dams and above-ground tanks in Xavier. This is where you two can help out. I would like you both to go to Xavier and handle whatever technical support we need over there."

Joseph raised his hand and asked politely, "I looked over the aerials and I could not find any potential targets. There are no populated areas that would suffer damage from a dam explosion. Overall, I could not see the potential for loss of life."

Sattler leaned back in his chair with his hands folded and countered, "You have an extremely one-dimensional view of this. You only look at the potential 'human' loss of life. You forget that Harrison County is one of the most prime areas for horse breading in Kentucky. Since the horse industry is one of the largest businesses in the state, accounting for over one billion dollars in sales and employing over one hundred thousand people, I'm certain there will be immeasurable economic impact from any dam breach. One of the past winners of the Kentucky Derby is housed in a barn downstream of the dam. That horse is worth several million dollars by itself. So don't sit there and insult me by saying there are no potential targets in the area."

Joseph replied in a dry, unemotional voice, "I don't think he is after horses. I think that is the last thing..." Sattler broke in and continued his tirade, "I'm positive there're lots of potential targets out there. You cannot spot everything from an aerial photo. You need to scout out the terrain. Obviously, Young is not going to send us a list of targets he wants to destroy. That's for us to figure out. But we definitely need to be there."

"What I am really curious about is why you really need me in Xavier at all. I figure I can do whatever support work that is required from my office in the mansion,." Joseph said apprehensively, while taking a sip of coffee.

Sattler thought he was doing Joseph a favor and was not going to change his mind. "No, I think it is better if you get the perspective from being in the field. You seemed bored working here in the mansion, and I thought you would appreciate this assignment."

"No, I am quite happy here," Joseph said with a phony smile on his face.

Dickey was keeping quiet, hoping Joseph would win his argument and finally said, "I think Dr. Hamiz has a valid point. There is no use wasting his valuable time doing the fieldwork. I can do it alone. I have all the information on the dam. I can handle any requests."

Sattler looked at Joseph and Dickey. "Is there a problem with you both I don't know about?"

Both Joseph and Dickey nervously shook their heads.

"I expect you both to be in Xavier tomorrow morning at eight at the dam site, and you'll stay there the entire day. Just get it done." Sattler picked up the folder in front of him and abruptly left the room. This left Joseph and Dickey glancing at each other awkwardly from across the table.

"I heard where you are living," Dickey said snidely. "I've got my state car, so I will pick you up at your place at six. Don't be late," he admonished.

Joseph retorted, "I am looking forward to it; two hours with you going to Xavier. Don't worry, I will be out front."

Sam stood up from the chair. "I hope you boys don't need any adult supervision. I've got better things to do," he said as he left the room.

***

As Joseph lay in a partial dream-state, he felt a cold dampness against his face. Still groggy, he turned over and then the wetness was on his back. Thinking he was dreaming, he tried to brush it away, but it returned. He finally opened his eyelids and discovered Ralph's nose stuck against his cheek. Terrified, he rolled off the sofa onto the carpet, hitting his head on the floor. He screamed in pain, "Get away from me, you filthy animal!" Ralph had the quicker reflexes and was halfway across the room as Joseph lay sprawled on the floor. Annoyed and rubbing his head, he grumbled, "I asked you to keep him in Toby's room."

Jesse was in the kitchen making bacon and eggs. She woke at five and had already eaten breakfast. "I don't keep you cooped up in a room, so how do you expect me to do that to Ralph? He's a member of the family. Anyhow, he did you a favor and got you up. You were about to be late for work. Didn't you mention Bob Dickey was supposed to pick you up this morning at six? It is quarter to six and you don't have much time. I've already used the shower, so you might as well take one."

Joseph showered for five minutes, grabbed the first towel he could find, and quickly dried off. He ran in the living room, took shelter behind the sofa, and put on his shirt and pants as Jesse piled eggs and bacon on his plate. "Not that I am ungrateful," he prefaced. "but isn't my car done? You promised me that it would be ready yesterday."

"I finished it up yesterday after work. I parked it out front."

"Oh, that is great—really nice to have it back," Joseph said, pleasantly surprised. He sat down at the table and started to eat his bacon that seemed to be blackened. From outside he heard a car horn. He was about to pick up a forkful of runny scrambled eggs when it sounded again. He checked the clock on the wall. It was five minutes to six. "He is early. He can wait a few minutes while I finish my breakfast."

Jesse pulled up the blinds and checked out the window. "Joseph, there is a car with a state emblem blowing its horn. You better get out there before he wakes up the entire neighborhood."

"Oh alright, I am coming." Joseph abruptly put down his napkin and picked up his briefcase. "I am sorry I won't be home till late so you will have to make dinner yourself tonight," he said as he hugged Jesse.

Jesse said, "I will find a way to survive," as he closed the door.

After Joseph exited the apartment, he saw Dickey sitting in the car looking angrily at his watch. Dickey had parked about five feet in back of his K-car and continued hitting the car horn. People in adjacent houses were beginning to look out the windows. "C'mon, get in," Dickey said. "If we are not there by eight, the FBI will have our heads." Joseph crossed in front of the white Plymouth Neon state car and was about to get in the front seat when he heard Jesse call out the kitchen window to him, "Oh shit, I almost forgot your lunch." She stood up against the screen and held up a paper bag.

Joseph threw his briefcase in the front seat and looked back at Jesse in a moment of indecision. Her food was generally inedible, he thought, but remembered the consequences. It would be more convenient if I ignore her and leave, but she took some time to pack the food and was going to be angry if I don't take it, he thought. He poked his head inside the car. "I am sorry; I need to retrieve my lunch."

As Joseph went back into the street, Dickey banged on the dashboard and yelled out the car window, "Make it quick! I would like to get out sometime this morning."

Jesse called out the window again, "Can you do me one more favor, and fetch my toolbox from your car while you are there. I think I left it in the front seat."

Joseph stopped in his tracks, flipped the handle and the rusty car door opened with a groan. He searched the front seat and could not find the box. "Are you sure the box is in the front seat?"

"Oh, maybe it is in the back," she called out the window.

Joseph leaned over the bench seat and could see only a couple of quarters he left on the floor. He came out and shook his head.

Jesse ducked out of the window and started to search the apartment while Joseph stood in the street. She looked under the kitchen table and spotted the gray, metallic box. "Sorry honey for the false alarm, it's right here."

Dickey's face was red with frustration as he watched Joseph fumble with the car. He leaned against the car horn. Joseph closed his car door and took a few steps before it popped open again. Joseph turned around and saw that it was ajar and slammed it closed and ran across the street to the brick vestibule of the apartment building to retrieve his lunch. He opened the apartment door and stepped inside when he was thrown to the ground by a powerful explosion. From the floor, he saw the car the K-car leap five feet in the air. Before the remnants of the car were able to hit the ground, the gas tank exploded, sending a fireball back toward Dickey's car. The Neon was lifted up and catapulted into the middle of the street, thrown backward onto its top. The interior was engulfed in fire with its windshield blasted out. Joseph kicked open the vestibule door with the mistaken belief something could be done about Dickey. The inside of the Neon was an orange inferno. He got up and stumbled out the door, immediately feeling the intense heat from the car on his skin. The acrid black smoke stung his eyes and he had to drop back to the ground, coughing.

He turned back, looked at Jesse's apartment and saw the blast had blown out the windows. He got back up and ran into the door and up the steps. He opened the apartment door, but did not find anybody, except the debris from the windows on the floor. The force of the explosion had slammed the kitchen table against the wall, dishes and glasses broken on the floor. There was no one there. Fear took over his mind. He screamed out, "Jesse where are you?" There was no response. He surveyed the living room and saw that the sofa was overturned. Hearing movement underneath, he flipped it back up onto its legs. Jesse was sprawled on the floor with Toby. Toby had blood streaming down his face from a cut above his eyes caused by the flying glass.

Shaken and on the floor with her shirt stained from Toby's blood, Jesse looked up, relieved to be seeing Joseph. With tears coming down her face, she got up and put her arms around him. "Am I ever happy to see you. What about Dickey?"

Joseph shook his head, and Jesse clutched him tighter.

***

Agents Sattler and Jefferies sped to the scene where police had cordoned off the neighborhood within a radius of five blocks of the blast. A half dozen ambulances arrived, taking people cut by debris to the hospital. Sam heard the police report on his car radio on his way to work, and looked worried as he got to the apartment. He looked on anxiously as the fire department EMT examined Jesse and Joseph. Finding nothing, the EMT moved on to Toby who was sitting up silently and unresponsively. Shining the flashlight in Toby's eyes, the EMT said somberly, "The boy has received a deep facial laceration. He needs to be checked out for a possible concussion at the hospital."

Jesse grabbed her purse and trailed the technician as they placed Toby onto the stretcher and into a waiting ambulance. Joseph wanted to go with them, but was held back by Sattler who said, "We need you here to answer some questions."

Dazed, but maintaining his concentration, Joseph found himself sitting on the sofa stained with red splotches of blood, recounting in painful detail the events of the previous twenty-four hours to Sattler and Jefferies. The other agents went door to door asking if the neighbors had seen anyone around the car. Mercifully, one hour into the interview, the forensic team chief came up to the apartment and briefed Sattler on the progress with the collection of evidence. The blast was strong enough to embed pieces of the K-car chassis in the brick of the apartment building. Dickey had received most of the force of the explosion and nothing more than badly burned bone and teeth fragments were found adjacent to the shell of the car. The best Sattler could figure was that the bomb was planted in the mid-morning hours, and the perpetrator was long gone from the area.

Sattler stood over Joseph, holding a clear plastic evidence bag with what seemed an innocuous looking piece of burnt plastic given to him by the technician. "You know what this is?" he asked.

Joseph shook his head.

"It is the remains of the switch that controlled the fuse of the explosive placed under your car. You must have jarred the two metal connections in the switch together when you slammed your car door. The fuse had a delay so that after you started the engine and got the car moving the explosive would have gone off. It was intended to kill you and anyone else in the immediate area. I'm grateful no one else was seriously hurt, that it was early in the morning, and that no one was out mowing a lawn. I admit we've had our differences; however, Dickey did not deserve what happened to him. I hope you know how lucky you are. You realize that had you not been running back to the vestibule, you would be dead. If you had taken two steps less and were still outside, unprotected by the thick, wooden door, your body would be splattered across the block like Dickey's."

Joseph stared down at the carpet, not wanting to be lectured.

Sattler continued, "We must be making them nervous, but I'm curious as to why they had chosen you? Do you know something about them that we don't?"

"I know nothing...I just told you everything I can remember," Joseph said plaintively.

"Are you working with them?" Sattler asked in an accusatory manner.

Sam, who was quietly observing the questioning, shot up from his seat. "I've heard enough from this prick. Don't answer that question, Joseph." He pointed a finger at Sattler, "You know that you're fucking nuts. Joseph has been responsible for all the progress we have been making. They probably saw he's vulnerable. So give him a break. Before you blame someone, you should look at yourself. You've been mismanaging this investigation from the beginning. Admit it, you have taken on much more than you can handle. I knew he was staying here. I'm just as responsible for what happened as he was. Why don't you get on my case, shithead? We all share the blame. If you guys were not sitting, jerking-off on the sidelines, you would have found this Young character. Then nobody would have had the opportunity to place a car bomb."

Sattler turned red and stood a few inches from Sam's face. "You fucking think you can do better, Sheriff?"

Not backing away, Sam said, "I've seen trainees from the police academy that would've made more progress than you."

"I haven't heard any suggestions from you recently. All I see is some small-town asshole that lets his emotions get in the way of his job. If you would have done it back at the Kendal River Dam three weeks ago, we would not be here in the first place."

Blind anger and rage took over and Sam punched Sattler squarely in the nose and. with both hands, lifted Sattler's body and slammed his head against the wall. Stunned by the suddenness of the attack, but not incapacitated, Sattler broke Sam's grip and landed a blow on Sam's jaw with his right hand. Sam grabbed Sattler again and drove him against the wall, the force dislodging the remaining pictures that survived the explosion. Slow to react, Jefferies tried to get a grip on Sam's arms and pull him away from Sattler, who landed a fist to Sam's stomach. The other two agents had rushed in and put their arms around Sam's wide shoulders. Sattler sensed he had been given the advantage and put enough distance between himself and Sam to kick him sharply in the groin. Sam, doubled over in pain, coughing and trying to catch his breath, crumbled to the floor as the group of agents finally loosened their hold.

Jaw bruised and his nose bleeding, Sattler stood over Sam and shouted to the agents, "Get him out of here! I don't want to see him!" They lifted Sam off the floor and helped him out of the apartment building. Joseph watched the fight in disbelief. Sattler pointed to him, "I don't want to see you either. Get the fuck out of here!"

Joseph stood up and slowly exited the building. He was without any transportation, and wondered to himself how he would get back to the Lakemount Motel outside of Pope's Mills, where he had been staying with the other agents. Outside, Joseph looked through the pandemonium of police and fire vehicles and noticed Sam sitting on the hood of his police cruiser talking to Jefferies who was trying to be the peacemaker. "Now calm down," he said, "You shouldn't have taken a swing at him."

"I'm not going to be calm. He crossed the line talking about what I did the day my friends died."

"You shouldn't have challenged his authority," Jefferies said, without the emotion that was charged in Sam's voice.

"I never recognized his authority in the first place," Sam snapped.

"Whoever is in authority is a moot issue. I recall it was you who begged to be onboard with the investigation. Best remember, your future, as well as ours, hangs on the outcome, so I would find a way to work with us. Let us handle things today, and you do something else. I'm going to talk to Sattler about letting you come back to work tomorrow, so just keep cool."

As Jefferies walked away, Joseph asked Sam sarcastically, "So what ever happened to being a professional?"

"Oh shut up and get in the fucking car," Sam said as he opened the passenger door. Joseph gratefully got in. Sam carefully navigated through the stopped ambulances and fire engines. Once clear, he gunned the engine, quickly putting the scene of the bombing behind him.

***

Jesse sat in the waiting room of the Mid County Memorial hospital and watched as the middle-aged emergency room nurse, dressed in light blue scrubs, endlessly chattered over the phone, ignoring the commotion around her. The combination of pale green paint on the walls, the harsh fluorescent lights, the oblong waiting room smelling of bleach, and her anxiety about her son, made her sick to her stomach. All she could do was sip on a lukewarm bottle of water while leafing through a six-month old *Time Magazine*. The waiting room had been filled with the victims of the bombing staring ahead with empty looks on their blood-stained faces.

She had been waiting five hours for the results of the Toby's CAT scan. Earlier, she held his hand as the doctor gave him twenty stitches on his forehead. She was proud that he barely whimpered as the doctor cleaned the cut and pushed the needle through the skin. She looked down and watched as he soundly slept on the waiting-room bench beside her, a large, gauze bandage around his head. Feeling helpless and bored of hearing the muzak version of "Tie a Yellow Ribbon Around the Old Oak Tree" for the fifth time, she put her head in her hands, hoping for some form of salvation.

Feeling a hand brushing her neck, she turned around and saw Joseph holding a bouquet of red roses and yellow daffodils. She said, "How thoughtful of you to wait here with me, and bring me the flowers."

"Actually, the flowers were Sam's idea," Joseph said modestly. Sam was behind him with his back turned, surveying the waiting room, trying to allow for a private moment of affection between Joseph and Jesse. Jesse stood in the middle of the room, and, while holding the roses, hugged Joseph for the longest time. She finally noticed Sam, walked over to him, and put her head on his chest. Sam smiled approvingly, "It has been quite a while since I've had gotten a warm embrace from such a beautiful young lady."

"Aren't you the big flatterer, Sam? I'm glad that you both showed up. I was getting depressed waiting here alone."

"Any news on Toby yet?" Joseph asked, patting the boy on the legs as he slept.

"Absolutely nothing. I think they have only one doctor taking care of twenty people. I don't know how much longer my nerves can take this waiting." Changing to another topic she asked, "How is my neighborhood doing?"

"They are still cleaning up," Sam said, picking up the month old *Time Magazine* and giving it a brief inspection. "I think it is going to be a while before the forensics people are finished with the long process of cataloging the evidence. It will probably be a couple of days before things are returned to normal, and all the utilities are turned back on."

Jesse put down the flowers and shot back a stern glare. "I don't care if the electricity is off and there is no running water, I have lived under a lot worse conditions. Someone is not going to force me from my home. They're going to have to bring me out feet first for that to happen."

Sam could sense that she was still angry and upset. He was about to discuss the situation rationally, when a young doctor in his early thirties approached her. "Hello, I'm Dr. Knowles. I've some good news for you. I just reviewed your son's CAT scan, and there is no evidence of brain trauma. It looks like he will be okay in the next day or so. However, as a normal precaution, I want to keep him here tonight for observation to make sure."

"Can I make arrangements to stay here overnight with him? I don't want him to wake up in the morning with strange people around."

"I think we can do that for you. I will mention it to the admitting nurse. If you excuse me, I have some more people to see. I will be checking on him in the morning. In the meantime, if you have any questions, just have me paged." As quickly as he arrived, Knowles walked down the corridor, and spoke to a nurse while pointing to Jesse. The nurse nodded, saying, "Yes, sir."

The phone hanging on Sam's belt rang and he walked a few paces away and answered it. Jesse took a seat in a yellow plastic chair as people injured from the explosion still milled aimlessly about the waiting room. "That news is a big weight off my shoulders." She took a big swing of water. "I've been thinking so much about Toby that I haven't even considered your situation. Are you going back to stay at the motel? Why don't you sleep here with Toby and me tonight? I think it will be a big morale boost for him to see you in the morning."

"I don't know if I should," Joseph said, a questionable look on his face.

Jesse felt his anxiousness. "Why not?" she asked.

"Because I am a danger to you. I do not want you to become further entangled in this business."

She reached out and held his hand. "That is really a quite noble sentiment, but I became involved when that wave took out my shop, which also happens to be the only way I put food on the table."

"I am not talking about that. For some reason I can't figure, they are going after me. I never wanted to be part of what was happening here from the start. I tried telling that to the FBI during the initial interview, but they wouldn't listen to me. Someone has a vendetta against the government for what went on here ten years ago, and I am being pulled into it. I've become part of the closed circle of what is happening, and if you are not careful, you will become part of it, too."

Jesse became indignant. "It must be convenient being at the center of your own little fucking universe. If you are too dumb to understand, I just want to let you know that this is the second time in seven days they tried to kill my son. It doesn't matter to me how fucking involved I become, because if I have anything to do with it the sonofabitch out there will not live long enough to try it a third time."

Sam got off the phone. Jesse's voice was becoming loud and was carrying down the hall. He heard the brunt of the conversation, walked over and said, "I hope I'm not interrupting anything."

"No, Jesse was being overtly melodramatic."

"You think I'm fucking bullshitting you. I mean everything I say. I'm not afraid to take matters into my own hands, especially when it comes to my son."

Sam grinned at Joseph. "That was our friend Agent Jefferies. He tells me they just had a meeting about you. They want you to go immediately into protective custody. They have your personal items from Jesse's apartment. I've been directed to drive you back to the motel so you can gather the rest of your things. They've arranged for a federal marshal to take you to an undisclosed location and baby-sit you until this whole thing gets resolved. I'm happy for you. You're going to get your wish and be free of all this horseshit."

"They want me to go at this moment?" Joseph could not believe the news.

"Yes, that is what 'immediately' generally means," Sam said.

Jesse's face dropped when she understood what was going to happen. "Excuse me Sam, I need to talk to Joseph in private." Jesse grabbed his arm and dragged him into an empty examination room.

"I suppose we will not be able to finish what we were just arguing about. I am sure I will have an opportunity to drop you a line from wherever they take me." Joseph said, looking into Jesse's eyes that had become moist.

"I've got a suggestion. They don't need to take you far. Why don't you simply go back to your 'lab,' or whatever hole you climb down at the Kentucky Institute of Technology and retreat? You seem to be pretty good at that."

Throwing his hands up in frustration he yelled, "*What do you want from me?* I am just following the FBI's advice, and staying alive."

"Survival's one thing. But what we're talking about is isolation. Is that what you really want?"

"I don't know," Joseph said, trying to search his own feelings.

"You fucking act like you don't have a mind of your own. I hear you speak your endless bullshit about 'cycles of violence' and 'closed circles,' but you're afraid to deal with the problem. It must be rather convenient for you not to have any beliefs strong enough to fight for."

"I believe in many things," Joseph said, bordering on anger.

"You talk a lot but don't have the conviction to follow through. Look at me. I'm not wealthy, and I work at some shit gas station. But it's something I own. Something I'm part of and that is part of me. I tuck Toby into bed every night thinking about someday owning a garage with six service bays and hiring top-notch mechanics to work on cars. I wake up at five o'clock every morning pursuing that dream, and one day it will happen. What's your dream, Joseph? What do you sit up at night thinking about?"

"I want to teach college in America and do state of the art research," Joseph said, as if responding to a question at a job interview.

"Yeah, you told how well that's going. You have a single class with ten students."

Joseph said, "I am also doing a lot of research; I have a big contract with the Corps of Engineers."

"*Yes*, you sure are doing that. *Yes*, you are doing the research. *Yes* you spend long hours in the lab doing tedious trials, and *yes* you let everybody front your work."

"I didn't tell you that."

"Yes, you did, just not in so many words."

"That's the game you play in academia when you don't have a permanent teaching position."

"I wouldn't be taking that crap. You're thirty three years old, and have more degrees and schooling than some medical doctors I know. Don't you think you should be treated better?"

Joseph could only stand in silence, knowing that Jesse was right, that he was in active denial about the way he was living his life. He had only pretended to be happy in his dead-end position at the Kentucky Institute of Technology, spending endless hours in the lab only to come home to a dark and damp basement apartment. A self-respecting individual would have left the job long ago. What was keeping him there? Was it the fear of change?

Jesse put her arms on his shoulders, looked into his eyes, and said, "I know that you are scared of what will happen. I am, too. But we're in the same boat. That bomb almost killed me. Wouldn't it make sense that, since you really have nothing much to go back to, you should stay here. We can deal with the threat...together."

PART THREE

CHAPTER 18

The farmer in grey overalls and dark cowboy hat shifted his position on the green John Deere tractor as he cut the hay in the field shrouded in the early Saturday morning fog that blanketed the countryside. The rumbling sound continued to get louder. The horses trotting in the dense grass across the road, behind a maze of white wooden fences, seemed spooked. Annoyed, the farmer stopped the tractor in the middle of the field and walked over to the crumbling asphalt that comprised Route 989, a narrow county road that threaded itself through the patchwork of green pastures and quaint, well-maintained country estates north of Xavier. The farmer looked ahead, seeing a string of glowing headlights in the white mist. He could finally discern the vehicles; they were National Guard Humvees, with some sheriff's jeeps thrown in. He counted every one of the forty-eight vehicles as they passed the farm.

Beyond the farm fields was a blind curve in the road. After the trucks navigated the curve, they stopped where five state police cars with their lights flashing blocked the road. The state police cars moved back to clear the way, revealing a black SUV parked along the shoulder. Agents Jefferies and Sattler sat in the front seat of the SUV, drinking coffee out of their thermoses as they watched the procession speed toward the dam. Jefferies took a long sip of coffee, and said to Sattler in an almost irreverent voice, "So, you think you have enough reinforcements here?"

Sattler said, "No, I requested thirty more National Guard units, but this is all I could get from them."

Jefferies took a last sip of coffee from the metal cup. The fog started to lift, and he could start to see the grass-covered dam embankment, the objective of the mobilization. To Jefferies, the dam itself was the easy part of the problem; the real challenge was to provide protection for the twenty-mile perimeter of the reservoir, to guard against any attack coming from the water. "You know what we are doing is creating a thirty-mile detour for the locals," he noted casually.

"I'm not a traffic planner, so I'm going to let someone else worry about that. We have no other choice but to pursue our current course of action," Sattler said, unconcerned.

"I hope the people who live around here understand. They haven't been told anything yet."

"The only people who have been informed are the mayor and the sheriff. I trust they can keep everything quiet. I don't want create a panic by advertising we think someone is planning to blow up the dam outside of town. The cover-story we sent out to the press of the embankment leak will be convincing enough for the time being. In another couple of days, we ought to have the situation under control and then it won't matter what everyone believes."

Jefferies turned back to reading the morning surveillance reports when he spotted a boy not more than fourteen years old biking down road towards the roadblock. Attached to the back of the bicycle was a fly rod and net ready for a day of fishing. A state policeman manning the roadblock walked over to the boy to direct him away from the area and after a five-minute discussion, the trooper escorted the boy over to the SUV. The trooper tapped his finger on the window. When Sattler and Jefferies got out into the crisp morning air to meet them, the trooper announced, "This is Gabriel Morgan. He lives a few miles up the road. I think you should listen to his story."

Gabriel repeated the story for Sattler and Jefferies. While fishing a month before, he had met a long-haired man with a camera taking pictures of the dam. The man taking the photos also had a fifty foot surveying tape and was measuring the embankment, noting the measurements on a sketch. The man, who did not show any ID to the boy, said that he was from the River Authority. The boy did not notice a car with an insignia, only a yellow Camaro. The man was very pleasant and polite and spent half an hour talking about fishing.

Sattler went into his pocket and laid the computer photographs of Suspects #1 and #2 onto the hood of the SUV. "Recognize any of these people?" he asked.

The boy pointed to Suspect No. 2. and commented, "I would remember him anywhere."

Sattler bent over the boy, putting his hands on his shoulders. "Thank you, Gabe, you were a big help. One more thing, don't tell anyone else what you have said to us. You think you can do that?"

The boy nodded and then left with the state policeman. Sattler turned to Jefferies and with a broad smile said, "Now, there's no more room for doubt. The son of a bitch was here casing the place."

***

Sam leaned over the black metal railing that framed the top of the dam and lazily extended his hand to Joseph, who had just finished climbing up the slippery, dew-covered slope. Joseph was exhausted from the dam inspection, which had included walking through the ten–foot diameter concrete spillway-pipe in the center of the embankment. Walking the two hundred and fifty foot spillway, flanked by two FBI agents with electric lanterns, was a terrifying experience after they had found a water moccasin in the shallow water on the perimeter of the pipe.

Joseph took the large hand and was pulled up to the top of the slope. Breathing laboriously, he sat next to Sam, who, in a leisurely fashion, looked up at the clear blue sky and said, "Fog's starting to lift; this is going to be a nice day after all."

Joseph, trying to catch his breath, said, "You could have helped me down there. We had to fight off a water moccasin in the pipe."

"I'm only supposed to provide protection from terrorists, not snakes. I've made a simple arrangement with the FBI that you would be in my protective custody instead of the Federal Marshall's, and snakes are definitely outside the scope of services." Sam thought about the agreement he had made with Jefferies the day after the car bombing. At the time he had negotiated it, he had thought it to be fair, but was now giving that a second consideration. The deal was obviously slanted toward the FBI. The simple agreement was that Sam provide twenty-four hour protective custody for Joseph in return for the both of them staying on with the investigation. On the surface, it had offered both of them what they needed; Joseph could be close to Jesse, and Sam could follow the investigation to its conclusion and stay away from Agent Sattler. The physical arrangements were simple enough. Joseph, Jesse, and Toby were to stay at Sam's house outside of Pope's Mils. Three of his deputies were to guard the house. Sam had implicit trust in the people that worked for him. If anything else happened, the responsibility was now on his shoulders.

It was getting toward noon when one of the FBI agents handed Joseph a box lunch made up of a stale ham and cheese sandwich, a cellophane-wrapped brownie that felt like rubber, and a small apple. Joseph tasted the ham sandwich and quickly discarded it, stuffing it back into the bag. Instead, he took a loud bite out of the apple.

Sam looked over and said, "If you are not interested in the sandwich, I'll take it."

"Something tastes funny. I wish I could get my own lunch in town," Joseph replied, with a look of disgust on his face.

"You know you can't do that. It's against the rules."

"This twenty-four hour protection thing hampers my mobility and makes me feel like a prisoner. I am not used to having to ask to go to the bathroom. I have not done that since I was six years old."

"Congratulations, you finally understand that you're essentially a prisoner in my protective custody. Remember, you nearly begged to stay with the investigation. This is something you wanted."

"Yes, I know the old saying 'be careful what you ask for because you may get it.'"

"Exactly. I know Jesse put you up to this. You were ready to leave, but I understand relationships with women will make you do things you would not normally do."

As Joseph finished his apple, he saw a large backhoe and dump truck slowly move up the access road. A crew of construction workers with shovels and yellow hard hats and River Authority shirts stood on the embankment awaiting thier arrival. A small, burly man who appeared to be the foreman directed the backhoe to take a position on the end of the embankment. The bucket of the backhoe stuck in the ground and with a groan started to remove the soil. Methodically, the backhoe excavated a trench from the downstream end of the dam to upstream end. Joseph watched this process for about fifteen minutes and then asked Sam, "Who gave the instructions for the dam to be breached?"

"It was at the River Authority's direction, but actually it was the FBI's idea. I got the telephone call this morning saying they were going to take the structure out of the equation."

"But this dam never presented a threat from the beginning," Joseph protested. "The flood wave would never have reached a populated area, and would not cause a significant amount of damage to the town."

"I don't know. I just work here," Sam said, as he reclined back onto the grass, closing his eyes.

"They are a good fifteen feet above the lake surface. At this rate, it's going to take them at least two days before they start draining the reservoir."

"You're right again. That's how long Jefferies said it would take."

"To me, it seems that the FBI is wasting a lot of their resources on nothing. This field exercise is completely futile, and demonstrates that what I said in the meeting was correct. There are no targets of any importance in this town. I cannot see anybody wasting their time on this facility."

"Look man, I agree with you and I give you a lot of credit. You were right about this whole thing being related to Reverend Adamson, and you gave us our suspect, Evan Young. But I'm also stumped as to what could be the next potential target. So here we are in Xavier, nearly one hundred miles away from Pope's Mills. My friendly advice is that you should enjoy this beautiful day and let the FBI worry about everything else. "

To Sam's amusement, Joseph stood up, angry and defiant, "No, I am sorry. I cannot relax when someone is planning to murder more people. This Evan Young may be obsessed with revenge, but also seems to be fairly smart and does not do anything haphazardly or carelessly. He knows we see the pattern he has established of having the dates of the bombings coincide with Jake's trial and arrest. He has always made sure to be two steps ahead of us. There is a definite objective to what he is doing, but it has nothing to do with Xavier. Something tells me there is more involved here than retribution for the death of a father figure. There is something we are all missing, and we need to it figure out before May 20th, or a whole lot more people will be dead."

***

After a day in the field, Joseph was tired and had kept quiet on the two-hour trip back to Pope's Mills. The day was uneventful as he crisscrossed the dam all afternoon with FBI agents in tow. It was seven o'clock in the evening by the time Sam had driven him back to the Clark mansion to grab some dinner before returning to his house for the evening. While en route, Sam called ahead for take-out from the Collins Hotel. The living room and dinning room of the Clark House were filled with papers. Sam looked around for a place to eat dinner when he saw that the large, circular entry foyer was nearly empty, except for the small wooden desk that served as a reception area. He removed the blotter and telephone and proceeded to clean off the desktop with a couple of swipes from his arm. Joseph sat slouching in an uncomfortable wooden chair across from Sam

The food arrived in platters with gleaming, stainless-steel covers. Almost ceremoniously, Sam uncovered them to reveal sliced white meat turkey, stuffing and gravy, peas, and sweet potato pie. He said jubilantly, "Remember when I bailed you out after your fight with Dickey; I wanted to get a turkey dinner. I've finally got it." Sam dug into the pile of white meat and corn bread stuffing, making two large piles on his plate, and then poured a generous amount of gravy from the steel gravy boat. He muttered appreciatively, "My oh my, this is good chow we got tonight. I bet it beats whatever the FBI is having by a mile. It almost makes up for me being here baby-sitting your sorry ass. I even had them get a bottle of your favorite hot sauce." Sam offered Joseph the tray of turkey as Joseph waved it off, sitting back stoically in his seat. Pretending not to be offended at Joseph's refusal, he said, "Well screw you if you aren't hungry. Hey man, I may be your bodyguard, but I'm not your mother. That means there is more food left for me."

"I was thinking about the missing element of the investigation," Joseph said, head in his hands.

Sam tried to brush him off. "Oh, that again. You kept quiet for the two hours we were in the car. For seven days a week I have been sleeping, eating, and shitting this investigation, and now, during the only time I decide to take a break and partake of this heavenly repast in front of me, you decide you're going to talk business." Sam leaned over the table and with knife and fork in hand said, "Now, I really find that downright rude." Sam sat back, proud of his overaction.

"I remember you telling me Jake Adamson had a 'cult of followers,'" Joseph said.

Sam looked up from his plate. "So, I see despite all my advice to the contrary you're not going to let this go. Okay then, yes, so what?"

"That would imply it was a rather tightly-knit group. Our discussions have been about Jake's influence over everyone in the group. What we haven't talked about was the relationships between the other people. It is safe to say everyone knew each other fairly well."

"That's fairly obvious. You've yet to break any new ground here."

"All the core members of the group were over the age of twenty with the only two teenagers being Evan and Theresa."

"You still haven't said anything worth a shit. You're wasting my time."

"From all the pictures I have seen of Theresa, and from everyone's description, she was fairly bright and good-looking girl. Evan was her age, and being two intelligent teens with similar interests, they must have been attracted to one another." Joseph got up and started to pace the circular room.

Sam watched in amusement. "Now that's a broad supposition. I knew plenty of really beautiful girls when I was in the youth group at church, but I never really dated them."

"Yes, that's a church group; these people did a lot of work together. Let me say that they must have been a lot more 'intimate.'"

"So, you've interrupted my dinner to discuss the social habits of teenagers?"

Joseph stopped in his tracks. "At the very least, they probably knew each other fairly well. Let me go further to say there is a possibility that not only was Evan attracted to Theresa, but in love with her. How would that impact his motives?"

"I don't see what difference that would make, since Theresa is dead."

"It makes a very big difference. The puzzle we think we have all solved now falls apart because, according to everyone, Jake was some sort of psychotic who molested her. Why would Evan go on some rampage for someone who had violently abused his girlfriend? It simply doesn't add up, does it? It is obvious he believes someone else was responsible. Maybe that is the person he is angry with."

"You still haven't said anything new. We all know Evan is avenging Jake's death and is not blaming anyone except for the federal government. The problem is, you are trying to make sense of someone who is not playing with a full deck. It's a well-known psychological principal that crazy people like to hang with one another, and Evan is crazy like Jake. Everything you have said is speculation, and you have yet to show me anything tangible. So I'm going to go back to eating this beautiful turkey supper in front of me."

Joseph thought for a moment and then looked over the oak table intently at Sam. "There is something else around here that smells other than your supper. Every time I mention Theresa around Pope's Mills, people shut up. Why?"

Sam picked up a gravy-coated slice of turkey and was about to eat it. "People simply closed their minds because what happened to her was so socially repugnant."

Joseph got up again and nervously paced around the foyer. "We sat down with Sally for nearly an hour. She knew all the details about Evan; someone who she barely spoke to. When I brought up Theresa, the daughter of one more notable people in the community, she hardly utters a word. Don't you find that interesting? That was the only time she ever appeared to be nervous."

"Yeah, you seemed to be fixated on her necklace," Sam noted, trying to tease Joseph.

"*Yes, I was.*" Joseph put his hands to his forehead trying to visualize the stone. "It was one of those cat's-eye stones. There was something very familiar about it."

"You said your father had one."

"But there was something else about it that got my attention. I have seen it somewhere else."

"Just like you thought you saw Evan somewhere else," Sam added, playfully trying to throw Joseph off balance.

Joseph continued pacing around the perimeter of the foyer. Joseph knew that he was prone to forget something whenever he strained to remember it. He cleared his mind by looking at the oil paintings on the wall. There was a wide painting showing a quail hunt with the sky gray and the dark red blood of the bird staining the ground. Another, a vista of the town in the 1920's showing the Collins Hotel and townspeople wearing black hats and coats strolling down the dirt road. Taken in all at one time, the paintings seemed to be dark and have a foreboding texture. Joseph crossed to the other side of the room where there was the oil painting of Clark overlooking the river valley.

As Sam watched Joseph curiously move around the room, he thought he could safely return to eating dinner without further interruption. Sam had a piece of turkey on a fork when he noticed Joseph had stopped in front of the Clark family portrait. Joseph's face became flushed with excitement as his index finger pointing right at the portrait.

* * *

The room was dark like a womb, except for the light from a single bulb illuminating Sally's face and hands. The harsh light made the ridges on Sally's face seem deeper. Sally read a book on the sofa as the clock on the wall struck eight. Butch took his prime spot next to Sally and napped while the other dogs found their resting places on the papers scattered around the living room. Unexpectedly, there was a knock on the door. Sally got up, lethargically crossed the living room, and looked through the peephole. It was Sam and Joseph. "Isn't this is quite a surprise," she said. There was an artificial, sugary sweetness in the tone of her voice that covered her fatigue from the day's activities. Generally, people did not come visiting unannounced at nighttime, and, out of courtesy, she opened the door even though she did not want the company.

"Mind if we come in? I know it's a little late," Sam announced, almost unapologetically.

"No problem, Sheriff. Where're your friends Agents Sattler and Jefferies? I thought all of you traveled together."

"I thought it would be easier if they were not here," Sam said with a grave tone to his voice.

Sally did not note the seriousness in Sam's speech and instinctively turned on the light in the kitchen to put a kettle of water on the stove. "Then come on in. It's still chilly out there. I'm sorry I can't offer you any cake. Do you gentlemen want any coffee or tea?"

"I think I will take some," Joseph said, as he gingerly stepped around the sleeping dogs, trying to make certain he did not wake any of them.

"Do you take cream and sugar?" Sally said as she moved items in her ancient refrigerator.

"Black will do fine," Joseph called back.

"Strong, black coffee it is then." Sally brought out a bottle of instant coffee coated with thick layer of dust from of the cupboard, and put a heaping teaspoon of the contents in a cup of hot water. As if in slow motion, she brought the cup over to Joseph, who stood next to the couch, and, with a groan, she sat down next to the hound dog. "Now, what can I help you boys with?"

"I think you know, Sally," Sam said, eyeing Sally suspiciously as she sat on the couch.

"No, I'm sorry. I'm not clairvoyant, so I don't know. I've told you everything I knew about Evan Young."

"Yes, you have. You left out one person from the story though, Theresa."

"I told you everything about her...she died in the car accident outside of Phoenix."

"Is that everything?"

"What else do you want to discuss?"

"You said you did not know her very well. Is that the way you still remember it?"

"Yes it is," Sally said, beginning to sound defiant. She clasped the cats-eye necklace around her neck.

"Why are you fingering the necklace? May I inquire where you got it?" Joseph asked.

Sally thought for a few moments. "Several years ago, at some flea market."

"It was not a gift from Theresa?" Sam asked.

"Why do you think that?" Sally responded.

Sam pulled out a picture from his jacket pocket. "I had one of Theresa's yearbook pictures scanned and blown up. You see the necklace she's wearing in the photo? It matches the one on your neck exactly down to the crack to the left of the star. It's also the same necklace she had in the family portrait hanging on the wall at the mansion. It must have been a real treasured item for her to be wearing it all the time. Now you're wearing the same piece of jewelry."

Joseph got down on his knees and looked at Sally directly in the eye. "I know why you wear the necklace. You were very close to Theresa, and because you feared some kind of reprisal from Matt Clark, you kept your relationship with her hidden for all these years. You have wanted to tell everyone about it, but couldn't, so you display the necklace as a subconscious way of letting everyone know."

Sally held the picture close to her face, ignoring Joseph's comment, and said, "I cannot see very well, so you have me at a disadvantage. But, I trust your observation, Sheriff." She calculated her next response carefully, "That's certainly a coincidence. She must have sold it to the flea market where I purchased it."

Sam asked, "Which flea market? Is it the one located just north of Gottlieb on Route 23?"

"Yes, I believe so," Sally said, trying to sound polite.

"I just made that up off the top of my head. There's no flea market there," Sam said as we walked around the sofa so his face would be in the light.

"Big deal. I have a faulty memory as to where I got a necklace ten years ago. An old woman like me is entitled to forget a few things," she said, quickly losing her patience with him.

"Do you know what the charges 'Perjury' and 'Obstruction of Justice' are?"

"Yes, it is something that applies to criminals."

"Don't think you are being a criminal? If you have been lying to us, that is what the FBI will charge you with. People spend years in prison on the charges that you potentially face. Now, do you want to tell us the truth?"

"What does the FBI want with an old lady like me?" Sally's eyes were becoming wet and there was hostility in her voice. Her hands were beginning to clench. She was used to seeing Sam as a benign child, having watched him grow up. She counseled him on several occasions regarding his education and now could not believe that this was the respect she was receiving. She considered herself a friend and mentor to him and, with this relentless interrogation, she realized the relationship had dissolved. "You don't scare me with your legal lingo. Your daddy thought he could be intimidating, too. It doesn't work on everyone."

"Is that what you really want, the FBI coming here, asking the same questions but not being as nice as I am? They will start by combing through all your records for the past ten years. I mean everything, your electric bills, telephone bills, credit card records, video rentals, everything. They will interview all your neighbors. None of your life will be private anymore."

"That would be fine and dandy. There's nothing interesting they can learn about me."

"Then they will start investigating Theresa. They are going ask everyone she knew what she did after her kidnapping, including her friends from school, and they will retrace everything she did prior to her accident."

Sally thought that Sam was being ignorant and had the audacity to think he knew what he was speaking about. She desperately wanted to tell him how stupid he was. The anger she was feeling finally came to the surface. *"Leave her alone, she's been through enough!"* Sally shouted in a hoarse voice.

"Oh my god, she's alive," Sam was stunned. His face became flushed as he sat down in an overstuffed armchair. "Why have you been keeping this a secret for all these years? Why are you protecting her?"

"Sam, I really feel sorry for you. You have such a Pollyanna, naïve view of things that happen here. All right, you truly want to know about Theresa, I will tell you about her. You want to know how a sixteen-year-old girl was put through vile physical and mental abuse for little or no reason; how she was made a virtual outcast afterwards, and how it took all the courage in world for her to stay and then to leave. Even though she suffered through a lot of pain, all she thought about was her invalid mother. She didn't want to go leaving her in a nursing home. So she gave me her necklace to remind me to take care of her. So now I'm guilty of the awful crime of helping a young woman in need? So take me away! Lock me up!"

Sally sat on the sofa, tears running down her cheek. Joseph went to the kitchen and retrieved a tissue. "Can you tell us where she is, Sally? It is very important. She may be the only person who knows Evan's whereabouts," Joseph asked imploringly, kneeling next to her.

"I honestly don't know where she's living." Sally wiped her face and re-gained her composure. "But if I were her, I would have moved as far away as possible. I've spoken to her on the telephone up until about a year ago. She didn't tell me where she was calling from and I didn't want to find out."

Sam pointed his finger at Sally. "You lied to us about Theresa when you should have come forward. Do you realize that Evan has killed nine people? Four of them you knew personally, and still you have the damned audacity to sit here playing your petty games?"

Sally was about to get up out of her seat and about to show the two visitors out of the house, but remembered her manners. Instead, she sat back in the sofa and said casually, "Sheriff, is it really lying when you are simply repeating the fiction everyone believes to be true? It all depends on your point of view, doesn't it? You come here all self- righteous about the nine people who have died when you do not even know about preserving even one life. You never had anyone depend on you. I pity you never held a child in your arms, knowing you were the sole source of their existence, never having that love or intimacy. I mourn your loss of Tonya, but there is nothing I can really do about it. I made a blood-oath many years ago never to tell anyone about my relationship with Theresa."

Sam gave Sally a hard look. "How really amusing that you pity *me*, when you yourself are incapable of telling the truth. Let's go, Joseph. I think I've got all I need. I don't want Ms. Richmond to break any of the promises that she has made." Joseph hesitantly got up as Sam opened the screen door for him.

As Sam was about to exit, Sally said, "When you do find her, please tell her that I love her and I miss her. I would give everything to see her again."

Sam gave Sally a disgusted look and closed the screen door behind him.

Sally wiped a tear from her eyes and petted Butch as she watched them leave. She hugged Butch and spoke directly into his wrinkled, saggy face. "Aren't people silly? They ask questions about things they really don't want to know about."

CHAPTER 19

The black car rolled through the neighborhood of pristine rancher houses; it was suburbia at it's finest. The grass in the yards was cut and the shrubs trimmed. Some of the housewives were out watering the grass, or jogging, while their husbands worked. The car stopped in front of a white brick rancher with redwood beams running across the roof. The modest looking house was surrounded by a white picket fence had some detailed architectural touches, including matching blue, wooden shudders and blue brick around the windows. In the yard there was a toy fire truck engine that was big enough to be ridden by a five year old. Jefferies checked his map and said, "168 Northview Lane, looks like we've arrived."

The trip to San Diego had been hastily arranged. Sattler decided to stay behind to manage the investigation, and Joseph was left at Sam's house with Jesse under the guard of the three deputies. Sam and Jefferies were forced to take a five-hour red-eye to San Diego from Louisville, stopping in Atlanta. Stumbling out of the car, Jefferies put on his black suit jacket, wrinkled from the flight, and Sam put on his sun glasses and hat. As they both strode up the stone walk, Sam hit his leg against the fire truck, nearly tripping over it. A slender, tanned woman in her late twenties with long, straight blonde hair and yellow tee shirt greeted them at the front door. A thin, silver necklace reflected in the sunlight as it hung around her neck, the pendant hidden under the rim of her shirt.

The woman waited at the door and shook Jefferies hands as he entered. When Sam walked in, the woman stepped back and curtly said, keeping her hands at her side, "Hello Sheriff, I've heard a lot about you from Sally."

Sam took off his hat and nodded, "Nice to finally meet you, Theresa. I've heard a lot about you too." As Sam looked around, he noted the sunken living room with red and white pueblo blankets hanging on the wall, which gave the room a warm feel. The adjoining kitchen had an oak table still filled with dishes from breakfast.

A small boy holding a metal airplane dashed up to Theresa. "Mom, can we go to the playground?"

She went down on her knees and spoke to the boy, while combing his hair with her fingers. "Not now. I'm sorry, if you are nice and play outside and let me speak to these gentlemen, I will take you to the zoo after lunch. How does that sound?"

The boy nodded his head in immediate approval, and scampered out the front door making a zooming sound while holding the airplane in the air.

Theresa pointed to a picture on the coffee table. "He looks just like his father, doesn't he?"

"He seems like a very nice boy," Jefferies said, trying to make pleasant conversation.

"I appreciate you meeting with me after my husband left for the office. He would freak if he knew you were coming," Theresa said, as she sat on the reddish-brown leather couch, her legs crossed.

"You are Theresa Clark aren't you?" Jefferies said with a note of hesitation.

"In the flesh. The name on my marriage license is Theresa Owens Brewer. I changed my name back to Theresa Owens about nine years ago. 'Owens' was my family name before it became 'Clark.'"

Jefferies noted, "You've certainly put on a good disappearing act."

"I did what I had to do to survive. I would do it again, too. But, before I answer your questions, I'm curious how you found me," Theresa said, walking over to the kitchen to fetch a coffeepot and some cups.

"Oh, that was easy," Sam volunteered. "When we found out you were talking to Sally, we pulled her phone records. We didn't know the name you were living under, but 'Theresa Brewer' was the only person she spoke to in California. We looked up the name in the California motor vehicle records and the license photo matched your yearbook photographs."

"I came out here to escape everything going on in Popes' Mills. I figured eventually someone would find me. In my mind, I've always dreaded talking about what happened. But now, it doesn't seem so bad. It's a relief I'm finally confronting it after all these years," Theresa said without looking at anyone in the room.

"We understand everything you have been through having been kidnapped," Jefferies said.

Theresa glared back Jefferies, her eyes filled with anger. "No, I'm sorry, you don't understand anything. There never was a kidnapping. It was all a lie perpetrated by my father and the sheriff. I freely went to live with Jake."

Jefferies sat on the couch, staggered by the statement. He quickly went into his leather briefcase and produced a plain, manila folder. "We have the sworn written deposition you wrote saying that you were walking home from school when he picked you up in his Chevy Nova, offering you a ride home. Instead, he took you back to the farm house. He handcuffed you to his bed for three days and eventually molested you." Jefferies looked up from the paper and passed it over to Theresa for her inspection.

Theresa glared back. "Get that pile of shit away from me. I know what it says."

"Isn't this your signature at the bottom of the page?" Jefferies asked mechanically.

"Yes it is," Theresa responded as if insulted.

Jefferies retrieved several eight-by-ten glossy, color photographs showing the thighs of a young woman covered with black and blue marks and welts. Sam caught a glance of the photos and had to close his eyes. "Weren't these the photos taken of you at the hospital?" Jefferies demanded.

Theresa saw the color glossies spread out on the table and the rage welled up in her. "You sons of bitches took the whole file on the case. You guys must get your jollies looking at this shit. Think you can break me down by showing me. If you believe I will sit here demurely and tell you things you want to hear, you're greatly mistaken," she said, glaring back at Jefferies.

Sam, trying to be objective, said, "Something ain't right here. The beating you took isn't imaginary, and now you're saying you had lied."

"I didn't lie. I didn't write the deposition you have in front of you."

"Who wrote it then?" Jefferies asked.

Without hesitation, Theresa responded, "It was the Sheriff." She gave Sam a cross, accusing glance, as he shifted uneasily in his seat. Theresa considered herself to be a loving, forgiving woman but she never expected Sam Johnson Jr. to be sitting on her couch. The image of his father flooded her mind, the man who sat her on the wooden chair in a cold hospital room while she was wearing a thin hospital gown and feeling vulnerable. She felt violated when he told her to lift the gown up her thigh so that he could photograph the bruises on her legs. She could still felt the threatening way he spoke to her, thrusting a pen in her hand, and telling her to sign the paper set on the table.

"Why did you sign something that you never wrote? Didn't you read it first?" Agent Jefferies asked.

Theresa laughed, "It really didn't matter if I read it or not. I wasn't allowed to leave the hospital without signing it. The sheriff told me if I didn't put my John Hancock on the statement, they would get a psychiatrist and have me committed into Burwood Mental Hospital."

Jefferies broke in, "When you say 'they,' you mean the sheriff and your step father."

Theresa nodded.

"You believed what the sheriff told you?" Jefferies asked.

"Yes, my step father had the power to do that. He owned most of the fucking hospital back there, and I was certain he could easily persuade a doctor to sign the papers. Anyhow, I was tired, having been up for twenty-four hours, and I would've signed anything. The whole thing was a made-up piece of fiction. Jake never touched me. He was a gentleman to me at all times."

Sam's face turned pale and his hands became cold and clammy. He said in a low voice, hesitantly, barely muttering the words, "I know my father. He would've never done what you just described. It violated everything he believed in."

"Maybe you didn't know him the same way I did. The truth hurts like alcohol on an open wound. It stings, doesn't it Sheriff?" Theresa shot back.

"If it wasn't Jake, then who beat you?" Jefferies asked.

"I don't know the people who did it," Theresa said.

Jefferies put his pen down after taking a page of notes. He stroked his forehead with his hand. "I'm generally a patient individual, but I'm overwhelmed by this bullshit. We find you living here across the country living under some alias after having perpetrated the fraud of faking your own death…"

Theresa's body tensed as if struck by a blunt object, "You guys are so full of shit. I didn't fake my death."

"Let me finish," Jefferies said, like a lawyer trying to his make his closing argument. "You ask us to believe everything you have said at face value even though it contradicts all your previous sworn statements. I don't even know where to start verifying what you have just told us. You can't even name one name for us regarding the people who assaulted you. None of this seems to gel, so you had better start making some sense."

Chapter 20

For Theresa, there was no sense or good reason for the many things that happened in Pope's Mills. It was about human nature, hubris, and the wanton need to control others while getting rich. At the age of fifteen, she was just beginning to adjust to her new life in Pope's Mills after the tragic death of her father from colon cancer. She had left Louisville, where her mother was director or volunteer services. Her mother had met Matt Clark at a convention of community planners, and moved to Pope's Mills six months later. Theresa had lived in the town for two years, but still felt like an outsider. Kids were known to be more judgmental than adults, and Theresa did not have as many new friends as her mother did, but she had managed to maintain a small circle of relationships. She made one very good friend, Beth Hamilton, who would periodically come over to the mansion to listen to music in her room. Overall, adolescence was an awkward time for Theresa. She was at that age that her body started to change; she spurted two inches in height within six months. When she came to Popes Mills she was chubby, but then became tall and graceful. Coming of age, she felt much older than her years. Theresa felt comfortable spending time with more mature, older people. She had met the Mayor of Louisville along with several congressman and senators, while helping her mother with the needy in Louisville. She had more experience in the adult world than the other kids. Boys would come up to her in homeroom and start conversations. She would be friendly with them, but never went beyond talking about music groups or sports. She understood that she had little in common with the other kids in school. In her heart, she still was a stranger, something no boy really understood.

Theresa did not understand the influence of outside factors on her life. In the coming year, there was an economic downturn in the state. The decreased demand for new houses reduced demand for construction products, and, in turn, lowered the demand for paper. Initially, the number of hours everyone worked at the mill was cut back. Then there were layoffs, with twenty employees terminated every week. In the meantime, the marital relationship between Matt and Lillian Clark became more tenuous. The evening dinners would be quiet with Theresa sitting at the dinning room table, watching her parents silently eat dinner. Theresa had grown to respect and trust her stepfather and understood the problems at the mill. She was pragmatic and understood the intense pressure to boost business. The success of her father's company impacted the entire community.

The competition for customers was intense. Clark would spend time trying to entertain them at the mansion. Her step father would return back to the mansion at three to four o'clock in the morning from the small parties he would throw for his select clients. One night, a group of people came back to the mansion and were playing loud music into the morning hours. Theresa was awakened from a sound sleep and her mother trod downstairs to show them out, only to be told not to interfere by Clark. Lillian was a strong person, but did not like confrontation, and calmly went back upstairs.

Much to the relief of everyone in Pope's Mills, the factory orders increased. With the economy slowly improving, Matt Clark decided to open a new wing of the hospital. Sometimes Clark would come home with plans and sketches. There would be heated arguments about the design of the addition. Lillian thought that she would be an equal partner in the planning, but in the end, felt he was just patronizing her. After a year and a half of planning and construction, the wing was finally completed. A three-story structure sheathed in glass, designed by the best architect in Louisville, dominated the main building. There was a long list of dignitaries who attended the opening of the Clark wing of the Pope's Mill Medical Center. Theresa stood with her stepfather on the red tile imported from Mexico. They glibly spoke to a senator about the number of additional patients that could be accommodated in the wing, while Lillian sat on the couch in the corner of the atrium lobby, unhappily drinking champagne. It would be one of the last times Theresa would see her mother healthy.

The stress of life in Pope's Mills had finally extracted a terrible price from Lillian. Two days after the opening, Matt Clark returned home one evening and found his wife collapsed on the floor of the bathroom. She had suffered a stroke. It was ironic that her mother would be one of the first patients in the new addition constructed by her step father. She had the deluxe suite on the third floor of the hospital, waited on constantly by her own private nurse. Theresa would come after school and tearfully sit beside her mother in the hospital room, while her mother stared ahead unresponsively. Clark would put his arms around her and reassure her that he would make certain nothing would happen to either of them.

Jake Adamson came to town two months later. If it hadn't been for her mother's illness, he would have gone unnoticed: just another face in the crowd of new arrivals. Meeting Jake Adamson opened her mind to the many possibilities of what life could offer in Pope's Mills. She desperately needed an adult friend who understood her needs and feelings, and Jake soon became her teacher and confidant. Theresa was still lonely, and Jake recognized this in her. It was no coincidence that Evan was working the counter of the mission when she was invited to visit. Theresa realized later that Jake had arranged for it to happen. When Theresa saw the boy with the thin muscular build and the smoldering brown eyes, she knew she was in love.

Theresa and Evan knew how kids spoke about romances in school and they decided not to advertise their affection for one another and become just another part of the town rumor mill. Evan would show up at church dances and would be introduced as a classmate, with no other status mentioned. Matt Clark would always pick up her from the dances and would scout the room for any potential boyfriends for his daughter. He was interested in finding a younger version of himself; a scholar-athlete-type who would go to college, and then return to take over the business. No one in the room had ever fit that mold. Clark was oblivious to the subtle changes in Theresa; not realizing she had already found her first boyfriend.

Evan and Theresa would walk back from school together, taking the long and scenic way home by way of the Kendall River. In the late afternoons, before preparing supper at the mission, Jake would periodically fish the river below the dam, hooking catfish and croakers. One particular afternoon, they did not find Jake happily in the water as they usually did, but instead, found him on the bank, overcome by a rotten smell of decay. There were dead fish on the shores and catfish floating in the water. Catfish were the sturdiest of the species inhabiting the river, and were able to tolerate sudden changes in temperature. The weather that spring had been rather temperate. Jake had told them something drastic must have occurred to kill catfish in the spring; and it was no coincidence that they were downstream of the discharge from paper company plant. He contacted the state, but heard nothing. Theresa saw Jake growing angry that no one seemed to notice or care.

Theresa felt her life coming apart. She could see Jake growing more despondent with time and less optimistic about conditions within Pope's Mills. Theresa herself had second thoughts about her friendship with Jake when the Council met regarding the zoning for the mission. Jake, who had always spoken about how much he cared about her welfare, now had seemed more interested in dominating her. She wanted nothing more to do with him, and was convinced he had misled her all along. Even Evan did not talk about his friend and mentor, Jake, after his arrest in the melee at the mission.

In Jake's absence, Theresa still went on dates with Evan. Evan had just gotten his driver's license and would pick her up in his parent's car in town. The relationship was mostly platonic; they would go to the movies, holding hands and kissing in the back of a movie theater in Gottlieb. She continued to keep the relationship secret from her stepfather. Clark did not want her to be friends with anyone associated with Jake.

Clark continued to throw parties at the mansion for his clients. The parties would take place on Saturday nights and he would arrange for Theresa to stay with her friend Beth for the evening. Clark would give strict instructions he did not want Theresa to be there. The justification was that a teenager in attendance would jeopardize any business with his future clients. Her stepfather was always secretive with regard to his dealings with his customers, and only spoke in generalities.

One Saturday evening in early April, there was yet another party at the mansion. Theresa and Beth scheduled themselves to go to a supper at the Antioch Baptist Church, followed by a sleepover at Beth's house. The menu choice at the church supper would start a chain of events that would forever change Theresa's life. There was either chicken, or fish, as a main course. Beth would have the chicken, while Theresa ate the fried catfish. The chicken this night was undercooked and at about ten in the evening, Beth became sick with food poisoning. Theresa had no other choice but to walk back home.

By the time Theresa arrived, the party was in full swing. There were about twenty cars parked in the driveway and loud country music blasting from the speakers. Theresa opened the front door and was greeted by a blonde in fishnet lingerie. Rather than the usual greeting, the woman eyed Theresa, who was dressed in a blue cotton dress. "Can I help you?" she said, "You don't look like the girls that usually show up here."

"I live here," Theresa answered curtly as she swung the door wide open.

Theresa went into the living room. Men were wearing black cloth masks on their faces, cowboy hats and blue jeans, and were dancing with woman wearing various types of lingerie. The partygoers looked her over quizzically, not knowing the new face, as Theresa headed up the staircase to her room. The house was filled with strangers. She needed to find her stepfather. She looked in her father's bedroom. No one was there. She heard a muffled cry from the guest bedroom across the hall and tentatively pushed the door open. She had walked in on a couple having sex, a naked woman straddling the man beneath her. Embarrassed, she slammed the door. She realized then that she needed to stay somewhere else that night. She rushed into her own bedroom, made a phone call to Evan, and asked him to come over and pick her up.

Evan's house was only about five minutes away. She decided to go outside to wait for him. Hoping to avoid the partygoers, she went down the back stairs that led directly to the kitchen, and then out to the patio. She walked across the fieldstone and saw bodies laying the ground. Repulsion took over when she saw a woman with a dark hood over her eyes and nose, on the ground with two men. The three of them were nude with one man keeling, putting a phallic object in and out of her mouth, while the other man was sitting on her legs and putting his fingers in her pubic area. The woman on the ground stared mindlessly at the sky, as if drugged. Theresa stood on the patio and covered her mouth in shock; the woman on the ground was chained at the ankle to the patio railing, as if she were some inanimate object, a piece of equipment that was being used. As the woman moved her legs the chain made an eerie, clinking noise. A photographer appeared from behind and started shooting flash pictures of the threesome. They were illuminated by the harsh light momentarily, as if under a strobe.

As Theresa was about to walk away, a bearded man wearing a black mask stood behind her to block her path. "Where are you going lil' lady?" he asked, grabbing her by the wrist. It was a strong grip that Theresa could not break.

"I don't belong here. I'm leaving," Theresa said emphatically.

"Let me get you a drink. You'll feel better," the man said, his breath smelling of whiskey.

"I don't want a drink. I just want to go."

"The party just started lil' lady. Why don't you stay?"

"Let go of me."

"You're certainly spirited. Not like the other women here."

"Let me go!" Theresa screamed. She started kicking at the man with her sneakers. She felt some of the kicks connect, but the man barely flinched. Some of the men from the party heard the scuffling and came out of the patio doors.

One of the men pulled out another pair of handcuffs and snapped them around Theresa's wrist. "You think you're better than us?" A bearded man pushed Theresa to the cold fieldstone, while the others cuffed her to the patio railing. Theresa felt her clothes being ripped off her body. The cold evening air was like knives hitting her skin. She started to plead, "Please let me go. I won't tell anybody. I swear."

Theresa heard Evan's voice from the other end of the patio. "Theresa, where are you?"

"Help! Help!" Theresa screamed.

Theresa was on the ground yanking at the cuffs that cut into her wrists. She could see Evan standing on the patio being restrained by three people. His face was red as he yelled at the top of lungs, *"Release her, you sons of bitches!"*

One of the men punched Evan in the stomach, and as he fell to the ground, the masked, bearded man stood over him saying, "I don't know who you are, young man, but you're trespassing."

Now that the momentary distraction was dealt with, the group turned their full interest toward Theresa. The bearded man stood back and with a smile on his face, said to her, "Now spread your legs and show us what you got."

Theresa still twisted defenselessly on the cuffs, keeping her legs tightly together.

The men made a semi-circle around her and started taunting, *"C'mon, show us"* as they pulled down their pants to expose themselves. The tall man with the beard went over to Theresa's prostrated body and said, "You think you can kick us with your feet. We'll show you what stomping really is." The man with the beard came over, raised his foot and kicked Theresa in the lower abdomen. Theresa felt a sharp pain in her hips. As she yelled out in pain, the phalanx of men started to take turns kicking her thighs.

The pain became unbearable and when Theresa started to lose consciousness, she heard a distant voice that sounded like Craig Brommel from the plant. "Oh my god, it's Clark's step-daughter."

The next morning, she woke up in her room wearing a pale pink nightgown that had been in her closet. Her head ached and as she felt disorientated. She remembered the events of the previous evening, thinking it must have been a nightmare. As she pushed away the bedspread, and gasped when she saw her thighs covered with a mosaic of black and blue marks. The stench on her body gagged her. Dark red covered the middle of the mattress where she had vaginally bled during the night. She rushed to the closet and searched for the blue dress she wore the night before. It was gone.

The nightmare was true.

Theresa picked up the phone and called Evan. Evan's uncle Terry answered saying that he was "not available." He continued to explain that the Sheriff's deputies brought him home the previous evening, and Evan was being punished for trespassing on private property and getting into a fight. Theresa tried to explain that she was with Evan, that he never hurt anyone, and that he was trying to help her. Terry brushed her off saying, "If you were with Evan last night, then you were in a place you should not have been," and hastily hung up.

Theresa started to cry as she put down the receiver. It seemed no one in town would believe her, or come to her aid. She was scared, felt alone, and needed sanctuary. She knew could not stay at the mansion any longer. There was only one person now she could talk to, and that was Jake.

Theresa hid the bruises with a pair of blue jeans, a departure from the dresses she usually wore, and went to school the next Monday. She called Jake and he agreed to pick her up a quarter mile from the high school so that no one would notice. When he took her back to the farm and saw the bruises on her thighs, he pounded the wall with his fist and cried about how people had lost their humanity. He talked about bringing the matter to the sheriff, but concluded that Sam Johnson Sr. was somehow involved in the activities at the mansion, if not directly then tangentially. Theresa did not want to be sent back to her stepfather. She knew he needed time to consider the options. In the interim, he tried to make her as comfortable as possible, giving her the best bedroom in the house to stay, his own room, and providing her antibiotic ointments and cold compresses for her thighs. Jake was headstrong about the course of action he undertook, and did not fully understand the consequences until Sam Sr. broke though the door.

After Sam Sr. had liberated Theresa from her supposed "captor," they drove her to the hospital where they gave her a full physical. She was asked to disrobe and was given a flimsy white gown. A doctor spread her legs in stirrups on a bare, white examination table and gave her a full gynecological examination while two nurses looked on with expressionless faces, taking notes. She was then asked to sit in a smaller examination room where the sheriff came to visit. Tired, bruised, and beaten, she signed the deposition laid on the table in front of her. Theresa was then taken back to the mansion where everything had begun two days before.

Theresa tried to pretend that things had returned to normal following her "abduction." She was constantly reminded of the drastic changes in her life. Other kids at school would not speak to her and even Beth kept her distance. She avoided contact with her stepfather, eating dinner in the dinning room at five in the afternoon. Before he would come home from the plant, she would run upstairs to her room and lock the door, staying there for the rest of the evening. Sitting alone in her room was torture. The feelings of guilt plagued her. Her weakness in signing the deposition had put Jake into jail. She desperately wanted to speak to him, or send him a note, but knew that was impossible. The coming months would be more difficult; with the trial approaching, Theresa decided she would not cooperate in the prosecution.

It was difficult to stay away from Matt Clark. The Sunday morning after Theresa's return to the mansion, she woke early to go to church. Matt Clark was downstairs sitting on the couch in his formal, pinstriped suit. He said casually, "I thought we ought to go to church together today." Clark knew everyone in town would expect to see him sitting with his daughter in Church, praising the lord and rejoicing in her safe return. He had pulled the blue Cadillac Coup De Ville out front and waiting for Theresa. Realizing she had no choice but to go with her stepfather, she opened the back door and sat on the opposite side of the car and hoped Clark would not make any conversation on the way to the church.

That morning, Theresa felt the eyes of two hundred people on her. She was drenched in sweat but this time there was no place for her to go seek refuge from the heat. She kept her eyes on the prayer book. The service felt like an eternity. Matt Clark struck out his hand to grasp hers as a token show of affection for other people to see, but she kept her arms at her side throughout the entire service. As Reverend Berky dismissed the congregation, she strode out quickly into the harsh sunlight and desperately wanted to go somewhere alone, but instead, chose not to make a public display and got back into the backseat of the Cadillac parked on the side of the building in a spot reserved for Clark.

Theresa could not wait until she got back to the mansion so she could retreat again into her bedroom. This time, Clark exited the car quickly enough to intercept her before she reached the front door. He grabbed her by the arm, led her to his study, and firmly sat her down on the leather couch. "There're a few things I want to discuss with you before you go back up to your room," he said. Clark showed no outward emotion as he sat next to her. His voice was unwavering as he spoke.

Theresa closed her eyes and could not even glance at him as he explained that she should not have come back to the mansion on that night; the "entertainment" he provided for the clients was not unusual in a major manufacturing industry. If she had followed his simple instructions about staying away, nothing would have happened, and she would have not gotten hurt. She should not have gone behind his back and involve Jake. It was her fault he was sitting in jail. Keeping his voice low, Clark continued on with his tirade: She should not to try to retract the deposition she had signed in the hospital...its purpose was to provide everyone protection...if the public would find out about the "entertainment" there would be a scandal that could potentially close the plant and would throw many people out of work. He concluded with a false, somber face that he could not guarantee her safety if certain people in town found out that she was the source of the story.

Theresa finally found the courage to open her eyes and confront the man who she at one time thought was someone with integrity, but now considered soulless and conscienceless. There was a moment of clarity when she realized he was responsible for her mother's stroke. He drew the strength out of her mother, and was now going to do the same thing to her. She stood up and yelled, "*You won't control me like you did to my mother. I'll leave first.*"

He calmly responded, "You're still legally my dependent. You're sixteen and have no place to go. What are you going to do for money? No one will hire you. Just remember, you can leave here but wherever you go, I'll find you. I've more law enforcement connections than you can imagine, and I will bring you back. You will keep living here under my auspices. You have no other choice."

She looked down on him, and spat on his face. "I would rather die, you son of a bitch!"

***

Jake had made his own choice about life or death. About two weeks later, Theresa had found about his suicide from Beth during homeroom period in school. Beth had awakened that morning and had found out from her father, an attorney, who had heard it from the chief of police in Xavier, who in turn heard it from the commander of the state police barracks the night before. Theresa was on the verge of an emotional breakdown as she sat in the classroom, pretending to listen to the teacher. Earlier in the week, Evan had shown her a letter on dirty, yellow legal paper he had received from Jake. Part of it was addressed to her and it included a brief statement written in red ink

> "*Do not worry about anything Theresa; the Lord will take care of you. I understand why you needed to do what you did, and the constraints you live under each day. This is neither the time nor the place to tell the truth. I will not barter my life for someone else's, and therefore, I will not allow you to endanger your future by forcing you to testify on my behalf. I have made my own plans regarding the trial. We are apart, but in a brief time we have created an inseparable bond. Whenever you need me, I will always be there for you. May the Lord always be with you, Theresa.*"

When Theresa recalled the note, she understood the finality of the phrase "made my own plans." She felt responsible and thought that she should have foreseen Jake's suicide. She sunk even deeper into guilt. She could not hold back anymore and ran out of the classroom into the spring day, leaned against the brick wall, and cried. When she looked up, she found Sally Holliday standing across from her. Sally saw Theresa's sadness and said, "I've just heard about Jake's suicide over the radio." She put her arm around Theresa's shoulder and whispered, "I think we need to have a long talk."

Theresa found empathy and unconditional acceptance from Sally. Much to Theresa's surprise, Sally believed everything she had said during thier discussions, and even collaborated parts of her story. Sally said she had known about the activities of her step-father for a long time. He had used the parties as a way to gain power over other people. Clark would hire the women who worked the party from other states so they could not be recognized in town. He would have photographers take photos of the clients during sexual activity. A few days later, they would receive copies of the photos along with a note on the back saying, "hope you enjoyed yourself on Saturday evening." It was a less than subtle way of telling someone that you had embarrassing information. Sally had found it cruel and disgusting, but there was no way she could stop it since no one complained, and so it had been accepted as part of doing business with Matt Clark.

Sally would reserve parts of her normal school week to talk to Theresa. Theresa became an office aide, so teachers or students would not find all the time they spent together unusual. Many of the conversations they had were about nothing significant: clothes, friends, and music. At times though, Theresa would admit to having considered buying a razor and committing suicide in her bathtub. Sally would throw a concerned look at her and Theresa would smile and say that she nixed the idea so as " not to give the fucker who owned the house the satisfaction of finding her body." They would speak as two women, even though Sally started to consider Theresa the daughter she never had.

Senior year came to a quick and uneventful end for Theresa. She did not hear from Evan in the six months after Jake's death. She would periodically see Evan pass by in the hall. He never said anything to her. On the last day of school, the seniors would get their yearbooks and, by custom, would gather in the main corridor to exchange signatures. Theresa got the requisite messages: "good luck in the future" or "best wishes" and was about to leave when Evan walked up to her smiling, wanting to sign. He snatched her yearbook and in the empty spot where his photo would have been, he wrote, "You were my first love, Theresa. We spent a lot of beautiful, carefree days together. I hope we find peace and can be together again." He gave her a peck on the cheek and walked out the metal doors, without relating to anyone his future plans. Everyone had posted their after-high school plans on the bulletin board: "Lehigh University" or "U.S. Army;" he simply wrote, "Follow the path given me."

Theresa had her own plans for after high school, which included no financial support from Clark. For her, it was all blood money. Sally had found her a waitress job in Louisville, and a cheap furnished basement apartment in a Victorian house. The apartment was only a few miles from the colonial where she grew up, and Theresa felt that she was finally coming home after a long dark journey. Sally's last contribution was helping out with transportation, having a brother-in-law sell her his 1985 Oldsmobile for two hundred dollars. Within a week of graduation, Theresa drove away with all her clothes in the cavernous back seat of the car, and, as she traveled down I-64 with the skyline of Louisville in the windshield, she knew she was finally free of her step-father.

CHAPTER 21

Lost in thought, Theresa watched her son from the kitchen window as he played in the back yard on the swings, holding the plastic airplane in front of him and pretending that it was flying in space. She came back to reality when she saw the reflection of the men in the window sitting in the dining room, staring at her back. She calmly rinsed out her orange juice glass in the sink, filled it with water, and joined her visitors at the dining room table. She resumed telling the story, "My son of a bitch stepfather was true to his word. A few months after I took the waitress job, my co-workers reported that men came to the restaurant asking about me."

Jefferies, who was taking notes, broke in, "So you thought your step father hired some private detectives?"

"I was damn sure of it. I found a man in a parked car, watching me as I came home from work. I knew I had to move on. So early the next morning, I headed west in the Olds."

Sam asked, "You left that quickly?"

Theresa swigged some water. "You have to understand, I wanted the change. Everything in Kentucky reminded me of my step father. I desperately wanted to be somewhere else. I desperately wanted to be *someone* else. Going on the road was the only way I could accomplish that, and I nearly did it. For the next six months, I found jobs here and there. I also found out that I could never stick in one place, thinking I was being followed. Eventually, the jobs became fewer and farther between. After six months of living on the road, I was nearly flat broke. That's when I got a truck stop in the middle of nowhere, Arizona. I believe it was a town named Tenpost. There, I met a woman named Vanessa, who promised me a night in her motel room if I would give her a ride. She gave me a sob story about being raped by her father and now wanted to go to California. I wanted to believe her. She was my age and also a blonde. We could've been sisters. When I woke up the next morning, she was gone—along with my wallet, clothes, and car. I was stranded in the middle of the desert with only my clothes on my back.

"Given, our physical resemblance, Vanessa was able to use my ID and pretend to be me. Maybe she did me a favor. It was quite a liberating experience. I went out there wanting to lose myself; to find a new identity, and the lord answered my prayers."

"How did you ever get out of the desert?" Jefferies asked.

"The man who had pulled over to pick me up turned out to be my future husband. At the time, Jordan was an architecture student on his way back to San Diego State from visiting the Grand Canyon. Jordan was the kindest man I ever met, and we hit it off in five minutes. I told him I wanted to go California, and he took me back with him to San Diego. There, I found a job as a waitress at a local restaurant while I went to college to study counseling. We were married four months later," Theresa said.

"What about the report of your death?" Sam asked.

Theresa took another sip of water and answered in matter-of-factly, "A day after she stole my car, Vanessa was killed when she hit a pickup truck head-on while flying down Route 60 at ninety miles per hour. Given that speed, her remains were not readily identifiable. She was carrying my driver's license in a car registered in my name; and, since both she and I were blondes and were the same age, the police had assumed she was me. Being efficient, they notified my next of kin, my step father, who was no doubt happy to see me out of the picture. It was front page news in Pope's Mills." Theresa threw her head back and laughed, "It wasn't until a week later when I had called the Arizona police to tell them that my car was stolen that they realized they had made a mistake. Anyhow, since that time, only two people from Pope's Mills knew I was alive… Sally and Evan…so, now does everything make sense, Agent Jefferies?"

Jefferies looked up from his notes and looked into Theresa' eyes to ascertain whether or not she was lying. He sat back in his chair, confident she had spoken the truth.

Sam had his head in his hands, staring ahead in disbelief while Jefferies noted, "It's quite a story that you have told us. However, there is no way of easily collaborating it."

"The only person who could do that would be Craig Brommel. I heard his voice at the party, but I would guess that he wouldn't be a very reliable witness, since he was part of everything that happened. I doubt he would admit to any wrongdoing. So, it's my word against everyone else's. Then, of course, there's Evan, who would confirm everything I have described. But then again, you're still trying to find him. I imagine that is why I've become so important to you."

"When was the last time you saw him?" Jefferies asked.

"Let me see…he came and visited me about two years after I had arrived in California, while I was living in an apartment outside of San Diego. He was obsessed with what happened in Pope's Mills. At that time I had been going to a therapist, and I advised him that he should also seek some form of professional help. That's when he stood there in my living room and told me it was the town that would need the 'professional help.' I gave that statement little thought, until now."

"Did he say where he was living?" Sam asked

"He did not really tell me where. My recollection was that he went from place to place, and had never really established a permanent address. But then again, he did say that he was considering purchasing a large tract of property somewhere in eastern Kentucky."

"Eastern Kentucky, huh? You just have narrowed down our search to approximately ten thousand square miles and about fifteen counties," Jefferies said sarcastically.

An idea struck Theresa, "But hold on. Maybe I can still help out. " She left the living room and walked back into the den, to a wooden secretary desk. There was a rustling of papers. After a few minutes, she walked out carrying a postcard showing a cabin in the mountains. "I got this a couple of weeks ago. I had nearly forgotten about it."

Jefferies handled it by the corners and read the message written in large capitol letters:

"THERESA,
I AM DOING WELL.
HOPE YOU ARE ABLE TO FIND PEACE AND PROSPERITY."

Jefferies examined the post card for a moment, handed it over to Sam and noted, "He doesn't give his address. It's postmarked April 19th; he sent it about two days after the Pope's Mills bombing. From what I can tell, the mark reads 'Morehead.'" That's where Morehead State University is located, in the northeastern part of the state, about one hundred and fifty miles from Pope's Mills. It adjoins Cave Lake, a large recreational facility built by the Corps of Engineers in the 1970's. Do you remember receiving anything else from him?"

"Maybe a half-dozen cards in the past five years. All of them with messages like that one. I threw them all out. You are lucky that I didn't clean out the desk earlier, or else that one would also be in the trash," Theresa said.

"Do you mind if I keep the post card?" Jefferies asked.

"By all means," Theresa said, relaxing on the sofa with her legs crossed. "I want you to find him so that no one else gets killed. I've already seen the man who saved my life die, and I didn't even get to go to his funeral to have the chance to say goodbye to him. I still wear the silver crucifix he gave me." Out of reflex, she took it out from under her tee-shirt and kissed it.

It was close to noon, and the front door suddenly opened with her son back from the backyard. He said, "Can we have lunch now, mommy?"

"In another minute, Jake, I'm just finishing up with these gentlemen. Theresa walked over to the sink and poured him a glass of milk. Why don't you read your books and play your CD's. I will have a tuna fish sandwich ready for you in a flash." The boy obediently ran into a bedroom down the hall. The sounds of the nursery rhymes soon could be heard from the CD player. "As you can see, I named my son after Jake. I would say that Jake had a big heart, which transcended anything he might have done wrong in this life. I feel terrible Evan has chosen retribution as a way to deal with his demons. He said to me once that 'we have to follow our own path' in life. I guess that's what I've done, even though it was much more circuitous and tortuous than I expected it would be. Gentlemen, I can say I'm now at peace with myself, and that's what Evan always wanted; but, given what's happened, I don't think we'll ever be together again."

CHAPTER 22

Evan sat in the dining room of the cabin atop the mountain, reading the black, leather-bound Bible Jake had given him on his sixteenth birthday. The only furniture in the dining room was a small plastic table with two matching, discount store chairs. The floors were covered with books, and the white, plaster walls were decorated with pasted pages of the Bible. The afternoon he spent in silence and reflection clarified his thinking. Evan closed his eyes for a moment, allowing himself to *feel* the words on the page in front of him, and then he scribbled a few notes on a sheet of yellow, legal paper. He could here heavy breathing from in the living room, a few feet away. "I'll be with you in one moment, Henry. I just want to get this thought down on paper." He wrote one more sentence, after which he walked out to greet his guest.

Henry Demurs rested on a wooden crate draped with a blanket, patiently waiting for Evan to finish. People were not normally invited into the house to talk, and Henry was on edge.

Evan saw that Henry was red in the face from the physical exertion of his outside activities, "I know you have been working hard, helping out Carl. Is there anything I can offer you? I've got a couple of Cokes left in the fridge. You don't mind if I get one?"

Henry stood up like a soldier at attention, "No thank you. You said you wanted to see me."

Evan went to the kitchen and came back with two bottles, handing one to Henry. "You might as well take one. I've been saving these for a special occasion, and I hate drinking alone. How are things going with Carl?" he asked.

Henry tried to relax, anxiously taking a sip, thinking hard before giving his answer. "Pretty good. Everything's set up and completed according to your plan."

"That's good. I feel very close to our great confrontation with our enemies, and we need to be prepared for the worst. I just finished meditating on it."

"Is there anything else I can do for you? I was just going back to the bunkhouse to wash up." Henry said, as he swallowed another gulp.

"How many years you figure we've known each other?" Evan asked, knowing the answer.

"About five."

Evan set his Coke down on the floor. "That sounds about right. I remember when we started. It was the two of us running this place, doing all the chores. Things were much simpler back then. But I am afraid it's all going to come to an end soon. I'm going to miss it here. I like the quiet. I can really that God hears my prayer here. But now, I need someone I can trust completely, and I feel you're that person."

"I am ready to do what is necessary to accomplish the goals you have set," Henry responded modestly.

Evan put his arm around Henry, sitting him back down on the crate, trying to make him feel at ease. "I know you're loyal to me. That's why I have a special mission set aside for you."

***

Two hours after the interview with Theresa, Sattler and a team of twenty agents arrived—in force—in the town of Morehead in Rowan County, Kentucky, with a court order for county records. The timing could not have been better. It was on a Monday evening and Morehead State was playing their basketball rival, Austin Peay College. The streets of the town were empty. Agent Sattler instructed Jefferies to charter a corporate jet to fly himself and Sam to a small airport about twenty miles away. They would be picked up in unmarked cars after touching down and shuttled back to the town. Not wanting to make the same mistake he did with Pope's Mills, Sattler decided to use unmarked sedans rather than the usual black SUVs, so that the FBI could maintain a low profile.

As the late-model, brown Mercury pulled up in front of the low-rise County District Court building, Sam got out and stretched. Troubled by what Theresa said about his father, Sam did not get any sleep on the airplane. Looking out the window as the jet made its final approach, Sam understood why Evan would want to purchase land in Rowan County. The area surrounding Morehead was mostly mountainous and wooded, with a dense canopy of trees. The only open areas were the town, the campus, and the lake. There were endless places for one to disappear, and Cave Lake, one of the prime fishing spots in the state, had over one hundred miles of coastline to fish—without being seen by anyone. Sam also thought about Morehead's large, transient population associated with the college. In short, Morehead was a place a strange face could blend in without drawing too much interest.

It was already seven at night when Sam and Jefferies walked into the County Building. The entire group of twenty agents, dressed in blue jeans and button-down shirts, were busy in the basement sorting through the real estate records stored in dusty file cabinets. Sam took off the uniform coat he had been wearing for the past twelve hours and quietly started going through the records. He gave no acknowledgment to Sattler, who was working a few feet away. Sattler, dressed in a green, corduroy shirt ignored Sam as well, but gave a faint smile toward Jefferies from across the dimly lit room. "Good job in San Diego. Now all we have to do is go through this mountain of papers to find him," Sattler said, looking at the fifty boxes spread out in front of him.

Jefferies had done a preliminary database search of the county residents on the airplane and found that there were three Evan Youngs. One was a seventy-year-old retiree, another had lived there for thirty years and had six children, and the third had died earlier that year. It was a daunting task to find someone living in the area under a fictitious name. Theresa stated that she had been receiving the post cards for approximately five years. Assuming the figure to be accurate, they needed to check the real estate transactions for the same five years. It was also apparent that no mortgage company would be involved, that the purchase would have been a straight cash transaction. Cash transactions were recorded on paper records. Agents would need to go through each of the real estate documents to find the one they were looking for, a painstakingly tedious process. For the current year alone, there were eighteen hundred real estate sales. Of those, two hundred were over one hundred thousand and involved more than one acre of land, two hundred fifty were for cash, and twenty were by a single male property owner.

It was two o'clock Tuesday morning before the members of the assembled team finished sorting through the boxes of records. Sam was soundly asleep on the floor, while Sattler leaned over a small, oblong utility table, drinking his eighth cup of coffee. He was looking over the list of fifty names in front of him, the product of eight hours of work by twenty agents: The names all seemed to run together: Philip L. Adranson…Milton Hathaway…Mason J.

Kadare…James Post…Steven K. Pelton…Lawrence Rutherford…Andrew K. Wallace…Percy Young.…

Jefferies stood over his shoulder and commented, "Maybe, he's not here in Rowan County. Maybe he dropped the post card in a mail box while traveling through the state."

"No, he's here," Sattler said confidently. "This place probably has sentimental value for Young. It's probably no coincidence that Rowan County is one of the best Muskie and Bass spots in the state. I bet Adamson took him up here to fish."

"How do you know he bought property here? With the Daniel Boone State forest here, there's a lot of wilderness for someone to hide."

Sattler shook his head. "I don't think he would choose to be a squatter on government land. A ranger would eventually find him. When Evan wrote to Theresa, he said he was interested in acquiring some property. He would stick to that." Sattler closed his eyes, deep in thought. "I bet Young chose an alias related to Adamson."

"I searched the directories for Jake Adamson and even Jack Brown, Jake's birth name. There is nothing," Jefferies said, a note of exhaustion in his voice.

"He wouldn't be obvious in choosing an alias matching either of those names," Sattler said, as he quickly copied the names down on a legal; pad. "It's only fifty people and we are just going to have to check out each one." As he made the statement, the name "Mason J. Kadare" drew his attention. He immediately saw that the first name "Mason" was a rearrangement of the last five letters of "Jake Adamson." Sattler wrote the remaining letters of the name out on a piece of paper "J. Kadare" and noted it was an anagram for remaining letters, excluding the "R." He turned around to Jefferies and asked, "Do you recall what Adamson's middle name was?"

"I believe it was Robert," Jefferies muttered.

"BINGO!" Sattler shouted out loud.

***

It was mid-Tuesday afternoon and Evan could hear the wind pick up in intensity as it shrilly whistled through the wooden slats in the shed just ten feet from the side door of the house. The shed was a ten by fifteen structure with a pitched roof supported by a thick oak beam. Evan took great comfort in the manual labor involved in the maintenance of the property. Sweat beaded off his face as he rearranged the items sitting on the ground, trying to maximize the storage space. He heard the door open as Taylor slowly, anxiously, entered. The sunlight came through the door, magnifying the particles of dust scattered in the air.

"I've been thinkin'…don't take this personally… I really don't know how to say this," Taylor said, leaning against the wooden wall by the plastic bags of mulch and fertilizer.

"Well what," Evan said, with a note of impatience to Taylor, who had a tendency to stutter when nervous. Evan, trying to pace himself, was busy lifting a crate of spare bolts from the middle of the floor to the perimeter of the shed in order to make room for the new items outside. He pointed his finger to the crates sitting outside and directed Taylor, "Do you think you can bring those in here without dropping them on the ground?"

Taylor stood with his arms at his sides and asked, "What's in the boxes?"

"Oh, it's some nitro I had Carl brew up," Evan said casually, while walking with a box.

Taylor's face became white with shock. "I hope you're shitting me."

"When I ask you to do something straightforward, just follow instructions and no one will get hurt. You ask too many questions."

Taylor picked up one of the crates and gingerly placed it in the middle of the shed. Evan quickly went over to the doorway and took the other crate, depositing it next to the previous one in the middle of the floor. "That will do nicely," he commented. "Now, you were about to say…"

Taylor swallowed hard. "Putting it in simple words, I want to leave the group."

Evan continued his chores. "Go ahead and leave. No one is going to stop you. But, are you really sure? It's only a short time before they come." Evan stopped and outstretched both his hands in almost an overt plea, "You need us. You cannot survive out there in the real world without my protection."

"I know how much you've helped me…and I understand I'd be a common drunk without you…and…I'm very grateful for everything you've done for me. I don't know how I could have lived without your guidance and everyone here's been like a family to me; the only family I've had in a long time…but…"

"But what?"

"I'm tired of hidin' out. I think it's time we give up."

"Surrender's not an option," Evan said curtly.

"When they find us they're going to surround the place with a few hundred FBI thugs and the state police. Then what are we goin' to do?"

"Do you trust me?"

Taylor hesitated before answering, "Yes, I…I do."

"I have foreseen everything. They do not concern me, so they should not concern you. Their forces will come against us, wave upon wave, but we will overcome them. "

"You've got no chance. All we have are five assault rifles, a thousand rounds of ammo, and some explosives. This is nothin' compared to the resources of the federal government."

"I would call your attention to the seventh chapter of Judges. If you spent more time reading the Bible, you would know the story of Gideon. He had harnessed a force of three hundred Israelites to drive out an army of one hundred and twenty thousand Midianites, using nothing more than trumpets. I would say that's about the same odds we face."

"But that's the Bible. There's no such thing as those types of miracles anymore."

"I thought you just said you trusted me. For the year and half I have known you, I have been straight with you. Have I ever mislead or lied to you?"

"No, you've never done that. I just think if we turn ourselves in then you could plea bargain your way to a reduced sentence. I am sure you have become a folk hero to people who're also fed up with government and all the immoral decisions they make every day. You've already won; there is no reason to keep on fighting. You have shown everyone that the courage and determination of one person can change how everyone thinks. Your story will appear in news around the country, and the world, and you will be fendin' off all the book and movie offers."

Trying to act surprised, Evan said, "You really think so? I've never really thought about that, Taylor."

"My last bit of advice before I leave is you should reconsider surrenderin' to them," Taylor said while walking to the door.

"Goodbye to you, Taylor," Evan said, smiling with an outstretched hand. Taylor was surprised at how well Evan had accepted his departure, turned around, and shook Evan's hand.

"Oh, there is one more thing you can do for me," Evan said offhandedly, as if it were a nearly-forgotten item at the bottom of a list.

"What's that?" Taylor said, almost reaching the door of the shed as he saw Evan with a 38 snub nose Remington handgun leveled at his head.

***

The valley was covered with the wispy, early morning fog as Sam stood in the stream. He had just slipped down the bank, twisting his ankle, and landing in a deep pool. Putting his hands in the cold, muddy water, he unsuccessfully tried to massage his legs to relieve the pain. Agent Jefferies approached from behind, tapping his shoulder. Sam, taken in surprise, nearly lost his footing. Jefferies grabbed his shoulders and steadied him. "Are you alright? I can get someone to walk you back up the road."

"Don't worry about me," Sam said wincing. "I've played two quarters of football with my ankle feeling worse." The nearest highway was an unimproved dirt road one mile away, and he did not feel like trekking back through the heavy brush. Sam could nearly see the outline of the three structures up ahead, and was not ready to abandon the mission with the objective so close.

"You look winded. Are you sure you don't want to go back to the road and wait?" Jefferies said, concerned.

"Yes, I'm sure. I'm just not used to wearing a vest." Sam felt the chill of the morning's cool crisp air as the sweat pored down his face. He was overheated from wearing a full camouflage suit, which added twenty pounds to his two hundred and fifty pound frame. Sam thought he could easily tolerate the extra weight, but the bulletproof vest was like a corset, restricting his breathing.

"They're standard issue on these operations. I'm surprised you didn't have your own," Jefferies said.

Sam became defensive, "Every cent I spend I have to justify with the Town Council. I've enough trouble getting a new radio for my car, let alone an expensive piece of clothing."

"Respect it. It's more than clothing; it'll save your life," Jefferies tersely muttered, showing no sympathy.

A call came in on Jefferies' radio, "Is your team in place yet? I would like to begin the operation."

"Nearly there," Jefferies whispered back into the receiver.

"Keep me apprised," Sattler's voice shot back.

Getting a cue from the message, Sam asked anxiously, "Are we really almost there?"

Jefferies pointed to a notch in the slope. "The sharpshooters are setting up about two hundred feet ahead." Sam figured Evan enjoyed the tactical advantage of being on the higher ground. The sun was rising above the hill, and finally, he could see the terrain around him. He was in the middle of a grove of small evergreen trees. They glowed in the light as the early morning dew still clung to the branches. He rested, knowing he was at the end of a journey that started halfway across the state in Pope's Mills. Sam closed his eyes, seeing the faces of his friends in the rubble after the dam failure. He was secure knowing he had no other course of action. Everything he had done was dictated by feelings of responsibility to the people of Pope's Mills, to bring some closure. Evan Young was hiding in a house somewhere five hundred yards ahead; the man who had callously murdered nine people, including two children; a crime against humanity that in his mind justified death. Sam griped his shotgun as he climbed out of the stream. Would he shoot to kill if he came face to face with Evan? He was a professional, and before now, such things were not a consideration in the performance of his job. Was it all about revenge now? Revenge sanctioned by society?. Initially, he thought he was on the legal and moral high ground, continuing something his father had started. But now, his father's actions have been called into question. Were they personally motivated? Was he continuing his father's personal vendetta against Jake Adamson? He decided simply to follow orders, hoping he would not have to make any life or death decisions.

Jefferies took a long swig of water from his canteen and offered some to Sam. Sam gulped it down as Jefferies whispered in his ear, "We're going to spread out twenty feet apart to establish a defensive perimeter. More than likely they will be successful in taking him from the front, where they have some clearer shots at him. We're here as an insurance policy if they're able to get clear of the house."

Jefferies went to his spot kneeling behind a pine tree and saw that everyone else had taken their positions, looking ahead. "We're all set up," he radioed in.

Sam dug into the dirt, watching as a squirrel squirmed in the bushes five feet in front. Beads of sweat dripped onto the ground as he tried to focus. Instead, he daydreamed about being home.

***

Sattler took shelter inside the grey, armored troop carrier that served as a temporary command post. He listened intently to the briefing being held around a laptop computer displaying the color infrared aerial photographs of the site taken during an airplane flyover. The carrier stopped about one hundred feet from the property's dirt entrance, beyond the view of the house. The photography showed a relatively simple layout with all three wooden structures facing a gravel parking area in the front. There were four cars in the lot, including the yellow Camaro, all showing in the photo as black. Had they been used recently they would have appeared as red or yellow, indicating head from the engines. Behind the rectangular structure, on the far right, was a pile of wooden crates and a hundred or so seemingly discarded barrels. Some of the barrels had rolled into the woods.

A group of three other people were gathered around the monitor displaying the images: Major Gredling; Gary Morrison, the agency photo interpretation expert; and Harry Boyd, the commander of the FBI SWAT team. Boyd, with his crew cut and muscular build, was the youngest of the group. He had been promoted rapidly through the Bureau had gained a reputation for taking risks; Sattler asked specifically for him to be at the stake out.

Sattler quickly scanned the photographs on the monitor. "Three guesses where they have set up their explosives lab? I bet it is in the rectangular building."

Everyone nodded in concurrence.

Sattler continued, "Let's try not to direct any fire at that building. I don't want to make any more of a mess than I have to." Sattler drew his attention to the tiny splotches of dark brown that circled the compound; they didn't match the color of the ground around it. Sattler pointed to them, "I wonder what these are?"

Morrison enlarged the areas on the screen but found no more detail. "They are probably areas where the soil does not have the same density as the rest. It looks that's where the ground has recently been excavated and refilled."

"Refilled with what?"

"The resolution of the photo does not allow us to figure that out," Morrison said.

"What do you think, Major? Have you had any experience with something like this?" Sattler said to Gredling. Gredling had been quiet during the debriefing, trying to size up the situation to determine his best strategy.

Gredling, admired by others in the state police as being a deep thinker, liked to err on the side of caution. "My frame of reference is Vietnam, where I dealt with all types of booby traps. I've seen kids blown to pieces by unexploded, buried ordinance. So, I wouldn't go near them. I'd find a way to go around them if I could, before I'd do anything else."

"Unfortunately, we don't have that luxury. I'm certain Mr. Young will not give us free reign of his property to send in explosives technicians to make an evaluation. We're running out of time. It is becoming light, and we want to maintain our element of surprise," Boyd said, wanting to resolve everything as quickly as possible.

Sattler turned to Boyd to ask what he thought to be the defining issue on which he would base his judgment. "Do you think we can contain him if we create a fifty foot no man's zone around these areas?"

"I'm confident," Boyd said. "I already have a dozen people up ahead who have clear shot of the house. They have training in spotting land mines."

Sattler got up from his chair. "Okay, let's proceed then. According to our infrared photographs, there are three people in the house. I want them captured alive. No one is to fire first. I don't want to provoke him. Is everyone clear on that?" The group of men nodded their heads and left the carrier to direct their subordinates, while Sattler remained behind.

Finally, after twelve hours of preparation, at quarter of six on Wednesday morning, Sattler picked up a microphone from the public address system in the carrier. His voice echoed throughout the mountain, "Evan Young, this is Agent

Sattler from the FBI. We've got a warrant to take you into custody. Come out with your hands above your heads. No one will get hurt. You are surrounded on all sides by FBI, ATF, and the state police. Your best chance is to surrender."

There was no reply.

Sattler waited five minutes and began again, "We want to hear your side of the story. I want to talk. I can be reached at..."

An agent at Sattler's side tapped him on the shoulder. "We've got him on the phone. He just called into the Louisville Office. They are transferring him over."

The voice over the intercom was pleasant and eerily stress free. "Hello Agent Sattler, and all the people from the FBI, police and ATF—and a very good morning to anyone else who is here with us. How nice of you folks to drop by. I wish I could invite everyone in for coffee and donuts so we could all chat, but you will have to forgive me. I don't have enough cups for all of you."

Ignoring the sarcasm, Sattler went on, "You know that you have no means of escape. So why prolong the pain by holding out on us? We want to hear what you have to say. We are ready to provide you with an attorney during questioning. You will get fair treatment."

"Oh really, that's so generous of you. 'Fair treatment,' huh...the same thing Jake Adamson got."

"I know how close you were to him; but you have to understand that Jake got the full benefit of our justice system, and he would have gotten everything he was entitled to. He did not allow the system to work."

Evan, who initially sounded amused, now seemed annoyed, "Please spare me the canned civics lecture. Maybe he knew he was going to get screwed by the kangaroo court system that already determined him to be guilty. And maybe he was courageous enough not to 'prolong his own pain,' as you would call it. You have no comprehension of what he tried to do."

"Okay, explain it to me," Sattler said.

"I have nothing against you personally, but you are so brainwashed by the bullshit they've been feeding you, it would be a waste of time."

"You're a smart person, so I hope you understand that we don't want any violence. The only way to reasonably resolve this situation is for the three of you to come out with your hands in the air and we take you in custody. I'm giving you my guarantee that no one will get hurt."

"This conversation is leading nowhere."

"Hold on, don't hang up. Maybe, I can speak to the two other people you have with you. Maybe, they will want to surrender."

"They don't want to talk to you. I'm speaking for them now when I say to get off my land before I take drastic measures."

"Mr. Young, you are in no position to issue demands."

"If you do anything to even attempt to take us, I will show you what I'm in the position to do."

"Mr. Young we can work this out…"

Evan shut off the phone, opened the living room window, and threw it out onto the gravel lot, hitting one of the parked cars. It shattered into little pieces. It was a symbolic gesture for the people who surrounded the house. Carl and Randy were standing with him in the living room, smiling in amusement. Evan commented, "Standard FBI technique to keep us on the phone and occupied, while they figure out ways to capture us. I'm no idiot. There will be no more talking. No more bullshit. You two know what we have to do. They have their main contingent towards the front of the property. They will try to flank us where they think we are vulnerable. Good for them. We've got a few surprises of our own."

"Yes, we sure do," Carl said eagerly. Carl was outfitted with a military surplus store helmet and a flak jacket with six hand grenades hanging from it.

"I'm going let them advance on the house a little before I give you both the signal to proceed. I suggest you both take positions as discussed," Evan said.

Carl scrambled out the side door of the house toward the bunk house, while Randy undid the safety of his soviet-made AK-47 semi-automatic rifle and exited via the rear door.

Evan put on a helmet of his own and crouched behind the sand bags and cinder blocks in the front part of the living room they turned into a makeshift bunker. There he waited. He followed the relaxation exercise of breathing in through his nose and out through his mouth. He did this for about twenty repetitions and felt his pulse slow down. He focused on the section of trees that were on the left and right sides of the house. It was there he asked Carl not to excavate any ground so the FBI would use the openings to gain entrance to the property. The wind kicked up, moving the tree branches back and forth. He concentrated his attention on the lower tree branches, which were moving more erratically than the other branches in the wind. With his AR-15 rifle, he sighted and pressed the trigger. The bullets sliced through the trees as the smoking cartridges discharged onto the floor. He heard Carl fire his gun from above, taking shots at the same area. The trees lit up as fire was returned. Bullets ripped through the front window and glass exploded onto the floor. The hail of bullets from the outside continued for five minutes and then suddenly stopped.

Sattler's voice could be heard from the public address system. "This is your last chance to come out peacefully."

Evan withdrew a remote from his pocket and pressed a few buttons. There were a series of loud explosions from outside as the soil pits blew up in a deafening staccato. The house vibrated as the air became smoky and filled with soil particles.

The impact threw Sattler onto the ground of the troop carrier. "Oh shit, he mined the entire mountain." The SWAT team that occupied the woods made a retreat to the road as the trees seem to explode.

Major Gredling opened the door to the carrier. "I don't want to put anyone in jeopardy. We can't take them from the ground; let's try the air."

Taking brief cover below the sandbags, Evan lifted his head and smiled. He had succeeded in intimidating a larger, more equipped force. The onslaught by the FBI had peeled the plaster off the walls, revealing the wooden planks underneath. The walls of the house were filled with bullet holes, hundreds of them, showing the early morning light in dotted patterns on the floor. Evan's nostrils burned from the smell of gunpowder as he rested, leaning against the sandbags. The explosives had served their purpose, confusion reigned, and now it was time to make his move before the FBI regrouped. He took a long, deep breath and went onto his belly, crawling through the debris, to reach the kitchen. The bullets had ripped the cabinets off the wall, obstructing the side screen door. Evan muttered a prayer as he scanned the walls of the house, and, improvising, he made for a two-foot hole in the brick. As he did, the floor stared to vibrate from a helicopter hovering above. There were two sets of explosions from the helicopter guns. The outside walls buckled from the ten millimeter shells. Finally, there was a groan as the walls collapsed inward and the second floor came crashing down to the first floor. The air outside was still filled with smoke and dust as he looked over in anticipation toward the shed.

Meanwhile, in the adjoining bunkhouse, Carl took note of the helicopter, and kept aiming his rifle at the moving target with little success. He needed something more substantial. He pulled out a grenade launcher from a wooden crate, and aimed the green tube toward the copter. Loading it with a grenade from his vest, the apparatus made a "poof" sound and, three seconds later, there was an explosion twenty feet from the tail rotor. Smoke poured out of the tail section and the copter made a quick retreat from the site. A second copter appeared and hovered down towards the second floor window. Carl was in the midst of loading the grenade launcher a second time when bullets came flying through the flimsy, wooden exterior of the bunk house. The bullets hit his flack jacket, throwing him onto the floor. Carl's leg had been blown off and he lay crumpled against the wall. With all his remaining energy, he removed the pin from the grenade and was about to heave it out the window towards the helicopter when another fusillade of bullets came through the wall, striking Carl in the face and neck as he dropped the grenade on the floor. There was a loud explosion as a red mist came out of the second floor window.

The helicopter pilot radioed in, dryly noting to Sattler, "We've got a confirmed hit here."

Sattler said, "Copy that. Do you have a visual on the other two?"

"Cannot see the ground—too much smoke," the pilot radioed back. Suddenly, the door to the shed opened and closed. "One of the suspects just entered the shed."

"Hold fire. We're going to give the other two an opportunity to reevaluate the situation and surrender," Sattler radioed back as he walked out outside, surveying the terrain that had been drastically altered in the past fifteen minutes. The lush pine forest surrounding the house had been leveled, trees laying flat on the cratered ground. Smoke and flames poured out of the main house and bunk house. Sattler now wanted a quick resolution, as the fire was threatening to spread to the adjoining woods. The debris from the house blew in the wind that picked up on the mountain. A burnt piece of Bible blew past him. Sattler's throat burned as he inhaled the smoke-filled air. Sattler said tersely to Boyd who was standing next to him, "Get your men and surround the shed. I want him bottled up tight."

Boyd got on the phone and five men in camouflage gear joined him. They crouched low as they approached the shed. Sattler spoke into the bull horn "Young, we know you're in there. You've got no recourse but to surrender. Come out with your hands in the air." As Sattler stepped a few more paces forward, there was a loud boom as the shed exploded, the oak planks that comprised the walls rained over the hill. The shed had completely disintegrated and all that remained was smoking ruins on the dirt foundation. On the ground, stunned from the suddenness of the explosion, Sattler looked up and saw Evan Young's bloody, burnt clothes laying on a downed tree.

***

Sam's legs ached from crouching as he glanced up the hill, noting how much it looked like a war zone. Smoke had filtered down the slope, making any view of the top impossible. He saw Jefferies looking up anxiously and shifting nervously in his spot. Jefferies moved out from behind the tree, clutching his radio. "Can get we get an update?" he asked, as he started walking up the hill to get a better view, as a helicopter circled overhead.

Sattler was walking through the shed debris when he replied, "Copy that." Sattler's voice came over the speaker in the helicopter. "We have two of them. What about the third?"

The helicopter pilot leaned over in his seat to get a better view. "There's too much smoke down there. I've got no visuals."

Not willing to wait any longer, Jefferies waved his arm forward, directing everyone to move up the hill. Sam was still crouching. "Let's stay here, and wait for him to come to us."

Jefferies had moved about fifty feet ahead and another series of explosions sounded. Dropping the shotgun, Sam dove onto the ground with his hands on his head, feeling the impact going through his body, jarring his bones.

The blasts were not from the top of the hill; they were on the nearby slope.

They were not going to be casual observers anymore; someone was taking the battle to them. Hearing a scream of pain from Jefferies, Sam stood and dashed up the slope as the explosions continued to blanket the hill. Barely able to see ahead, he tripped on a downed tree, and fell face first. Getting up again, dirt stinging his eyes, he ran blindly ahead, trying to feel for any obstacles. There was an outline of a body ahead—a man clutching his leg. Sam put his arms around the man's shoulders and pulled him down the slope. Sam got him past the explosions and rested the man's body against an oak tree. Overcome by the smoke, Sam collapsed on the ground, coughing, trying to get air into his lungs. Through his coughs he said, "I told you Mike. You shouldn't have gone ahead."

He looked back at the tree. The man was not Jefferies; it was Randy, dressed in a camouflage outfit.

Randy forced his mouth into a scowl and pointed his AK-47 at Sam. Sam reached for his sidearm, a Remington pistol, and aimed it forward. His finger froze on the trigger. In his brief moment of hesitation, Sam thought how absurd it would be to die helping one of the people who killed his goddaughter.

Bullets cut through the air past Sam from both directions. After a few seconds, he put his arms out and looked at himself. Miraculously, he was untouched. A sharpshooter's bullet had hit Randy in the center of his forehead. The back of his head had exploded into a shower of grey and red on the trunk of the tree. Jefferies came limping down the hill, rifle ready, a green piece of shrapnel in his leg. The blood slowly trickled onto his boot as the both of them stared at the corpse ahead. Randy's face had a vacant look, like a mannequin in a store window.

Jefferies got on the radio. "All's clear. Third suspect's down." As he did, a group of sharpshooters gathered around the tree in a semi-circle, eyeing the trophy. Sam always thought he would feel vindicated and triumphant at this moment, but somehow the sadness returned, and he felt empty.

CHAPTER 23

Joseph sat on the swing, reading a hard cover book, *Analysis of Water Systems using Laplace Transforms*, occasionally looking over the cover at the two legs protruding from under the sheriff's car in the driveway. The legs had not moved in about five minutes and he was about to start getting concerned when he heard a clicking of tools. A voice tersely muttered, "Oh, what the fuck is this," followed by more sounds of tools being dropped onto the driveway pavement.

For the past three days, everything had been relatively peaceful, Sam's house serving as the proverbial port in the storm. All Joseph could do was to wait with Jesse and Toby for news of the FBI operation in Morehead. Sam had given him a courtesy call before he left San Diego to tell him to stay at the house, to follow the deputy's instructions, and to keep out of trouble. That was just about the only thing he had said. When asked about the interview, Sam said nothing. He responded to questions with one-word answers. Joseph could tell that Sam had felt like the entire universe had collapsed around him. Sam needed time to put the recent events into proper perspective, and, as a friend, Joseph decided to give him the space to do so.

Joseph himself was feeling worn out and physically exhausted from working eighteen-hour days for the past three and a half weeks. He needed time to relax and to do nothing. In contrast to his sluggishness, Jesse was a ball of energy, doing many of the chores around the house, including the yard work and the laundry. Life had almost returned to normal: in the late afternoon, when Toby would come home from school, Joseph helped him with his homework, and the three of them would then make dinner. Joseph would then read to Toby before going to bed. For Joseph, staying at a house with a woman and child was surreal. Being there with Jesse and Toby made him feel part of a family; but, he was a bachelor, not a man with a wife and kid. He had only known Jesse for ten days, but with the investigation coming to a close, everything would have to start changing. He asked himself the future of his relationship. Was he going to drive off and simply say, "Good bye, everything was nice, and please keep in touch?"

Joseph heard more tools clanging and cursing coming from under Sam's Thunderbird, and finally, he decided to ask, "Are things okay down there?"

The disembodied voice said almost in a mumble, "What? I can't hear ya."

Joseph slowly got up from the wooden swing, as if just awakening from a deep sleep, "Do you need any help?"

Jesse's head popped out from the undercarriage, her eyes squinting in the sunlight of the early spring afternoon. Knowing that Joseph would be of no aid, she said, "Thanks for the offer. Can you fetch me some lemonade from the fridge?"

"No problem. I think I will get some for myself, too. Do you think that you ought to be working on Sam's car?"

"Why not?"

"Remember the last time you worked on the car of someone you knew?"

"I've complete confidence this time it won't blow up." Jesse smiled.

The statement was intended to be humorous, but Joseph was much more serious and replied defensively, "I didn't mean that. You had the engine taken apart. It was in two hundred pieces on the floor of your garage. You wanted to do a complete overhaul."

"You don't need to worry. This time all that is needed is an oil change and a minor tune up. I can see that Sam has had this thing professionally maintained, not like your car. His mind seems to be rooted in reality. I need the work. I can't spend all afternoon on a porch swing reading books. Remember, I need to do something physical. That's the way I am."

"I don't know how I should take that comment?" Joseph said, brooding.

As Jesse got up from the Thunderbird, her blue jeans had patches of dark oil that reflected in the light, and there were smudges of grease on her face. She gave Joseph a smile and put her face only inches from his. "It's a compliment. I love how your mind works; it's completely different than the other men I've met." She unexpectedly kissed Joseph on the lips, leaving dirt marks on his face with her fingers. "If you have any doubts about how much I respect you, come have some lunch with me, and we can discuss it a little more." She playfully took his hand and then led him to the house. "If you haven't noticed, we've got the place to ourselves. Maybe I can clean up, and we can pretend that we are back at the park and have a picnic lunch on the porch with the leftover roast beef from last night."

Joseph got to the kitchen and searched the refrigerator for the plate of roast beef while Jesse went upstairs. He heard the water run in the bathroom, and started to pile the bread and mustard onto the counter. The telephone rang and Joseph dutifully picked it up. The familiar voice on the other end said, "Don't ask any questions, just turn on the television. I think all the local channels are carrying it. Is Jesse with you? She would want to see this, too. I'll be back soon. Bye." The line went dead and Joseph went to the living room and flipped on the television.

Jesse ran down the stairs. "Who was that, Joseph?"

"It was Sam. I think something important just happened and he wants us to watch it on TV."

Jesse quickly turned on the VCR next to the Television. "Maybe we should record this for posterity."

It was a live news conference from the courthouse in Morehead. Sattler was standing at a dark, mahogany podium with the FBI symbol, along with Colonel Frank Gredling. Looking rather wooden in front of the assembled reporters, with a hint of perspiration on his bald head from the television lights, Sattler said, "I have a brief prepared statement to make, and then I will take questions from the press." He continued reading from the paper on the podium. "At 5:45 am today, the Joint Federal State Task Force headed by myself and Colonel Gredling of the state police surrounded a house in the vicinity of the town of Morehead in our attempt to apprehend the suspects in the Pope's Mills and Gottlieb Heights bombings. The suspects put up armed-resistance and, following a fifteen minute firefight, two men that we have identified as Randy and Carl Andrews, were shot and killed. Another man, who we have identified as Evan Young, the main planner and participant in the bombings, took his own life to avoid capture. A member of the task force, ATF agent Mike Jefferies, received minor, non-life threatening injuries during the siege and was flown by helicopter to a local hospital for treatment, where he is currently listed in good condition. In our subsequent search of the property, we found equipment typically used to create explosive agents. We have made a preliminary identification of the materials on the site as being plastic explosives similar to those that had been used in the bombings. We are currently testing the materials and will be completing a lab analysis within the next two days. I would like to thank the state police and local authorities for their cooperation in making today's operation possible. That's all I have. At this time, I'm going to throw it open for questions."

Jesse, who had been watching with wide eyes, jumped in the air and made a whelping sound. "Woo, Woo, They finally got the fuckers." She then hesitated, having a dour look on her face, "Whatever happened to them sounded much too good for what they did. I would have preferred that they had died much slower and more painful deaths."

Joseph, who was calmly sitting in Sam's easy chair, put out his hands to try and quiet her. "I would like to hear the news conference, if you don't mind."

"Did the FBI ever determine the motive for the bombings?" a reporter in a red sweater asked.

"We believe the motive was to obtain revenge on the communities of Pope's Mills and Gottlieb for the arrest and subsequent suicide of a Mr. Jake Adamson.. He was a cult figure in the area, and Mr. Young had been a member of his group. In the house, we found writings relating to the destruction of the federal government, and the creation of a society based on Mr. Adamson's religious views."

A tall woman in a grey business suit stood up, "Does the FBI believe that the conspiracy was limited to the three individuals that died in the raid?"

"Our preliminary assessment, pending further investigation, is that Mr. Young and Mr. Randy Andrews matched the descriptions we had from eye-witness accounts of the bombings, and from other evidence we have obtained during the investigation. All the information we have received so far seems to point to only two perpetrators setting the explosive charges. We have accumulated other evidence, which I won't discuss at this time, that would confirm this. We believe that Carl Andrew's role was primarily in the fabrication of the explosives. That leads us to believe that all the conspirators are dead. However, we will be investigating any other leads that turn up."

Photographs of Evan Young and the two Andrews brothers appeared on the TV screen. As Jesse watched, she said in disbelief, "That's weird. They must be old pictures. I don't recognize any of them. If the FBI wasn't so certain that they were the bombers, I would've sworn I had never had seen any of those men at my station. I can't imagine I was standing within a few feet of one of those people."

Joseph noticed Jesse's reaction as a note of concern came across his face.

A reporter stood up. "With all the suspects dead, are you going to recommend to the governor that the National Guard be called back from protecting the dams? They have been on duty for the past twenty five days."

Sattler gazed into the TV camera and, with a crooked smile, glibly answered, "That's a call for the governor to make. I would say that the threat has now been significantly reduced."

The television anchor broke in and summarized the news from the morning, showing an aerial view of the compound prior to the raid. The anchor explained that the compound had been used as hunting lodge, while a computer block diagram of the compound indicated the location of the main house, the bunk house, the shed, and the dirt access road was shown on the screen. The block diagram was replaced with the current view, including the burned out remnants of the houses that were still smoking, and the dirt foundation of the shed. The anchor went on to say, "We have exclusive photos of the early morning operation provided by the FBI." A tape ran, showing a sweeping close up of the three buildings in the compound through the trees. Joseph, who had been leaning forward in the flowered, cloth armchair, suddenly stood up as if something hit him. The image that got his attention was quick enough to be almost subliminal. In the few seconds it took for him to run to the TV, the news had switched from the tape to a reporter at the news conference. The reporter on the scene made some closing remarks, and then the program turned back to a soap opera. Joseph quickly went to the controls of the video recorder.

"What's wrong?" Jesse asked.

He quickly rewound the tape and paused it when it showed the close ups of the buildings and a series of faded white letters on the sepia background of the weathered wood of the shed. "Did the news say the compound had been used as a hunting camp?"

"I believe so. Why?" Jesse asked.

Joseph went to the paused view. He put his fingers on the screen, tracing the outlines of the letters. "Come over here. I think I see remnants of a name on the shed. What does that look like to you?"

Jesse came over and squinted at the grainy image on the TV. "I think I can faintly see the word 'Cann.' I can't make out any letters after that. Maybe it's an 'E.'"

"I am glad I'm not seeing things," Joseph said, as he got his briefcase out of the closet, and started out the front door.

"Where are you going?" Jesse asked incredulously.

Joseph hesitated for a moment. "The public library. The Gottlieb Heights Public Library. Do you have Sam's keys to his Thunderbird?"

"Can I come along?" She said, as she threw the keys over to Joseph.

"Remember, you need to be here when Toby gets back from school. You have to hold down the fort. This is something I have to research myself," Joseph said as he gave Jesse a peck on the cheek.

Jesse angrily sat down on the sofa, crossing her arms. "I'll never figure out that man," she said, as Joseph quickly shut the front door behind him.

***

It took Joseph almost a full day of leaving telephone messages to finally hear back from Sattler. When Sattler did call, Joseph practically had to beg to meet with him. What he finally got was twenty minutes over lunch.

When Joseph arrived in Lexington for his appointment, the office buildings of glass and brick glinted in the mid-day sunlight. Black briefcase in hand, Joseph shuffled across the street to avoid a car speeding through a red light. It was five minutes after twelve and he was late for his appointment. After running the last five hundred yards, he arrived at his destination, the Federal Building that housed the FBI. Joseph was asked to wait for Sattler in the first floor lobby. It was not until one in the afternoon when Sattler strolled out of the elevator, carrying a yogurt and an apple. Sattler warmly shook hands with Joseph and said, "Sorry, I'm late, but I've got a lot of paperwork and reports from the investigation to write up. People don't understand how much of it we have to contend with." Sattler was making a conscientious effort to be more relaxed than he was in the field. "Do you have your lunch? We can get something at the cafeteria they have in the building?"

Joseph had eaten enough Federal Building cafeteria food over the past weeks for a lifetime and politely refused. "I grabbed something on the way over here."

"Did you drive here from the university?"

"I am still living in Gottlieb," Joseph said, not wanting to discuss his ongoing relationship with Jesse.

"That's okay by me. It's a really nice day. Why don't we talk outside?" Sattler gestured toward the door with his outstretched arm as the two exited the double glass doors of the Federal Building and started briskly walking in the direction of Gratz Park, a block-wide, green space in the middle of town. There they found a bench in the shade and sat looking toward a bronze fountain of children playing. Sattler took a plastic spoon out the breast pocket of his suit jacket and started to dip it tentatively into the cup. "I'm not a health food fanatic, but I noticed this morning I've put on a couple of pounds. Stress will do that to you and I have to think about my annual physical. Before you start talking, I just want to say that I know I've been tough on you, but I hope you understand it was not personal. I had to keep us focused on the tasks at hand."

"I understand the pressure you were under," Joseph said. At that moment, Sattler appeared more human and fallible than any other time during the investigation. Joseph did not know how to start the conversation and began by asking, "How is Agent Jefferies doing?"

"Thanks for your concern. I visited him in the hospital today and the doctors have a good prognosis for him. The piece of shrapnel went though the muscle of his leg, fracturing his fibula. If the shrapnel had hit his leg a quarter of an inch over, it could have shattered the bone entirely and would have required major reconstructive surgery. But as of now, he is scheduled to be getting out the hospital in a couple of days, and after two to three months of physical therapy, he'll probably be getting back to field work."

Joseph was still trying to be casual. "That's good news. At one time, he asked me about some Lebanese food, and I thought that I ought to bring him some spinach pies while he was in the hospital."

"You did not make the trip over here to talk about Agent Jefferies or Lebanese cooking. I bet you're curious about the promise I made to you at the beginning of the investigation, to help your relatives come over here if you helped us out. I think that you made a huge difference, and I'm writing a letter of commendation to the President of the University regarding your performance. Most importantly, I intend on keeping my word about helping you bring over some of your relatives from Lebanon. I've got a contact at the INS for you, and I can schedule a meeting. You just tell me the time, and I will get it arranged."

"Thank you, Agent Sattler. I appreciate that. I need to call some of my relatives over in Beirut and find out what their feelings are."

"I see. Sounds like you still need to figure out your own plans, too."

"I didn't come here to talk about my relatives. I came here to talk about the investigation."

"As I said, we have a lot of paperwork to do. You must be relieved with Evan Young and his confederates dead, the investigation is closed. You must be looking forward to going back to teaching."

"Yes, I certainly am. But, there are some unresolved issues preventing me from going back with a clear conscience."

"For example?"

"Motive, for one thing."

"Of course. The motive was revenge for the jailing of Jake Adamson. I remember you were the person who helped clue us in to that one."

"I was convinced of that originally, but after the interview with Theresa, it became evident that he had a completely different purpose."

Sattler seemed surprised at Joseph's tenacity in getting information. "So, you've read the transcript, too, and you believed everything she said at face value?"

"It seemed to explain all the events that had happened ten years ago."

"Having not been there, I can't judge whether or not she was telling the truth. But reading what she had said has not swayed my opinion. I still think Adamson was guilty. The bottom line is, I don't believe her version of the story. The entire interview simply demonstrated that she hated her stepfather. That's normal in many families when the mother remarries, and the children do not want a new authority figure. I know this from experience. I dated a divorcee for a while, and, I was going to get engaged, but I didn't get along with her son. I eventually broke up with her."

"What about the events at the mansion?"

Sattler shined his apple with a napkin. "Oh, the story of the wild parties, the orgies, to entertain clients. I think that sounds way over the top. You have to ask yourself the question, why we never heard about this from anyone else in town? We spent over two weeks there and interviewed over two hundred people. I think she believed she was speaking the truth, but I think there was a more rational explanation. Have you ever heard of Stockholm Syndrome?"

"Isn't that where the kidnap victims becomes sympathetic to their captors and wind up aiding them?"

"That's part of it. The victim becomes vulnerable to whatever the kidnapper says and does. In that vain, you have to consider everything in that context—she spent three days with Jake. I've met many criminal personalities like Jake; they can convincingly blend truth and lies. I'm sure one of the things he convinced her of was that he was there to save her from her 'evil' stepfather, and then planted in her mind the idea of the parties where women are beaten and abused. After a few days of being sermonized, it's not surprising Theresa would believe it to be fact."

Joseph got up and paced around the park bench where Sattler remained seated. "No. I completely disagree. The fact is, all along we have been dealing with someone who had witnessed his girlfriend being molested, saw a father-figure being prosecuted and then ultimately committing suicide over a crime for which he was innocent. I think Evan wanted us to find this out. He wanted the FBI to visit Theresa so we could discover it for ourselves. We have been assuming Evan put the blame on the federal government, but I think it was Matt Clark. Clark had the reputation of being able to get the government to do whatever he wanted. He got the government to build a dam for Pope's Mills, and then was able to maintain control of a company town, down to hiring a town council and sheriff that would follow whatever he dictated. Clark regarded Jake as a threat and acted accordingly. I have no doubt it was he who set up Jake during the hearing in Pope's Mills, and it was Clark who framed him for the kidnapping charge. Evan always wanted people to think there was some sort of higher motive for all the bombings, some sort of religious crusade against government. However, that could not be further from the truth."

Sattler thought for a moment, and said with a deprecatory smile on his face, "That theory is interesting, but you have nothing to support it. It's just another interpretation of events." At that moment, a young brunette in her early thirties, wearing a thin white cotton shirt, sat on a bench next to them along with a young boy who Joseph gauged to be Toby's age. Sattler watched amusedly as the mother tried to encourage the boy to eat a tuna fish sandwich.

Instead, the boy went over and started to play in the fountain. As the mother tried to pull the boy out, she got her sheer shirt wet.

Sattler seemed distracted, and Joseph stood up and intentionally blocked Sattler's view of the young woman. "But I do have evidence. I went to the Gottlieb Library and looked through their archives. I found a newspaper article from May, 1962." Joseph went into his briefcase and pulled out a set of pages printed from microfilm. The first page had a grainy, black and white picture of a line of people with shovels on top of a hill overlooking the town. The second page was the text of a newspaper article. Joseph handed them to Sattler, who seemed more interested in his yogurt. Joseph said, "This is simply a newspaper piece about the ground-breaking for the new water system. I would call your attention to the person second from the end. Do you recognize him? It is Matt Clark. If you read the article, you'll find out that the town engineer at the time had little experience with projects of that magnitude, so they hired Clark to manage it for them. That would explain why when I looked at the water system plans, they had some one else's initials on them. However, Clark was still closely associated with the project. That was the link between the two bombings, and as it turns out, it was fairly obvious, but you had to know what you were looking for."

Sattler examined the copies briefly, and then let them fall to the ground. "I cannot accept that all of this is because of one person."

"It wasn't because of what Matt Clark specifically did, but rather, how he did it. You don't see the poetic justice involved here. To Evan, Matt Clark was a symbol of the hypocrisy and the immorality of government. Clark used government to create his fortune, and would eliminate anyone who got in his way. Now Evan is using government to destroy Clark, through the obliteration of the major projects he built."

"It is essentially an academic argument since Evan himself has committed suicide."

"I think you need to consider some of the loose ends before you make that statement."

"Loose ends? I don't exactly know what you mean?"

"When I was with Jesse, she said she did not recognize any of the men that were killed. We both know she had a close up view of one the suspects at the gas station before the tanks were blown."

"Sometimes eyewitness descriptions are inexact, even when the person making the ID is only a few feet away. From what I remember of her description, the man's hair was covered by a baseball cap and he wore dark glasses. It is fair to say that most of the facial features were obscured. Randy Andrews matches the general description of height and weight of the man seen on the Pope's Mills dam, and we definitely believe that he was Suspect Number One,

315

the person who aided Evan Young in the placement of the explosives." Sattler threw up his hands as if to dismiss Joseph. "You don't need to worry; we've got this thing wrapped; everything's covered."

"I am sorry. I see everything from a different perspective. I think the entire shoot-out was a set up to get everyone to believe that the threat is over."

"A set up, huh," Sattler said incredulously.

"Evan Young wanted you to find where he was hiding."

"Oh really, he wanted to get apprehended?"

"No. His intent was far from getting caught. But I am certain he wanted the FBI to find him at that specific location. That's why he sent all the post cards to Theresa, so you could trace them back to Morehead."

"We spent a day researching the property records in the area to find him."

"What did you expect him to do? Give his address and say 'I'm here, come and get me?' That would have been a little obvious."

"You still have not explained the reason for all the subterfuge? If this was some sort of ploy, then it certainly backfired since Evan wound up committing suicide."

"Exactly. There is no better way to commit suicide than in front of the one hundred FBI agents and state police officers who had surrounded the property," Joseph said.

"I don't understand your point. You had better make it quick." Sattler finished his yogurt and started methodically pecking at his apple. He checked his watch, feigning boredom. "I appreciate all the thinking you put into this, but I need to get back to work."

"Did you consider the significance of location where Evan Young was hiding out? It was Rowan County, approximately two and a half hours away from Popes Mills and Gottlieb. Why choose a place so distant from his intended targets?"

"He wanted a place that was remote, where he could fabricate and test explosives," Sattler said, distracted by a blonde woman in a short skirt crossing in front of the bench.

"But there are other remote places within the vicinity of Gottlieb and Pope's Mills, places hidden in the mountains where he could have done all the bomb fabrication, places that were much closer than the town of Morehead. Evan had ten years to plan the bombings, and a lot of cash— this was the property he bought? There must have been other factors that decided it for him."

"I still don't see your point. I don't know how someone like Evan made his decisions. He was not a rational person. Maybe he liked the color of the house or the view of the countryside."

"No, quite to the contrary. I believe he left nothing to chance; everything he has done was very well planned and thought out. Did you ever investigate the geology of the area?"

Sattler broke out in a smile at the seemingly academic question. "Geology? No, I'm sorry. I was not interested in mineral rights."

"Maybe you should have. If you would have looked at the geologic survey, you would have found that the area is underlain by Pennsylvania Rock; the rock from which they mined anthracite coal. I contacted the U.S. Geological Survey and there are several abandoned mines scattered throughout the area. Of course, we all know most of the existing coal mines in Kentucky are located to the east of Rowan, in places like Floyd, Morgan, and Martin Counties. Remember, I worked for a mining company in the town of Pikeville before I became a teacher, so I have driven through these places. You need to realize that, in the late 1800's, they were still mining coal in Rowan County. After the coal ran out they simply sold the mining camps as they were, and never removed any of the buildings they used. When I saw the videotape of the site, I noticed the name "Cannel" and I remembered from a book I saw at the library that Biggstaff Cannel was one of the largest mining companies of the era." Joseph went into his briefcase and pulled out a massive, leather book with a yellow tab on one of its pages.

Sattler took it and gave it a brief inspection before laying it down on the bench. "I'm not blind either. I saw the letters 'Cann' on the shed. Aren't you going off the deep end a bit when you say that the property was owned by them? I can think of plenty popular names that begin with 'Cann' such as Cannon, Cannan, Canner, and so on. And so what if the property was owned by Biggstaff Cannel, by some remote possibility?"

Joseph took a breath and continued, "It would conclusively demonstrate that before it was a hunting camp, it was a mine; and the old wooden building to the right of the house was probably not originally a shed, but an entrance to a shaft so the miners could gain access to the coal. Generally, one of the constraints to mining is the amount of air air circulation so the miners would not suffocate. It was not uncommon for them to create another portal at another location, so that there would be adequate airflow. You could enter a portal a hundred feet below the surface and wind up several thousand feet from where you started. That's why Evan purchased the property, because it had a 'back door,' so to speak."

"So what you're saying is that Evan Young got the FBI and the state police to surround his property so he could fake his own death? And he's is still at large with his confederates. Having witnessed the entire event, I don't buy your theory."

"You need to ask yourself why Evan blew himself up when he could have used his gun to commit suicide."

"Perhaps he wanted to be dramatic, or thought he could take a few FBI agents with him."

Joseph shook his head. "There were two reasons why he blew up the shed: so visual identification could not be made of the remains, and to eliminate any evidence of the entrance to the mine. How long of a delay was there from when he entered the shed to the explosion?"

"About four to five minutes."

"That gave him plenty of time to get to a safe distance underground beforehand. The explosive charge was a perfect diversion to draw everyone's attention to the compound while he got away. He probably had a car parked near the other portal, where ever that was, and was able to drive away from the area unnoticed."

"Okay, I will humor you and let's say the DNA of the remains does not match the DNA of the hairs that we got from his house, and that somehow he had escaped. What then is his target? I would say that he wanted to destroy the dam at Xavier. But we have just finished draining the lake behind it, so it's not presently a threat to anyone."

"I don't think the dam at Xavier was ever an objective."

"I know, you have said that before, but we have eyewitnesses. He visited the town and reconned the dam. We even found the sketches of the dam back in his house showing where he wanted to place explosives. You can't get any better evidence than that."

"Again, he wanted you to believe that he was going to destroy that particular dam. He purposely made himself seen by an eyewitness, and he got all the photos and sketches of the dam and marked them up. I would say that he got a good return for all his play-acting. I think that he had something else in mind all along, something that was directly connected to Clark."

"Now you really have me curious. What are you talking about?"

Joseph pulled out a glossy photo he had in his briefcase. Sattler took a brief glance. It was a picture of a concrete gravity dam that was one hundred and sixty feet high and had walls that were twenty feet thick. "So what's this?" he asked.

"It is the Racoon River Dam in Cummings, Ohio."

"Did you say it was in Ohio?" Sattler asked.

"It was the last project Clark built for the Louisville District of the Corps of Engineers before he went into the private sector," Joseph said, pointing to the photo.

"And you think that Young is going to be able to take it out? I don't think that even a cruise missile would be able to destroy the dam. Even if he were alive, he wouldn't have access to any more explosives. We've got his laboratory, he cannot create any more," Sattler said, about to walk away from the bench.

Joseph put all the exhibits back in his briefcase. "Oh yes, that was another loose end. I had a brief conversation with Dr. Schelling, your explosives expert, and posed the same question to him. He figures Evan had used a total of roughly one thousand to fifteen hundred pounds of explosives for the destruction of the Pope's Mill dam, the Gottlieb Water Tanks, and the mining of his compound. During the inventory of the various drums of chemicals left at Morehead, he had estimated he had enough material to create about two thousand pounds. So, doing some basic arithmetic, there are about five hundred pounds still unaccounted for."

"Schelling's a very conservative fellow, very cautious, and tends to overestimate amounts. We do have some agents looking for another stockpile, but we're not going to make that publicly known. We don't want to unnecessarily alarm anyone. Anyhow, I don't think that five hundred pounds would do a significant amount of damage to the dam."

"So, you are not going to take any action?"

"Are you proposing that the Ohio State Police provide round the clock protection for the dam? Do you want to venture the cost of providing protection for the fifty dams in the Commonwealth of Kentucky that you put on the list?"

"I am sure it was expensive."

"It was over fifteen million dollars," Sattler said, getting angry, "and that's not including the cost for overtime salaries. I've got a lot of people out there trying to crucify me for my recommendation to use the National Guard. Now, based on your hunch, you want me to risk my career and contact the Ohio State Police to tell them that this dam, one could probably withstand a collision from a jumbo jet, is in danger of being destroyed by someone we've presumed to be dead, and who at most could only have a couple hundred pounds of explosives? Do you have any thoughts on how someone could take out a structure that size with the resources he has at hand?"

Joseph shook his head. "No, that's why I am here talking to you. I thought that you might have some ideas. All I can say is that whatever Evan has planned, it will take place on the ten year anniversary of Jake's death, May 13th, which is tomorrow."

Sattler hesitated for a moment, and then gave an uneasy look. "I might be able to act on it with the resources at my disposal. I really hope you're wrong."

"I hope I am wrong too. There is a community of about twenty-thousand people about five miles downstream. Most of the town is elevated only about fifty feet above the stream, making it well within the danger reach if there was a catastrophic failure. It would be an event very similar to the 1889 Johnstown Flood, where a reservoir dam broke from an intense rainfall and over twenty-two hundred people in a community of twelve thousand died. No one heeded the warnings that the dam was about to break, and many people stayed in their homes and were washed away with the flood waters— along with the hotels, factories, and everything else in the town. I read a description of a stream valley filled with bodies."

"I know about Johnstown. You don't need to lecture me about it," Sattler said, red in the face.

Joseph stood up to leave the bench, his face drenched in sweat from the afternoon heat. "It doesn't take a genius to figure if the same thing would happen to Cummings, there would be hundreds to thousands dead. It would certainly rank as the most significant terrorist act to hit the U.S. since 9/11."

CHAPTER 24

Sheriff Rob Valentine, a heavy-set man in his early fifties, sat in his squad car at the entrance of Raccoon River Park. He contently drank his coffee and ate a sweet roll, trying to forget it was six am, Saturday morning. He was annoyed that the FBI had contacted him one hour earlier about a "lead on a potential threat to the community." Valentine had worked law enforcement in the area for about thirty years and never heard from anyone in the Lexington Office before. He was more curious about the circumstances of the call, than anything else.

The park was approximately one mile away from the center of Cummings and was considered to be a major recreational area for the people of southern Ohio. It was one thousand acres in area, and had about fifteen miles of roads, making it one of the largest facilities of its type in the region. He wondered how anything at the recreation area could be a threat, except for the dam. The dam was maintained by a staff of twelve people, and to his knowledge, was in excellent operating condition. The FBI agent mentioned the possibility of closing the park. Valentine was half asleep when he said there should be "a tangible reason" for the closure other than a "half-baked threat." Even partially asleep, he understood that later in the day there would be a line of sail boats on the lake as county residents took to the water on what was being projected to be a beautiful spring day. On a typical May weekend, over five hundred people paid the ten dollar entrance fee to use the facilities. The park's closure would be a big news event, and he knew the mayor would question him about it when his contract came up for renewal in June.

Several black SUVs approached and a short, bald-headed man raced up to the sheriff's car flashing his badge. The sheriff made a quick exit from the car and brushed off the crumbs from his pants.

Sattler said in hurriedly, without introducing himself, "Is this the only entrance to the park?"

"Yes it is. You still haven't told me why you're here."

"Have you seen anyone here today? Any pickup trucks? Any vans?" Sattler asked, while doing a quick, visual inspection of the area.

"Nobody," Valentine said without hesitation. "I only got here fifteen minutes ago, though. Should I've seen something? There was a note of recognition that came over Valentine's face. "Hold it there for a second. Aren't you the fella from the FBI who just solved the bombing of the dam out there in Kentucky?"

Sattler walked back to the SUV, ignoring the Sheriff. He got back into the truck and drove one thousand feet ahead, where the principal part of dam was located. Sattler could hear the rushing of water going through the spillway pipe, discharging downstream as a white jet. He got out of the SUV and was immediately amazed at the scale of the project. There was a grey, rectangular building that housed the turbines. He could hear their hum as they turned, creating electricity. He glanced upstream and the early morning sun reflected off the lake. It had been a wet spring and the water was high. There was no wind and there was crystal clear visibility around the lake. Sattler could see little picnic areas that had been created along the shore with grills and picnic tables. He went across the road and leaned over the concrete railing, feeling dizzy as he looked down the one hundred and sixty feet. The town of Cummings was off in the distance. He could see the green grass of the river park and the large wooden dock jutting out into the river. There were bright red, wooden concession stands, which would later have lines of people wanting hot dogs and french fries. The park was the focal point of the community with a pavilion where orchestras would play on warm summer nights.

Sattler turned around and saw that Valentine had followed him in his car. Sattler looked over the structure, trying to see any areas vulnerable to attack. "I called your office yesterday and told the secretary I would be in the area today, but never received a call back."

Valentine stood on the asphalt, enjoying the breeze from the lake, still trying to wake up. "I have to prioritize, and general information inquiries, even if they are from other law enforcement agencies, have to take a backseat to my usual duties. Yesterday, I was busy with a robbery and a domestic abuse call. But it seems that with you calling me today at home—on my day off—to ask me to come here, you finally got my attention. I'm sorry, but after only four hours of sleep, I'm going to be direct. Why the hell are you here?"

"I don't have time to explain it fully to you, but there's a small possibility that someone in the group from Kentucky may be interested in this dam."

"We followed the events over there and we beefed up security. I've had deputies come around at all times of the day. In short, there is nothing going on around here. If you would have told me this over the phone and not been so fucking secretive this morning, I could have saved you the trip. It must have been an hour and a half long ride from Lexington."

"It was two and half hours," Sattler tersely corrected him. "Let me understand this: you have over a thousand acres of park with more than fifteen miles of road and you're fully confident no one else is here? I don't believe that."

"Yes, this is my backyard and I implicitly trust my deputies. Don't you have full trust in the people you work with from day to day?" As Valentine finished speaking, the three other agents Sattler had brought with him started fanning out around the dam structure, making a regular search pattern. One of the agents went into the powerhouse. Fifteen minutes later, the most senior agent came back to Sattler, who was still taking in the view from the dam. He announced, "The area around the dam and the powerhouse appear to be secure."

Valentine said, "Of course it's secure."

"Do you mind if I check out the rest of the facility?"

"Check it out to your heart's content. You're here already, so you might as well take the nickel tour."

Sattler drove down the road with the Sheriff, while the other agents followed in their SUV's. As the road twisted and turned, something caught Sattler's eye and he pulled over. It was a fresh pair of tire tracks in the grass trail. Sattler got out and examined them more in detail, touching the tracks and rubbing the mud on his hands. He motioned for the other agent to come over. "Agent Brown, what do you think of this?

"Looks like these tracks were made in the past hour by a pickup truck," he responded crisply.

Sattler stood up and said, "My thoughts exactly. I'm glad we looked things over and did not listen to the sheriff's bullshit. Where does this trail end, Valentine?"

Valentine said, "It goes back towards the lake. I wouldn't worry. We've all types of people coming back here in the mornings. Sometimes they just like to have a campfire breakfast."

"Right, you don't mind if I find out for myself." Sattler hurriedly walked down the path with the phalanx of agents on either side in a triangular formation. Toward the shore, there was a canopy of trees shading the shoreline. Sattler crouched on the trail, saying between breaths, "I think I hear five of them." He quickly motioned over towards the trees and silently signaled the agents to take the sides, while he took the front. Drawing his gun to a ready position, he quickly ran through the trees and held it with the two handed grip. "I want everyone to freeze," he yelled.

The four boys in the middle of the clearing, all wearing scout uniforms, abruptly dropped their kitchen utensils on the ground adjacent to the fire, while the man in the scoutmaster uniform next to a double cab white pickup truck trembled. A trickle of urine suddenly dropped on the ground from under his kaki shorts. The scoutmaster quickly put up his hands causing his dark thick glasses to fall off his face and he said breathlessly, "Take anything you want mister. We'll give you no trouble."

Huffing, Valentine got there one minute later. He saw the scene and said calmly, "Claude Humphrey, I want you to meet Agent Sattler from the FBI. Claude is president of our savings and loan association in town, and is the leader of Troop 105." He turned away to control himself from laughing. Sattler put down his gun, his face flushed with embarrassment. By the time he got back to his SUV, Valentine had already gotten back in his car. Valentine started his engine and pulled over to Sattler, who was looking to the ground in humiliation. Valentine couldn't resist saying as he drove off, "Do you still need me, or do you want me to stick around and help you bust some more... boy scouts?"

***

The red Mustang with a bumper sticker that read, "I work for a Jewish Carpenter" sped away from the gas pumps as Joseph helplessly watched.

"People certainly are in a rush," Joseph noted. "I will do better with the next customer."

"It's the nature of the business; people don't like it when you try to fill their oil via the automatic transmission fluid. It pisses them off," Jesse noted dryly, mounting a tire in the service bay.

Joseph scratched his head, "Oh, that is why he gave me the finger."

"I appreciate your offer to help me out, but I think I can go it alone. I've done that for a long time. I know now that PhD's make bad service station attendants," Jesse said, returning to her repair in the service bay.

Joseph followed her to the car on the lift. The last time he was in the station, it was chaos with the front window smashed and debris everywhere. Now the plate glass window in the front had been repaired, the roof was fixed, and the cinder block walls were patched where the cars had busted through. Above the desk, behind a new glass frame, was the poster of the redhead holding a wrench, sitting on the Corvette.

Joseph was mesmerized as he watched Jesse move smoothly and methodically around the car, mounting the tires. He was still a little distracted by his meeting with Sattler. He was certain that Evan was going to fulfill Jake's prophesy of being "resurrected to bring justice to the world. " This time, the justice would be the murder of innocent people to demonstrate the immorality and ineptness of government. He was still searching his mind as to how Evan was going to collapse a one hundred and sixty foot high concrete dam, and had not gotten any sleep the previous night thinking about it. If Evan was true to the pattern he established, he would plant the explosives in the mid to late afternoon. The dam would fail as people were still out shopping in downtown Cummings.

His bags were packed and were waiting in the corner of the office. He wished he were confident about his decision to leave. "To be honest, I didn't stop by to watch you work. I came over to say goodbye."

Jesse proceeded with the repair, trying to be unemotional. "It's Saturday, so why don't you stick around for one more day. I usually take Saturday afternoons off. We can go see a movie or somethin' like that. Toby's in 'Play Care' 'till five at the Church."

Joseph leaned against the freshly painted pillar in the service bay, picked up a wrench from a toolkit, and out of boredom, twisted it in his hand and watched the jaws move up and down. "That sounds tempting, but I have to catch a 12:50 bus out of town. The next one is at six in the evening and I need be back to school this afternoon. I can't do anything more to help out."

"We had this conversation last night. Why don't you let me drive you back?"

"You have done enough for me already. Anyhow, I have already bought my ticket."

"Joseph, I have to say this one thing about you, you have to be the most fucking stubborn man I've ever met," Jesse said as she lifted the tire off the body of the green Chevy. "I don't know what you're trying to prove. The semester is half over. You can't go back to teaching the class. Remember, someone else took it over from you. You might as well be taking it easy."

"I have lab work to do," Joseph said, almost as if he was making a declaration.

"For something they postponed until next year. You want to go back to that damp shit-hole and have your allergies act up again. Within the past week, you have not sneezed or had to blow your nose once. When we first met you were doing it constantly."

"So what do you want me to do? You want me to stay, do nothing all day, and watch you repair cars?"

"I'm sure there are things that even a PhD can do around here. You know about math and physics. Maybe you can teach in the high school."

Joseph became defensive, "I am *not* a high school teacher; I work at a *University*. It took me six months to find my present position."

Jesse turned around and put down her air hammer. "You seem so damn fixated about keeping your present status. If that's what you want, then I can go where you are. I can sell the station."

"Why are you going to do that? You are not making any sense. This is your home, and you have Toby in school here?"

"You are a firm believer in scientific and mathematical principals, that everything follows logic, but you don't seem to understand that most relationships don't work that way. They're based on feelings and emotions. You have trouble reading the writing on the wall. Okay, since you are being so stupid, I will spell it out in very basic terms that even you can understand…I love you Joseph. But I am realistic, and can face it that you don't seem to feel the same way about me."

A tear came down Josephs face, "I am sorry. I am not afraid to say it. Yes, I do love you. But I don't know about our relationship; we are completely different."

"I don't know why you are saying that. Maybe we aren't that different. Maybe it was 'kismet' that we met like we did.

"'Kismet?' I am not familiar with that word."

"It means 'fate' or 'inevitability.' I still do not understand why you say it was a random chance that we met. There is something I've not told you. Toby told me you sang 'Amazing Grace' to him when he was stranded on the river. I used to sing that to him all the time. He knows it quite well, but he did not expect it to be sung to him by a stranger. You see, the likelihood of two people who never saw each other selecting the same song to sing to a boy is quite remote considering the thousands of tunes out there. There must be some sort of divine intervention going on here. I'm not especially religious or superstitious, but you cannot fight something like that."

"There are always thousands of everyday coincidences, none of them 'divine intervention,' as you would put it."

"Okay, let's forget about 'kismet', Joseph. I've been good to you, fixing your car, providing for you a place to eat and sleep, trying to make you feel comfortable and at home. You don't seem to notice any of that."

"You know that is wrong. I have shown my gratitude in many ways. That doesn't seem to be enough."

"Yes, you have said 'thank you' but those are just words; what I am talking about is your attitude. Sometimes I think all I see in front me is someone who only thinks about himself and no one else. I'm a positive person; I think anyone can transform their life given the proper motivation. Growing up, I was very self-centered, but Toby changed that. I had a shit marriage with someone who lied to me and treated me like a doormat. For about six months, I was in denial about it, but raising a child forced me to have self respect. Joseph, you do have the ability to reinvent yourself. I can help you, but you need to lower whatever is shielding your ego. Sometimes…when we are talking about something personal…you seem to back away. Are you scared of me?"

Joseph started to laugh out loud uncontrollably.

Jesse started to get red in the face. "What are you laughing at? I'm being serious and I don't see what is so goddamed funny."

"I have been dealing with a terrorist who has been trying to kill me, and I am scared of a woman?" Joseph said, trying to catch his breath.

Jesse glared back. "I asked, 'Are you scared of me?' Do I intimidate you? You don't seem to want any physical intimacy."

"You are one of the most beautiful women I have met in along time."

"I didn't ask you if I was pretty. I asked if I intimidated you. You don't seem to want to touch me, or even kiss. There were a lot of times when I have wanted you to do that. But you walk away or ignore me."

"I find you very attractive and I want you very much but…"

"But…"

"I imagined romance to be completely different than this, that's all. Women don't act the way you do where I come from?"

"Most men I know get their ideas about women from their mother. Tell me about her. You always speak about your father."

"What do you want to know?"

"Anything. The kind of qualities that set her apart from other people."

"She was quiet, intelligent, dignified, and very graceful in her mannerisms. She was the only one of her family of three sisters to have a college degree. She was more charismatic than my father, knew more about psychology, and had more insight into politics than my father, but would never embarrass him or try to act smarter than him in front of others. I would never hear them fight or show any public affection, except for holding hands. She was a very private individual, but knew when to show outward strength."

"I can't be anything like her. You seem to have created this unobtainable standard for people. If someone gets near meeting it, you raise the bar again. It is self defeating." Jesse put her arms around Joseph's neck, looking him straight in the eyes, "I have a feeling this it isn't about me, or how I talk. You know the person I am on the inside. Maybe it's good that you're leaving. Give you sometime to think. I know what I want to do in life, and who I want to do it with. But I think you're still unsure. I believe in you, Joseph. You can make a big difference in this world. You think you've got a sure thing playing the role of college professor. So go ahead, go back to your job, have people walk all over you, and then in thirty years look back and see what you have missed. I can go most of the way in this relationship, but you need to believe in yourself, and I'm sorry, I just can't do that for you. It's a gap that you will have to close." She held onto Joseph for another moment, staring into his eyes and letting the spring breeze wash between them. "I guess this is goodbye then." She put her head on his shoulders and then kissed him on the lips. It was a long, soft kiss with her lips moving over his mouth. As quickly as she embraced him, she had let go and walked across the lot. "If you want to say goodbye to Toby, he's at the church up the street." Another car came in to get gas, and she briskly went about her business.

✱✱✱

Joseph saw the church steeple on the hill peeking above the homes, its silver cross glowing in the morning sunlight, and walked steadily towards it. It was a modest, dark-gray structure with bricks that looked as if they had not been cleaned in years. The front doors were open and three red candles burned in the sanctuary filled with plain wooden benches. He followed the sound of the children's' voices to the basement. He went down the stone steps on the outside of the building and found the basement buzzing with children playing with a myriad of plastic toys and on the floor and doing finger painting. A pony-tailed blonde girl chased a boy holding a fire engine. She flew around the corner and tripped over Joseph's feet, landing on her hands when she fell onto the brown linoleum floor. Joseph leaned over to help, but instead the girl smiled, picked herself up and continued in her playful pursuit of the boy. He scanned the room to find Toby piling Lego's one on top of the other in the corner.

There was a deliberate intensity as Toby tried to press one of the curved pieces onto a finished wall. Toby seemed to be ignoring everything around him. Then Toby noticed Joseph standing in the middle of the activities. Smiling, then motioning for Joseph to sit next to him, he said, "Good, we can build together. You make the roof."

Joseph was in the midst of a sea of multi-colored pieces. "What are you building, Toby?"

"A fort with gun turrets," Toby said, searching for some more circular Lego's. "I want about twenty gun batteries to blast away all invaders."

"That seems like a big project. I can help out at least for a few minutes," Joseph said, as he looked over the Lego's on the floor and started to construct the second wall.

"I watched the people rebuilding Mom's gas station. It was pretty cool how they put the cement blocks one on top of the other. Maybe I can build buildings when I grow up."

"You can do anything you want, Toby. The sky is the limit."

"Maybe I will build skyscrapers, one hundred stories high."

"Probably by the time you grow up there will be buildings one hundred and fifty stories high. In Taipei, Taiwan, they have built a building that is seventeen hundred feet high and over one hundred stories."

"I want you there to see me do that," Toby said, picking out some more blocks.

"I probably will. Right now, though, I am going back to the university. You know that's where I live. You can write me there, or email me, and I can come back to visit."

Toby put down the plastic piece, saying with a pouting expression on his face, "I don't want you to leave, Mr. Joseph."

Joseph, on the hunt for some flat Lego's, was amazed how succinct and blunt the comment was. As sincerely as he could, he responded, "Don't worry, I will see you again. I promise."

"Okay, I understand," Toby said, making a quick recovery and looking over his available pieces.

"Good. Give me a hug." Joseph held out his arms.

"Guys don't hug. My mother likes to hug. I don't let her do that anymore. Let's shake."

Joseph stood up and extended his open hand. As he did, Toby said, "I want to play a game."

"I just played Lego's, and now you want to play another game? I need to go." Joseph got up from his knees.

"Just a quick game. Then you go."

Joseph examined his watch impatiently. It was already 12:10, which still gave him forty minutes to gather his bags from the station and catch his bus. "Okay, what game do you want to play? It has to be a quick one."

Toby looked around the room. There was a set of large black dominoes resting on the floor. He pulled out the large cardboard box of the black pieces, upending the box, and scattering them amongst the colorful Lego's.

Amazed how quickly Toby made a mess on the floor, Joseph said, "Here, let me see them. I used to play these with my father when I was young."

"Is it really a game? I just like to set them up and watch them fall down."

Joseph tried teaching Toby the rules of dominoes. After a couple of minutes, it was apparent Toby was not interested in learning the game, and instead started to set up the dominoes up in a circle. He pushed the lead domino over, watching gleefully as they all fell down. He took some more of the tiles from the floor, created a larger circle, beginning the process over again.

As Joseph watched the dominoes slowly fall down in front of him, he felt a strong anxiety. The solution to the problem of taking out the Raccoon River Dam had become clear. The physics of the blocks were abundantly obvious. The theory, so straightforward that it was even taught in high schools: the energy of one block becomes kinetic, and then that energy is transferred to the next block. It had taken the simplicity of a child's game to demonstrate that all one needed to do was push one smaller object over to initiate a series of events. Joseph had thought the collapse of the gravity dam would be a single, large-scale event, rather than the result of a smaller failure. As the last domino toppled over and lay on the floor, he had finally understood how Evan Young was going to destroy the Raccoon River Dam.

CHAPTER 25

Jesse was filling a car when she saw Joseph out of the corner of her eye running down the street from the church. He quickly shuffled past her into the station office and punched out a number on the telephone. She saw him moving his arms gesturing in wide circles, speaking animatedly, being as excited as she had ever seen him. She finished up with the customer and went to the office in time to hear him scream into the receiver, "*It is a national emergency. I need to speak to him. What the hell do you mean he is unavailable? You need to find him.*" Joseph abruptly slammed the phone down and turned to Jesse. "They put me into his voice mail. The FBI acted as if I was some stupid crank, or something like that. Don't they know who I am?"

Jesse put her arms around him, speaking in a hushed, motherly tone, trying to comfort him, "Now settle down, and lets talk like rational people," she said, both hands on his shoulders, trying to get him to sit on vinyl couch opposite her gray metal desk.

He became excited again. "*Don't you do that to me! I am not crazy! I know how he is going to do it!*" he yelled, as he strained out of her grip. He abruptly walked away heading for the phone, hastily punching numbers on the keypad. This time he connected with the other party. After an animated five-minute conversation, he finished by saying, "Get here as soon as possible. You are the only chance we have."

Looking concerned, Jesse watched as Joseph grabbed the notebook computer and portable printer he had resting against the wall along with his luggage. Quickly setting up the computer and printer on Jesse's desk, he started accessing a database of dams. After reviewing several sites for half an hour, he came to the one that he was ultimately interested in, and set the printer in motion to output a map. While it was printing, a Ford Thunderbird pulled in front of the station, which Jesse immediately recognized to be Sam's personal vehicle.

Sam and Travis slowly exited the car. As Sam walked towards the door, he stopped in the middle of the lot, admiring the new paint job on the Richmond's Auto Care sign and the improvements that had been made to the station. They both wore their tan uniforms; Travis's displaying a sheriff's badge on his shirt, visible from under his jacket. Travis looked tired, with bags under his eyes. Jesse was surprised that Sam had taken what Joseph had said seriously enough to bring another person, obviously as a backup.

It was now after one o'clock, and both Sam and Travis were hungry. They poked through a paper bag filled with bagels and cream cheese they had found on the office desk, remnants of breakfast. "Mind if we eat?" Sam asked.

"Help yourself," Joseph said, and proceeded to brief them on his theory as they chewed their bagels and sipped their coffees. Sam felt the nervousness and anxiety in Joseph's voice and decided to try easing the tension. Looking down at the bagel, he commented, "These are really good? Where'd you get them again?"

Joseph smiled, realizing that he needed to relax. He picked up an onion bagel and, taking a bite out of it, responded, "At Murray's Bakery down the street." They cook them fresh every morning. I think Murray is an excellent baker, on par with some of the places I have been to in New York City."

Annoyed, Jesse broke in, "Why don't you quit the bullshit with the stupid goddammed bagels? Sam, why don't you tell him he is out of his fucking mind? Tell him to let the FBI handle it."

Speaking with his mouth full, Sam turned to her, "I wish I could. In reality, I know that the FBI is not going to do anything for Joseph because at this point he has zero credibility with them. Whatever points he had earned over the past few weeks he has now lost, and now he's in the negative score. That's why he hasn't been able to reach Sattler. Joseph is the very last person in the world he would want to talk to," Sam said, as he finished swallowing the mouthful of bagel. "Anyhow, Travis and I are the ones out of our fucking minds for being here on a Saturday." As Sam looked over his shoulder and saw that Travis had finished his bagel and was soundly asleep on the couch. "I've scheduled myself a day of watching baseball on the tube and drinking beer; a well deserved vacation after everything I've been through in the past few weeks."

Standing next to Sam, with his arms around her shoulders, Joseph said, "All we are doing is some field reconnaissance. If Sam sees anything suspicious, he is going to call the Ohio State Police. That is it. We are not going there to try to arrest or capture anyone."

Sam knew that he was about to get pulled into an argument and purposely walked away to the other side of the office to avoid it.

Jesse stood in the middle of the office and said defiantly, "What ever you're up to, I'm coming."

"No, you are not!" Joseph said emphatically.

"Yes, I am. You need me. What are you frightened of? That we may meet up with Evan? You needn't worry. After I'm finished with him, I'll leave enough of a souvenir for the FBI to take back with them."

"We already have three people on this expedition, and we don't need a fourth."

"But you don't know who's going to be there," Jesse said, trying to stare him down.

"It is not going to be you."

"Then let me ask you a question. We are taking Travis on this jaunt to back up Sam. So who is backing you up?" Jesse said. Travis was now snoring loudly.

"I don't need the protection. I am sorry, you are not going."

Jesse shifted the "Open" sign on the station to "Closed" and said, "You stay here while I get some things from the apartment."

As Jesse left, Joseph asked Sam, "Why are you saying that I have zero credibility with the FBI?"

Sam smiled back with a coy look on his face. "I know because I spoke to Sattler about an hour ago. He called me at home."

"Sattler? He called you?" Joseph said with a surprised look on his face.

"He said he wants you back at the university, doing your work and out of the way. He told me to cuff you and to forcefully bring you back if you resisted. He said that if I did not do it he would send someone from his office."

"Was he serious? Why would he say something like that?" Joseph asked innocently.

"Something about being sent on a wild goose chase to the Raccoon River Dam, and being made to look foolish. Something involving the Boy Scouts." Sam raised his coffee mug to Joseph in a mock salute. "I would've laid down a week of wages to have seen that. Anyhow, in some form, I do agree with him. It's time that we got you got back to the university. Do not worry, you're not free of me. I'll be in the area, and all of a sudden you'll get a phone call asking you to cook Baba Ghanush. I would still like to try some of your famous Lebanese food. Remember, you owe me a few favors."

Joseph said in a concerned voice, "But you do believe me, don't you?"

"Yes, I still respect your theories, but in my mind they are like a rubber band. They can only stretch so far and cover enough area before the rubber snaps. We're at that proverbial breaking point," Sam said.

"Does that mean we are not going to go to Ohio today?"

Much to Joseph's relief, Sam responded, "Yes, we're going, but I hope you realize that my being a sheriff means almost nothing over there. I've got very little law enforcement authority."

"I know, but you are the only resource I have left."

"Now I'm just a *resource* to be used," Sam said, feigning being insulted. Joseph was about to speak in rebuttal, but Sam raised his hand stopping him. "I just want to have a basic understanding that I've not released you from my protective custody, and I don't want you to do anything on the trip—nothing whatsoever—I'm going to handle *everything*…me and Travis. If anything happens, Travis will cover my back. You're going to sit there in the car and look at the scenery, while I check out your site. On the way back, you're going to take us to this steakhouse I know outside of Lexington, where you are going to buy Travis and myself the biggest porterhouse they sell, smothered in mushrooms and onions, with a giant baked potato piled high with sour cream and chives. I don't care how little money you make. I hope that the dinner bankrupts you for the month, because *you are going to owe us—big time*. Then tomorrow, we'll drive you back to the Kentucky Institute of Technology."

Joseph knew that he was finally cornered. "Okay, I agree," he said with a serious tone to his voice; putting out his hand as if making a binding legal contract.

Sam's large fleshy hand enclosed Joseph's when he shook it. "I'm going to really miss you, my man, mostly because you are such a piece of work. I hope you take that as a compliment." Sam checked his watch. It was getting on half past one. "We ought to start out if we expect to get there by the late afternoon. Let's see what you've got."

Joseph brought over the maps he had printed out from the internet and laid them on the desk. After a couple minutes of discussion, Sam, satisfied as to the route of their destination, gave Travis a tap on his shoe. Travis lazily opened his eyes and then proceeded to sit groggily on the edge of the couch. Taking his last sip of coffee from the Styrofoam cup Sam crumpled it in his hand as he asked Joseph, "What did you two decide?"

"She's not going," Joseph said as he quickly scribbled a note on a parts order form on her desk, hoping that Jesse would not come back in the next minute.

Sam said, "Good, then let's hit the road. We're burning daylight. Let's get this thing over with."

·

Fifteen minutes later, the glass door slung open as Jesse came back dressed in her green camouflage pants and jacket with her compound bow arrows slung across her shoulder. "Okay, I'm ready to go," she announced to an empty room.

She read the brief note left on the desk in almost undecipherable handwriting:

"Do not have time to argue with you anymore. Hope you understand. Will be back by 9 pm. See you then."

Frustrated, she ripped up the note and cursed under her breath, "The *fuckers*." She was about to leave when she noticed that in his haste Joseph left his computer on. She walked over to the screen and saw the last maps displayed. She printed the maps, ran out to her Taurus, and sped out of the lot.

***

Joseph was sitting in the front passenger seat staring ahead as Sam drove north on Route 68 towards Maysville, where they would cross the river into southern Ohio. Sam knew all the back roads in Kentucky, but had limited knowledge of the Ohio roads and relied on Joseph, armed with a pile of weathered AAA maps, to navigate. Travis went back to sleep in the passenger seat, his head resting on his hands.

Joseph heard Travis snore loudly, and turned around to see him sprawled across the back seat. "He must have had a hard night last night," he said sarcastically.

"Oh, give him a break," Sam said in a weary voice. "He's doing you and me a big favor being here on a Saturday, which happens to be his day off. He's had a tough four weeks. The job and having to raise two kids have tapped him out. He didn't realize that you can put in eighteen hour days six days a week. He's a young man; and I'm certain he'll get adjusted to it all, and find whatever help he needs."

"I'm confused." Joseph said, "Haven't you gone back to being the sheriff and Travis the deputy?"

"Not by tomorrow. I have resigned the office, gave the letter to Williams two days ago when I came back from Morehead. I was surprised that, given our relationship, he actually sat there for about two minutes thinking about it before verbally accepting it. He tried to act regretful about it and gave me the speech about my 'long years of service to the community, my father's service to the community, and that I should reconsider.' While he was saying all that bullshit, he was filing the letter and making all the copies for distribution to the Town Council. I'm certain he was as happy as a pig in shit and that my resignation was truly a godsend for him. Anyhow, it is effective this Monday, so I can proudly say that this trip to Cummings is my last, unofficial act as Sheriff of Pope's Mills."

"I still don't understand why you resigned. The emergency is over and you did what you set out to do…help solve the case. You should feel proud of yourself," Joseph said.

They arrived in Mayville, a quiet industrial town with a large paper plant on the Ohio River. As they crossed over the Ohio, traveling over a graceful, green suspension bridge Sam said, "You're not the only one who is saying that. Most people I talk to, including the Reverend and Thelma at the Collins Hotel, don't understand it either. Personally, I don't expect them to. I gave them, and the people of Pope's Mills, my life for the last four years, like my father did for the fifteen before me, so there is nothing I owe to anyone. After the interview in California, I had what most people would call a "moment of clarity." I thought a lot about what Theresa said on the airplane ride back, and somewhere over the Rockies, a lot of things in my life came into focus. Have you ever been to a party where everyone knows a story or a joke that you are not clued into, and you feel like an outsider, a complete fool? I'm that outsider. I feel everything in my life has been a lie. There are two components to a lie, the person who tells it, and the other person, the chump, who believes it. I'm the chump who has believed everything that has been said without question. People have tried to clue me in throughout my life, including my friend Charlie, but I was too stubborn, too proud, to listen. Now I'm paying for it. The day my goddaughter died, I sat on the side of the road in my car, trying to sidestep responsibility. I made a mistake. As you so rightly noted Joseph, my mind was overwhelmed with guilt, which accomplishes nothing. Up to now, I've done everything to compensate for that moment of weakness, except for taking the ultimate responsibility to make a change in my life. So now I'm doing that. I'm not going to look back to judge my father for what he had done. I'm certain that somehow he felt justified in his actions. I forgive him. I understand he was trying to protect me, to provide me the best future he could. But I have learned now that I have to follow my own inner voice, and not lead my father's life."

"You are not going to make the same mistakes your father did. Sam, you have to the ability to change things, to create your own future," Joseph said as he focused on Ohio Route 41, a two lane country road.

"I know I do. But every time I walk down the street, people don't see me, they see my father. They want things to be like they were when Matt Clark was in charge at the plant, but in all good conscience I can't be part of that anymore. I'm sorry, but there is no argument you can give me for staying in Pope's Mills."

"So what are you going to do now?" Joseph asked

Sam sat back in his seat, announcing confidently, "I've given it some thought and I've decided to go back to school to become a teacher."

"A teacher? You mean teaching kids in a classroom? Chalkboards, erasers, lesson plans?" Joseph asked.

"Don't act so surprised. I've always liked being around kids, and I've wanted to coach high school football for ever. So I thought I'd give it a shot. I've contacted Kentucky State and they're going to count some of the credits I did in undergrad towards a teaching degree."

"What would you teach?"

"Who knows? Before I wanted to be a cop, I was a victim of a liberal arts education. I was, however, thinking about taking up American History. A real bitch of a woman taught me history in Junior High, and maybe I could do a better job of it," Sam said. "Come to think of it, maybe I will meet some nice young woman there. It still isn't too late for me to try to have a family..." His voice trailed off as he stopped talking and concentrated on getting to Cummings.

They were making good time on Route 41, until they started to follow a fertilizer truck going fifty. Joseph had an apprehensive look on his face as he glanced at his watch. Sam suddenly gunned the engine and passed the truck, left of a double yellow line and barely missing an oncoming station wagon. Joseph covered his face with his hands while Travis slept. Relieved, Joseph said, "Traveling with a cop has its benefits." Sam smiled broadly, but said nothing.

When they reached Route 32, an east–west, four lane highway, Sam, who was known to be a conservative driver, had the car up to eighty-five. Joseph, distracted by Sam's seemingly erratic driving, almost missed directing him to the turnoff. Route 281 was a commercial, two lane highway lined with auto dealerships and tacky-looking clothing outlets. Joseph knew he was headed in the right direction after crossing the Raccoon River when he a spotted a sign directing them to Cummings. Sam asked if he should go towards the town and Joseph looked over the map and nodded. It was already four fifteen in the afternoon.

***

Their objective was to the north of town, and Joseph navigated Sam to Center Street, which took him through the modest-sized business district. The center of Cummings was composed of older, granite historic buildings surrounded by brick-faced newer businesses, like the rings of a tree core. It was nearly the end of a lazy spring day. People bustled about, taking advantage of spring sales and enjoying each other's company.

Joseph looked at all them attending to their business, not knowing that soon there would be a fifty-foot high flood wave filled with mud and debris hitting the center of town, crashing through the buildings, washing away foundations and flattening the newer brick face structures along with the old granite blocks, shattering the store windows, and washing the cars down the street. People would not see the wave coming, and although there might be a few to have the awareness try to outrun it, there would be nowhere to go. In a manner of minutes, all the buildings would be under water, and the town would be dead. Joseph could not clear his mind of these images.

"You don't get any more middle-America than this. I counted five churches," Sam observed. "If I wasn't finished with small town life, I could settle down here."

After Center Street had turned into County Route 976, they could finally see the gray monolith of a dam in the distance, glowing majestically in the light of the spring afternoon. Jets of white water tumbled out of the gates at the base and voices of teenagers rafting below the dam in flimsy inner tubes could be heard. Joseph realized it had been a wet spring, and for them to be releasing any flow, the water level must be toward the top of the dam. All of this drastically increased its vulnerability to overtopping.

The dam dwarfed the houses and the oak trees located in its immediate vicinity on the river. Sam slowed the car and looked up. "How high did you say it was?"

"One hundred and sixty feet," Joseph responded.

Sam scratched his head as he gave it a final look and then passed the sign for the entrance to the park. "It's difficult to believe someone can cause something of that magnitude to go into, what did you say, 'catastrophic failure,'" Sam said.

Joseph explained, "All types of dams from twenty feet high to two hundred feet in height are be prone to 'catastrophic failure.' To quote an over-used phrase 'Size doesn't matter.' In more technical terms, this facility is what is called a gravity dam. Gravity dams hold the water back by the sheer weight of the embankment and are usually composed of concrete. The biggest enemy to a gravity dam is overtopping. If enough water goes over the crest of a dam, the foundation can be undermined and the dam could tip. These types of dams have fairly large spillways designed to bypass unusually high rainfall, up to something exceeding a thousand-year storm, so the possibility of overtopping is extremely remote."

Travis got up from his sleep and asked groggily, "Are we there yet?"

Joseph answered, "Almost."

Sam asked, "So where's this second dam?

Joseph felt foolish that he was so focused on the Raccoon River Dam itself, he forgotten there was a another dam only five miles upstream. When Clark had constructed the Raccoon River Dam in the early 1960's, it was designed to replace a smaller, ninety foot dam, Whiting County Dam Number 54, a concrete block structure built in the 1930's by the Workers Progress Administration. For its day, Dam Number 54 was a significant civil engineering achievement, overshadowed by the highways and buildings that were built during the depression. From the photographs on the internet, he noted that Dam Number 54 was anchored between two massive concrete columns attached to a bedrock outcrop in the stream. Number 54 had simple, yet elegant, vertical lines on its curved concrete face with ornate Bas Relief's attached to the top depicting people working in the fields. Architecturally, it could be described as minimalist combined with an art deco flair. Now, it was a nearly forgotten relic that no one appreciated.

Usually, when a new dam is built, the original structure is removed. This time, however, it was maintained. Dams are sediment collectors, which limit their lifespan, and Clark must have considered it a masterstroke to keep Dam Number 54 in service as a sediment trap for the Raccoon River Dam, to extend its design life. The problem that was overlooked in the design strategy was that a catastrophic failure of Dam Number 54 would create a wave that would overtop the Raccoon River facility, causing it to fail with a domino effect.

"We are just about ten minutes away," Joseph said excitedly, while he examined the aerial photograph and the U.S.G.S. topographic map.

Sam quickly looked over and noted the location.

Joseph continued, "It is in a fairly remote area surrounded by farms. You see, everything makes sense from a tactical point of view. The location of the Raccoon River dam was a highly visible park used by many people, making it not so prone to attack. This Number 54 dam is located by country roads that are only used by a dozen cars a day, making it an optimum target."

As they turned off of Route 976 onto County Route 953, a modest blacktop farming road, they finally got their first view of the crest of Dam Number 54 poking through the tops of the trees in the distance. Sam slowed the car to cross an old open, grate metal bridge that spanned the Raccoon River. Instead of crossing, he pulled over toward the left of the entrance, onto a gravel access road where a large wooden sign hung from a rusted metal swing gate reading, "U.S. Government Property, U.S. Amy Corps of Engineers— No Trespassing."

All three of them got slowly out of the car, trying to reinvigorate themselves from their long trip. As Sam popped the trunk latch open and took out his field clothes, Joseph walked over to the bridge and tried to get an unobstructed view of the dam. All he could see was the middle-third of the structure. There were no tell-tale signs of anyone there.

By the time Joseph returned to the car, Sam and Travis had put on their jackets and were examining the large, round padlock on the gate.

Joseph went into the Thunderbird to retrieve a printout of the quadrangle map. He noted, as he visually surveyed the area, "This gravel road goes back for two to three miles to the dam. It is more secluded than it shows on the map." He folded the maps away in his pocket and said in a doubtful voice, "It looks like this place is dead after all. Nothing is going on. Maybe I was wrong."

Travis already had a piece of granite in his hand that he had picked off the shoulder of the road. He lifted it, and after a couple of token swipes, the heavy rusted padlock came falling to the ground with a small thud. "We won't find out standing here, that's for sure." he said.

The three of them went back into the car, and as Sam drove through the gate, he reminded Joseph and Travis, "Remember, all we're supposed to do is scout things out. If something looks suspicious, I'm going to call the state police. This ought to take all of fifteen minutes to check out, and then we'll turn back and get those steaks."

The access road was cut in the side of a hill that paralleled the river. The road was perilous, without a guard rail and a thirty-foot, steep incline down to the river. The loose gravel road was not maintained, and there were large rills that had formed where runoff funneled down from the adjacent hills. Sam took it slow as the car bottomed out in the ruts, but was able to maintain a steady pace without getting stuck in the mud. Sam pointed to the individual saplings that were crushed, indicating that someone had been there recently. After a few minutes, the road came to a dead end with another chain across the gravel. Beyond the chain, the road was overgrown with weeds and small trees, and was impassable by a car. "This is where the road ends gentlemen," Sam announced. "Joseph you stay here while we go and check this place out. "

"But I need to come with you. You don't know the layout like I do," Joseph complained.

Sam pointed his finger at him, cautioning him, "I don't have time for your shit. It was our agreement that you would follow my instructions to the letter. You're going to stay back here in the car, and that's all there's to it."

"Yes sir, Sheriff," Joseph saluted, as Sam and Travis disappeared ahead into the brush.

Joseph sat back in his seat and shut his eyes, trying to relax, hearing the sound of rushing water from the river fifty feet to the right in the woods. It was only about five minutes later when he heard a tapping on his window. Expecting it to be Sam, Joseph's heart nearly stopped when he opened his eyes and found it to be was a clean-shaven man, wearing sunglasses and with a cap bearing the

Corps of Engineers emblem. "Hello, may I assist you?" he said genially. "May I ask who you are?"

Joseph caught his breath. "We were curious about the dam," was all he could do to explain.

"You're trespassing on Federal Land. Where's everyone else?" he asked.

Joseph pointed towards the dam as the man opened the car door and motioned for him to get out. As Joseph walked ahead, the brush started to clear and after a couple hundred feet he could see the dam more clearly. Part of the surface was covered with vines, the concrete spalled, and the bas relief of the workers chipped and weathered, but as Joseph judged it, the dam was still in good operational condition for being more than sixty years old.

Ahead sat a gravel parking area before the crest, where Joseph could see a half-ton green pickup truck with the Corps of Engineers emblem. Sam and Travis stood next to the truck, cupping their hands over the passenger side glass to get a look inside. As Sam looked up from the truck, he saw Joseph and the man with a Corps of Engineers cap walking toward him. He approached them saying, "You scared the shit out me, sneaking up on me like that."

The man wearing the cap asked, "What is your business here? This is government property."

Sam gave a broad smile, trying his best to amicable, and said, "I'm here scouting out a fishing spot. You know these old dams are good at trapping the fish. Who are you?"

"Name's Bruce Pellington, Maintenance Engineer with the Louisville District Corps of Engineers. I'm here doing some work on the outlet structure," the man officiously. "But it really doesn't matter who I am in particular, because you're trespassing, and I have the right to call the Federal Marshall if you don't leave."

"Don't worry, I won't interfere with what you were doing," Sam said, looking over the top of the dam, trying to visually verify the word of the engineer. "I'm just impressed that you're here on a Saturday at four doing maintenance work."

"It is not very impressive. Ever since the budget cuts, they've got fewer people to do the work, and I've found myself working on Saturdays to get it all done. We're trying to patch the outflow structure," the man in the maintenance uniform said, as he pointed ahead toward the center of the dam. As he did, Joseph caught a glance of his right arm. Unmistakably, there was a tattoo on his forearm in the shape of a black cross with red letters. Joseph stared ahead and remembered that Jake Adamson had tattooed crosses on the people who worked for him at the mission.

With a jolt, Joseph realized that this man was Evan.

Evan had forgotten about the tattoo. Joseph's heart raced at the sight of it; he debated running…or confronting Evan. He wanted to alert Sam, who was standing only five feet away, but was afraid that Evan would kill him on the spot. The best thing to do would be to leave and alert the authorities.

"So, if you don't mind, I need to get some things done before the end of the day," Evan said, eyeing Sam and Travis.

"Oh certainly, go ahead with your work, we're going to leave and let you get it all done," Joseph said, turning around toward the woods, hoping Sam and Travis would follow suit.

Sam tried to look disinterested, but things were beginning to look more and more suspicious.

As Sam was about to leave, a scraping noise emanated from the side wall of the dam. Travis went over to the metal pipe rail, close to where Evan was standing. As he looked down he saw a short blonde haired man in a harness suspended by rope. Travis quickly took out his revolver and pointed it down. *"Stop what you are doing!"*

As the man in the harness lifted his hands, Travis pointed the gun at Evan, who was standing only a few feet away from him. *"You put up your hands too! You think I'm stupid. I see the gun in your pants. Throw it down and drop to the ground!"*

"Don't get yourself tied in a knot. Just calm down, that's my assistant down there." Evan said, still acting as a maintenance engineer would. "I got robbed out here once, and I am licensed to carry a firearm for protection. I can show you my ID and my gun license, if you let me."

"Throw the gun on the ground! I want to see it!" Travis said, making a locking grip on his gun with his two hands in front of him.

"Okay mister, anything you want. Just keep calm." Evan slowly retrieved his Remington 38 snub nose and dropped down on the gravel.

"Now GET TO THE GROUND. I want you to assume the position. Hands behind your back!" Travis yelled.

"I just want to show you my ID," Evan said, his hands still up.

Sam pulled out his wooden gripped Smith and Wesson 38 revolver and moved towards Travis to assist. For a moment, Travis took his eyes off of Evan to watch Sam. Within a split second, Evan moved the two steps ahead, within striking distance of Travis, pulled out a long, silver object from his vest. In one swift motion, he slung the knife against the side of Travis's neck. Travis made a high pitched scream as a spray of crimson came from the sliced carotid artery. There was a gurgling sound as the blood sprayed from Travis's neck. Evan took the revolver out of Travis's blood soaked hands and aimed it at Sam. Using Travis's body as protection, he fired. As Joseph watched helplessly as the bullet exploded into Sam's left shoulder. His body writhing in pain, Sam raised his right hand and fired way left of Evan, the bullet striking the gravel access road. Evan fired again, this time hitting Sam in the center of his chest. Sam was thrown backward to the ground; his body lay motionless on the gravel.

Evan moved towards Joseph, aiming the gun squarely between his eyes. "How you doin' over there, good buddy?" he said, reprising his hillbilly accent.

Joseph put up his hands. Evan stared him down. Joseph finally realized that he had eaten lunch with Evan at Christine's in Pope's Mills, and felt nauseas at the thought. "So what are you waiting for? Get it over with."

Evan glanced at the hardened steel handcuffs on the belt loop of Sam's pants and took the cuffs off. He attached one end to the circular metal railing of the dam and called Joseph over and, waving his gun, told Joseph him to attach the other cuff to his wrist. He continued in the hillbilly accent as Joseph sat on the ground, secured to the railing. "I wish I had the time to buy you some lunch in town, but as you can see I'm real busy with my current project." Pleased how easily he controlled the situation, he smiled, and in his normal voice added, "You're so damned insignificant, and I have already wasted enough time on you— you seem hardly worth the bullet. It especially bothers me that you have been feeding off of the excesses of government by studying something like dam collapses. It just occurred to me that since you have spent so much time coming over here, I should at least satisfy your intellectual curiosity, and let you see one…first hand. Don't worry, you won't have to wait very long. I have the charges set for about twenty minutes from now."

Joseph looked over toward Sam, searching for some form of help that would obviously not be coming. Evan noticed and said, as he walked over to other side of the dam, "Don't concern yourself, fairly soon you will be joining him. If you're lucky, they'll find all of your bodies together—about ten miles downstream."

"Evan, what you are doing won't work. You won't create nearly the wave you want to take out the dam," Joseph called out.

"So, is that why you're here? Trying to stop me? You're a liar," Evan called back. "I can spot one a mile away, Dr. Hamiz. I'm the only person here with any personal integrity. But I'm just a man…lets say…a visionary…who can see the cancer that government has become, and knows that it is going to take a catastrophic event to bring the denigration of society to people's attention. I'm operating under divine instruction. I'm a messenger of god."

"You are neither a visionary nor a messenger. You are a cowardly murderer who kills women and children as they sleep."

Evan went and stood over Joseph as he lay on the embankment, "It's government who kills millions of men, women, and children every day by wasting their souls. *I* know exactly who *I* am. *I* am going to be written up in the history books, while *you* are going to be a forgotten piece of garbage in the sediment of the Raccoon River. But just think: you are going to be a witness to the beginning of a new age, one without the vestiges of government immorality."

"Look at what you are doing. You are ready to destroy a community of thousands of innocent people because of the actions of one person. There is nothing moral about murder."

"You're in no position to argue morality with me. I wish I could stay and chat some more, but unfortunately, I have a few odds and ends to take care of before I leave. In the meantime, don't go anywhere. You don't want to miss the show."

Joseph strained at his handcuffs as Evan disappeared again. He saw the keys on Sam's belt. He called, "Sam! Sam!" but there was no response. Even extending himself, he was still five feet away, not even close. Cupping his hand, Joseph tried to draw it through the steel, but the cuff was on too tight, cutting into the flesh of his hand as blood started to drip down his arm. Joseph thought that there was always some way out of a trap. If he could not get out of the cuff, he would simply have to remove the railing post. Examining the base carefully, he saw a rusted spot. He leaned back and kicked it with all his might. The steel post was more solid than it looked and did not budge even with repeated kicks; after the third strike, the bottom of his foot got bruised and Joseph winced with pain. He tried to think calmly. He needed a tool, any tool. Spreading out on the ground, he tried to reach into his pocket, having watched countless movies that showed people picking locks with paper clips. The contents of his pockets spilled haphazardly on the ground: his wallet and keys, but nothing he could use. He needed a more basic tool. He searched the area for rocks and found a palm size piece of granite on the embankment. Hitting the granite against the railing vibrated it but didn't break it. He looked at the adjacent section of railing, which was also rusted through. Kicking at the bottom post, he managed to dislodge the section. He held the two-foot section of pipe in his hand, the trophy for all his work. He extended it out toward Sam to get the keys dangling from his belt, but still was short of his objective. Cursing to himself, he laid on his back and heard Evan giving orders to Henry, knowing that fairly soon they would be completing their work and leaving.

Nearly out of ideas, he looked upward, noticing that the other cuff was fastened loosely around the post. He put the pipe into the cuff, trying to use leverage to break the lock. The cuff was too large and Joseph realized that he was not applying enough leverage. He put a small piece of granite into the cuff and the pipe fit snugly in the fulcrum. With all his strength, he bent the pipe back, feeling the lock begin to give, and after a minute, leaned back on the ground, out of breath. One more time he told himself. As he pulled the pipe, he felt the granite crack and both halves fell on his face. The cuff fell to ground.

Crouching, Joseph surveyed the area and saw that the crest of the dam was vacant. He heard the voice from below on the concrete wall, "I have six more charges to place before I am finished." Still crouching, Joseph moved to the railing where the harness was tied and started to loosen the knots. Henry noticed the line becoming loose. "Hey Evan, What the hell you are doing? He climbed up a few steps. He saw Joseph standing at the railing, took out his handgun, and fired. The shot ricocheted off the metal railing. As Joseph loosened the last knot, the entire climbing apparatus came loose and Henry screamed as he plunged down to the river. Joseph leaned over the railing; there was no sign of life in the void of the rumbling river.

Hearing the gunshot, Evan raced out of the woods to the railing where Henry was suspended. He turned around and saw Joseph poised with the pipe in his right hand, ready to pounce. Grabbing the end of the pipe, he said, "You are much too slow and obvious." Joseph instead raised his left hand to strike Evan on the jaw. Evan moved to avoid the blow, not knowing there was a metal cuff attached to Joseph's wrist at the end of the chain. The cuff struck Evan squarely in the eye, and he was knocked back in pain, releasing the pipe. Joseph raised the pipe again, this time making contact with Evan's temple. Evan fell to the ground, unconscious and bleeding.

Joseph knew he had only a very short time before the explosives were set to go. He leaned over the embankment and with the pipe, dislodged the circular charge attached to the wall closest to the railing. It fell onto the rock in the river. There was a small "boom" as it exploded on contact. He thought to himself that he did not have enough time to dislodge all the charges. He would have to run to get to a minimum safe distance.

He heard Sam's voice, "Joseph, behind you."

Joseph turned around and Evan, blood running down his face, was standing at arm's length holding Travis's Glock in his hand. Joseph instinctively moved to the side and grabbed the top of the gun with the palm of his hand. The gun fired a few inches from Joseph's ear. The explosion was deafening as it reverberated in his head. He did not loosen his grip until he twisted out of Evan's hand, the gun dropping harmlessly to the ground. Evan threw his left hand solidly into Joseph's jaw. Joseph was dazed as he was thrown back onto the railing. Evan quickly connected again with his right hand to the middle of Josephs' chest, forcing all the air out his lungs. Joseph was still on the railing as Evan put his two hands around his neck in a choke hold, bending him backwards.

Joseph was powerless to break the lock with his hands. Evan said, "I hope you die knowing everything you've done was for nothing. I've already placed enough explosives on the dam to cause a catastrophic failure. Everything downstream will disappear. Only God can stop..." An explosion from below ripped away part of the concrete. Then more of the charges exploded, this time choreographed in a group. Joseph was thrown forward, breaking Evan's grip. The both of them landed on the gravel. Evan tried getting up, but was thrown down again by another series of blasts. Stunned, the two of them got up from the ground and Joseph took a swing with his handcuffed hand, only to miss broadly. Evan caught the cuff and spun Joseph around this time, wrapping the chain around Joseph's neck like a garrote. Turning blue, Joseph sidestepped, and with all the leverage he could muster, threw Evan over his hip. The two of them, tethered, tumbled back to the ground. Evan still had a grip on the chain, but Joseph was able to force his left hand under it. Facing each other on the ground, near the rope that dangled from another climbing harness, they rolled around on the gravel as the smoke from the explosions billowed above them. Evan kept the pressure on the chain as Joseph reached for the rope and wrapped it around Evan's neck, trying to limit his mobility. Evan spotted his own discarded Remington nearby.   With his left hand, he hit Joseph in the mouth. The Remington out of reach, Evan got up to retrieve it, and as he did there was an explosion of water coming out of the base of the dam. Out of balance, Evan stumbled and was thrown off the ledge. Joseph heard the "snap," as the rope went taught. Rubbing his neck, Joseph got up from the ground and saw Evan's body dangling from the railing next to the concrete wall; his head hung crookedly over the rope.

Joseph looked over to Sam and saw him sitting on his knees. "I thought you were dead. You sure took that gunshot straight on."

Sam opened his shirt to reveal a bullet proof vest with a large indentation. "I feel like I've been kicked by a horse. I think my ribs are broken. The next time I see Sattler, I'll give him a big wet kiss for being a dumb shit for not asking for it back after Morehead. I never thought I would ever have to put it to use again." Sam groaned after he got up on his feet, "Is he dead?"

"Yes, I don't think he is going to be resurrected anytime in the near future. His partner is somewhere in the river. I don't think we have to worry about either of them."

"What about the dam? I see it's still standing."

Joseph stood and looked down at the blast damage. There was concrete debris everywhere and water seeping out of fissures at the base. "I don't know. This time I agree with Evan. This thing is going to collapse."

Sam asked, "Can't we do anything about it?"

"We have to relieve the pressure behind it. We have to lower the water level."

"Don't they have controls to do that?"

Joseph pointed to a concrete tower standing in the lake. "I was about to run over there and check it out."

Sam got up, wincing. Joseph asked, "How is your shoulder?"

"On fire. I'm lucky, I think the bullet only grazed the top of the bone. I'll survive."

They walked over to the concrete tower on the metal catwalk. Sam took his handgun and shot the massive lock off the door. Inside there was an array of circular wheels controlling the valves. Among them, Joseph guessed the large metal wheel on the right controlled the gate for the principal outflow pipe. Joseph strained to open the valve, but the wheel would not budge. "It's jammed. The explosions must have done it."

"So what we're going to do now?" Sam asked.

"I don't know. It needs to be breached."

"Just like Xenon?" Sam asked

"Yes, just like Xenon," Joseph repeated.

"Okay, I will call the police to get the equipment." Sam went into his pocket to retrieve his cell phone. He looked at the screen for a second. "Oh shit, we're out of range. What about your phone?"

"I was so rushed to leave this morning, I left it back at Jesse's apartment."

"That's great. For lack of a better idea, we should get the hell out of here, and try to get help."

Joseph said, "I think I saw Evan amble in the direction of our car. Being the way he was, I would say it is a certainty that our tires are flat. I don't think we are going to be able to find the keys to Corps truck. Anyway, it will take a half an hour to get back to town, and there is a high probability that this structure will be gone by that time. My best estimate is that I would give it an hour...tops."

Sam threw up his hands. "So this is great. This is really terrific. We're stranded out five miles from the nearest populated area, and are about to become an active part of a dam failure."

"Our problem is not here. It is downstream, where thousands of people are going to be flooded by the dam break, and we have no way to warn them."

Sam was becoming more unraveled, "So you haven't answered the question. What can we do, other than watch it happen?"

"I have already told you. We need to drain the water from behind the dam. We need to lower the spillway by about twenty feet."

"Be realistic. You need construction equipment to do that. I am sure that it's going take days to do something of that magnitude, and we don't even have an hour."

Joseph nervously moved along the railing, watching the seepage along the base go from a trickle to a heavy piping. As he walked, he nearly stumbled over the blue nylon duffle bag left by Evan. Out of curiosity, he opened it finding a dozen circular explosive nodules. Displaying them for Sam, he seemed deep in thought for a moment, and then his opened his eyes wide..

Sam saw the explosives and the expression on Joseph's face. He understood what Joseph was planning. As he did, his mouth opened wide. He blurted out, *"Oh my lord! You're fucking crazy!"*

Joseph thought a little more. "Oh yes, I am fucking crazy. But I am not going to stand here and do nothing as people get murdered, and their property destroyed."

"You're going to finish the job that Evan started?"

"No, I am just going to blow a twenty foot hole in the spillway."

"But there is the possibility that when you do that, the rest of the dam will come down with it."

"I have an approximate idea of what will happen, but I can't guarantee anything, if that is what you mean."

"That's exactly what I mean," Sam said, still in shock.

"I think I can do it if I can place the explosives properly," Joseph said, as he started rummaging through the bag of explosives and timers.

"What experience do you have with explosives anyhow?"

"I worked with them for about three and a half months."

"So that makes you an expert?"

"Enough to make the FBI think I was dangerous."

"*Was* dangerous? You still are." Exasperated, Sam said, "Show me where to place them. I'll take the responsibility."

Joseph stood across from Sam with his arms crossed. "There is no way you are doing anything. You can barely walk, let alone get down a rope."

"You're not fresh as a daisy either, Joseph. You took a good beating from Evan," Sam said, looking at the blood coming out of Joseph's nose and mouth.

"I still have arms and legs, and I can climb down a rope."

"Yes, but can you get back up?"

"Let me concern myself with that."

"The problem is, you'll only have yourself. I can't help you at the bottom of the rope."

Joseph went over to Evan's discarded climbing harness, picked it up and examined it. "So how does this thing work?" he asked.

"Who do I look like to you, man, Sir Edmond Hillary?"

"We have five minutes to figure it out," Joseph said. "That should be long enough."

Joseph started putting his arms in the holes and immediately felt awkward. Sam took a look and immediately started to take it off. "You have it on backwards, Einstein. You really sure you want to do this?"

Joseph nodded and leaned over as he proceeded to adjust the digital timers in the bag. "I have set the timers to go off in about twenty five minutes."

Sam said, "Aren't you cutting this a bit tight. Why twenty-five minutes?"

"Because I figured twenty minutes is too little time to place the explosives. By thirty minutes, the dam may be beyond any help.

Joseph climbed over the rail, feeling dizzy at the thought that he was ninety feet above the ground. He tentatively started to lower himself to traverse the vertical concrete face. As he did, a buckle snapped loose and the harness slipped. Joseph felt himself falling backwards. An explosive popped out of the pouch and fell to the streambed, exploding on contact. Sam took his left hand, seizing Joseph by the collar, yelled, "I have you." Joseph grabbed the top of the concrete wall until his knuckles on both his hands started turning red. Sam made a quick adjustment to a strap. "Whew…that was really a close one. Why don't you give it another shot?"

Joseph hesitated, and Sam said, "I wouldn't worry. With all the explosives you're carrying, the fall won't kill you."

Releasing his lower hand, he went down a few feet. Nervously, he repeated the process and descended another five feet. Even though Sam flashed the okay sign from above, Joseph felt alone. He set the first explosive charge in the middle of the spillway, the timer reading 20:19. He needed to speed his progress. Swinging on the rope, he set the next charge a few feet on the same level. He saw the ground move below him and again felt dizzy.

Sam stayed above to coach. "Concentrate on what you're doing," he said.

Joseph swung to the right, setting the third charge with the timer reading 17:05.

His hand was beginning to get sweaty, threatening his grip. Joseph started to think of the cold and damp comfort of his basement lab in the Kentucky Institute of Technology. Here he was risking his life to preserve something that was part of another man's legacy; a dishonorable man who simply wanted to control others to create his fortune. What if that legacy was intertwined with the lives of innocent people, so that they were inseparable? Yes, it is moral to preserve the legacy, even if it is a false one, to maintain life. What of his own contribution? He had his own reasons for isolation, but was he going to stay alone, without children. Jesse was right; he had been rigid about his own thinking and about changing his own life. Yes, there needed to be changes, and if he got off the wall and the dam alive, he would do things differently.

"You need to push yourself. You're running out of time," Joseph faintly heard from above. Applying the sixth change in the center of the circle, Joseph, arms numb, struggled to continue.

"C'mon, you can do it, Joseph," Sam shouted from above.

"I don't know. Maybe this was a bad idea," Joseph said, under his breath. As he placed his ninth disk, the numbers looked fuzzy, but he could makeout 6:45.

"You're almost there."

Stretching over, he nearly lost his balance. He corrected himself, placing the final disk that read 1:40.

Joseph tried climbing up the rope, but was out of strength. Sam noticed Joseph stranded and just hanging there. "I'm going to pull you up."

He yelled, "There is no time for you to pull me up. You need to get clear."

Sam felt a déjà vu, "I won't leave you here."

"I have an alternative. If I can't come up, I will go down."

"I don't know about that idea…"

"Get the *fuck* out of there, Sam," Joseph screamed.

Startled at the curse, Sam responded, "Yes, sir."

Joseph eased his grip and slid to the end of the rope. He looked down and realized that he was still fifty feet above the water. Out of options, Joseph started to swing over the channel. As he swung, he started to undo the straps holding the harness in place. Feeling his bodyweight transfer to the rope, he continued to swing in greater arcs until he was over the main channel of the river. There was no room for error. If he dropped in the shallows, he would die for sure. It was time to leave everything to chance and let go. As he dropped into space, he felt the force and heat of the blasts. He remembered to tuck his legs under his body and the water hit him like concrete as he went under. Coming up, gasping for air, he found himself swept indiscriminately downstream along with the other debris.

Above, a cloud of white smoke hung over the dam. Sam peered over the crest, straining to see the hole that was created by the explosion. The dam had hardly vibrated. Then he heard the sound of running water and debris coming out the fissure like a high pressure nozzle. "My god, it's working," he said out loud and walked from the embankment toward the access road. Suddenly, the earth embankment washed away under his legs and Sam slid down the slope. He was able to grab onto a tree before dropping to the water. He winced in agony from his shoulder wound as he hung to the wood, his feet dangling in space.

Below, Joseph gasped for air, still being swept downstream, taken by the current. He was forced over a large, submerged rock.   The rock's jagged point entered his chest and he felt his rib cage break. He screamed in pain, the sound muffled by the water. He needed to get to land before he got washed completely downstream. Through the water, he saw a tree branch angled over toward his direction. He grabbed it. Using all his remaining strength, he pulled himself onto the bank. Shivering, and coughing up blood, he picked up his head and saw Henry standing over him with a gun that dripped water onto his face. Henry mashed his foot into the wound on Joseph's his chest and pressed the wet, cold gun to his temple. "You think you're pretty smart doin' that to me back at the dam, so now I'm goin' to blow your head clean off."

Pain pulsed through his body as he closed his eyes, resigned to his fate.

"Didn't you forget someone," a voice called out from behind.

Out of instinct, Henry stood up from his crouch, and as he turned his body towards the voice, Joseph lifted his head to see a woman by the edge of the trees, pulling back a bow with all her might.

Taken by surprise, Henry shifted the gun towards the woman, trying to discern who she was when she yelled, *"Remember me in hell. You sonofabitch!"*

Over the sound of raging water, Joseph could hear the clicking sound of a cocked pistol, and then of a hissing projectile cutting through the air. He saw Henry's body thrown back five feet into the water as the arrow hit between his ribs, nearly cutting him in half. The body floated on the river as the water slowly turned red.

Dropping the bow, Jesse ran over to Joseph and knelt by his side.

"You need not have done that. I could have easily handled him myself," Joseph said with a faint smile, still not believing that he was alive. "How…How the hell did you get here?" he asked, shivering.

She looked into his eyes. "You aren't going to change, are you? If you really didn't want me to follow you, you shouldn't have left your computer on back at my station, you absent-minded prick. It was lucky thing for you I'd spotted that guy in the woods when I got here. Can you stand?"

He nodded weakly and she picked him up by the shoulders. As she did, she noted all the bruises on his cheeks, his bloody nose and lips. "Joseph, you look like shit," she said.

"I feel like shit," he said, trying to walk.

Jesse heard Joseph's labored breathing and noticed a blood stain on his soaked shirt. Instinctively, she put her hand on his ribs, and Joseph erupted in pain. "You've got some broken ribs. Where are Sam and Travis?"

Joseph's face turned to sadness. "Travis didn't make it. Evan killed him. Now he is dead too."

"Then where's Sam? I haven't seen him."

"Sam should be here with us. I hope he's not back at the dam…I told him to get clear…but he was stubborn and wouldn't leave me."

"You've hit the nail on the head. He is fucking stubborn, just like you, Joseph."

They walked back to the access road through the thick white haze of the explosions. Through the stinging smoke, they saw a figure and they both immediately picked up their pace.

It was Sam. His tan uniform stained with a dark mixture of blood and mud.

The three of them, overcome with joy, smiled as they hugged each other. As they did, Sam and Joseph screamed in pain from their broken ribs.

"You both need a doctor," Jesse said, holding up the men like a human crutch, walking between them.

"I can't speak for Sam, but I just want to go home," Joseph said.

"And where would that be?" Jesse said.

With no hesitation, Joseph responded, "It's wherever you want it to be."

After a pause, a coy smile came to her face, "Is that a proposal?" she asked.

"We can talk about it on the way back to Cummings," he said.

They heard police sirens coming toward them in the distance as they slowly ambled down the gravel road toward Route 953, where Jesse parked her car alongside the road. The sun sank beneath the trees in the horizon; it would be dark when they finally reached town.

ACKNOWLEDGEMENTS

Scott Hitchcock was the editorial consultant for this book. Scott had the laborious task of proof reading and polishing the manuscript prior to publication.

I would like to thank all the friends and family who read the very wordy first draft, and provided such wonderful feedback. I especially want to thank Sara Green, Kathy Sparks, Nydia Finch, Leonard Eskowitz, and James Maxa for their support while writing this novel.

Finally, I want to thank Mayo Lucas who many years ago e-mailed me, telling me to "Write the book." Not only did she start me on the journey, but mentored me throughout the writing process.

Printed in the United States
147390LV00002B/37/P

9 781438 963921